ONE NIGHT OF LOVE

Gideon ran one hand over Tess's hair, down her spine to the small of her back. With the other hand he turned her chin upward so her eyes met his. "I would have to be stone," he said furiously. "Do you think I am stone, you willful, prideful girl?"

His hands moved to her breasts. At his touch Tess's knees went as weak as water. She heard him mutter, "Oh, my lovely—" Suddenly her head was filled with the scent of him, warm spice and musky sweat. Her body reeled with wild sensation as he lifted her into his arms and carried her to a bed of pine boughs and ferns. . . .

JERICHO'S DAUGHTER

Mallory Burgess

AN ONYX BOOK

ONYX
Published by the Penguin Group
Penguin Books USA Inc., 375 Hudson Street,
New York, New York 10014, U.S.A.
Penguin Books Ltd, 27 Wrights Lane,
London W8 5TZ, England
Penguin Books Australia Ltd, Ringwood,
Victoria, Australia
Penguin Books Canada Ltd, 2801 John Street,
Markham, Ontario, Canada L3R 1B4
Penguin Books (N.Z.) Ltd, 182–190 Wairau Road,
Auckland 10, New Zealand

Penguin Books Ltd, Registered Offices:
Harmondsworth, Middlesex, England

First published by Onyx, an imprint of New American Library,
a division of Penguin Books USA Inc.

First Printing, November, 1990
10 9 8 7 6 5 4 3 2 1

*For Dr. Rebecca S. Conrad,
who delivered our daughter.*

And Jephthah came . . . unto his house, and, behold, his daughter came out to meet him with timbrels and with dances: and she was his only child; beside her he had neither son nor daughter. And it came to pass, when he saw her, that he rent his clothes, and said, Alas, my daughter! thou hast brought me very low . . .

—Judges 11: 34–35

I

1

Windber-on-Clun, Shropshire, England—April 1670

Benjamin Jacob Ezekiel Jericho heard the end of the world and let out a groan, clapping his hands to his ears in a desperate attempt to stave off the Apocalypse. The four horsemen charged him, the earth quaked, the trumpets of the angels blared, and the woman atop the seven-headed scarlet beast rose up before him, arrayed in purple velvet, decked with gold and precious gems and pearls.

He trembled helplessly before her. She reached down, grabbed the collar of his nightshirt, and shook him, her voice like the cold steel of a sword slicing through the tumult as she cried out:

"For God's sake, wake up, Dad! You're having a dream!"

"What? Who's there?" Ben started, opened one eye, then recognized the heart-shaped face framed in red-gold curls that hovered above him. "Tess! Thank God it's you!" He fell back on his bed. "I thought 'twas the Judgment Day. What in Jehovah's name was that awful racket?"

"The church bell ringing noon," Tess told him, and almost smiled. But she set her mouth sternly instead, propping him up against the headboard, handing him the towel she held, and reaching for the pitcher. "Lean over, if you please. I just changed the bedclothes Wednesday a week; I don't care to have to do it again."

Ben dutifully leaned out over the floor with the towel circling his ruddy neck, though the alteration in equilibrium made him shudder. "Oh, Tess, lass," he moaned, "you don't know what 'tis like to suffer such fearsome dreams."

"That's right, I don't. And that's because I also don't know what it's like to down ten pints of ale at a sitting."

"I didn't have any ten pints."

"You did too, Dad. Backus told me so. Stop twitching about. Are you ready?" He nodded faintly, and Tess let a torrent of chilly water from the pitcher stream over his bushy white hair. He gasped and shook himself like a dog coming in from a storm. When Job saw his master he howled in sympathy and leapt from the cot to cower by the door of the cottage.

"It's all right, boy," Tess told the hound, who went on howling mournfully. "Christ, Dad, what's he doing in here anyway?" She went and opened the door to a bright stream of sunlight yellow as butter, and Job bounded into the yard.

"Mind your tongue, lass." Ben raised callused hands to shield his eyes from the sun, then sat up with a start. "Noon, did you say? Great Jehovah, what about the horses?"

"I already did the feeding—*and* the mucking. No reason they should suffer for your sins—though I do think that if you're to be called Lord Halifax's stablemaster you might do your own work for a change. Here's your potion, then." She gave him the bowl she'd mixed up at dawn, when she woke and saw the signs of his carousing: jacket and shirt and belt scattered hither and thither, mud making a trail toward the discarded boots at the hearth, and Job draped over his unconscious master's chest, drooling blissfully. When he was sober, Ben heeded his daughter's decree that the dog sleep in the stables, but when he'd been drinking, Job always managed to slip into the cottage with him somehow.

Ben took a deep breath, then downed the bowl of milk, raw egg, crushed fennel seed, beet juice, garlic, and hollyhock water in one gagging gulp. "No one makes that recipe like you do, pet," he told Tess fondly, wiping his mouth with a corner of the bedsheet.

"No one else would make it for you at all, you old fool," she said, and snatched the sheet away.

" 'Tis hardly becoming for a young girl to call her dad such things," Ben observed, "nor go about using Jehovah's name in vain—not to mention oaths such as 'bloody.' "

"Aye, well, it's not becoming either for you to sop yourself stone drunk, is it?" Tess examined the sheet, sighed, and flung it onto the mound of laundry that was growing, mushroomlike, at the foot of his bed. Her father's father, who'd died long before she was born, had been a preacher and had seen to his son's education. She never could decide if the advantages of that—Ben had taught her to read, for one, and she even knew a bit of Latin—were worth the drawbacks. Why did Ben have to be so impossibly upright? "Anyway, I hardly see the difference between my saying 'Christ' and your saying 'Great Jehovah.' "

" 'Tis a matter of respect," he told her. "But then, that's something you know precious little about."

"I respect how much ale you can drink," said Tess, and started out to the yard.

Her father called her back. "Here, now, did you say you'd seen Backus already? What were you doing at the Swan before noon?"

"Slinging back brandy."

"Don't sass me, Teresa."

"I wasn't *at* the Swan," she said with a sigh. "He came round here, as you'd know for yourself if you hadn't been sleeping the morning away."

"Backus came round here?"

"Aye," said Tess, and headed for the door once more.

Her father stumbled up from the bed, boot half on. "Well . . . why'd he do that? Is something amiss? Did something happen?"

She turned to him, her slim straight figure silhouetted against the dust-laden slice of sun. "You must be jesting. When was the last time anything happened in Windber-on-Clun?"

"If you'd seen as much of life as I have," Ben began, "maybe you'd be grateful to live in a place such as this, that's blessed with peace and quiet."

"Maybe I *would*, but I haven't, have I, so how would I know?" She looked at him pleadingly. "Honestly, Dad, it's beyond me how you can stand to waste your whole life away here. As good as you are with horses, you could work anywhere—in Stafford or Shrewsbury, even in London!"

"Don't tell me what I could do, lass; I know better than you do. Didn't I once head a stable for a great lord, with twenty men under me, and one hundred horses?"

Tess sighed; if he'd boasted about that job to her once, he'd done so a million times. "That's just what I mean, Dad! Why not get such a place again?"

"I'll tell you why," he said, grizzled chin thrust out. "Because I like it here in Windber-on-Clun."

Tess threw up her hands. "Then all I can say is, you're daft."

He lowered a blunt finger at her. "Honor thy father, the Good Book says, lass!"

"Tell me, what does it say about great stablemen who sleep until noon and make me do all the bloody work around here?"

"You mind your tongue, Teresa!"

"Oh, what the hell? Why don't you just sleep the rest of the day too? See if I care." She turned to go.

"Tess!" She kept going; he said her name again, with the small hitch in his gruff voice that always stopped her. "Don't be cross with me, pet, I can't bear it. Jehovah knows you've a right to think me a lazy old sot—"

"Dad, don't." If he starts to cry, Tess thought, I will kick myself.

"All I want is for you to be happy, pet. That's all I've ever wanted. I've tried so hard to do my best by you, but it's been hard. If your mother had lived—"

"Oh, Dad." Tess crossed the room and kissed him, felt the stiff whorls of muscle beneath his leathery skin. "You've done perfect by me, honestly you have. No one could have done better. You've got to understand, just because I get tired of Windber sometimes doesn't mean I don't still love you."

"There's naught wrong with Windber," he said, and she was glad to hear his voice steady again.

"You're right. There *is* nothing wrong with Windber," Tess agreed, and laughed. "That's why 'tis so bloody dull! Now, wash up, why don't you, and put on a clean shirt." She kissed his cheek.

"A clean shirt? Why should I?"

"Because Lord Halifax wants to see everyone up at the big house at four. That's what Backus came to say."

"Wants to see us? Whatever about?"

"I don't know."

"Well, did Backus?" he pressed.

"I didn't ask," said Tess, and at last made it into the yard.

"Well, why the devil not?" her father bawled. Her voice floated back to him on a ribbon of sunshine:

"Because I knew it wouldn't be anything interesting, whatever it was!"

"Cheeky little chit," he growled at her, and shut the door.

Tess drank in a deep draft of April air scented with apple blossoms from the tree by the well and green grass from the pastures. Job loped toward her, his long ears swinging, and she cupped his snuffling snout in her hand. "What do you mean letting Dad stay out all night," she chided, "not to mention your slobbering all over the bedclothes? How would you like to do the laundry for a change, eh? What do you say to that?" He didn't say anything, just looked pitifully sad—but then, Job always looked sad. "Never mind, then," she told him, and gave him a pat. A low-flying woodcock crossed his field of vision; without the least change in his woeful expression, he tore off after it, squeezing like a sausage to fit beneath the rungs of the pasture fence.

"Job, no!" Out of the beechwood thicket behind the cottage a young man came running with a drawn bow, his yellow hair disheveled, a grimace on his broad bronzed face. "That bird is mine!"

"*Was* yours," Tess called. "Jack, don't you dare shoot into that pasture or I'll have your head!"

The young man wheeled to a stop, his hazel eyes

alight. "Tess!" He unslung the bow and came toward her. "Hard to believe I could miss seein' somethin' as lovely as ye, but the truth is, I did."

"And are sorry you did, too, I reckon, since if I hadn't been here you'd have shot at that cock."

"Faith, how could I ever be sorry to see ye?" He gave her a disarming grin. "And I'd never risk shootin' into that pasture with yer precious Linzy in there."

"Oh, hell, no—not unless you thought you wouldn't be seen."

His grin faded. "Tessie, don't curse. It doesn't make ye sound worldly, ye know, only coarse and vulgar."

"I like cursing."

" 'Tis just like the high-blown way ye talk. Ye only does it to be different."

"I *am* different," said Tess in the clipped Kentish cadences she'd learned from her father, which were so unlike Jack's lazy Shropshire drawl. She'd clung to her father's accent against all odds, like a badge or brand. "I wasn't born in Windber-on-Clun, you know. And I surely don't—" She stopped. Don't intend to die here, she'd nearly told him. But it wouldn't do to say that to Jack. "Surely don't see anything wrong with trying to speak properly," she finished instead.

"Airs," Jack sniffed, to her fury. "Nothin' but airs." She turned her back to him.

"Why don't you mind your own business, Jack Brady?"

"Ye are my business, Tess."

He'd come up close behind her, so close that she could feel his breath ruffle her hair as his hand caught her elbow. Tess wriggled away, whistling for Linzy and leaning her arms on the pasture fence. The pony's head snapped up from the patch of grass she'd been cropping; she came galloping toward her mistress, nickering happily.

"Hello, there, pretty lady," Tess crooned softly, stroking her silvery mane. "Hello, my darling."

"D'ye know what I'd give," Jack said at her side, his voice very low, "to have ye look at me just once the way ye look at that horse?"

"If you were as good a ride as she is, I would," Tess said without thinking.

"Oh, Tessie. Just say the word and I'll give ye a ride ye'll never forget," he whispered, his mouth at her ear.

Blushing furiously, she moved away again. "Who is being coarse and vulgar now?"

"There's nothing vulgar about what I feel for ye, love. All I want in this world is to wed ye, to hold ye 'n' look after ye for the rest of my days."

Tess felt a familiar tug at her heart; she felt it more and more often now when he talked that way. She and Jack had been sweethearts for a dozen years, since she was four; everyone in Windber-on-Clun knew they'd marry someday. For months he'd been pressing her to set the date and have the banns read at St. Jude's. She looked at him now, at his warm hazel eyes, the thatch of corn-colored hair, that broad smiling face with the slight crook of the nose, broken at ten when he'd fallen out of the apple tree while showing off for her.

He loved her; there wasn't any doubt of that. He was a good man; he would make a good husband. He worked hard for Lord Halifax—or at least, as hard any Shropshireman; they were not a race known for diligence. She'd never seen him drunk. And she loved him too. Wasn't that why her heart gave that little leap when he spoke of their future together, of the endless years of happiness that stretched ahead?

Endless . . .

Linzy nuzzled her apron pockets, searching for treats. "I've got nothing for you," said Tess, her voice unaccustomedly sharp.

"Here, Linzy girl." Jack had bread and jam in his pack, and he fed her a bit. "Well, Tess, how about it? Ready to name the day?"

"I'll tell you what I am ready to do, Jack—ask what you're doing shooting at his lordship's woodcocks."

"You know old Andy wouldn't mind. He's the right sort, he is." His jaunty tone didn't quite conceal his impatience at the way she evaded the question.

"Oh, Jack." It occurred to her quite suddenly that the leap of her heart might be guilt instead of love. "You're the right sort too. Really you are."

"Then why not set a date?" he asked persistently.

"What's the hurry, pet? It's not as though anything ever happens round here."

"Shows how much ye know. Haven't ye heard about his lordship's summons?"

"Oh, that." Tess's red mouth curved in disdain. " 'Tis likely nothing more than a meeting to pray for the sowing. Or perhaps he's heard someone's poaching his woodcocks."

"Well, it's not me, is it? Thanks to Job." He squinted at the sky. "Not half-past one yet. Fancy a walk in the woods on such a lovely afternoon?" He caught her hand; Tess saw the bulge in his leggings and knew well enough what he had on his mind.

"Speaking of sowing, isn't that where you should be?" she asked quickly.

He shrugged, a lazy Shropshire shrug. " 'Twill get done. In time." Tess found her neighbors' attitude toward work exasperating, and yet she understood it. The land fate had dealt them was the devil itself for farming, harsh and rock-strewn and unyielding. She supposed a few dozen generations of hacking at it with a hoe would have worn down her ambitions too.

"Well, anyway, I can't go walking," she lied, giving Linzy a last pat. "Dad had one of his nights. He's not even up yet. I've got to tell him about his lordship asking us to the house." Please, Dad, she prayed, whatever you do, don't walk out here now . . .

Jack frowned. "I should think ye'd be dyin' to wed me, Tess. After all, once ye do, ye won't have to nursemaid that old codger."

"I don't mind doing for Dad."

"There's doin' and there's doin'. 'Tis a danged shame the way he carries on with his drinkin'."

"Shut up, Jack."

His jaw clenched; he stood for a moment, then shouldered the bow again. "Right," he grunted, stalking toward the wood.

Tess watched him go, nibbling her lip, wanting to call him back and apologize, but unwilling to pay the price for his forgiveness. She pictured the cavern high up on the ridge, its entrance hidden by rocks and a screen of deep moss and high ferns and pine. The secret place, he and she called it, using it first as a castle, a ship, a fortress, whatever their whimsy declared it on a given day. Only much later, just two summers past, had they dragged fresh ferns into the cool, echoing darkness and begun to play, breathless and timid, a new sort of game.

Tess found it quite as thrilling as Jack did that first summer, when all they dared were long, awkward kisses and vague, clothed gropings. The summer after that, he'd reached her bodice buttons; she could still hear in her mind his sharp, awed intake of breath as his hand first slipped beneath her petticoat to cup a breast. For a time he was content with that; then he'd wanted to kiss her there, and she'd let him, despite a small qualm of misgiving. It seemed from his wild, panting eagerness that he was getting something more out of all this than she. Suddenly the sultry evenings when they'd sit and talk for hours, the lazy days of fishing for trout, the afternoons of If-I-were-king—all were gone, swallowed up by Jack's all-consuming passion to get her alone in the cavern again.

They'd fought that summer, last summer. He'd pressed her to go farther, let him show how much he loved her, prove that she loved him. Tess remembered those months as a blur of tears and bitter words and recriminations. Jack swore he could never, ever in his life want anything as much as he wanted her. And she—she felt as though somehow she'd lost her truest friend. For once, she'd actually been glad when the winter came.

And now spring was here. The apple tree was blooming, the cuckoo was singing, the sap was flowing—and it was all going to begin all over again. Her dad would be coupling Lord Halifax's fine bay stallions and mares. Job would find a bitch to bear him. Perhaps, at their moment of joining, he would even be happy; that would be something to see. Tess would put Jack off until they were married, or else she wouldn't. Either way, the world wouldn't come to an end. She didn't even know why she'd held out so long.

Unless it was to postpone, however briefly, the moment when she knew once and for always that in the pattern of her life, just as in that of Windber-on-Clun, there would be no surprises, no astounding changes, no unforeseen bolts from the blue. And really, what was the sense in delaying the inevitable? Might as well wish for wings, you silly girl, thought Tess, and went to do the wash.

The sun was still well above the humped, crooked heights of the range of hills called the Forest Clun when Tess and her father set out for the big house later that afternoon, but its light had changed from butter-brightness to the thinner hue of whey, filtered through a fine sieve of clouds. The rays reflected from the long windows of the manor were paler still, but even so Ben groaned and shaded his eyes as he trudged up the path. "Tess, lass . . ." he began.

"Yes, Dad?"

"I've done some hard thinking, pet, and I'm giving it up."

"Yes, Dad," said Tess, and whistled Job back from the brim of the river that ran through the village and down by the pasture.

"I mean it this time, I swear it," Ben insisted. " 'Tis naught but a waste of time and money, after all. It steals a man's steadiness, and if there's one thing a good horseman needs, 'tis steady hands, wouldn't you agree?"

"Yes, Dad."

Ben gave her a sidelong glance. "You don't think I can do it, do you?"

"Oh, I've no doubt you could do it, Dad. I just don't think you will."

"Well, you're wrong there, Tess. I've learned my lesson. I've had enough of waking up in the morning all fuzzy and confounded, with my pockets empty and my mouth tasting like wet sheep. And Jehovah knows I've had enough of dreaming of the end of the world. So I'm quitting. Right here and now. Never again will a pint pass these lips; you've my solemn word on it."

"Yes, Dad."

He jabbed her shoulder with a thick, blunt finger. "Wait and see, sassy lass," he told her, and stumped off ahead, with Job running gloomy circles around his heels.

From the outlying fields and the barn, the swine pen and dovecote, the Black Swan tavern and the tiny cluster of cottages around it, the forty-four residents of Windber-on-Clun were ascending to the big house. There was not among them a man, woman, or child whom Tess could not describe to a tittle; she knew their likes and dislikes, every item in their wardrobes, what they called the cats curled by their hearths.

There were Backus and Missus Backus, that ran the Swan, and Dad's drinking buddies, Robbie and Mungo and Sam, and Jack's father and mother, Mort and Ellie, with their other five youngsters, and Widow Jonas, who made herb tonics for the sickly, and Shepherd Tom, and Tim Whitaker, and Jack, still looking cross, and Millie Fish, who would marry him in a minute if he ever asked, and all the others, cozy and familiar and well-beloved and so bloody boring that sometimes Tess found herself wishing the earth would open and swallow the lot of them whole.

The two houseboys and three maids and Missus Wallace, the cook, and Prince Oren, the butler—Ben had nicknamed him for his airs—were ranged along the steps to the portico as usual for one of their master's summonses. The villagers gathered on the drive below them, calling greetings, shaking hands. Jack saw Tess and pointedly put his back to her, chatting with Millie. So that's how it's going to be, Tess thought with a sigh. Already Ellie had noticed her son's snub and was whispering to a neighbor; in two minutes everyone there would know she and Jack had had a falling-out.

Tess lingered on the fringe of the drive, toeing a bit of gravel, pretending not to notice Jack and Millie and occupying herself by studying the big house, though she knew its every angle and line by heart. When she was small she'd thought it a castle, and Lord Halifax the King of England. Ben had long since told her there were other houses he'd seen that were far more grand, but it was still the finest Tess knew by a long, long way. Three stories up, it reached, each with acres of windows; the enormous front doors were of polished brass, set back beneath the smooth-hewn columns and vaulted arch of the portico.

Tess had never been any further inside than the kitchens, and the front hall at Christmas, but the housemaids had told her all about the manor's interior: the beds big as cottages, the satin draperies, the carpets on the floor that had come all the way from Persia, and had leaves and flowers woven into them, lifelike as could be. At the moment Lord Halifax was in the throes of redecorating; everyone had seen the carts of furnishings rolling away. Speculation was rampant as to whether this meant his lordship might be planning to remarry after all his years of lonely widowerhood.

"Quiet, everyone!" That was Prince Oren, clapping his hands for silence and then bowing so low his nose nearly scraped the stair as his lordship emerged from the house. The rest of the villagers followed his lead; as they straightened up from their obeisances, there was a hum of comment. Tess heard Backus mutter, "Gor, he don't look well, does he?"

She had to agree. Ordinarily Lord Halifax appeared sober, kind, and distinguished, his well-fed chest attired in severe black velvet, his white wig caught back in a braided tail. He had thick jowls, and a nose made red with boiled beef in sauce, and merry pale gray eyes between crinkly lids that always made Tess think of Jack's mother's special pie crust with the scalloped edge. But on this fine spring day the master of Windber-on-Clun's clothing was disheveled, his peruke askew, his thick jowls quaking; he stood before his tenants at the top of the stairs and wrung his small plump hands.

"My dear—" he began, and was stopped by a fit of coughing. He pressed a snowy kerchief to his face, paused, and started again. "My dear, dear friends. I hope that, through the years, I've earned the right to call you all my friends. Indeed, you've been something more than friends to me in this solitary life I've led; you've been my family." Tess supposed that was true; his bride had died young, and without giving him an heir. And he certainly was father to the village, always looking after his people, making sure Widow Jonas had wood for her fire in winter and the Backuses cider and ale for the Swan.

He'd paused again and was twisting the kerchief back

and forth, wringing it tight as a pig's tail. "I really do find myself at a loss as to how to tell you . . . what I must tell you," he went on at last. This isn't about praying for the sowing, Tess realized suddenly, nor about poaching either. She could see from the tense, silent faces of her neighbors that they knew it too. Her stomach coiled like his lordship's kerchief. "The fact is," Andrew Halifax said, "I am going away."

"Going away to London?" Jack's brother Billy piped. "Will ye bring us sugared almonds again?"

His lordship smiled. "No, Billy, not to London. To someplace much farther than that, I'm afraid."

"Where, then?" asked Billy, and his mother, pale-faced, pulled him to her.

"Hush, lamb," she told him. "Let his grace have his say."

"Why, to the New World, Billy my boy!" Lord Halifax announced heartily. "To the colonies!"

"The wot?" asked Meg Mullen, cupping her ear.

"The colonies!" Mungo shouted at her.

"The . . . Well, why the devil would his lordship go there?"

Again their master smiled. "Why does any man decide to do such a thing? For the thrill—the adventure! For a new beginning!"

"Begging your pardon, sir," Ben Jericho said, "but you're not really the sort, are you, that craves adventure? And I daresay you're a mite old for new beginnings, too."

"Aye," Robbie chimed in, " 'tis sixty-three ye'll be, come Martinmas, just the same as me."

Lord Halifax held out his hands. "Come, now, my good men, do you mean to say you think I'm not up to a bit of adventure?"

"More'n a bit, sir," said Ben, "sailing ten thousand miles away."

"Just over three thousand, actually," his lordship corrected him. "It averages a two-month trip. I'll be leaving tonight, and come mid-June, I'll be landing in his majesty's colony of Delaware."

"Tonight!" Prince Oren gasped, and nearly fell off the porch.

"But ye can't just leave!" Missus Backus cried. "What will become of us?"

"Don't you worry," Lord Halifax said soothingly. "Would I go off without first making sure my friends—my *family*—were taken care of? Of course I wouldn't."

"Well, what *is* to become of us?" her husband asked.

"Why, there'll be another lord coming to look after you." An astonished chorus of "Another lord!" filled the air; he had to shout to finish: "A very honorable gentleman by the name of Gideon Cade!"

An awful racket greeted this news; Tess was tempted to cover her ears, but didn't dare miss what else might be said. Her knees were trembling; she swayed and found that somehow Jack had made his way to her side. He put his arm around her and she leaned against him, grateful for his strength. "Whatever does he mean, another lord?" she asked.

Jack's jaw was tight. "I don't know, love. But there's more here than meets the eye."

Tess's father clearly agreed with him, for he thrust his way to the foot of the porch and bellowed, "Just one blessed minute! I want to know what the dickens is going on here!"

The uproar died away. Lord Halifax smiled cheerfully, but Tess saw that the knuckles on his hand as he clenched his kerchief were stark white. "It's just as I told you, Ben. I'll be going away, and—"

"Aye, sir, but why?" Ben demanded, and then added, as he heard the women gasp, "Begging your pardon, of course, for breaking in that way."

"Of course," said his master. "There's no mystery about it, Ben. It's just that, as you say, I'm getting older. If I've a notion to see the world, it's time I got on with it. And as I've no family to hold me here—"

"But ye just said we was your family!" Meg Mullen cried, and then clapped her hand over her mouth at her audacity.

His lordship smiled down at her. "And I meant it, Meg, my dear. You must believe that. I could never express how much all of you mean to me."

Jack took a step forward, still hugging Tess. "If that's

so, sir, then why spring this on us all sudden, when ye're leavin' tonight? Why not give us some warnin'?"

"Jack and Tess." Lord Halifax looked at them for a moment. "How I'd hoped to be here for your wedding day." He coughed into his kerchief again, so violently that he had to dab his eyes dry. "Lovely Tess, with your hair like fire . . . you must look after her, Jack. And perhaps . . . perhaps when she gives you a son you might name him Andrew. For me." His voice cracked; he shrugged his velvet-clad shoulders and then went on speaking quickly, embarrassed by his emotional display. "I meant to tell you all ages ago, honestly I did, but the attorneys said I mustn't give up ho—" He clamped his mouth shut in mid-word, his face flushing red. "I mean, they said I mustn't . . . mustn't . . . that is . . ." Floundering helplessly, he stared at the toes of his cordovan shoes and mumbled, "Oh, dear."

Ben faced him, arms akimbo, like some compact avenging angel. "Give up hope, that's what you were going to say. And I for one want to know what that means."

"I misspoke myself, that's all."

"Horse manure!" his stabler snapped.

"Mind your tongue, Ben Jericho!" his lordship thundered. "I may have lost my title and my lands, but by God, I hope I'm still worth some respect from my men!"

As one, the tenants caught their breaths. Ben rocked on his heels. And then it happened—something every soul in Windber-on-Clun would remember till his dying day: proud Lord Halifax, legs buckling, sat down heavily on the portico step, buried his face in his hands, and dissolved in tears.

It was horrible, awful to watch him, Tess thought—like seeing God naked, or hearing Ben tell bad jokes. It made her want to run and hide; she burrowed against Jack's shoulder instead. No one said anything for the longest time, for hours and hours. Then Lord Halifax dropped his kerchief. Billy Brady darted forward and picked it up, handing it back to him. "Please, yer lordship, sir," he begged, "please don't cry!"

"Billy." Lord Halifax took the kerchief and patted the boy's blond head. "All right, Billy, I won't." He blew his nose once, loud as a trumpet, and rubbed his eyes with his thumbs. "I'm very sorry, all of you," he apologized. "I don't know what could have come over me."

Ben said quietly, "Won't you tell us about it, sir?"

"There's not much to tell, really." Lord Halifax drew a deep breath, tucking the kerchief into his doublet. "Men have been fools since Adam; I'm nothing new."

"But how could such a thing happen?" Jack's mother wailed.

His lordship smiled wanly. "I'm still not sure myself, Ellie. The attorneys say I should have been more careful, spent less time here and more in London looking after my interests."

"Why, ye already spend most o' the year there!" she said indignantly.

"I know—and hate every moment of it." His lordship gave a rueful laugh. "I don't think I've ever reached the city gates without wishing straightaway that I was back here. But the attorneys tell me if I'd been closer to the king, to court, I'd have seen this blow coming. Well, it's not the way my father brought me up, God rest him—"

"God rest him," the tenants murmured.

"—to have to play the lackey for what's mine by right. But it's a new age, isn't it, this Restoration? And I guess it's true what they say about teaching an old dog tricks."

"Begging your pardon, sir," said Ben, "but just what *did* happen?"

"Oh, this Cade fellow put forward a claim that my lands were his."

"How's that?" Meg Mullen asked, frowning.

"The new lord," Mungo bellowed in her ear, "says Windber is his!"

"Stuff and nonsense!" the old woman cried. "Why, Windber's belonged to the Halifaxes since King William come over from France!"

"That's what I thought too," said his lordship. "But Cade had it heard in the courts, and the courts said I'm wrong."

"He's cheated you, that's what he's done!" Robbie declared, and a host of others took up the cry: "Aye, he's a rotten swindler!" "He's crooked, he is!"

"Here, now!" their master said sternly. "Let's have no talk of that! It's the law says 'tis his now, fair and square, and an Englishman's bound to abide by the law."

"Then call me a bleedin' Dutchman," Backus barked, "for I'll not stand for this! I'll go to London myself to fight it. We'll get up a what-ye-may-call-it—what's that, Ben, where we all sign, like Magna Carta?"

"A petition." Ben's face lit up. "Aye, that's what we'll do!"

"A petition!" the villagers echoed him. "Let's make a petition!"

"We'll get Windber back for ye, yer lordship," Jack promised, "just see if we don't!"

Lord Halifax's jowly face creased with emotion as he raised his hands for silence. "My friends," he called above the commotion. "My dear, *dear* friends—"

"Everybody shut up!" Ben shouted.

His lordship smiled. "Thank you, Ben. What I wanted to say is, I'm more grateful than I could ever tell you for your loyalty to me, for your faithful service. But you must believe this: you can serve me best now by transferring that loyalty and faithfulness to Gideon Cade."

"In a pig's eye we will," Mungo growled.

"Never!" cried Missus Backus.

"Please!" Lord Halifax begged them. "Please, no acrimony—"

"No wot?" Meg Mullen asked.

"Gideon Cade is your lord now," their master went on, "and you must be fair to him; you must let him begin with a clean slate. Just as I shall start my life anew in the colonies."

"The man's a saint," Missus Backus sobbed, "a living, breathing saint!"

"But you can't just walk away from the work of a lifetime," Ben protested, "of your lifetime, and of your father and his father before you—"

"I can and I will," Lord Halifax said sternly. "And if you men and women have ever . . . have ever loved me, then you'll prove it now by welcoming Gideon Cade with open hearts and minds."

"I'll welcome him with a bleedin' bludgeon, I will!" Backus said.

His lordship stood, drawing himself up to his full height, such as it was. "You'll do no such thing, Backus! Let this be my last command to you as your lord. I order you to serve Gideon Cade with all the strength and purpose and fortitude you have shown to me and my family. Now, is that clear?" No one spoke. "I said, is that clear?" Lord Halifax demanded again.

Tess heard her father mumble, "You can lead a horse to water, right enough . . ."

"What's that you say, Ben?" his master asked.

For a long moment Tess saw Ben Jericho torn between his heart and his duty. Then he hung his head. "Nothing, sir."

"And you'll do as I ask?"

There was one more lengthy pause. Then, as though the words were being dragged from him, "Aye, sir," Ben said.

Lord Halifax beamed. "Thank you, Ben. Now I shall rest easy at night. Remember, all of you, I pray you: your behavior toward Gideon Cade will only reflect on me."

"He'd be a fine one to pass judgment on others," Robbie spat out, "the filthy rat!"

"Now, Robbie, none of that," Lord Halifax said. "I haven't much time, I'm afraid; I must be in London to catch my ship the day after tomorrow. So, Ben, if you'd kindly saddle two of the bays and bring them round, so that Oren and I can get started—"

"Me?" Oren asked in surprise.

"But I'll come with you, sir!" Ben offered.

"Let me come!" cried Jack.

Lord Halifax shook his head. "I need you to look after the stables, Ben, and Jack for the sowing. I want everything in order when Cade arrives."

Oren was preening at this proof of favor. "Very good, sir. Shall I go upstairs, then, and pack your things?"

"My things?"

"Aye, sir. Your belongings."

His lordship looked rather embarrassed. "I'm afraid I haven't made myself clear. I haven't any belongings any longer. It all belongs to Gideon Cade." He laughed self-consciously. "So much so, in fact, that I'll be selling the horse I ride to London to pay for my ship's passage." He reached into his doublet pockets. "Hold on one minute; I've just found . . . Billy, Molly, Joe!" He gestured to the children in the crowd. "Come here, my pets. I've a little something for all of you, to remember me by." One by one they came up to the portico, and he pressed something into each tiny hand. Billy ran back to show his mother.

"Here, Mummy, what is it?"

" 'Tis a shilling, pet," she told him, and burst into tears again. "Oh, yer lordship, sir—"

"No scenes, my dear Ellie. Please," he said softly. "For the children's sake. We must all be very brave. Will you do that for me?" She nodded, squaring her shoulders. "Good girl. Now, how about those horses, Ben?"

Jack went to the stables with Ben to help with the hitching, while Lord Halifax shook the hand of everyone there. When Tess's turn came to climb the portico steps, the master reached into his doublet again, pulling out a delicate gold chain. He held it in his pudgy palm, turning it so it caught the flashing rays of the fading sun. "My Eugenia wore this on the day we were wedded," he said, his voice thick and hoarse. "I shall never forget that day. It was the happiest of all my life."

"It's very beautiful," Tess told him.

"And so are you, my dear. That is why I want you to have this."

"Oh, sir, I couldn't!"

But he lowered it gently over her head, smiling into her wide green eyes. "Ah, Tess, you must! I want you to wear it on your wedding day, and to think of me."

Tess dug her nails into her hands, tears streaming down her cheeks. "I shall think of you every day, sir. I can promise you that."

"Lovely Tess." He brushed her tears away with his finger. Jack and Ben ran up the drive with the horses. "Well," Lord Halifax said. "Well. Time for me to be going. Oren, I do have just one bag upstairs, with my personal things. If you could bring that down—" The Prince bowed low and hurried off; in a moment Tess could hear a loud clunk-clunk-clunk as he brought the baggage down the stairs.

"Ye ought to have let me pack for ye, m'lord," one of the chambermaids said mournfully as she helped Oren heft the bag onto the porch. "Sounds as though ye've got everythin' all topsy-turvy."

"I must learn to do things on my own, Frannie, mustn't I? And I couldn't have you suspecting that I was going away before I was ready to announce it to everyone." Jack and Ben slung the bag onto the back of one of the bays. There was the undercurrent of sniffles and sobs in the air.

"I wish you'd let me come along," Ben said again.

"And me," Jack put in.

"Far be it from me to separate two lovebirds!" his lordship told Jack, winking at Tess. "And as for you, Ben, I want to make certain you're here when Gideon Cade arrives."

"Pah!" said Ben, and spat in the dust. "When is the blackguard coming?"

"Now, Ben, you gave me your word—"

"Aye, that I did, more's the rue. Right enough, then. When's his lordship arriving?" Tess's father asked, giving the title a twisting sneer.

Lord Halifax plainly thought it best to leave well enough alone. "I'm not certain, but it won't be long," was all he said. "Remember, all of you, I am counting on you to welcome him properly to Windber-on-Clun."

"Aye, m'lord," a few glum voices chorused. He nodded briskly and walked to the horse. On his first try at mounting, his foot slipped from the stirrup and he half-fell. Ben rushed forward to help, but Lord Halifax waved him back; Tess heard him curse beneath his breath before he managed to climb aboard successfully and pull out his kerchief again. "I detest good-byes," he said, and blew his nose.

"Good-bye, yer lordship!" "Good-bye, sir!" "God bless!" cried the citizenry of Windber-on-Clun. He waved, and Oren got up on his horse, and they both rode away. Billy and the rest of the children ran after them, shouting farewells, with Job at their heels. The women sobbed, and the eyes of the strongest man there were burning with tears.

"A saint, a living saint," Missus Backus said over and over again, clinging to her husband.

" 'Twill be a cold day in hell," Mungo intoned mournfully, "before we see his like again."

As the horses galloped down the road, the children dropped from the chase one by one. Finally only Job was still running; Ben let out a piercing whistle that summoned him back. "Where'd ye get that?" asked Jack, noticing the gold chain circling Tess's throat.

"He gave it to me," she told him, "the poor dear man."

Ben cleared his throat. "Backus, my friend. Would the Swan happen to be open?"

"Soon as I get back there," the publican announced, and held up a crown he'd clutched in his hand. "Ale's on Lord Halifax, may God save him, though he asked me to keep it a secret."

"Well, ding me and dang me," said Ben, starting toward the village. "Was there ever such a man?"

"Dad!" Tess caught his collar. "What about what you promised me not an hour ago?"

"What's that, darling?"

"You know!" She hissed it in his ear. "About giving up ale!"

"Great Jehovah, child!" Ben burst out. "Our whole world's been stood on its end and you're bringing that up? Why, I wouldn't be half-surprised if all of this was your fault!"

"*My* fault?" Tess echoed incredulously.

"Aye, yours! Aren't you the one was always blathering about how dull it was in Windber, and wishing something would happen? Well, I daresay you've finally got your wish."

"Dad, that isn't fair!"

"*And* now she's wanting me to turn down Lord Halifax's last gift to me on this earth—a pint or two of ale!" Ben shook his head in wonder. "Honestly, Teresa, how can you be so cold?"

2

If there were a worse way for a day to begin, Tess thought viciously, shoveling up a load of steaming-fresh manure, she surely couldn't imagine what it might be. She'd been wakened by rain trickling onto her head from a new hole in the thatched cottage roof—and cold rain at that. Her father's clothes were scattered all over the floor; he lay curled on his cot fighting off dream-demons, with Job stretched atop him, drooling gloriously onto the sheets that Tess had washed just the afternoon before. No amount of poking or shaking or shouting could waken Ben for his potion; finally she left him to sleep and stomped off to the stables through the torrential downpour for her second morning straight of doing the feeding and mucking alone.

God only knew how late he'd stayed at the Swan last night, at the wake for Lord Halifax. That was what it had been, really, Tess mused, digging in with the shovel again. Everyone sat about saying over and over how wise his lordship had been, and kindly, and generous, and noble, and virtuous, as though he'd died instead of riding off to London and the New World. Tess left early, brushing off Jack's offer to walk her, bothered by some feeling she couldn't quite put into words. It came to her now, though, as she stood in her father's cut-down trousers and shirt, ankle-deep in dung, her fiery curls caught back in a damp braid. She was jealous of Andrew Halifax. So what if he'd lost his title and his lands and all his worldly possessions? At least he was getting out of Windber-on-

Clun. At least he was going somewhere. At least *something* was happening to him.

The instant she articulated the thought, Tess tore off her glove and knocked on the wooden wall to ward off the bad luck it was sure to bring her. What was she, daft, to be thinking such things? She wondered fleetingly if what had happened to Lord Halifax really could be her fault, the way her father had said, but then dismissed the notion. It didn't seem likely God would go to the lengths of ruining his lordship's life just to teach her a lesson. Still, they did say God worked in odd ways.

In her stall at the front of the stable, Linzy whinnied— the high, contented sound she made when she'd just been fed sugar or jam. Jack, Tess realized, hearing his footsteps. No doubt he was coming to try for a quick grope and kiss on his dinner break. There was nothing she felt less like at the moment, covered in muck as she was. If he really wanted to give her a thrill, she thought crossly, he might pitch in. After all, he'd been with the bunch that kept Ben at the Swan till all hours.

The footsteps came closer. He knows perfectly well I hate being sneaked up on, Tess fumed, and noiselessly thrust her shovel into the pile of hot, reeking dung, then lifted it up, fading back into the dark stall. He paused, seeing the open stall door, no doubt, and then kept coming. Tess balanced the shovel, waited until she saw his shadow fall across the doorway, then let the dung fly over the side of the stall.

"What in bloody—" Tess heard a lengthy, expert stream of obscenities that left no doubt at all the visitor wasn't Jack Brady. The deep, growly man's voice wasn't even familiar to her; it bore neither a Shropshire drawl nor her father's curt Kentish clip, but was entirely different, dark and rich somehow, like burnt-sugar pie. Curiosity conquering her better judgment, she peeked round the stall door to see who was there.

"Why, you little . . . I'll skin your hide, boy!" the deep voice swore, and before Tess could even get a good glimpse of him, the man sprang at her. She scuttled back into the stall, clutching the shovel as a weapon, and answered indignantly, with wounded pride:

"I'm not a boy, idiot!"

He stopped short in the doorway. They faced off in the shadowy stall, each taking stock of the other for a moment in silence, while rainwater dripped from the eaves.

Tess saw a man who was older than Jack but a good deal younger than her father. He was tall—*very* tall—with long black hair plastered tight to his head by the rain. He was dressed all in black—black cape, black boots, black gloves—and had thick black eyebrows above black-lashed eyes that slanted upward at the outer corners; they were like no one's eyes that Tess had ever seen before. His nose was long and straight, his mouth wide and unsmiling, with a full upper lip that seemed pushed together in the center, so that it curled upward. It was the most wonderful mouth she had ever seen, Tess decided, and pondered what color those strange slanting eyes might be.

He was still staring her up and down, and she grew painfully conscious of the sight she must make in her father's old clothes, reeking of dung, with the long fire-colored curls that were her best feature bound back. Every insult the other girls in Windber-on-Clun had ever hurled at her—Spindle Legs, Skinny Minnie, Cat's Eyes—surfaced in her mind. No wonder he'd thought her a boy.

"Really?" he asked very coolly. "Well, I'm no idiot. Do you always welcome strangers so charmingly?"

Tess's embarrassment made her tart-tongued. "If they skulk in on me, aye."

One of those thick black brows, the left one, arched upward in the center. "I didn't skulk in. I knocked."

"If you had, I would have heard you."

He stepped into the doorway and blocked it, so suddenly that Tess caught her breath and inched backward. She would not have thought so big a man could move as quickly as that. "Are you calling me a liar?" he asked, and now his voice was silk-smooth.

"I'm not calling you anything," said Tess, and heard her own voice break. It was just that all at once she was unnerved to be alone here with him. After all, he could be anything—a thief or highwayman or murderer—and probably was, from the looks of him. Would Ben hear if she screamed? She wished she hadn't mentioned that she wasn't a boy.

"Is something wrong?" he asked, lounging against the post. His upper lip curled in something that could have been a snarl or a smile.

"Of course not," Tess told him, clutching the iron shovel with both hands. "Why should there be?"

"I don't know. You seem . . . jumpy." He stretched out a long, long arm toward her throat. Tess let out a tiny cry and backed all the way to the stable wall. "I beg your pardon," he said. "I was just admiring your necklace."

"My what?" She reached up and touched the gold chain she still wore. So he *was* a thief! "The lord here gave it to me. He . . . he's very fond of me," she added bravely, hoping that might scare him off.

He nodded, withdrawing his hand. "Ah. I see."

"Look here," said Tess, her fear giving way to temper, "what do you want?"

"I'm looking for a man. A man named Jericho."

Tess's fear returned with a vengeance, coiling tight round her bowels. What in the world could this grim stranger want with her father? "Jericho?" she echoed, playing for time.

"Don't you know the name?"

"Aye, I do. But he isn't here."

"Perhaps you know where I might find him."

"No," she blurted out. "No, I don't. I haven't any idea."

He gestured toward the stable doors. "Is that his cottage I passed out there by the well?"

"I don't know which one you mean."

The man snorted like a horse at the transparent lie. "Come along, then. I'll point it out to you." Moving with that lightning quickness, he grabbed the shovel from her, put his hand on her elbow, and pulled her from the stall with such force that Tess had no choice but to let herself be tugged along.

He paused in front of Linzy's stall; the silver-gray pony had stuck out her muzzle and was watching him with wide, unblinking eyes. "There's a pretty girl," he said softly, reaching into his cloak, bringing forth a sugarloaf. He held it out to her on his palm; she took it eagerly and whinnied her thanks. Tess gave her beloved horse a dirty look as the man led her past.

"There." He trained his finger on the cottage. "Is that Jericho's?"

"Aye," Tess acknowledged. "But he's not there now. I know that for a fact." Just then she saw an enormous black stallion tied at the railed fence, with bulging saddlebags slung over his withers. "Is he yours?" she asked, unable to keep a note of admiration from her tone.

The man beside her nodded. "We've had a hard ride; he needs a good rubbing down. I was told this man Jericho would see to him."

"Who told you that?" Tess asked in surprise.

"The fellow at the tavern. Backus, that was his name."

Backus—that figured! Tess had had just about enough of him *and* the Swan, between this and her dad's drinking. "I can rub him down for you," she told the stranger tartly, "but you'll have to pay. It's not a bloody livery stable, you know. I've got my plate full enough at the moment without catering to you."

"Do you," he said very coolly. "And who might you be?"

"Jericho's daughter."

Again he arched one brow. Then he untied the stallion and gave her the reins. "Here, then. He's called Satan. See he gets oats, not hay." He slung the bags down from the saddle and over his shoulder, reached beneath his cape, and flipped something at her. She caught it on the fly, opened her hand, and stared at the coin lying there.

"What's this?"

"A crown. Since you seem in the habit of taking gold from lords. When you see your father, tell him I am looking for him. I'm Gideon Cade," said the stranger, and stalked off toward the big house through the pouring rain.

Tess didn't even wait for her father to wake up and lean over the floor; she dumped the whole pitcher of icy water onto his head as he lay sleeping. He and Job yelped simultaneously; the hound leapt for the cottage door, Ben for the stout cudgel he kept at the head of the bed. "Run, Teresa!" he cried, laying about with the bat as he strained bleary eyes to see his attackers. "Run for your life! 'Tis the Armageddon!"

She caught the cudgel and twisted it away, then pushed his potion on him. "Christ's sake, Dad, drink this quick and listen to me. I've seen him!"

"Oh, I've seen him too, lass, and 'tis a fearsome sight! His beady red eyes, and his cloven feet, and his mouth that breathes fire—"

"Not the devil, Dad," Tess said impatiently. "Gideon Cade!"

Her father stopped flailing. "Gideon . . . Why, now, who's that?"

"The new lord, Dad! The one cheated Lord Halifax out of his lands!"

Ben sat on the soaked bed in his underdrawers, then quickly jumped up again. "Oh, Tess. I thought all of that was just a bad dream!"

"Well, it wasn't," she told him grimly. "Lord Halifax is gone, and there's no mistaking Cade's here. Didn't waste any time, did he, coming to claim his ill-gotten gains? He sneaked up on me in the stables while I was mucking, and near made me jump out of my boots. Been to see Backus already, he had. And, Dad, he was looking for you."

"For me?" Wet bed or no, Ben sat. "Did he . . . did he say why?"

Tess shook her head. "Just that I should tell you he's looking for you. I'll tell you one other thing: he's got a devil of a fine stallion, as black as midnight. The bloody biggest horse I've ever seen. He calls him Satan."

Ben's blue eyes bulged. "What does he look like, this Gideon Cade?"

"He's a great huge fellow, dressed all in black. He's got black hair, too, and the strangest eyes—"

"What do you mean?"

"It's hard to say, exactly." Tess knit her brows. "He just doesn't look like anyone from round here."

"Great Jehovah." Ben's voice dropped to a whisper. "That's it, don't you see? Just like in my dreams, it's the end of the world! He's Beelzebub—the devil! The Old One himself's come to Windber-on-Clun!"

"Oh, Dad." Tess couldn't help it; a giggle escaped her. "Don't you think maybe that's going a little too far? Why in the world would the devil want to come here?" As she bent down to hand him his boots, the crown Gideon Cade had thrown her fell from her sleeve to the floor.

"What's that?" Ben demanded.

Tess picked it up again. "A gold piece he gave me."

"For the love of heaven!" He snatched the coin from her. "Don't you know once you take gold from the devil, your soul is his?"

"Dad, give that back; I earned that money!"

"There's only one way to earn money from Old Scratch, Teresa, and I pray heaven you haven't done that!"

"All I did was rub down his bloody horse."

"Mind your mouth, young lady!" her father roared, struggling into his trousers and shirt.

"But you've got no right—"

"I've got every right to protect my own flesh and blood from having truck with Lucifer!" He grabbed his oiled coat and hat from the peg by the door and whistled for Job. "Now, you stay right here in this cottage until I've had a look at this fellow myself. Come on, Job!"

"But, Dad—"

"Just do as I say!" He stomped out the door, turned around, and came back for the cudgel, tucking it under his oilskin. "Like to see him try to pull one over on Benjamin Jericho!" he was muttering as he went out again.

Tess stood in the middle of the cottage, rain trickling down her neck from yet another new leak in the thatch, and pictured her father confronting Gideon Cade protected by gloomy Job and the hidden cudgel. Without even realizing it, she began to laugh. Once she started, she couldn't stop; she laughed until she collapsed on a stool, holding tight to her sides. The devil in Windber-on-Clun! Only her father could come up with a notion like that.

"And if he is the devil," she told the leak in the roof thatch, "more power to him!" For it had been a very long time since she had felt so filled with expectation, since she had felt so—alive.

"Wot did ye say to him then, Ben?" Mungo demanded, his eyes big as pie plates.

"Well, what do you think I said? 'Benjamin Jacob Ezekiel Jericho's the name,' that's what I tells him. 'I hear you've been looking for me.' "

"Ooh, my, I don't know how ye had the gumption," Missus Backus marveled, holding tight to her blackjack of cider, "if he's so demoniac as ye say."

"So wot?" asked Meg Mullen.

"Demoniac," Missus Backus repeated, leaning toward her. "Didn't my Backus say, too, he had the look of the devil about him?"

"I don't know how a man can look like the devil," the Widow Jonas objected, "less'n he's got hooves and a pitchfork and a long red tail. Had he got a tail, Ben?"

"Not that I could see," Ben admitted, "but mind you, he was sitting down."

Tess sat cross-legged on a bench by the big fireplace in the Swan, Job's head in her lap, and bit her lip to keep from giggling. "Honestly," she whispered to Jack, "the way they're carrying on!"

He shot her a disapproving look. "It's no laughing matter."

"Oh, Christ, Jack, of course it is. The man's not the devil!"

"The Good Book says the evil one wears many disguises."

"Where does it say that?" Tess asked, but he hushed her, trying to hear Ben. She scratched Job's long silky ears and listened as well. Ben hadn't got back from the big house till nearly four o'clock, and wouldn't say a word to her about what had gone on. "I need a drink," he'd insisted, heading for the Black Swan, "and anyway, I can't stand to tell a story twice."

He was relishing the telling now, though, with them all

hanging on his every word. "He says something then about being pleased to meet me, and holds out his hand. Well, you can bet I wasn't about to shake hands with that one, not me! I just says, 'Accosted my daughter, didn't you, down in the stables?' "

"Oh, Dad, you didn't," Tess moaned.

"Dang me if I didn't. 'White as a ghost and all shaking she was when she found me,' I tells him."

"Dad, I was not!"

"Hush up, Tessie, and let him tell it," Backus chided her, refilling her mug.

"Wot did he say to that, then?" Robbie wanted to know.

"Had the nerve to tell me she didn't look the kind that scared easily. *And* asked about his horse."

"His wot?" Meg Mullen demanded, and was answered by a chorus: "His horse!"

"Why, wot about his horse?"

"I saw the creature," Backus asserted, while Missus Backus nodded eagerly. "Huge, that horse is. Why, ye'd have to be the devil to ride him."

"Calls the beast Satan, Tess says," Ben added darkly.

"Why, I calls that cat of mine Tiger," said the Widow Jonas, "but it don't make him so."

"Drink yer cider, pet," Missus Backus told her, shoving the cup toward her mouth. "Ben, what happened then?"

"I told him I brought my girl up to know how to take care of horses proper. And then I gave the gold piece he gave Tess right back to him."

"Dammit, Dad," Tess cried, "you'd no right to do that!"

" 'Course he had, love!" Meg admonished her. "Ye can't be taking gold from the devil or he'll own your soul!"

"He's not the bloody—"

"Tess!" Jack broke in, highly shocked.

"But I was going to use it for my wedding dress!"

"Even if Gideon Cade ain't the devil," Jack said grimly, "he's a thievin' bastard. And I'll not have a man like that payin' for yer weddin' clothes."

"Oh, you won't have it, won't you?"

"That's right."

"Well, it just so happens, Jack Brady, that I don't take orders from you!"

"Listen, ye two!" Backus roared in their ears. "Take it outside if you want a spat, but shut up if ye're stayin' in here!" Green eyes flashing, Tess pulled Job closer and leaned against the hearth. Jack put his back to her and gulped down the rest of his ale.

"Then," Ben said loudly, trying to take control once again, "I told him just what I thought of his cheating poor old Lord Halifax out of his place with that crooked lawsuit of his!"

"Ooh, Ben, ye didn't!" Missus Backus squealed.

"Aye, I did!"

"Well, wot did he say?" Robbie asked in awe.

Ben's voice dropped to a whisper. "He laughed."

"He wot?" asked Meg, cupping her ear.

"He laughed—just like he was sharing a jest with the Old One!"

"God bless us and keep us," said Missus Backus, and crossed herself.

"I knew he was a bad 'un the minute I clapped eyes on him!" her husband insisted.

"The shameless cur," Jack spat, his hands curled into fists.

"Someone ought to take a horsewhip to him, that's what I say!" Meg cried.

The door to the Black Swan opened in a gust of freezing wet wind. A huge figure loomed on the threshold, surrounded by a swirl of jet-colored wool. "Ladies. Gentlemen. Good evening," said Gideon Cade.

Dead silence dropped over the room, like the sudden fogs that came down in the marshlands. No one moved or breathed; Ben sat with his mug halfway to his mouth. Then Job rose up from Tess's lap, growled with a show of bared teeth, and sprang at Cade's throat.

"Down!" the caped man commanded in a truly terrible voice. Job jerked in midair like a silver trout caught on a line, fell to the floor, and then slunk, cowering and craven, back behind Tess's skirts. Missus Backus promptly crossed herself again.

"Is this the devil, then?" Widow Jonas asked loudly.

Gideon Cade threw back his head and laughed.

Tess hated to admit it, but there was something unearthly about his laughter; it was a low deep rumble that seemed to begin somewhere in the ground beneath his black-booted feet. The fact that no one joined in didn't bother him a whit; she understood as she listened to his private amusement what Ben had meant about his sharing a jest with Old Scratch.

Backus found his tongue first, as was only fitting, since it was his tavern. "Yer lordship." Either Jack or Job growled; Tess couldn't be sure. "Was there somethin' ye wanted?"

"Aye, Backus. I'll have a mug of ale."

"Ah—ale, sir?"

"Ale. You sell ale, don't you?"

"Y-yes, sir."

"Well, then." Gideon Cade straddled a bench, as calmly as you please. Smiling, he scanned the staring faces that were turned to him, nodding at Ben. "Mr. Jericho. Nice to see you. Wretched weather, isn't it?"

"Excuse me, sir." That was Backus; Cade turned to him questioningly. "It's just that . . . Lord Halifax never came in here."

"Never came to the tavern?" Tess recognized the slow arch of the new lord's left eyebrow. "How peculiar of him."

Jack stood up slowly, thumbs hooked in his belt loops, with a look in his eye Tess had thought he reserved for her when she really provoked him. "Not really," he told the interloper. "See, he knew this was our place. Not his."

"You don't say." Cade's deep voice was studiously pleasant. "That's peculiar too. Because the documents I received from Lord Halifax state that he held the lease on this building, was responsible for upkeep, and supplied the ale in return for ninety-two percent of the profits."

"Ninety-two percent?" Missus Backus echoed, looking at her husband. "Is it so high as that?"

"Which makes it my tavern now, and my ale," Cade went on, still ever so politely, "which I am understandably eager to sample. If you would be so kind, Mr. Backus?" He looked at the tavernkeeper expectantly.

Backus didn't budge. Tess heard that low growl again and knew it was Jack this time. She had the curious sensation that the minutes were ticking by with infinitesimal slowness, the way they did sometimes in dreams. When her father pushed himself to his feet, everyone gave a start, so lengthy had the impasse seemed.

"Bring him his ale, Backus," Ben told the barkeep. Then he set his own mug on the table. "You needn't bother bringing me another, though. Gone right off my taste for it, I have."

"Aye, so have I," said Jack, following Ben's meaning. "Ye, Mungo, Sam, aren't ye done as well?"

"Damn straight we are," Mungo declared, grabbing his hat and coat and catching the arm of Widow Jonas. "Come along, then, woman, we'll see you home."

"But I'm not done my cider."

"We're all finished here, pet, all of us," Meg Mullen told her, pulling her toward the door.

"Tess." When she didn't move instantly, Jack called her again, more sharply. "Tessie, come on!" Realizing this wasn't the best moment to remind him they were having a row, she flounced up from the bench and let him bundle her into her cape. As she knotted the thongs at her throat, her gaze met that of Gideon Cade. His long, hollow-cheeked face was expressionless, but beneath the beveled black brows his pale eyes burned. Then Jack steered her out into the cold rainy darkness with the rest of the tenants, leaving Backus and his wife to tend to their unwelcome guest.

Once outside the tavern, the residents of Windber-on-Clun became highly vocal. "The nerve of that bleedin' bastard!" Sam declared, his voice loud enough to carry through the closed door.

"I've got his number, all right," Jack muttered, and spat in the mud.

"I still don't see why I couldn't finish my cider," Widow Jonas said crossly.

"Because he's run us out, ninny!" Mungo told her. "Honest to God, wot's the world comin' to when a hardworkin' man can't have a mug of ale in peace?"

"He didn't run anybody out," Tess tried to protest.

"Shut up!" her father barked, and yanked her toward home.

Meg trailed after them, pulling at Ben's sleeve. "Did ye see the way Job went for his throat there? They do say animals have a sixth sense, don't they, about these things? I reckon ye're right, Ben, about wot he is."

"Aye, I knew it the moment I saw him," he told her, plunging on through the rain.

Speaking of Job—Tess looked for him in the darkness, but didn't spot him. Even when she whistled, he didn't come loping toward her. He'd got left behind in the Swan somehow, she realized, a strange little tingle running up her spine.

Ben and Meg were walking five yards ahead of her, locked in conversation. She peered back at the tavern. The knot of neighbors had vanished, everyone gone on to his home.

"Tess!" her father called, turning round to find her.

"I'm right here. I'm coming," she answered, and ran back to the Swan as fast as she could.

She pushed the door open only a crack, and what she saw within promptly quelled her nerve. Cade had gotten his ale. The mug sat on a table by his elbow, while he bent over something he had cupped in his enormous hands. Job was stretched out on the bench beside him, but Backus and his wife had disappeared. Hardly in a rush to be alone with the new lord again, Tess decided Job might as well spend the night there at the tavern; it was warm and dry. She was just about to shut the door when Cade turned and saw her, and smiled.

"Hello," he said. "I thought you might be coming back."

"Why?" Tess blurted, feeling as though she'd been caught snatching cakes from a windowsill.

"Because you forgot this magnificent specimen of *Canis familiaris*. Your dog," he added, when she didn't move.

"I know what *Canis* means," Tess told him tartly, entering the room. "Come along, Job."

Job didn't move. "So that's his name—Job," Cade said thoughtfully, scratching the hound's long ear. "It surely does suit him. Does he always look so morose?"

"You needn't make sport of him. Job, come here!"

"I wasn't making sport. Names should suit those they're given to." His pale eyes surveyed her closely. "Yours does. That young man called you Tess. A very beautiful name. Not from the Bible, though. That puzzles me, given your father's string of prophets and patriarchs."

"I'm named for my mother."

"Ah. Was she here tonight?"

"She's dead."

"I'm sorry," said Gideon Cade.

Tess shrugged. "It wasn't long after I was born. I don't remember her or anything."

"Then I'm even more sorry." He patted Job's withers.

"I don't need your pity, thank you. I *would* appreciate your letting go of Job."

"I'm not holding him," he told her. "It seems he's fascinated by what I've got here. He may look morose, but he's got the devil of a nose on him. Caught the scent the instant I walked in. For a moment I thought your father might have trained him to tear out my heart."

Tess almost giggled. Instead she inched closer, looking at the hand he held cupped on the table. "What have you got?" He raised up his hand. She caught her breath. "Oh, the poor wee thing!"

"Exactly," said Gideon Cade, frowning at the tiny wet kitten that mewed and batted his finger. "I heard it crying as I left the stables not half an hour ago. Thought it was a baby at first."

"It couldn't have been a baby," Tess scoffed, letting the kitten sniff her hand, smiling as its rough tongue brushed her. "No one in the village is in a family way. But then, you wouldn't know that."

"No," he agreed. "Anyway, once I'd found it, I didn't know what to do with it. There wasn't any mother cat around. I stopped by your father's cottage to see if it might belong to you. When you weren't there, I thought perhaps you'd come here."

Tess scratched the kitten's matted black back. "It must be the Widow Jonas'. Her Tabitha had a brood two days past. Three black and one gray."

"My, you certainly do keep track of the village cats. Are you especially fond of them?"

"No. But a new litter is enough to set the whole village buzzing for a week."

He arched that brow. "Surely, Mistress Jericho, you're not implying that life is a trifle dull here in Windber-on-Clun?"

" 'Dull' is too mild a word."

Gideon Cade picked up the kitten by the scruff of its neck and stared into its unblinking eyes. "You must have been very sorry to see Lord Halifax go, then."

Something in his voice put Tess on guard. "Why do you say that?"

"It must have served to relieve the tedium quite nicely when he gave you gifts like that chain." He parted the front of Tess's cloak with one hand and ran his gaze over the green skirt and white smock that she wore. "I do hope I've inherited all of the former lord's privileges."

She snatched her cloak away. "You inherited nothing. You stole it all, like the low, conniving thief that you are. For your information, Lord Halifax gave me this necklace to wear when I get married to Jack. He said I reminded him of his wife."

"And of what he used to do to her, no doubt."

"Why, you—" Tess put her hand up to strike him. He caught her wrist, quick as lightning, in his iron grip. "Go to hell," she spat, trying to twist free.

"All I meant was how he used to love her, Mistress Jericho," he told her. "What did you think?"

"I know what you bloody well meant. Let go of me or I'll scream."

"I beg your pardon." He released her hand. "But even a low, conniving thief has a right to defend himself from a slap in the face."

"Not when he deserves it so richly as you do. Get over

here, Job. *Now!*" Recognizing that she meant business, the hound slouched to her side. "I've never in my life met anyone so rude and churlish as you."

"Then your life *has* been sheltered," he told her. Then, as she turned and stormed out, green eyes flashing, he called after her: "At least I don't bore you!" And his laughter, dark as the deep waters of the River Clun, followed her into the night.

3

Gideon Cade's invasion of the Swan had one salutary effect: Tess's father was cold sober for the next week, and awake even before she was. On the seventh day after the new lord's arrival, when she called Ben down from the stables for his breakfast, he came into the cottage looking cross and preoccupied.

"Anything wrong, Dad?" she asked, setting a bowl of oatmeal before him.

"Aye. I don't like oatmeal."

"Well, it's either that or gruel, and you hate that more. If you think you get tired of eating the same thing every morning, think how I feel cooking it."

"I've a taste on for bacon," said Ben, pushing the bowl away.

"Do you really? I've a taste on for being Queen Catherine, and there's as much chance. If you've complaints about the food, tell his lordship, not me."

"Gor, don't remind me of that one." He dug gloomily into his porridge. "We'll all be starving come midsummer if he has his way."

"What are you talking about?"

"I found him in the stables at dawn again, and he'd already been out riding. Looking over the land, he said. Oh, Gideon Cade has got plans for the village of Windber-on-Clun. Big plans."

Tess got her own bowl of oatmeal and sat down across from him. "What sort of plans?"

"The sort a madman makes, what else? Wants to build himself a house made all out of glass, and grow lemons and oranges—"

"What are they?"

"Fruits, pet. Sort of like . . ." He groped for a comparison. "Like gooseberries, only bigger and sourer. With a rind around them like a cheese."

"Are they good?" Tess asked, intrigued.

" 'Course they're good! But if Jehovah meant oranges to grow in Shropshire, I guess he'd have put them here, wouldn't he?"

"Why don't they grow here?"

"Because it's too cold!" Ben said explosively. "But he says he saw 'em growing in these here glass houses over in France, and so why not here?"

"Been to France, has he?" Tess stirred her porridge. "What else is he planning?"

"The craziest stuff that you ever did hear. Why, there's some kind of plant that the heathen Indians grow in the New World, he says—mars, he called it, or something—that's better than hay for cattle or acorns for swine. He wants to put in whole fields of that by the north wood."

And to the New World too? she wondered. "That doesn't sound so awful, Dad. You were just now wanting bacon. If the swine ate better, you could eat better too."

"You're missing the point, aren't you, Tess? How in tarnation could some red-skinned Indian on the other side of the world know what's good for Shropshire hogs? Or how could Gideon Cade, for that matter, who doesn't look like he's ever done an honest day's work in his life, much less slopped pigs?"

"I don't know. But just because something's new doesn't mean it's bad."

"Why do we need new, I'd like to know? What's wrong with the old ways?"

Tess bit back a smile. "You're starting to sound just like a Shropshireman, Dad. Afraid Gideon Cade's changes will make a bit more work for you, is that it?"

"I'm a mite surprised to hear you defending him, lass," her father said with sly complacency, "seeing as he wants to be breeding that devil horse of his to your little pony."

Tess stood bolt upright in her place. "To my Linzy?"

"Aye."

"He is out of his bloody damned mind."

"Isn't that just what I told him? Though not in such language, which, by the by, I've told you before is most unbecoming. But it's just another one of his newfangled ideas that you say I shouldn't be bothered by. Wants to breed racehorses, he does, with that black demon's power and your Linzy's grace. Says such a horse would best the king's own at the tracks in London. Tess, where are you . . . Teresa!" The door slammed behind her just as Ben let out a snort.

Tess flew up the hill to the big house like a racehorse herself, long legs striding, fiery mane streaming. She was so incensed that instead of going round to the kitchens she ran right up the front stairs to the portico and pounded on the brass doors. When Prince Oren, back the night before from his sojourn to London, didn't answer immediately, she thumped on them again.

The butler appeared at last, looking flushed and irate. "Mistress Jericho," he said haughtily. "As you're well aware, tenants are permitted to present themselves only at the rear entrance to the manor, unless by prior arrangement they have—"

"Save the airs, Oren; you forget I know you were born and bred right here in Windber. Christ, don't you ever get sick of being such a bloody prig? I want to see Gideon Cade. Now."

"That's quite impossible," the butler told her.

"Oren, is someone there?" a deep voice called from somewhere at the top of the long marble staircase in the center of the entrance hall. Tess recognized that cool, insolent tone by now.

"I'll see myself up," she told Oren, pushing past him.

"Mistress Jericho!" He caught her arm. "You can't go up there!"

"Can't I? Just watch me." She shook off the butler's restraining arm and ran up the stairs.

"Your lordship!" Oren cried in warning.

"What is it now?" Cade called back.

If he hadn't spoken, Tess never would have known which of the dozen hallway doors to look behind, but when she heard his voice she could tell to open the third one. With Oren huffing up the staircase behind her, there was no time to lose. She grabbed the shining crystal knob, turned it, and pulled. "Listen, you . . ." she began.

Across the room her eyes met Gideon Cade's in a mirror. He had his back to her—*all* of his back, Tess saw with a start, for he'd just stepped out of a tub of water onto the tiled floor. His black hair hung in damp ringlets to his shoulder blades; his skin was browned and gleaming from his broad back to his narrow waist, with only his taut, smooth buttocks more pale. His legs were dark again, sinewy and strong; along the right one a thick raised scar, red and shiny as a Welsh poppy's petals, ran from the bottom of his knee all the way to the top of his thigh.

"Mistress Jericho! What a pleasant surprise," he declared, his brow inching upward. Tess thanked her blessed stars the mirror was a small one; she'd seen no more of the front of him than his eyes and face. "Please don't rush off," he went on as she backed away and then found she couldn't, since Prince Oren had jammed into the doorway behind her.

"I'm terribly sorry, milord," the butler snapped, glaring at Tess, "but she just barged in.'"

"Don't give it another thought, Oren," his master said smoothly. "Mistress Jericho is welcome to join me anytime and anywhere she pleases. Mistress Jericho, would you be so kind as to hand me that towel?"

I . . . will . . . not . . . blush, Tess vowed, reaching for the towel on a chair at her side and flinging it toward him. After all, he wasn't the first man she'd ever seen naked. She used to spy on Jack and his mates when they swam in the Clun—though to be honest, she'd never dared get close enough to see much. And there was her father; she'd seen nearly this much of him plenty of times. Of course, there *wasn't* this much of her father, or of Jack either, she thought, her gaze drawn again to the seemingly endless expanse of broad back. Gideon Cade draped the towel around his shoulders and turned to her. Like lightning, Tess stared at the floor again.

"And my robe, if you would?"

Tess knew she was blushing now, and ducked her head lower. Any sort of gentleman—hell, even a peasant, in that situation—would have helped her graciously out of her plight. But Cade was clearly relishing it. Well, think of it as penance, she told herself, for being such a fool as to burst in this way. As steadily as she could, she held out the midnight-blue robe that lay across the chair.

"Thank you, Mistress Jericho. Tell me, have you breakfasted?" Tess said nothing; as he'd wrapped himself in the long robe and tied it at the waist, she'd caught the scent of him, warm flesh mingled with some dark exotic spice that was in his soap, and the strange musky fragrance made her flesh tighten in the most peculiar way. Beneath the linen smock she wore, her breasts grew taut and heavy; low in her belly, some muscle coiled like a spring. "No?" Gideon Cade continued when she didn't speak. "Then by all means, you must join me. Oren, set another place in the . . . What the devil do you call that room?"

"Lord Halifax referred to it as the librarium, milord. I must say, I hardly think—"

"Yes, I know, Oren, but that's just as well. Don't you agree, Mistress Jericho?" He dried his hair, tossed it back from his forehead with a raffish grin, and steered Tess past the openmouthed butler and down the hall.

"Here we are." He pushed open one of the doors. "The librarium—but don't ask me where the books might be." Tess saw that the shelves lining the walls of the room held nothing but dust. There wasn't any fancy carpet on the floor, nor much furniture either—only a table laid for a meal for one, with plain pottery dishes and tinware, and a few spindle chairs. Noticing the way she stared about her, Cade laughed. "Rather disappointing, I know. My predecessor seems to have disposed of everything that wasn't nailed down."

"No doubt he had to, to pay off the lawyers," Tess spat.

"The lawyers?" Cade echoed. "Oh, yes. The lawyers. Hired by Halifax in his noble efforts to save the estate from falling into my clutches, I suppose."

"You know damned well they were. I'm glad you find ruining another man's life so amusing."

"Won't you sit down, Mistress Jericho?" he invited, pulling back one of the chairs.

"I didn't come here to eat."

"Just to try to catch me naked?"

"Certainly not!"

"I hardly see why you should be angry with me, Mistress Jericho," he said imperturbably, taking his own seat, checking with great solemnity to make sure his robe was closed at the lap. "After all, I didn't burst in on you in your bath." He looked at her across the table. "Ah, so you *can* blush—and most becomingly. I did wonder." Tess was nearly certain he'd seen her blushing earlier, but decided it was decent of him to pretend he hadn't. And besides, he did have a point about who should be angry with whom.

"I apologize for that," she said shortly. "It was unspeakably rude of me."

"So it was. But please, don't apologize. I enjoyed it immensely—as I hope you did." He laughed again as she darted an angry glance at him and stalked toward the door—only to find her escape route blocked by Oren once more. This time he carried a big tray laden with covered platters. The smells coming from them were indescribably enticing; against her will, Tess turned, following with her nose as he bore it past.

Gideon Cade looked at her with that eyebrow raised. "Sure you won't do me the honor of joining me, Mistress Jericho?"

"I only wanted a word with you," she insisted, but her feet were moving toward those delicious aromas of their own accord.

"Please," he coaxed. "I know you came on business, but I make it a rule never to discuss work until I've breakfasted." Her resistance eroded, Tess sat. "You may go, Oren," he told the butler, who marched out with his upturned nose showing just what he thought of this unorthodox dining arrangement. "Christ, what an insufferable snob that man is," Cade muttered as the door clicked shut. Tess stifled a giggle; her host took his place again, smiling charmingly. "There's nothing in the world I enjoy so much as having breakfast with a lady this way," he went on, "unless it is breakfasting with a lady in bed."

"I'm not about to sit here and listen to you make lewd remarks," Tess said angrily.

"Lewd? It was merely a statement of fact."

Tess was about to get up again when he uncovered the first of the platters; instead she stared in wonder at a bowl full of orbs the color of the summer sky at sunset. "What are they?" she asked, her pique forgotten.

"Oranges. Have you never seen them before?" Tess shook her head as he set one on her plate. Its skin was waxy, dimpled like a baby's elbows.

"How do you eat them?"

"Some people take off the peel, but I find that a bother. I just manage like so." He took one and sliced it neatly in half, and the air was filled with a smell sweeter than eglantine blossoms. To Tess's surprise, the flesh inside the fruit was the same vivid hue as the skin. He raised half to his mouth and dug his teeth in. Juice ran down his chin; he laughed and wiped it away. "Not very elegant, but it gets the job done."

Tentatively Tess cut her own orange in half; as its scent engulfed her, she laughed too, for sheer pleasure. With Cade watching, she nibbled delicately at the segmented pulp and felt her eyes go wide. "Like it?" he asked, head cocked to one side. She nodded, sucking at the fruit so eagerly that its juice dribbled from her mouth too.

"It's wonderful. Indescribable!" She scraped out the last bit of juicy pulp with her teeth, seized the other half, and finished that as well. "I've never in my life tasted anything so good! May I have another?"

"Certainly. I'll see what else we have got." He uncovered another platter. "The mush!" he exclaimed. "Let's see if Missus Wallace downstairs has followed my instructions."

"What's mush?" Tess asked through a mouthful of orange.

"Ground maize boiled with water, then sliced down and fried. Why are you making that face?"

"Maize—that's what Dad said you wanted to feed the pigs."

"Aye. So what?"

"So how can you eat something that pigs eat?" she asked with a shudder. "We don't eat acorns, do we?"

"We could, you know, if that's all there was. I take it you don't care for any mush, then."

"No, thank you!" He shrugged, slathered the crisp yellow slabs with butter, and covered them with a thick golden-brown liquid he poured from a pitcher. "You eat them with honey?" Tess asked.

He shook his head. "Maple syrup. Brought all the way from the colonies." He took up a forkful, chewed, and swallowed, with an expression on his face of pure bliss. "Ah, Missus Wallace, you have done this mush proud."

"What does it taste like?" Tess asked curiously.

"Ambrosia. Nectar of the gods."

"No, I mean it."

"Some things in this life words can't do justice to, Mistress Jericho," he told her gravely. "You must simply experience them for yourself." He cut off a piece of the mush and held it out to her on his fork. "Try it. I dare you."

Dubiously Tess opened her mouth and let him feed her the morsel. "Oh!" she said. "Mm! Really!" She cleared the orange rinds from her plate and pushed it toward him. "More, please! And what else have you got on that tray?"

"Hickory-smoked ham from Virginia." He piled thin slices of that on her plate with the mush. Tess attacked it happily. "That's what a pig fed on maize will taste like," he told her, "if you cure it right. And Moroccan coffee." He started to pour her a cup of strong-smelling black liquid from a steaming pot, then paused. "I'm not sure you'll like this; it's rather an acquired taste."

"I'll like it," Tess said through another mouthful of mush. "I like it all."

"Well, just in case, you'd better try it with cream and sugar." He stirred them in until the drink was the color of fine tanned leather; his own cup he left dark.

Brimming with confidence, Tess took a hearty sip and promptly choked, sending a fine spray of the liquid into the air. "I beg your pardon!" she cried in horror, grabbing for her napkin.

But Gideon Cade only laughed, leaning back in his chair. "I tried to warn you. Do you think it's horrible?"

"Not horrible, exactly." Tess took another sip, much more circumspectly, and screwed up her nose. "It just doesn't taste at all like anything I've ever had before. What did you say it's called?"

"Coffee." He spelled it for her. "It comes from Africa. It's become all the rage in London. There are coffee-houses springing up everywhere, where a man can go and sit and read and drink it all day long."

"Does it get one drunk?"

"On the contrary. Most people say it gives them energy."

"If that's so, they ought not to waste it on those with the leisure to sit about and read; they ought to give it to farmers and field hands."

"I suppose you're right. How nice it is to watch a woman enjoy a meal! I'm used to seeing them peck at their food like birds." Tess flushed and quickly pushed her plate away, aware she'd been behaving like a pig herself. "No, I mean it," Cade insisted. He smiled at her over his cup. In the slanting rays of morning sun that poured between the room's striped curtains, Tess saw that his eyes weren't gray, as she had thought, but a clear deep blue, like an October sky. His smile was warm and winning, and made Tess feel as though the two of them shared some special secret no one else could know. He looked impossibly handsome and elegant lounging late over his morning meal. She thought again of the long, hard body she'd seen earlier, its muscular lines barely hidden now by a drape of indigo wool, and again her own body trembled, flesh contracting, breasts tightening, nipples growing round and hard against her linen smock. No one, not Jack or anyone else, had ever evoked so vivid a response from her—and this lazy, languorous man managed it with no more than a smile. She groped for something to say.

"Are you going to grow coffee too?"

"If I can. In the glasshouse. It's one of many things I intend to try here in Windber-on-Clun."

His words reminded Tess of the reason for her visit. "My father says another is putting your stallion at stud to my pony. I'll tell you right now, I won't have that," she said bluntly.

He poured himself more coffee. "Might I ask why not?"

"I'm not breeding my Linzy to anyone. I don't want her spirit broken."

"Breeding doesn't always break the spirit," he noted with a trace of a smile.

"It does often enough. I'm not taking chances."

The smile broadened. "Have you consulted Linzy on the matter?"

"I don't have to. I've looked after horses all my life. I know well enough the changes that breeding brings. She'd lose her will and her courage, not to mention her speed."

"You call her your pony." Gideon Cade scratched his chin. "It's my understanding that I own everything in Windber-on-Clun."

"Not Linzy," Tess told him, her own chin raised. "A friend of Lord Halifax's had a mare sick with horsebane fever last year. Dad cured her and he gave him Linzy as thanks. Dad's a genius with horses. He had a place once with a great lord, with twenty men under him and one hundred horses."

"You don't say. Whatever made him give it up?"

Tess bit her tongue, regretting her boasting. Though Ben had never told her, she assumed he'd lost the job because of his drinking, and it wouldn't do for Gideon Cade to find out about that. "He likes it in Windber," she said at last. "Anyway, the point is, the man gave Dad Linzy, and Dad gave her to me last year when I turned sixteen."

"And now you stable and pasture her at my expense. I wonder what an attorney might have to say about who owns her under those circumstances."

"You and your bloody lawyers." Tess shoved back her chair. "That may have worked with Lord Halifax, but it won't with me."

"And why is that?"

"Because before I see you breed Linzy to that stallion I'll cut off his balls with my own two hands," she said steadily, and put down her knife and fork. "Thank you for breakfast."

She felt his eyes follow her as she went to the door, heard the galling bemusement in his voice as he told her, "The pleasure was all mine, Mistress Jericho."

*   *   *

That afternoon when her work was finished, Tess went riding high into the blunt-crested hills of the Forest Clun. She rode the way her father had taught her when she could scarcely walk, on the small light saddle he'd made for her, knees hugging Linzy's withers. Ben had nothing kind to say for the fashion of women riding sidesaddle. "Good way to get your neck broke," he'd grumble. "If Jehovah meant you to ride like that, he'd have made you with two left feet."

The sun was still warm on her face as she left the valley, but further up, in the shadows of the bud-leaved beech and oak trees, there was still a bite of winter in the air. When she reached the summit of the White Moor she gave Linzy her head and let her scrounge for forage among the ghost-pale rocks that gave the pitch its name. From that height the River Clun was thin as a girl's hair ribbon braided through waves of green banks; the thatched roofs of the Swan and its neighbor cottages seemed like wisps of hay lost from a giant's pitchfork. The stable was small, her own cottage still smaller, stocky and square, a child's building block.

But the big house had character and definition even from a distance; the solidity of its stone and mortar was undiminished; its red tile roof stood out boldly against the smooth green carpet of lawn and trees. Rather like its occupants, Tess thought. Lord Halifax had always stood out in a crowd, and Gideon Cade surely would.

Cade wasn't really a lord, she reminded herself; he'd merely stolen the trappings. Without that fancy house and his elegant clothes he'd be . . . well, she'd seen that morning just what he'd be, and she'd only be lying to herself if she didn't admit what that was: the most glorious, magnificent male creature she had ever set eyes on. Even now the thought of his nakedness sent shivers through her spine.

Once, the summer before, when riding Linzy, she and the pony had hit some pace, some rhythm, that set loose a sensation in Tess's loins she'd never felt before. It had been painful and at the same time exquisite, made her want it never to stop and yet want to scream. She'd spurred Linzy on while wave after wave of the feeling pulsed through her; she'd been breathless, lost in wonder, riding in a blind fury toward some promised land. Then Linzy jumped a fallen tree, landed off-gait, and faltered. The sensation vanished, leaving only an imprecise imprint on her memory and a dull ache between her thighs.

In all the hours she spent atop Linzy, the feeling never came to her again. Eventually she came to think she must have dreamed it, the way she could only have dreamed her dead mother's face. But that morning, as she sat across the breakfast table from Gideon Cade and ate mush and maple syrup from his fork, the ache had come back to her, and some gossamer trace of the sensation too.

It frightened her to think what that might mean. She'd felt excited from time to time when Jack kissed her, when he tugged down her bodice and plucked at her nipples, fondled her breasts. But even when he tried to lie across her and reach beneath her skirts, rubbed her thighs with his, pressed that bulge in his trousers against her, it was as though she stood outside herself watching, not really there while he pawed her so frantically.

And all Gideon Cade had to do was brush her shoulder, smile into her eyes over a plateful of ham . . .

She yanked up on the bridle so quickly that Linzy neighed in protest. "Sorry, girl," she apologized, smoothing down the pony's silvery mane. Glancing westward, she saw that the sun was near setting. "Past time we started home to make Dad his supper," she said, and set off down the hill.

Back at the stable she gave Linzy a good brush and comb and then fed her, giving her hay mixed with oats and bran and a carrot to top it off. She hung over the stall door and talked to the pony as she ate, a habit she'd begun when Ben first gave her the foal, who'd been shy and skittish; now, "Spoiled, aren't you?" she murmured. "Won't touch your supper, will you, unless I'm right here?"

In the catercorner stall Gideon Cade's gleaming black stallion snorted and shifted, rocking the walls. Tess looked back over her shoulder. His ears were flattened, his nostrils flared, and his dark eyes lively; the last thing in the world that he seemed ready for was sleep.

"If you think I'm afraid of you," she told him, "you're sorely mistaken. I let that master of yours know what I'd do if you came near my Linzy, and I meant it, too." Unruffled, he stared back at her with something of Cade's cool arrogance. Tess laughed. "Oh, you're two of a kind, aren't you, you and he?"

She heard another sound then—heavy footsteps outside the stables. "Speak of the devil," she whispered, and felt the quickened pulse of her heart. She stepped back from the stall, facing the doors; they flew open with a crash, and Jack came in.

"Hello, Tess. Expectin' someone else, were ye?"

"Jack!" She laughed. "I wasn't expecting anyone at all. What are you doing here?"

He stood with his thumbs hooked in his belt, his sturdy legs apart. In the dim light it was hard for her to see his face. "I've just come from the Swan," he said.

"Christ, don't tell me Dad's there already! He hasn't had any supper; he'll be pickled on half a pint."

"Aye, yer father's there." How strange his voice sounded, thought Tess—as though his jaw were one of the traps Mungo and Sam set in the fens for boar. "Yer father and everyone else is there. They're all listenin' to Prince Oren tell how ye helped Gideon Cade take his bath this morning, and then had breakfast with him naked."

"Oh, Jesus." Tess put her hand to her mouth and giggled. "Oren! I should have known."

Jack took a step toward her. "Ye don't deny it, then?"

"Don't tell me you believe him!"

"*Do* ye deny it, Tess? Be careful what ye say. One of the chambermaids saw ye give him a robe, and swore he was naked as the day he was born."

"What do you mean, be careful what I say?" she demanded. "You act as though I'm on trial!"

"I'm waitin' to hear an explanation, Teresa."

"And if you'll stop sounding like the bloody Grand Inquisitor, I'll give you one! I went up to the big house in a rage because Dad told me Cade wanted to breed his stallion to Linzy. That shifty prig Oren wouldn't let me in, so I pushed past him and accidentally walked in on Cade in his bath. He was just getting out, so I handed him his clothes. He had his back to me, Jack. It's not as though I saw anything."

"And it never occurred to ye to turn around and walk out again once ye realized wot ye'd done?" he asked angrily.

"I already felt fool enough. I didn't want to make it worse by letting him think he'd embarrassed me."

"And so ye stayed to breakfast too—for the sake of yer pride?"

"Pride counts, Jack, and you know it."

"Ye're damned right I do!" He came for her, grabbing her arms, and she realized in shock he was shaking. "Wot about *my* pride? How in hell d'ye think *I* feel havin' the whole village know my girl was lollin' about with that scoundrel, laughin' and flirtin' with him, eatin' off his fork?"

"Whoever told you that was spying!"

"And that's worse than playing the whore?"

Furious, Tess twisted free and slapped him as hard as she could. "You've no right to call me such names!"

"Haven't I, then?" He caught her arms again and thrust her back against the door to Linzy's stall. "That's where ye're wrong, Tess. I have. I've got rights when it comes to ye."

Tess had never seen him like this, so fierce, so enraged. The force of his grip on her shoulders frightened her. "Please," she said more quietly. "You are hurting me, Jack."

"Wot about me? Wot about wot ye've done to *me?*" he cried, and shoved her into the wood so hard that Linzy whinnied in alarm.

"I'm sorry!" Tess gasped. "I surely didn't mean any harm to you, Jack, you know that. I love you—"

"Do ye, Tess?"

"Of course I do!"

His hold on her slackened. Panting, she rubbed her arms where he'd held her, knowing they'd be bruised. In the darkness she thought she saw him smile.

"I've been goin' about it all wrong, haven't I, Tess?"

"I don't know what you mean." She tried to brush by him, and he grabbed her again. "Let me go, Jack."

"That's wot I've been doin', isn't it? Lettin' go when ye tell me to." His voice was low and steady now, as though he spoke more to himself than to her. "Good old Jack. Steady Jack. Always does wot he's told." He brought up his blunt-fingered hand and caressed her cheek. "But that's not wot ye like, not really, is it, Tess?"

"I don't know what you—" She stopped because he spun her around and jerked her back against him, forcing her farther into the stables, toward the bales of hay stacked at the back wall.

Squirming in his grasp, she bit his palm; he laughed and brought his forearm up beneath her chin, snapping back her head, crushing her windpipe. She tried to reach his face with her hands, claw him with her nails, but he tightened his hold. Linzy was screaming; the black stallion was snorting, butting the sides of his stall again and again. Jack tore her cloak from her shoulders and flung it onto the hay-strewn floor. Then he flung her down too, in a tangle of skirts and hair.

"Jack." She raised herself on her elbows, searching the shadows for his face. "You don't know what you're doing."

"By God, I do. I just don't know why I didn't think of it before."

Tess's head was spinning; the horses were still neighing. She tried to scramble past him, but he caught her and pinned her spread-eagled on the cloak, his hands at her wrists, his knees on her thighs. Abruptly he brought her hands together above her head and held them in one fist; then he caught the other at the throat of her smock and ripped downward, straight through the waistband of her skirt and the top of her drawers.

"Jesus, Jack, stop!" she screamed, and felt his breath at her bared breasts, heard the click of his belt buckle as it fell to the ground.

"This is the way ye want it, isn't it?" he panted, scrabbling to yank down his trousers. "The way a lord would take ye, the way *he'd* take ye."

"For pity's sake, Jack!"

He grunted, rearing back from her, and she caught her breath in a sob. He'd only meant to frighten her, after all . . .

But no: he'd shifted his weight to tear her skirts aside. In an instant he was straddling her again, forcing his hand between her tight-clenched thighs. She screamed as long and hard as she could, but knew the sound was lost in the commotion of the crazed horses. "Please, Jack," she begged, "don't do this. Let me go. Please."

"No one else is goin' to have ye, Tess. Ye belong to me. Nobody else can have ye." She could feel his manhood pushing between her legs; she began to cry.

He let go of her hands then, putting his palm to her chin, making her raise her head to meet his mouth for a slavering kiss. Choking on her tears, on the taste of his spittle, Tess grabbed his hair and pulled it so hard that hanks came out in her fists. "Bitch!" he shouted at her. "Bitch, ye're supposed to love me!" He lifted her right off the ground by her own hair, then shoved her back onto the cape, face-downward this time.

Gagging, fighting for breath against the wool that muffled her cries, Tess felt him haul her upward by the buttocks, part her knees with his, and force his way inside her. Her eyelids seared with pain; she clutched the cape in her fists and screamed while he reared back and thrust into her again. He was saying her name, grunting into her ear: "How d'ye like that, Tess? D'ye like it?" She thought she would explode with her shame and rage.

And then, that quickly, it was over. He shoved against her one last time, driving deep inside her, and held her there while his body twitched and jerked. Then he let out his breath and released her, and she fell to the floor. She could feel some horrid sticky liquid flowing down her thighs, and smelled his smell on her, rank and cheesy and foul.

Behind her he'd gotten to his feet and was buttoning his trousers, threading his belt. "I reckon I showed ye," he said, and the complacent satisfaction in his voice made her cry harder than ever. "I reckon ye'll be good and ready to set the date now." Not looking at him, Tess wrapped herself in the cloak, curling into a ball. "Aye, well, I reckon so," he said. Then she heard his footsteps receding, and Linzy and the black stallion neighing wildly as he passed their stalls.

Tess bit down on the back of her hand until she tasted blood on her tongue. She could not stop shaking; her legs and arms were so icy cold that she did not think she would ever be warm again. Bile rose in her throat. She struggled to her knees and vomited onto the hay.

"Teresa."

Her father's voice. "Daddy," she whimpered. "Oh, Daddy. Help me." In the darkness she felt his hands; he raised her up from the floor.

"Come along, lass." He tucked the cloak tight about her, leading her toward the door. "Come along, then."

"Daddy, it was Jack! He hurt me. He—"

"I know, lass. But you're all right now; you'll be all right. Come on to the cottage, then; I've poured you a lovely warm bath."

"A bath . . ." The coldness in Tess's limbs crept into her soul. She pulled away from Ben's comforting arm. "You knew he was coming here," she whispered in disbelief. "You knew what he was planning and you didn't stop it." He said nothing. "Sweet Jesus in heaven, you're my father!" Tess cried. "How could you do such a thing?"

"You shamed Jack today with what you did at the big house," Ben said heavily. "You shamed him. You shamed me. You cannot flaunt God's laws and expect to go unpunished."

"And this was my punishment? *This*?" Outside in the chill April moonlight Tess threw open the cape, showed her tattered clothes, the bruises on her throat and arms. "Dad, look at me! Look at what he did to me!"

"Cover yourself," Ben said harshly, averting his eyes. "Go to the cottage. Wash yourself."

"He raped me!" Tess screamed at him. "He raped me on the ground, in the dirt, and you are blaming me!"

"There's no harm done. Don't pretend you haven't been dallying about together for the past two years."

"This wasn't dallying!" she raged. "He hurt me! He beat me, he made me kneel down like a dog—"

"Tess! Go to the cottage. Wash yourself off."

Green eyes narrowed, she clutched the cloak at her throat. "You don't want to look at it. You don't want to hear about it. How would you like it if it had been you that he hit and laughed at and groped at and rutted and—" Her breath caught in a sob so she could not continue.

"I hope it's taught you your lesson."

"What lesson am I supposed to have learned?" Tess cried in bewildered fury. "What law did *I* break?"

"You're my daughter, Teresa. A stableman's daughter. The meat they serve up in the big house, that isn't for you."

"You let Jack rape me because I had breakfast there?" she asked incredulously.

"Don't sass me, lass. You know that's not the meat I mean." She stared at him. He pushed her gently down the hill. "Go and wash yourself. There's horehound balm put out for your bruises. And you'll be marrying Jack on the feast of St. Barnabas. I've gone ahead and picked the day."

4

"Madness, that's what it is," said Mungo. "Lunacy. Delusions, as they say. The man's stark raving mad."

Inside the corral, Ben held tight to Satan's bridle while the horse snorted and tossed his head. "Say what you please about him," he grunted, tugging at the big black stallion's lead. "You'll get no argument here."

"I mean, look at the bleedin' thing!" Mungo waved toward the hillside, where a dozen of the village men were struggling to haul a huge hinged window into place on an iron frame. " 'Tis a monstrosity, a . . . a folly!"

"Cade's Folly. Hmm," said Ben. "You may have something there. Tess!" he shouted into the stables. "Bring the pony out!"

Mungo turned from the construction of Cade's Folly to watch as Tess led a high-stepping silver pony through the doors and across the yard. Her small heart-shaped face was set in an expression as bitter as bindweed root. Mungo whistled between his teeth. "So his lordship's really goin' through with it. I'm surprised she's lettin' him, crazy as she is fer that pony." Then he squinted, looking at the pony more closely. "Hold on, that ain't Linzy."

"No," Ben confirmed. "It's another from the same dam and sire. Cade sent me to Stafford to buy her."

"I'll be damned. How'd Tess ever convince that bastard . . . ?" Mungo began, and then stopped, seeing Ben's jaw tighten. "Well, I guess she's got her ways, our Tess!" he said cheerily. Ben's jaw grew tighter. "Oh, Christ, Ben. I didn't mean—"

Tess smiled grimly to herself at the old man's discomfiture. Fools and gossips . . .

Mungo had decided to change the subject. "Ye must be up to yer pretty little neck in weddin' plans, Tessie!" he called to her. "Wot is it now, another month to go?"

"Three weeks and three days."

The old man laughed. "Aye, 'n' ye know to the hour and minute too, I reckon! 'Twill be lovely to have something cheerful to celebrate, 'stead of worrying about how that madman Cade is bringing us all to ruin."

Tess said nothing. Her father dug his heels into the dirt as Satan reared up, catching the newcomer's scent. "Tether her," he directed his daughter. "Go on."

Very slowly she led the pony to the center of the corral, ran the lead through an iron ring sunk into the ground, and knotted it. The pony had seen Satan now; she edged backward, wide eyes ringed with white, as far as the rope would allow. Tess patted her forelock and murmured into her ear. The stallion was straining wildly against Ben's hold, snorting and bucking. "Best get out of there, girl!" Mungo warned Tess gleefully, hanging on the fence.

She gave the pony one last pat, then hurried past her father as he reached up to let Satan free. "I won't stay to watch," she spat as she went by.

Ben twisted out of the stallion's way and vaulted the fence.

"Odd how they come over all modest right before they wed," Mungo mused, watching Tess head toward the house of glass that was gradually rising, like a glistening phoenix, halfway up the slope.

For answer Ben only grunted. Satan circled the cowering pony, his ears laid back, and then galloped toward her, sending her flying across the corral till the rope pulled her up once more.

Trying not to hear the pony's frightened whinnies, Tess hurried up the hill and looked on as Robbie and Sam led the rest of the workers in their attempt to slide the first of the leaded-glass panels into place on the frame. "A little higher," Robbie instructed the sweating crew. "That's it, and now to the left—to the left, Colin, idiot! That's yer bloody right!"

"Well, I'm sorry," the chastised man puffed, "but I'm a bleedin' plowman, ain't I, not no glazier nor builder!"

"Even a plowman ought to know his right from his left. Get it up on yer end, Sam."

"Get it up yerself, ye arse! The friggin' thing weighs a ton!"

"Heh! Sam can't get it up!" Colin crowed.

"Well, at least he knows where it is!"

With a great deal more jostling and complaining and what seemed to Tess a modicum of effort, the men finally fit the panel in place. "Whew! Time for a break," Robbie decreed, mopping his brow on his sleeve, though he'd done no more than tell the others what to do. "Everybody over to the Swan!"

"Robbie." Sam nudged him. "Here *he* comes." He pointed to where Gideon Cade was striding toward them from the big house.

"Aye, well, like I says, heave to, men, 'n' let's get that next piece up here! Come on, ye slackers!" Robbie changed direction in mid-step and led them toward the pile of panels the wagon train from Shrewsbury had deposited on the lawn the week before.

Frauds, Tess thought scornfully. As they passed her she saw a few surreptitious glances, heard a murmured comment or two. She didn't know whether Jack had boasted or if her father had let it slip while he was in his cups, but all the menfolk in Windber seemed to know what had gone on in the barn that day. Their evident approval galled her, added insult to the injury.

She started back to the stables by a circuitous route, not wanting to act as voyeur to the pony's terror. When she reached the well she paused and hauled up a bucket of water, splashed her face, and then drank thirstily from the ladle. As she went to hang it on its hook, a hand reached over her shoulder and took it from her instead.

Terrified it was Jack, Tess drew in her breath to scream. "Do you mind, Mistress Jericho?" Gideon Cade's deep voice asked, and her taut muscles slackened; she turned, letting out her breath again. "It's so warm today that it might be midsummer instead of mid-May." He filled the ladle, gulped it down, and filled and drank again. Then he rubbed his mouth with the back of his hand; droplets of water clung to the curling dark hairs there and shone like glass in the sun.

"Yes," Tess said, "it is warm. Excuse me, please."

He didn't move. He wasn't blocking her way, exactly, but to reach the stable she would have had to duck beneath his outstretched arm. As he stood looking down at her, Tess could just barely smell the warm scent of spice he'd emanated as he stepped from his bath. "Excuse me," she said again, and turned the other way.

"I wanted to ask you something."

Wary, she leaned against the well. "What?"

"I haven't seen you around much since we had breakfast together. I wondered if you'd been ill."

"I'm fine." Self-consciously she tugged down the sleeves of her smock to cover the yellowed remnants of the bruises Jack had left on her arms. In the weeks since his attack she'd stuck close to the cottage, leaving only to do her work and ride Linzy each afternoon.

"Are you?" He reached down and brushed a hank of long red-gold hair back from her throat. Tess yanked it forward again, knowing the print of Jack's angry hand still showed on her there.

"I said so, didn't I? So if that's all you wanted to ask me—"

"It isn't. It's about the horses. No, not about Linzy," he hurried on, seeing her small stubborn chin come up. "You should know I've given up on that idea. After all, I sent your father to Stafford to buy her sister."

He acted as though she ought to be grateful to him, Tess thought, when Linzy was her bloody horse. Oh, they were all alike, all such pigs, were men. "Well? What is it, then?"

"I wanted to know why your father mates them the way he does. With the pony tied up, I mean. It's like a rape, isn't it?"

Tess flushed bright crimson. "You bastard," she spat. "Had your little jest now?" She shoved his arm and brushed past him.

He caught her hand and spun her back, his dark face bewildered. "What did I say?"

"As if you didn't know!"

"I *don't* know. Tell me."

Tess looked into his clear blue eyes and saw honest perplexity. It was possible, she supposed, that the news hadn't reached him. So far as she knew, he hadn't returned to the Swan since he brought the kitten there that first night; if he had, she was sure Ben would have mentioned it. "Nothing," she mumbled, more embarrassed than ever. "It's just . . . I thought you were such an authority on breeding horses."

He eyed her curiously for a moment, but when it was clear she wasn't saying any more, he laughed. "Actually, I don't know the first thing about it."

"Then why in the world did you decide to start breeding racers?"

"I don't know. It was just an idea I had."

"Oh, I see. It must be right lovely to have ideas and just give people orders and have them come true," Tess said cuttingly.

"If you really want to know, it's bloody damned boring. But when I try to do more than give orders, it's like that night at the tavern. There are times I feel like the leper of Windber-on-Clun." How odd, thought Tess. That's just the way I've felt of late. Gideon Cade scuffed the toe of his fine leather boot in the dust. "I only asked you—about the horses, I mean—because I thought anybody else would just laugh at me. Because I'd hoped we were friends."

"Us? Friends?"

"Well . . ." He smiled crookedly. "At least not enemies."

A glimmer of movement beyond his broad shoulder caught Tess's eye. Jack, she was sure of it, skulking around the corner of the stables to spy on her. The realization made her furious. She smiled warmly, gloriously, at Gideon Cade. "I suppose we are friends, aren't we?" If nothing else, she'd give Jack a show for his trouble. Cade still held her hand. She twined her fingers through his, pulling him away from the corner where Jack was lurking. "Let's get out of the hot sun, shall we? Over here, under the apple tree."

Cade followed her readily. It was a simple matter to

arrange appearances to her liking. She sat in the shaded grass; he crouched on his haunches beside her. Tess beckoned him closer, putting a finger to her lip conspiratorially. "I don't want to have to shout. This isn't the sort of subject I'm accustomed to discussing with men."

"Except for your father."

Tess tossed her head in a ripple of fiery curls, laughing gaily. "Of course. Except for him. Well. In a perfect world, Satan would run loose with all the mares in the stable until they got to know him, to accept him as their stud. But if Dad let him do that, the rest of the stallions here would either go mad or gang up and try to kill him the first chance they got. In a slightly less perfect world, Satan and the pony you bought would get put out to pasture by themselves, your stallion would eventually establish his mastery, and the rest would follow naturally. However, in the world we've got, if Dad doesn't get the pony mated in this heat or the next . . . you *do* know what a heat is?" He nodded. "Then it will be too late."

"Why will it be too late?"

"Because gestation for horses is eleven months. If the pony's colt is born any later than May of next year, it won't have time to build up before winter comes. It'll be spindly and sickly, and there won't be time to wean it, and nursing it will only sap the pony's strength. Dad and I would have to hand-feed it with cow's milk, which doesn't always work and ends up spoiling the colt most times. You told Dad you wanted a colt next year. And that's why the pony is tied."

"I see."

"Any more questions?"

"I guess not." He was frowning.

"What's wrong?" Tess asked. "You seem disappointed."

"I don't know. It's just not what I expected, that's all."

She cocked her head at him. "How do you mean?"

For a moment cool, haughty Gideon Cade looked almost bashful. "Somehow I just thought—"

"Teresa." They both turned to see Ben glaring at them. "I need you in the stables. Now."

"Mr. Jericho." Cade rose on his long haunches, smiling. "Your daughter has been kind enough to tell me a bit about horse breeding." He offered Tess his hand.

Ben jerked her up by the elbow. "I don't want her telling you about that or anything else. Get in the stable, Tess."

"I'm done my chores," she said defiantly. "I can do as I please."

"Don't sass me, lass, just do as I say."

"What will you do if I don't?" Tess demanded. "Get Jack to teach me another lesson?"

Ben took a step toward her, his fist curled and raised. She stared at him, feeling as though the earth was opening beneath her feet, as though the sky was spinning above her. In all her life her father had never put his hand to her in anger; she could not believe that he would do so now.

But he did. He swung and clipped her on the cheek, hard enough so that she stumbled back against the tree trunk. He seemed as surprised as she was; his arm dropped to his side and he stood there opening his mouth and closing it again. "Teresa," he said finally, hoarsely, with the tiny catch in his voice that always pulled at her heart. "Tess—"

"I might have forgiven you for the other someday," she whispered, touching her stinging cheek, "but I never will forgive you for that."

"Tess. Please . . ."

From the corral the pony screamed as Satan mounted her. Without looking at Gideon Cade, Tess walked past her father, past the stables, down the hill to the cottage. She went inside, and then she shut the door.

Ben didn't come home until after midnight, when he trudged in with Job trailing glumly behind him. Tess had waited up, sitting on a stool by the dying fire, her belongings tied in the rucksack that lay at her feet. When he opened the door she stood, not wanting to look up at him and thus be at a disadvantage, wanting to be ready to evade him whether he meant to hug her or strike her again. She started talking right away.

"Listen to me, Dad. I hope you're not so muddle-headed with ale that this won't sink in. I want to tell you all this tonight because I'll be getting an early start come the morning, and I doubt you will, after you've been so long at the Swan. Now. I've baked enough bread for at least a week, it's there in the cupboard, and there's a big bowl of oats in there too, with the cup I use to measure them with. You just add one cup of oats to two of water and boil them for an hour. You know where I keep the honey if you want that. When the bread's gone you'll have to make some arrangement with Meg or Widow Jonas to bake you more. Don't pay but half a penny a week, though, because so long as they're baking already, it's not much trouble to make a mite extra. As for the laundry—"

"Sit down, Tess."

She didn't. "—you can try to do that yourself if you like, but I'd recommend—"

"Please, Tess. Sit down."

"Dad, I've thought this all through. I've made up my mind to leave. I'm going to London, and then I'll make my way to the New World, just like Lord Halifax. Delaware, that's where I'm going. And nothing you and your drunken cronies at the Swan may have cooked up in the way of apologies can change it. So there's no use—"

"I've not been to the Swan, and I haven't been drinking."

"Why—" Tess looked at him more closely. Sure enough, his blue eyes were clear, and his weathered face was far from ale-ruddied. If anything, he seemed pale. "Where the devil have you been, then, for nigh on eight hours?"

"Walking." He eased himself onto a stool and pried off his boots. "Up in the forest."

"Gor, you must be done in! Let me get you some bread and cheese."

"I don't want any, pet. All I want is for you to sit down."

Still she stood her ground. "I told you, you can't make me change my mind!"

Ben Jericho sighed, stretching out his thick, stubby legs. He is old, Tess realized suddenly. I think of Robbie and Sam and Mungo as the old men in this village, but he is old too. How old? She really hadn't any idea. "I don't mean to make you change it, Tess," he said wearily. "I never meant to make you do anything. That's never been my way. If you're bound and determined to go, then I guess you'll be going. Before you do, though, I've something to tell you. Something I reckon you've a right to know. All these years I thought I did you a favor keeping it from you, but I wonder now."

Curiosity swamping her determination to remain aloof, she took the stool across from his, leaning forward. "What is it, Dad?"

He closed his eyes, took a long breath. "It's about your mother, Tess."

Her mother . . . Tess waited eagerly. Discussing his long-dead wife was so painful for Ben that she knew precious little about her. In answer to her questions when she'd been younger, and less conscious of how it hurt him to discuss the subject, he'd given her some tidbits to chew upon. She'd been a Catholic, the daughter of a potter; she'd given Tess her saint's name. She worked as a lady's maid in a big fancy house near London. Ben met her there when he delivered a coaching pair to her master; he'd been working for a breeder in the city, near St. Paul's. It had been, Ben said, love at first sight, for his Tessie was the prettiest creature he'd ever seen, with the red-gold hair and green eyes she'd passed on to her daughter. Within a month they'd been married. Within a year she gave birth to Teresa. Within another year she caught the plague as it swept through the country and died.

Heartbroken, Ben couldn't stand to stay in London. He'd packed up Tess and all they owned and headed westward, winding up with a job as Lord Halifax's stablemaster here in Windber-on-Clun. Those were the facts. But like anyone else growing up in those circumstances, Tess had entertained pretty fantasies about her birth in her younger days. At times she even imagined she wasn't Ben's at all, but the daughter of the king, Charles II, and his childless Queen Catherine, somehow stolen from them without their knowing she'd been born. And it was this absurd notion that popped into her mind as her father opened his eyes at last and, staring into the fire, said, "Everything I ever told you about her, Teresa—it was all lies. None of it was true."

"You're jesting," she said dubiously, once she'd stilled her fluttering heart by telling herself very firmly it would have been impossible for Queen Catherine to have had a baby and not notice it.

"Not quite everything," Ben acknowledged. "She did have your hair and eyes."

"Well . . . was her name really Teresa?"

"I never knew her name," he said very quietly.

"But that's impossible," Tess said after a moment. It had to be. She'd heard men parry jests about the identity of one another's fathers. But how could anybody not know who'd given birth to his daughter, when eventually, just like Jack's mother when she'd carried Billy, she'd be the size of a house?

"Oh, don't get me wrong, lass; I know who she was, all right," Ben told her. "It's just her name I didn't know. I knew her title, though."

Tess's heart beat faster. A title—that meant a noble-woman! Hadn't she always suspected, nay, always *known* deep in her soul that she was different from everyone else in Windber-on-Clun? She winked, giving him a tap on the knee. "A noblewoman! You old devil!"

"Great Jehovah, you stupid girl, don't make jests concerning matters you know nothing about! There's devil-women in this world, just like Eve in the garden, and that's what your mother was—nothing more or less." Tess flushed, staring at him. "Didn't you ever wonder, lass, why I left that place I had with the nobleman, with all those men working for me, and all those fine horses?"

"Aye, of course I did. But I thought—"

"You thought 'twas the drinking. Well, 'tis Jehovah's truth, lass, that I never in my life touched a drop of ale before I met that Jezebel."

Job had been creeping toward his master as he spoke, watching with sad eyes to see if another outburst was forthcoming. Ben beckoned him close, and the hound laid his head across his master's knee. "It all began with horses," Ben said, his blue eyes distant. "Sometimes I think: if Jehovah hadn't made horses, how different my life might be."

"How do you mean?"

"My father wanted me to be a preacher, follow in his footsteps," he told her. "But I was mad for horses. Always was, ever since I was a babe. Well, I pestered him and pestered him, the poor soul, until finally he got me a post slopping stables on a great estate." He smiled, remembering. "I was all of eight years old. He was sure the work would turn me against the creatures. But, dirty though it was, I only loved them more. By the time he and my mother died of the plague, when I was twenty, I'd worked my way up to groomsman. And the lord—oh, he was a great man, lass, a fine man, a saint—well, he treated me like his own son. As the years went by, we built those stables into the finest in England. He made me master of them, too—me, a poor preacher's boy! I owed everything to him." His face darkened. "And then he took it into his head he would wed."

He was still staring into the fire; his voice had turned soft and dreamy. "She was something to look at, Teresa. The loveliest woman I've ever seen before or since. Everything she wore on her was brand-new and fine. All lace and silks and velvet she was, with dainty little feet and a waist a fellow could circle about with one hand. M'lady, that's what everyone called her. That's all I ever called her too." Some strange note in his voice made Job turn to him questioningly. He patted the dog, and his tone turned hard-edged again.

"I was teaching her to ride, with his lordship's blessing. He'd have done it himself, but he was too stiff with the arthritis; he was getting on in years by then. Every day we'd go off by ourselves alone; that's how much his lordship trusted me. And as Jehovah's my witness, I never thought I'd give him cause not to. But then m'lady started in on me."

"What do you mean, started in?"

He waved his hand impatiently. "First it was just compliments. How well you ride, Ben, she'd tell me, or, how patient and kind you always are with silly little me! I won't pretend I wasn't flattered, because I was. But after a couple of weeks she started telling me things about her and his lordship. Things I didn't want to know."

"What sort of things?"

He looked embarrassed. "Oh, she said that her parents had arranged the marriage without her even meeting his lordship. That she hadn't known he'd be so old and feeble. That he was, well, a gelding, if you get my drift. She had a way with her, Tess, that made you feel sorry for her. She said how she didn't mind going to the grave a virgin on account of how much she loved his lordship, but how she couldn't help being curious about what she was missing. Oh, she talked a line, she did, and I swallowed it, fool that I was."

Tess shivered, remembering the pain and terror she'd felt when Jack raped her in the stables. "She wasn't missing anything," she said vehemently.

"Well, of course she wasn't," said her father, misinterpreting her words, "but how was I to know that at the time? I didn't know she wasn't really a virgin until she'd wheedled me into . . . into making love to her." Now he was flushing. "And by then it was too late. She threatened to tell his lordship that I'd forced myself on her unless I finished what I'd begun."

Tess shivered again, this time in horror at the thought of what an unnatural creature her mother had been. Imagine blackmailing someone to go on doing to you what Jack had done to her! "So there we were," Ben said miserably, "riding off every day to tryst in the woods, with her threatening to tell if I didn't please her. 'Tis Jehovah's truth, Tess, I've never been so unhappy in all my life. There were days I thought the only way to put an end to it was to put an end to myself."

"What happened?" Tess whispered.

"After six months or so, she stopped coming to the stables. At first I was happy as a clam, but then I got to thinking: what if she was only tricking somebody else the way she'd tricked me? So, brave as I could, I tried cozyin' up a bit to her maids. Most of 'em didn't have the time of day for the likes of me. But there was one, named Teresa—Tessie, they called her—who had a good heart. It was she that told me m'lady had got herself with child and was all in a dither lest his lordship find out."

"Couldn't it have been his child as well as anyone else's?"

"Apparently not. It seems that much of what she'd told me was true."

How incomprehensible, thought Tess. Here was a woman who'd had the best of everything—a husband who was rich *and* couldn't copulate with her—and she'd risked it all for a fling in the woods with Tess's father! She eyed Ben with new respect, wondering what he'd looked like then.

"Anyway," he went on, "Tessie told me m'lady hadn't time for anything except trying every which way she could to get rid of it."

"Of what?"

"She was trying to get rid of the baby," Ben repeated patiently, "before her husband noticed anything amiss. Only trouble was, she'd put off believing she was with child so long that she was already five months gone."

To get rid of the baby—he meant to get rid of *her*, Tess realized. The notion gave her a queasy sensation in the pit of her stomach. "How would she do that?" she asked, not at all sure she wanted to know.

Ben shrugged. "Oh, there are ways, long as a soul don't mind burning in hell for all eternity. She'd got some old woman like Widow Jonas making up potions of herbs for her, Tessie said. And there were other things she tried too, that were much, much worse. None of 'em worked, though." He smiled faintly. "Seems you were meant to be stubborn right from the start."

The story he told was bewildering. In all the fantasies she had concocted about her mother, Tess had counted on one constant: the woman had loved her totally, unquestioningly, the same way Ben did. Learning that the opposite was true shook her world straight to its foundations. "You," she said softly, fearfully, "did you want the potions to work? Did you want to be rid of me too?"

It was a long time before he answered. "I thought that I did."

"So." Tess did her best to act nonchalant, but her tears spilled over. "Nobody wanted me. All I was was a mistake and a bother. You didn't love her, and she didn't love you, and neither of you loved me."

"Lass, lass! There's a long time between the sowing

and the reaping," Ben said earnestly. "When Tessie first told me, I won't deny I was scared witless. His lordship was a rich, powerful man. He could have had me thrown into jail, even hanged. And I knew I could look for no quarter from m'lady; she'd gladly have seen me swing to save her own skin. But as the days went by, and then weeks, and Tessie saying her mistress was trying this and that and nothing was working, well, by the Great Jehovah, I started to be glad! I thought, well, what she did was wrong, and I was wrong too. I let myself be used. I betrayed everything my father ever stood for, and I betrayed his lordship, and worst of all I betrayed the Great Jehovah by breaking his commandments. But what had the babe done? Why should it suffer for being the offspring of two such fools? The weeks turned into one month, and then into two, and so help me, pet, I got to be proud as a pickle of you! I, a grown man, hadn't had the guts to defy m'lady, and here you were, a wee baby not even born yet, standing up to her!"

"You are only trying to make me feel better," she accused him.

"Teresa, how can you say such a thing? Why, I can't even imagine what my life would have been like without you. Every time I look at you—"

"You think of her, and you hated her!"

Ben shook his head, smiling. "Nay, lass. I wonder what in the name of all that's holy I could have done right to deserve such a blessing as you."

"I don't believe you."

He caught her hand and held it tight; she felt the hard crust of his callused fingers and palm against hers. "Believe it, Teresa. Until you came into this world I never knew what love was. And the love I have for you is something not time nor tide can ever wipe away."

Touched and yet embarrassed, Tess took back her hand. "What happened when I was born? What did his lordship say?"

Ben's expression turned grim. "He never found out. M'lady took to her bed, wouldn't let him see her, said she had the hives. The night you were born, she told Tessie to smother you with a pillow and bury you in the forest."

"Dear God," Tess whispered.

"Well, Tessie disobeyed, thank Jehovah. She spirited you out of the house and brought you to me, and I left that same night. I never went back there again." He was silent for a time, staring into the fire. Then one corner of his mouth twitched in a grin. "I never could understand how she managed to get you out of there alive without m'lady knowing. Seemed to me you did nothing but cry at the top of your lungs for the next two years."

"How did you know what to *do* with me?" Tess marveled. "If someone dropped a newborn baby in my lap, I'd have no more notion of how to care for it than of how to fly to the moon!"

"I'd had foals before that had lost their mothers. 'Twas much the same thing, really." He winced. "Except for the diapering."

"Where did you go?"

"Back to Kent, just for a bit, until you were strong enough to travel. And then I set out looking for the sleepiest village in all of England. I didn't want to meet up with m'lady or anyone like her ever again."

"So you settled in Windber-on-Clun." Tess nodded in sudden understanding as the pieces of her father's life fell into place. "Oh, Dad. Why didn't you ever tell me all this before?"

"There wasn't any reason to. So long as you were happy and contented, I hoped I'd never have to tell you. It's not something I'm proud of, Jehovah knows—"

"But you should be! You saved my life!"

"Nay, Tessie did that, pet; she was the brave one. Truth to tell, if she'd told me ahead of time she was bringing you to me, I don't know if I'd have had the courage. But once she set you into my arms—faith, lass, you were so tiny! And wrinkly! And *loud!*" He grinned at the memory. "Well, after that I knew there was no going back."

"I wonder . . ." Tess said before she could stop herself.

"Where your mother is now?" He saw her shamed look and patted her hand. "Nay, lass, 'tis natural enough that ye'd want to know. Tessie wrote to me ten years or so back that she'd died. I'd sent word to her where I was, in case m'lady ever regretted what she'd done. But she never did."

So long as you were happy and contented, he'd said. . . . "Why are you telling me about her now?"

Ben sighed. "What Jack did to you—that was wrong, Tess, I know that. He knows it too. And I only went along with it because I'm as certain as I am of Jehovah's grace that in his heart he loves you. That he's a good man, a decent man who'll care for you when I'm dead and buried, and give me a parcel of fine lusty grandchildren in the nonce."

"I hardly think he was showing he loves me!"

"Oh, he was, pet, in his way. He's not good with words, with telling you how he feels all wrapped up in flowery sentiment and such. But he loves you so much that it near drove him mad to think he might lose you to Gideon Cade. And it drove me mad too, because I know Cade's kind. He's cut from the same cloth your mother was; he's got the devil in him, the same way she did. I know the signs now, and I can see 'em in that man's eyes." Tess opened her mouth to protest, then closed it again. Ben would know, wouldn't he? And there wasn't any doubt Cade had wronged poor old Lord Halifax.

"I struck you today, Teresa," her father said sorrowfully, "and that's something I'm not proud of. I don't believe in breaking the spirit of another human being any more than in breaking that of a horse. But I'll swear this to you. If I ever found you'd bedded Cade, I'd do worse than strike you. For it would rip out my heart to see you make a shambles of your life the way I did of mine. So." He got to his feet. "Is there anything more you'd be wanting to know about your mother?" Tess shook her head. Ben started for the door, the hound at his heels. "I'll put this one in the stables. If you're still set on leaving in the morning, mind you wake me to say farewell. I just pray you'll know in your heart what's the right thing to do. Come on, Job." He stumped out into the night.

Tess sat stunned as the fire guttered down to ashes, numbed by the terrible tale her father had told. She tried to imagine him feeding her drops of milk from a cloth, cuddling her in his big rough hands, and the image she conjured up broke through her stupor, made her dissolve into tears.

He had given her life and then saved it. How infinitely simpler it would have been for him to have snuffed her out like a candle! That was what her mother had wanted. That was what most men would have done. But he had loved her too much for that.

And how did she repay his love for her? By being headstrong and willful, always complaining, turning her back on him now as he was growing old and would need her more and more.

He only wanted what was best for her. He wanted her to be happy. He'd given up his own chances for a normal life, a wife, a son, so he could look after her. Overwhelmed by his selflessness, all Tess wanted in the world at that moment was to make him happy in return.

He came back into the cottage, brushing raindrops from his white hair. "Pouring again," he announced with a grimace. "But I can just see the moon through the clouds. Tomorrow bids fair. Mind you show me where that roof is leaking before you go, so I can patch the thatch."

"I'll get Jack to do it," Tess told him.

Ben nodded, almost to himself. "Seeing him before you leave, eh? That's kind of you, pet."

"I'm not leaving, Dad. I'm staying here with you." She took a deep breath. "And fixing the roof is the least Jack can do, so long as I'm marrying him."

5

"I reckon ye're about ready to burst with excitement," Millie Fish told Tess, envy plain in her tone.

"Aye," Tess said. "I reckon."

Jack's mother beamed at her. "I can't tell ye how happy Mort and me are, Teresa. We've been waitin' for tomorrow to come for ages, it seems."

"So's Tess been, I'll wager," Meg Mullen put in with a sly cackle. "After all, she and Jack have been courtin' since they was babes in arms."

"I think this dress is ever so lovely," Jack's younger sister Joan said dreamily, running her hand over the pale green skirt her mother was hemming. "Ye'll be the most beautiful bride that there ever was, Tess."

"Not unless we get the bloomin' thing done, she won't," said Widow Jonas, handing her needle to Tess to be rethreaded. "The custom says we're just supposed to take a stitch in your wedding gown for luck, girl, not sew it for ye."

"I can finish it myself, really I can," Tess told her. "I know I shouldn't have let it go so long, but there were so many other things to tend to—"

"There, now, I'm only pullin' yer leg, pet." The widow took back the threaded needle and set to work on the waistline. "It's hard when ye ain't got no mother to help ye. Ben's not much good when it comes to weddin' plans, is he?"

"Not much," Tess agreed.

"Where is Tess's mother?" Joan asked her own.

"Why, she's in heaven, love! She died when Tess was

just a wee thing. Before Ben ever came to Windber-on-Clun." Missus Brady patted Tess's shoulder. "Ye can bet, though, she'll be looking down at ye tomorrow in the church and smilin'."

Tess got up from her stool and fetched the bottle of dandelion wine Widow Jonas had brought. "Anybody for more of this?"

"Aye, I'll have a bit, thank ye kindly," its maker told her. Tess refilled her cup and her own, then gulped the bitter brew down.

"Best watch yer step with that, Tess," Millie cautioned her sweetly. "If ye don't want to be bleary tomorrow."

"Why shouldn't she be?" Joan piped up. "Jack's been three sheets to the wind since this morning." Widow Jonas laughed so hard that she spilled her wine.

"Joanie, where in the world did ye ever learn such an expression?" Missus Brady demanded.

"From Jack," the girl said promptly.

Her mother sighed. "Ye try to bring 'em up right, but what can ye do? For yer sake, Tess, I hope you and Jack have all boys!"

"Oh, they'll have a packet of young 'uns—eight or ten or a dozen, I'll wager," Meg Mullen declared. "That Jack, he's built like a stallion."

"Meg, please!" Missus Brady clapped her hands over her daughter's ears.

"Well, so long as we're touchin' that subject . . ." Widow Jonas reached into her apron pocket and brought out a small cloth-wrapped bundle. "Here ye go, Tess. A bit of a weddin' present."

"What's this?"

"Go on and see." Tess unwound the little bundle, then stared uncomprehendingly at the pile of dried leaves and twigs that lay within. "It's my special love potion," the old woman told her. "Mandrake and wormwood and bittersweet—but I mustn't give away my secrets! Anyway, 'tis guaranteed to bind soul to soul when ye steep it in wine."

"What does Tess need with that? Jack's already crazy in love with her," Joan objected.

"Aye, that he is. But you never do know when a love

charm might be needed." Tess looked at the herb woman. Lord, but her dark eyes were shrewd!

"I'm glad to have it," she said lightly. "It's bound to come in useful."

"Marriage is forever," the widow agreed, "and forever's a mighty long time."

"Such stuff's the work of the devil," Meg Mullen sniffed. "If I was ye, Teresa, I'd throw it straight on the fire."

But instead Tess rewrapped the bundle and tucked it away in a drawer. Then she picked up her needle and sighed. "I swear, this dress is taking as long to finsh as that glasshouse out on the hill."

Widow Jonas laughed. "Cade's Folly, d'ye mean?"

"There's nothing laughable about it," Ellie Brady chided. "The time the men spent on that silliness should have been used to put seeds in the ground! Come this winter, we'll all be starving, just ye wait and see. I'll wager ye won't be laughing then."

"I don't know," said the widow. "They tell me the sense of humor is one of the last things to go."

Meg pursed her mouth. "Mockin'. Always mockin'. But Ellie's right as can be, and ye knows it."

"I'll tell ye wot worries me more'n that there folly of his," Millie announced, "and that's the crops Cade *has* got the men planting. Why, my pop says he's never seen seeds like them ones he put in up to the north side. Not even seeds, but little bits of stuff."

"Eyes, Cade calls 'em," Missus Backus said darkly. "Gives me the shivers, it do. Like filling a field up with body parts."

"And did ye taste wot grows of 'em?" Meg demanded. "Here, what's the name of 'em, Millie?"

"I can't remember. Poor tatters, or something like that."

"Had me ruin a perfectly lovely lamb stew by stickin' 'em in it." The tavernkeeper's wife made a frightful face while Meg nodded assent. "All nasty and tough they stayed, though I boiled 'em ever so long. Put me in mind of eatin' green apples. I could barely keep down one tiny bite."

"But *he* sat there and lapped it right up," Meg hissed. "Polished off a great bowlful!"

"Well, no one else would touch it," said Missus Backus. "In the end I fed the whole pot to the pigs."

"My pop says he's crazy," Millie noted.

"Faith, girl," Meg cackled, "d'ye mean to say ye need your pop to tell you that?"

"He brought me some of them things with the eyes when he brought me back my black kitten. Potatoes." Widow Jonas nodded, remembering. "I liked 'em. A little like chestnuts."

"Precious little," said Missus Backus, "if ye asks me. By the by, Tess, is he comin' to the weddin'?"

"I don't know, really."

"Lord Halifax would've been there," Jack's mother said sadly, "and wearin' bells."

"Now, Ellie, don't be so hard on Gideon Cade," the widow chided. "Didn't Jack tell me he went to see the man about rentin' the Harley cottage, that's been empty since poor Toby died, and Cade gave him the lease at half what Toby used to pay?"

"And well he should," Meg huffed, "seein' as we'll all be starvin' come Martinmas!"

"He's just out to buy our affections," Ellie Brady insisted. "Jack wasn't taken in by him, and neither am I."

"Could we talk about something else, please?" Tess asked.

"Why, of course we can, lass! And I can't say I blame ye for wantin' to, either," said Meg. "Wot'll it be, then?"

"Wot d'ye reckon the menfolk are talkin' about at the Swan?" wondered Joan.

"Never ye mind, child!" Her mother laughed, casting a knowing look at the other women.

"Ye got any questions 'bout that, Tess?" Meg demanded with a wink and a nudge. "I'd wager not, as long as ye 'n' Jack been sweethearts!"

"Look at that!" Missus Backus pointed. "I've heard of blushin' brides, but our Tess is gone pale!"

"I doubt this to be wot Tess had in mind when she suggested we change the subject," Widow Jonas said dryly. "Anyway, there's a lot more than that to a marriage."

Meg snorted. "Yer sayin' that just shows how long yer Ethan's been gone!"

"A lot more than wot? Wot's everyone talking about?" Joan asked plaintively.

The widow took the last stitch in the hem and tied off the thread. "There we are—finished at last! Now I'd suggest we all make ourselves scarce and let Tess get her sleep."

" 'Cause she won't be getting none tomorrow night," Meg crowed, "not if I knows Jack!"

"I am awfully tired," Tess told the widow thankfully, suppressing a yawn. "But I can't tell you how grateful I am for all your help. And for your company."

"We'd be happy to stay on," Missus Backus offered. "The men won't be done at the Swan till past midnight, most likely."

"Just come along," Widow Jonas insisted, gathering up her sewing basket and herding everyone toward the door. "What she needs right now is peace and quiet and a good night's sleep."

"Thank you again, everyone!" Tess cried, waving from the doorway as they filed out into the moonlight. "Oh, Widow Jonas, wait!" She ran after the old woman with the half-filled bottle of dandelion wine. "You forgot this. There's still plenty left."

"Ye hold on to it, pet. Just in case ye want another swallow or two." Those shrewd jet eyes searched Tess's face. "Ye're a good girl, Teresa, lookin' after yer father the way ye do. The Lord will reward ye for that."

"I'd say he already has," Millie Fish said tartly. "She's marryin' Jack, ain't she?"

In the shadows Tess felt the widow's crabbed hand squeeze hers. "Just remember, Teresa. He works in strange ways."

"Come on, Millie," Joan Brady said, "and don't be so jealous. Tess can't help it if she's a thousand times prettier than you. Good night, Tess! See ye at the church in the morning!"

"D'ye know," Widow Jonas muttered, staring up at the sky as the women headed down the hill to the village, "I think we may be in for a storm."

Tess watched them go. A cool wind from the north whipped their skirts up. Above their heads snatches of black cloud scuttled across a milk-white full moon. Let there be a storm, she suddenly prayed, a huge storm, worse than Noah's, and let it wash Windber-on-Clun right off the face of the earth, and take me with it.

But all that happened was that the wind died away to a whisper. Tess walked back to the cottage, the bottle clutched tight in her fist. "They say wine brings courage," she whispered. "Well, God knows I need it." She fetched her glass, sat on her stool, and began to drink.

Tess could not remember ever in her life having been so thirsty. She would have committed murder for a single sip of clear, cool, sweet water; her throat was parched as stale biscuit, dry as bone. High above her head was suspended the ladle from the well; it hung from the ceiling, twisting and turning, and with every twist a drop of water dribbled over the edge. But try as she might, she could not reach the drops before they spattered to the floor.

She stared up at the ladle and saw through a hole in the ceiling that it was Jack who held the string from which the scoop dangled. He was grinning down at her, teasing her, moving the string every time she came close to standing beneath it. "Please stop," she begged him. "Please. I'm ever so thirsty—"

"Wot will ye do for me if I give ye this water?"

"Anything. I'll do anything!"

"Very well, then. Take off yer clothes and dance."

She laughed. "Oh, really, Jack!"

"Really," he insisted, no longer grinning. "Ye said ye'd do anything, didn't ye? Take off yer clothes and dance naked for me."

"I will not!"

He shrugged. "Suit yourself." Then he tilted the ladle beyond her reach. Drop by drop, the precious water spilled down to the floor.

"Wait!" Tess cried. He straightened the ladle, looking down at her expectantly. "Dance just for you?"

He smiled, gesturing around the cottage. "There's no one else here, is there?"

"All right, then. Give me the ladle."

He started to lower it down to her, then jerked it up again, out of her reach. "No. After ye dance."

Tess reached for her bodice strings and found she was wearing her wedding gown. She unlaced it slowly, slid the sleeves down over her shoulders, unhooked the skirts. "Hurry up," Jack ordered from the hole in the ceiling. Biting her lip, Tess slipped out of the bodice, stepped out of the skirts. In just her camisole and drawers, she began to do a little jig. "Take *all* of it off!" Jack shouted down at her.

"Jack—"

"D'ye want this water or don't ye?" Tears burning her eyes, she nodded. "Well, then?"

Tess couldn't bear to look at him. Staring at the floor, she unbuttoned the camisole with trembling fingers and pulled it off. Then she untied the string of her underdrawers and stepped out of them too. Hating Jack, hating the thirst that drove her to this, she danced naked in the middle of the cottage, slowly, mournfully.

"Faster," Jack commanded. "I'll set yer pace." He began to beat time with the ladle. Tess obeyed him, tears streaming down her cheeks. The clapping sound grew louder. In the midst of a turn she glanced up and saw dozens more holes in the ceiling, and all the men in the village peering through them, clapping as they leered down at her.

"Damn you!" she screamed at Jack. "Damn you, damn you, damn you!" She opened her eyes, still screaming, and found she was sitting up on her cot, impossibly thirsty, with a new leak in the thatch dripping rain on her face.

"Oh!" Her heart was pounding; in the darkness it took her a moment to realize she had only been dreaming. It had all seemed so real! Even now she flushed to remember the faces of Jack and the rest of them as they egged her on. "Shouldn't have finished off that dandelion wine," she mumbled, stumbling over to the table, lighting the lamp so she could find the water pitcher. It was on the shelf, but it was empty. So was Ben's bed.

That's odd, she thought. The night had the feel of long

after closing time at the Swan. Even more odd, though she was wide-awake now, she still heard a sound like clapping. She checked the window shutters, but they were all latched tight.

Shrugging, she grabbed the pitcher and her father's oiled coat and opened the door to go out to the well. The clapping sound grew louder. It couldn't be thunder; the rain was only a thin drizzle. She hurried barefoot through the slick wet grass, hauled up the bucket, and filled the pitcher, drinking greedily.

The water cleared her thick head, so she heard the sound more distinctly. It was more of a banging than a clapping, and was coming from the stables. In the gloomy darkness she peered toward the building. Some flicker of movement there caught her eye. Straining to see more, she set down the pitcher and walked partway up the hill. Sure enough, someone had left one of the stable doors open; it was swinging on its hinges with each gust of wind, slamming against the wall.

Tess was certain she hadn't been so careless—and if she had, she would have heard the door banging earlier that night, when she came outside to say good-bye to Jack's mother and the rest. No, someone else had to have gone to the stables since then, and it could only be Ben. She went back into the cottage and picked up the lantern, then marched up the hill to the stables, wondering why, if her father had left the tavern, he hadn't come in to bed.

The moment she peered into the stable, she saw him, sprawled snoring on the pile of straw in the back with Job curled at his feet. Sighing, she walked toward him down the aisle. "Dad! Wake up, Dad!" Job stirred and wagged his tail in greeting, but Ben didn't move. Tess knelt beside him, shaking his shoulders, but still he never stirred. He just went on snoring, slow and steady, stretched out in blissful obliviousness across the heaped straw.

"Gor, I'd hate to be you in the morning," she muttered, aware of her own throbbing temples as she stood up again. In some muddled way he'd been trying not to disturb her by staying out there, she supposed. She fetched a couple of blankets from the tack room and tucked them around him. "There, you look after him, Job," she told the hound. "I'm going back to bed." She was halfway down the hill to the cottage when something struck her: why hadn't Linzy whinnied her usual greeting when she came in?

She must have been asleep—as I dearly wish I were right now, Tess thought, taking another step toward the cottage. Still, it wasn't like the pony to fail to recognize her mistress's voice and put out her head to beg for a pat and a treat. It *is* the middle of the night, she reminded herself, but she could not shake off a touch of apprehension. Tired though I am, I'll do nothing but worry till dawn unless I see for myself she's all right, she realized, and started back toward the stables again.

"Linzy?" she called from the doorway, and waited for that familiar nicker. There was only silence. "Linzy?" she called again, holding up the lamp. In mounting panic she ran to the pony's stall. "Where are you, Linzy?" She reached to unfasten the latch. It was already off. She yanked open the gate. The stall was empty, dark as the grave.

"Oh, God!" Cold, utter panic swept through her. What could have happened? Had her father somehow knocked the latch off? Or—Jesus, had the stable been visited by thieves? Frantic, she ran down the row, checking to see if any of the other horses were missing, and then up along the other side. One more was empty—the one catercorner from Linzy's. Satan's stall.

"Dad!" she shouted at him, pulling his arms, pinching him, but Ben wasn't budging. "Wake up, Dad, you've got to wake up!" Still he only snored on. "For the love of Christ . . ." Tess knelt on the straw beside him. "Dad, please, Dad, wake up and tell me what to do!"

"Mistress Jericho?" The deep voice from the doorway made Tess scream in fright. "Forgive me," Gideon Cade apologized. "I couldn't sleep—I saw the lamp coming and going again from my window. Has something happened to your father?"

Tess scrambled around in front of Ben, shielding him with her arms. "Don't kill him. Please don't kill him!"

Cade laughed. "Why the devil would I want to kill him?"

"It's Satan," Tess whispered. "He's got out somehow."

"He *what?*" Cade strode to the black stallion's stall and saw it was true. "Jesus bloody Christ. How did it happen?"

"I don't know. I only found out myself just now."

"Your father—" Cade advanced on them. "Is this his doing?"

"If it is, he didn't mean it!" Tess cried. "He's drunk, that's all. But he'd never do anything to hurt the horses!"

"All right, calm down." He glanced around the stable. "Any of the others missing?"

"My Linzy," Tess admitted miserably.

For some reason, that news made his lordship look almost cheerful. "Well. You don't say." He pushed back his hair with one hand. "I'll get some men from the village and go after them. Whom do you suggest?"

"None of them know much about horses. Anyway, they're likely all as bad off as he. I . . . I'm getting married tomorrow, you see."

"Aye," said Cade. "I know." He looked around her at Ben. "God, I'd hate to be him in the morning."

Tess laughed shakily. "When I saw him, that's just what I said." She got up from the floor, dusting straw from Ben's jacket. "I'll come with you to find them."

"You can't do that."

"Why not?"

"You just said—you're getting married tomorrow."

"I don't see what difference that makes."

He eyed the nightgown peeking out from beneath her father's coat. "Besides, you're not dressed."

"Well, someone's got to help you look; you wouldn't even know where to begin," Tess told him briskly. "Here, you ride Bobbin; he's good and steady in rain. I'll take Daisy."

"Who names these horses, anyway?" Cade demanded, taking the lead he was handed.

"I do." Tess's chin came up. "Why?"

"No reason," he said quickly.

"Tell me what you meant," she insisted.

"I don't know. They're such . . . well, such ordinary names."

"They're good solid names for good solid horses, that's what they are. Why do you call Satan Satan?"

He laughed. "Because he's a devil of a horse to ride. Why do you call Linzy Linzy?"

"Because I like the sound of it," Tess said coolly.

"Oh," said Gideon Cade. "What saddle should I use?"

He was quick with the tackle, Tess noted, working beside him; he had Bobbin ready before she was finished with Daisy, even though the gear was unfamiliar to him. "We'll each take a lantern," she announced, lighting another and handing it to him. "We're lucky it rained. Their tracks should be easy to see."

Once outside, she leaned down from the saddle and peered at the ground. "Only two sets are fresh," she observed of the tracks she saw there. "And I don't see any new footprints but yours and mine. That rules out robbers. They must have just gotten free from their stalls somehow."

"Your Linzy's in the lead. Look." He pointed to where the smaller set of tracks peeled off to their right; the other set had started left but then wheeled around. "She hasn't by some wild chance just come into heat, has she?"

"By God—" Tess realized, heart sinking, that she had. "Damn that bloody stallion!"

In the lantern light she saw his left brow arch. "You can't blame him for doing what comes naturally."

"Spoken just like a man," Tess muttered, and dug her heels into Daisy's sides.

The tracks led all the way down into the valley and past the cottage, then skirted the road to the village, circled back again, and headed west, up into the hills of the Forest Clun. The prints Linzy had made were wide-spaced and deep, showing how hard she'd run to get away from the stallion that nipped at her heels. Now and again the two sets of prints would merge and muddle as Satan cut off his quarry and tried to mount her. Each time, the evidence showed, Linzy had reared and bucked and then broken away.

Tess was riding hard too, eyes trained to the ground, ears cocked for a familiar whinny or neigh. Gideon Cade might have said he didn't blame her father, but the fact remained that the stables were Ben's responsibility. Should any harm come to the stallion on this midnight foray, it would be his fault. And should anything happen to Linzy . . . She pushed that thought from her mind. For her the pony was the single spark of light in a future that loomed increasingly dim.

Cade didn't speak as he followed behind her, or question her route; indeed, if not for the steady thud of Bobbin's hooves beyond her shoulder, Tess might not have known he was there. But that wasn't quite true. From time to time as they brushed beneath the dripping branches of an oak, above the green scent of the storm-washed forest she would catch a hint of his smell, the dark exotic mingling of soap and spice that she remembered from the morning when she'd burst in on him in his bath.

Suddenly she pulled in on the reins and halted. Cade rode up to her side, turning to her questioningly. She pushed back a tangle of damp red-gold curls from her forehead, put her finger to her lips, and pointed. Beyond the next thicket of trees, in a darkened clearing, shreds of light from the cloud-shrouded moon shimmered against Linzy's argentine coat as she knelt on the forest floor.

Cade started to speak. Tess threw him a warning glance. On the far side of the clearing, facing them, stood the stallion, a froth of white foam showing stark against his jet-black withers. Cade caught Tess's eye, dropped his lantern, and laid his hands on the rope coiled over his saddlehorn, gesturing that he meant to circle back behind Satan. She nodded, gathering up her own noose, but before Cade could move, the stallion charged Linzy, bellowing and snorting, threatening her with his hooves to frighten her up from the ground.

Linzy screamed, high-pitched and wild, and flailed in clumsy circles, like a waterfly pinned to a board. "She's hurt!" Tess cried accusingly.

"I can see that," Cade shot back. Tess's voice had alarmed the stallion; he backed off from Linzy, reared and roared, and turned to escape into the trees. But his master was already advancing, pounding into the clearing atop wild-eyed Bobbin, raising up the noosed rope and letting it fly. The throw was perfect; the snare fell around the stallion's neck and drew tight as he bucked and kicked. As soon as the rope tightened, Cade leapt down from the saddle, braced his boots against a rock, and held Satan there, talking to him in a low, quiet voice in a language that Tess could not understand.

"It's all right," he told her as the stallion stopped fighting and stood, straight-legged, nostrils flaring, not exactly calmed but more or less under control. "You can go in and get her." Tess looped Daisy to a tree, set down her lantern, then grabbed Bobbin and secured him too before approaching the pony and slipping the spare bridle over her nose.

"There's my good girl," she crooned, "there's my lamb. Hush, pet. I've got you." She smoothed her hands over the pony's neck and back, stroked her nose, patted her sides. "Let's see where he's hurt you."

"How do you know it was Satan?" asked Cade, coming up behind her. "She could have tripped on a vine, thrown a shoe—"

"Oh, shut up," Tess snapped. "You know as well as I do it's that bloody monster's fault; he's been hot after her since the day you showed up here. Come on, Linzy, love, can you stand?" Holding her breath, she tugged at the bridle, ready to let go again at the first sign the pony was in pain. To her astonishment, the silver pony clambered easily to her feet, shook herself dry, and nosed at the pockets of Ben's coat, looking for a treat.

"What the devil . . ." In disbelief Tess felt the horse's knees, checked her hocks, her shins, her hooves. "Why, there's nothing wrong with you at all!" At her shoulder, Gideon Cade had begun to laugh; she turned on him angrily. "And just what's so bloody damned amusing?"

"Oh, Christ, she's a horse in a million, your Linzy! And I'd pay a million pounds—if I had 'em—to breed her with Satan." He slapped the pony's side. "You sneaky little cheat, you ought to be ashamed! And you, Satan, you fell for it; you should be ashamed too!"

"Do you mean you think she collapsed like that on purpose?"

"Of course she did! She's female, isn't she? One can never put anything past a woman."

"Oh, I suppose you know everything there is to know about women," Tess said very coolly.

"Not quite everything," he told her, and grinned.

A sudden burst of sound split the air, like a shot from a musket, only a thousand times louder. The horses shied at their ropes, and Tess jumped. "Jesus, what was that?"

"Thunder," said Cade, and at the word the sky above them opened, letting loose a downpour of rain mixed with hail. "This village has got the damnedest weather I've ever known in my life!" he shouted above the raucous clatter of water and ice.

"We've got to get the horses home!" Tess called back, drenched within seconds despite her father's coat.

"Are you mad? Look at them!" A flash of cold green lightning illuminated the nervous animals. "We won't get ten yards down that hill without them getting loose again!"

"Well, what would you suggest?" Tess cried, struggling to hold on to Linzy as she skittered and flinched.

"We'll have to stay here!"

"And catch our bloody death of cold?" Already Tess's teeth were chattering; the pellets of ice pummeled her bare hands, clung stinging to her lashes and hair.

"Have you a better idea?" Gideon Cade shouted, and as lightning flared again, she saw his left eyebrow arch.

Tess searched the dark forest around them, trying to find her bearings; their circuitous route in following the tracks had thrown her off-kilter, though she knew every inch of those woods. The clearing in the trees, the big oak that Bobbin was tied to, the cliffs that rose up, forbidding and black, beyond Satan's broad back . . .

The cliffs. "As a matter of fact, I have!" she called into the fierce driving wind. "Follow me!"

"What's that?"

She gestured with one hand, clinging to Linzy's bridle with the other. "Follow me! This way!"

They were no more than a hundred yards from the cave in the cliffs that she and Jack had made their own. Fighting the icy sleet, Tess led Linzy toward the overhanging rocks that formed a roof above the hidden entrance, checking now and then to make sure Cade and Satan were close behind. "Good work!" he bellowed as they reached the precarious shelter. "At least it will hold off the hail. I'll go back for the other horses."

"Wait, I'll come with you!"

But he shook his head, tying the stallion to an outcrop of stone. "I can handle both those nags. Besides, you've got to protect Linzy's honor, remember?"

"Surely a storm like this would dampen even Satan's ardor!"

"I wouldn't count on it. Back in a minute!" He drew up the collar of his jacket, stepped into the tempest, and vanished from view.

Linzy was eyeing Satan suspiciously. Tess tied her as far away from the stallion as she could, on a very short lead. By the time Cade returned with Bobbin and Daisy, she was pulling at the stones piled across the mouth of the cavern; she started when he said, right in her ear, "I hardly think you need to build a wall between them."

"Don't be an idiot. There's a cave here, with flint and dry wood for a fire."

"I've told you before, I'm not an idiot."

Tess was too stiff with cold to bandy words out there any longer. Tugging the last of the stones from the doorway, she ducked low and hurried inside. "Keep a sharp eye out for Cerberus, Satan," she heard Cade mutter as he struggled to follow her through.

"Who's that?"

"The hound that guards the gates of hell. What the devil is this place?"

"I told you, it's a cave." Tess felt along the stone shelf to her right for the candles and flint that she knew would be there. "You can stand up inside; it's plenty big enough," she said over her shoulder, and promptly heard a thud and a curse. Lighting the candle, she turned to see him crouched over, rubbing the back of his head. "Well, big enough for Jack and me, anyway."

"Ah," said Cade, and again that damned eyebrow arched. In the flickering candlelight he took in the makeshift mattress of branches and ferns, the old blanket folded neatly beside it, the pile of ashes mounded in the fire pit. "Very cozy indeed."

Tess flushed. "We used to come here when we were children. It's not what you're thinking."

"How do you know what I'm thinking?" asked Gideon Cade.

He was right, of course. She couldn't know, any more than he could tell what her thoughts were. And a damned good thing too, she decided, showing him where the dry wood was stored, because she herself was shocked at the strange notions filling her head. As the thunder cracked and the wind and rain swirled past the entrance to their secret shelter, she was remembering the way he had looked stepping from his bath, the length of his hard brown body, his slim waist and firm, tight buttocks . . . Or could he read her mind after all? For when he took the candle from her to ignite the fire he'd built, his hand touched hers and—she was sure of it—lingered, before he smiled and moved away. And when he'd set the fire blazing, he unbuttoned his dripping jacket and shirt and peeled them off, stripping down to his breeches. Tess hurried to avert her eyes from the sight of his strong-muscled arms and broad chest with the dense thicket of curling black hairs that trailed down into a V just above his belt.

"You had better take off that jacket," he warned from the far side of the cave, "unless you want to catch a chill for your wedding." It did not occur to her to refuse the suggestion; she pulled off Ben's coat. Despite its layer of wool-grease, the rain had soaked through to her night-dress, making the sturdy fabric transparent as lawn. Realizing how plainly the tips of her breasts showed through, Tess reached for the blanket. But Cade was already there; he tucked it around her shoulders, raising up her damp curls and then letting them fall through his fingers. She heard her heart pounding even above the tumult of the storm, and wondered whether he heard it too.

"We may as well sit down," he said. "It doesn't seem as though it's letting up at all."

"I think it's warmer standing. Moving about." She proceeded to pace back and forth across the cave. Half-naked, he sat on the stone by the fire pit, the seat Jack always used.

"I'm sorry all this had to happen tonight of all nights," he went on. "You must have had . . . What's that expression you use? Enough on your plate without chasing after lost horses. Excited?"

Tess whipped to face him. "I beg your pardon?"

"Are you excited about the wedding?"

"Oh. Oh, aye. Very."

"He seems like a fine young man," said Cade. "Very much in love with you. I daresay you'll be very happy together."

Happy? Tess cried to him dumbly. How can I be happy with Jack? I hate him! I am only going through with the marriage for Dad, because of all he has done for me! But she could not swallow her pride enough to voice such thoughts aloud—especially not to him. "Aye, so we shall" —that was all she did say, and turned away.

"You seem young to wed," he mused. "But I suppose that's the way it's done out here. No doubt that very upright father of yours has been preaching the virtues of wedded bliss to you since you were born."

"Doesn't yours?" Tess countered.

"Oh, my father was a great believer in marriage. He had four wives." His fine mouth was twisted. "Were your father and mother happy together?"

"Would you mind talking about something else?"

"Forgive me," he said after a moment. "I forgot—you'll miss your mother a great deal tomorrow. I'm sure she would be very proud of you if she were here."

My mother . . . Tess swallowed a bitter laugh. What would her mother say if she saw her daughter now, alone in a cave in the woods with a man who was practically a stranger, on the eve of her wedding? Meg Mullen used an expression—"the apple doesn't fall far from the tree." The fact was that at that moment, as Tess watched the flickering firelight play over Gideon Cade's dark face, she felt less kindred to Ben than to the wicked, willful woman he'd called "m'lady" and coupled with in another wood.

Forever and ever, amen. God, it seemed a long time, forever. Tess looked across the leaping flames at Gideon

Cade. Jack had wronged her, horribly wronged her; even her father had admitted that. Didn't that give her the right to repay him wrong for wrong? And what better retribution could there be, what revenge more fitting, than to flirt with the man whose fault all this was in the first place? She could pay Cade back while she was at it. After all, if he hadn't come up with the notion of breeding Linzy and Satan, she never would have gone to the big house that morning and burst in on him. Then Jack never would have raped her, and she wouldn't be marrying him on the morrow. If Gideon Cade had never come to Windber-on-Clun, everything would have gone on just the same as before.

She knelt on the floor of the cave beside him, spreading the blanket beneath her. "I take it you're feeling warmer," he observed.

"Much warmer, thank you. It's a lovely fire." Tess leaned her head back, running her hands through her loose, tangled hair. She could feel how her nightdress pulled tight across her breasts in that position. Cade shifted on his hard stone seat; she was certain he had noticed too. "I didn't mean to be cross with you before, about my mother. But I can't help thinking of her," she told him. "Drat."

"What's wrong?"

"There's a leaf caught in my hair. Right here. Could you get it out, please?" She moved so she knelt facing him, bowing her head. "Do you see it?"

"Aye," said Cade, his deep voice sounding strangled. Tess nibbled her lip. This was easier than she'd thought it would be.

She felt his fingertips riffle through her curls, heard the dried leaf crackle as he tugged it free. "Ouch!"

"I'm sorry. I'm not much good at this sort of thing."

"It's not your fault. It's just that your hands are so strong." She smiled up at him, catching one wrist as he pulled them away. "Widow Jonas reads people's hands, you know. She says a person's whole life is laid out right here." He'd curled his fist closed; she pried it open and traced the lines on its palm with her finger.

"What do your hands say?"

"I don't know. Dad would never let her read them. He says fortune-telling is the devil's work."

"He's probably right," said Cade, and withdrew his hand from hers. "He's a very wise man."

"He's not so wise as all that," Tess said with a little pout. "But let's not talk about him."

"What would you like to talk about?"

"You." She sat back on her heels. "Let's talk about you."

"There is nothing to say."

"You mustn't be so selfish. A man who has been so many places as you have, done so many things, must have thousands of stories to tell. You might at least share a few with me. After all, I've never been anywhere or done anything." Wide-eyed, coaxing, she laid her hand on his knee.

He stood up abruptly. "The fire needs wood." Choking back a giggle, Tess twisted to watch as he went and fetched another log, then crouched down on the opposite side of the blaze and set it in place. A flurry of sparks flew into the air.

"You've burned me!" She held out her arm as he circled back to his seat, showing him where one of the cinders had landed and already turned to ash. "You must make it better!"

"Don't!" he said sharply as she stretched her hand toward him.

"Don't what?" Still wide-eyed, all innocence.

Gideon Cade shook his head, staring at her, his blue eyes blazing. "You look like an angel, kneeling like that with the fire behind you, making a gold halo of your hair. A Botticelli angel."

"What does that mean—Botti—"

"Botticelli. He was a painter. In Italy." His words were tumbling one after another. "Sandro Botticelli of Florence. He studied with Fra Lippi. He was a mystic, a disciple of Savonarola. He . . ." Cade stopped.

Tess smiled up at him. "Tell me more."

The man who stood before her sighed soundlessly, the muscles in his bared chest contracting and then unbinding. "I can't remember any more."

She shrugged prettily, twining a long curl around her finger. "I'll wait until you do remember."

"I never will, to see you kneeling there." He grabbed his wet jacket from the floor. "I'll go and check on the horses."

"Wait, I'll come with you. I don't want to stay in here all alone. Will you help me up?" Again she extended her hand, and this time he took it in his. He pulled her to her toes as though she were weightless, volatile as a bird— and then he pulled her into his arms.

He ran one hand over her hair, down her spine to the small of her back, crushing her body against him; with the other he seized her face and yanked her chin upward so her eyes met his. "I would have to be stone," he said furiously. "Do you think I am stone, you willful, prideful girl? Do you?" She shook her head mutely, unable to speak for the force of his grip. Of all possible reactions to her coquetry, she had not expected anger. "You're to be married tomorrow!" He slid his hand down over her throat to her shoulder and jerked her so hard that her jaw snapped. "Does that mean nothing to you?"

His hand moved lower still, across the bodice of her nightdress, brushed her breast, wrenched away as though burned, returned. At his touch Tess's knees went weak; she sagged against him, her cheek pressed tight to his chest. "Christ," she heard him say. "Oh, Christ . . ." Her head was filled with the scent of him, warm spice and musky sweat; her mind reeled with a surfeit of wild sensation as he lifted her into his arms and carried her to the mattress of pine boughs and ferns that Jack had assembled there in the secret cave.

He caught up the blanket and let it fall onto the high-piled greenery; then he laid her down gently atop the crazy quilt the leaves and branches made. Tess did not take her eyes from him as he knelt and pulled off her boots. Her toes were icy cold; he took each foot in turn between his hands and rubbed them to warmth. Then he yanked off his own boots and stretched out beside her. "Where else are you cold? Are you cold here?" Smiling, he touched her nightdress at the ankle, the calf. "Here?" Her thighs—his fingers trailed toward the V between them, and she pushed his hand away. "Here, then." He brought it right back, tracing the line of her lowest rib. "Or . . . here." Tess drew in her breath as his hand closed on her breast, plucking at the taut bud that marked it. He lowered his head, his mouth covering hers while he teased the rosy nipple with his fingertips.

His kisses were fiery-sweet, like camphor-root and honey; he thrust his tongue against her lips until they parted to welcome him, and his moistness mingled with hers as he tasted and explored. When Jack had tried the same thing, Tess had felt suffocated, but this man's touch was sure and unhurried; he knew just when to press and when to withdraw, tantalizing her so that she circled his neck with her arms to try to keep him near.

He shifted on the blanket so that the great length of his body lay tight against hers. Tess felt the bulge of his manhood hard at her thigh, the pulsing blood in the veins of his throat, and her mind warned: this has gone far enough. She had to stop him. But the small act of vengeance she'd planned against him and Jack was all but forgotten, lost in the swirl of longing his kisses unleashed in her soul.

"I want you," he told her, his mouth at her ear. "God, how I want you!" Tess put her hand to the side of his face, wishing she could put into words so readily the emotions that she was feeling: fear, wonder, happiness. Instead she stroked the harsh line of his cheekbone, the hollow beneath it, the stubble of coarse black beard that ran over the plane of his chin. "Sweet," he murmured, "so sweet . . ." And he seized her hand and kissed it, held the fingers to his mouth one by one and covered them with kisses, kissed palm and thumb and knuckles so greedily that she laughed and rolled away, turning her back to him.

He caught her, one arm at her waist, the other under her shoulder, and pulled her against him so that she curled within the curve of his body. The pulsing pressure of his manhood at her buttocks made Tess's muscles go rigid with the memory of how Jack had entered her, violated her there. She tried to pull free, but he would not let her go; he held her while he kissed the nape of her neck and fondled her breasts and belly, until she forgot her terror and lay against him quietly.

Not until then did he slip his hand beneath the hem of her nightdress. He ran it all the way up her leg, past her thighs and drawers and rib cage to her bare breasts, and all thoughts of Jack flew straight from her head as his flesh touched hers, as she let out a shivering sigh.

"Oh," she whispered, his long, strong fingers caressing each taut nipple in turn, while his hand cupped the soft weight of each creamy mound. "Oh . . ."

"Like that, do you?" He grunted, moving the arm that circled her shoulders down the length of her body until he could reach that hand too, beneath her skirt. "How about this? Do you like this?" Still stroking her breasts with one hand, he brought the other up to her belly and slipped it into her drawers.

"No!" Tess told him, trying to push him away.

"Wait," he murmured. "Wait. Let me." And again he did no more than touch her, trace feathery circles around her navel until her fear passed.

When he felt the stiffness flow from her shoulders and spine, he slid both hands down to her hips and turned her to face him. Eyes closed, lips parted, Tess waited for him to do with her what he would. Even if he takes me now roughly, crudely, the way Jack did, she thought, at least he has done his best to give me some pleasure, to show some concern for me.

She felt him catch the hem of her skirt and raise it up slowly, all the way over her head; he pulled her hands from the sleeves with great gentleness, the way a mother would help her child. Shy at her near-nakedness, she crossed her arms over her breasts. "Are you cold?" he asked, and she shook her head. "Look at me." Tess hid her face against the blanket, her eyes still clenched; he pulled her back, his hand caught in her hair. "I said, look at me."

Unwillingly Tess peeked through the fans of her lashes, ready to turn away again. What she saw made her eyes fly wide open instead. He'd stripped off his hose and breeches and lay stretched out beside her stark naked, without a jot of self-consciousness. But it was his private parts that caught her attention, the parts she hadn't seen when she walked in on him in his bath. His manhood rose rigid and hard from the bulging red sacs at its root, thick as a sapling, longer than the span of her hand; its smooth head pulsed with a life of its own, fed by the lace of blue veins just below the taut skin.

"You flatter me," he said wryly. "Is your betrothed so slight by comparison?"

"I've never seen . . ." Seen anyone's manhood before, she started to tell him, but he laughed, leaning over to silence her with a kiss.

"No words," he murmured. "No lies. Touch me." He drew back again, her hand in his, and laid it against that great rod. Tess shivered as he pressed her fingers around it, as she felt it grow harder still beneath her tremulous hand. "Will you kiss it?" he asked. Tess jerked her hand away, staring, thinking him mad. "So, that nicety hasn't reached Windber-on-Clun. Pity. Still, there's no harm in asking."

Apprehensive though she was, Tess was struck by the expression in his eyes as the firelight illuminated them: they were watchful, uncertain, as if he awaited some sign that she hadn't yet given. Not knowing what he wanted, she lay silent beneath his close scrutiny. The golden chain that Lord Halifax had given her hung at her throat, flashing and winking with the dancing flames. He hooked his fingers beneath the delicate links and tugged; fearful the necklace would snap, Tess came forward with it, her hand prying at his. He drew her toward him until their mouths nearly met, and then held her there.

"How earned you this chain?" he demanded, his eyes searching hers.

"I told you; it was a gift."

"Are you marrying Jack tomorrow?"

"I have to," Tess told him, and saw the uncertainty vanish from his eyes, replaced by a hard blue flame.

"And what am I?" he asked, black eyebrow raised. "One last swipe at pleasure?"

"I don't know what you are. I only know . . . what you make me feel."

"And what is that?"

"As if my life isn't ending," she whispered. "As if tomorrow may never come."

"Fair enough, Mistress Jericho." His mouth covered hers in a fierce burning kiss; the chain slid from his hand. Beneath the pressure of his embrace Tess fell back against the blanket. He followed, one leg sprawling over both of hers, and lowered his head, the trail of his kisses leading down along her throat to her breast.

For exquisite, agonizing minutes he lingered over its white softness, tracing each blue vein that showed against her pale beauty, savoring the taste, the scent of her pristine skin. Not until he'd explored that with infinite thoroughness did he take the taut rosy bud of her nipple into his mouth, sucking its tip, flicking his tongue back and forth across it with increasing speed. He'd moved one hand down over her drawers to cover the gentle curve of her mound of Venus; at first he barely touched her there, but gradually he increased the pressure of his hand, moving it in a slow circle, his palm brushing the mat of curls he could feel through the thin lawn.

Tess closed her eyes, abandoning herself to the soft breathless sighs that escaped her with each move he made, clutching his broad shoulders as he sucked hungrily at her breasts. To compare what he did to the rushed, fumbled gropings she'd endured at Jack's hands in this cave—much less to that harsh, hateful rape—was to compare day with night, light with darkness. Jack's hurried attempts at seduction had always made her feel soiled and vaguely shamed, but Gideon Cade's leisurely perusal of her body made her proud of its beauty, of the pleasure he took in touching and tasting and looking his fill. Jack's attack on her in the barn had made her feel less than human; Cade made her feel exalted, immortal, worshiped like some deity.

She longed to tell him so, but "No words," he'd said, and so she sought to exalt him in return. As bravely as she could, she reached down and touched his throbbing manhood, closed her fingers around it, and was rewarded with a groan of pleasure so deep it seemed to rise from his very soul. Unsure what to do next, she started to pull away, but he would not let her; he closed his hand over hers and moved it up and then down along his thick rod. She followed his lead, timidly at first but with more confidence as his body responded, his loins thrusting against her in the rhythm he'd established while he licked first at one breast and then the other, his tongue hot as flame.

"Past time we were rid of these," he grunted, his fingers finding the string of her drawers and loosing the knot. As he slid them downward, he groaned again, his hand running over her thatch of red-gold curls and cool ivory hips. "So beautiful, so white . . ." He pushed the last bit of linen past her knees, over her feet, and brought his hand up again ever so slowly, parting her legs a bit with each tender caress. When he reached her thighs, he slipped his hand between them. Tess held her breath as those long fingers inched upward, reaching, stroking, seeking her most secret place, that even she had never dared to explore.

"Are you ready for me?" he whispered. Tess said nothing, not knowing what to say, and he laughed, one finger climbing higher than the others. "Sweet sinner Teresa . . ." Then he touched her, and from his silken touch there spread a silken warmth, the first red-gold sparks of a fire. She fell back, trembling, shuddering, as within her belly she felt a shimmering, the start of the honeyed ache she had felt long ago as she rode atop Linzy high in the hills.

"Oh," she whispered in wonder as his finger probed deeper and deeper. With each movement he made, the warmth, the shimmering, spread, until it seemed a river of heat had enveloped her blood. "Oh, oh . . ." Then he thrust his finger far down inside her; her eyes opened wide, and she had to bite her lip to keep from crying out loud. He looked at her, his own gaze narrowed.

"So," he said. "So we know . . . for sure. Still, I'll give you a wedding gift, as Lord Halifax did. Something to remember the lord of the manor by."

His words made no sense to Tess, but she didn't care so long as he touched her, kept that fiery river flowing through her blood and bone. She felt as though every bit of hidden flesh he stroked turned to crimson satin, slip-

pery and smooth, like the vestments the priest wore on
the highest of holy days. There was something priestlike,
too, in the way he knelt over her now, watchful and
solemn, and bent his head to kiss her, tongue pushing
inside her just as his finger did. He kissed her mouth and
each of her breasts, then moved his hand away from her
parted thighs.

"No," Tess begged, catching his wrist, trying to push
his hand back to work its miracles. "Please, please . . ."

"Greedy little sinner, aren't you?" The words were
teasing, but his voice was strained. "Let me give you this
now." He reached down for his manhood and ran its
pulsing head over her belly to her mound of Venus, then
lower still, between her legs, until it stroked her as his
finger had. Back and forth he moved, that hot thick rod
sliding against her, while she closed her eyes and abandoned herself to what she knew was the summit of ecstasy.

Each time he shifted, beginning the slow sweet motion
again, she could not keep from moaning, a brief tiny cry.
"God help you, you were made for this, weren't you?"
he muttered. "And God help me, I can hold off no
longer . . ." He leaned back, his thighs clasping hers, and
then his hard shaft drove into her, penetrating her tight
satin sheath. There was no pain as when Jack had forced
himself on her; there was only a tingling pang of discom-
fort before the pleasure flowed through her once more.
He ran his hands over her shoulders and breasts, then
down to her hips, slid them round to her buttocks, cupping them, raising her up from the pine-bough bed. Moved
by tantalized instinct, Tess reached to clasp her hands
behind his neck, and thus straddled his thighs. "Oh, God.
Oh, Christ," he groaned, pulling her against him so that
thick rod plunged even deeper. "Oh, Tess. Tess . . ." He
began to move at a frenzied pitch, sliding her back and
forth along his haunches while he buried his face in her
hair. She held on tightly, craving this fierce wild ride, the
burning ache in her belly that flared with each white-hot
thrust.

"Now," he grunted, his mouth at her ear. "Now, love,
come with me. Now, feel it now . . ." His words were a
passionate incantation; though Tess did not know their

meaning, she sensed his heightening excitement, felt the taut strain of every muscle as he clutched her and buried his manhood deep in her sheath again and again.

"Now . . ." And her head fell back, her flesh ignited, her hands dug into his skin as the ache inside her became an unbearable fiery beauty. She screamed, her voice ringing from the rocks, with the awful knowledge that filled her at that moment: she could see all goodness and truth in a flash of bright radiant light. "Now!" cried the man beneath her, clasping her to him, the whole great length of his body shuddering as the light within her split and spread itself, magnified, refracted through the prism of their shared ecstasy into a hundred thousand sparks. He called her name once more; the sparks flared to flame, diamond-bright, bedazzling; mountains moved; seas rose; stars fell; and then all was still.

For aeons, ages, they clung to each other, breathless and panting. Then he shifted her on his lap, withdrawing his still-engorged rod, and pushed back his damp hair. "Did you hear that?" he asked, cocking his head toward the entrance to the cave. Tess didn't answer; she could hear nothing but the blood pounding in her heart and head, feel nothing but the fading glow of the fire in her soul. How had she ever, she wondered, imagined herself in love with Jack? That had been no more than childish infatuation; this, *this* was love, this mystical union she and Cade had shared. She looked at him, awed, adoring, and smiled beatifically.

He was frowning in return. "Someone's hound—your Job, I'd guess, from the sound of him. And hot on a trail . . ."

Tess could hear the baying too now, though she didn't know why he should find the sound so intriguing. "It could be Job," she said dreamily. "He might have gotten out of the barn somehow." Made bold by the warm glow inside her, she put her hands to his chest, catching her fingers in the thick black curls there, and tugged him toward her. "Give us a kiss," she begged playfully, tilting up her chin as the hound's baying grew louder. Instead he thrust her down to the floor of the cave.

"What mischief is this," he demanded, "or would you have me believe it is just mischance?"

"I don't know what you mean," Tess stammered. His eyes had turned flint gray and cold; she was reminded of the first time she had seen him, for despite the intimacy they had shared, he seemed a stranger again.

He flung her nightdress and drawers at her. "Put them on." Uncomprehending, she didn't move. "Put them on, damn you!" The hound was close at hand now, howling frantically. There was some other commotion outside the cave as well; the horses were neighing and stomping. Cade grabbed for his breeches. "Have you found her?" a man shouted, and Tess froze, recognizing her father's voice.

A tousled blond head appeared in the mouth of the cave. Hazel eyes took in the naked figures crouched on the makeshift bed of branches and ferns, turned wide in disbelief. "No," Jack whispered. "No. Oh, God, you whore, you filthy whore." Then he reared back and screamed, a long wordless scream of betrayal and fury and pain.

"Jack, lad, what is it?" Ben Jericho clambered into the cave beside him. First he saw Cade, who was putting on his breeches, and then he saw Tess. She had never in her life imagined anything so awful as the expression on his face. "Jehovah will damn you in hell for what you've done this night, you devil," he spat at Cade. "As for you . . ." His blunt finger trembled as he lowered it at Tess. "You're your mother's daughter, all right." He put his arm around Jack's shoulder. "Come along, lad. I'll see you home."

"We were to be married tomorrow!" Jack sobbed brokenly.

" 'Tis better wise late than never."

"But I loved her!" Jack cried.

"Aye, lad, I know, for I loved her too."

The terrible finality of his words broke through Tess's numbed daze. She stumbled up from the blanket, clutching the nightdress to her belly and breasts. "Dad. Dad, listen to me—"

" 'Come down and sit in the dust, O daughter of Babylon,' " her father quoted the prophet Isaiah, " 'thy nakedness shall be uncovered, yea, thy shame shall be seen.' "

"For God's sake, Dad!"

He turned his back to her and led Jack away.

Job's delirious howling slowly grew fainter. Tess stared at the mouth of the cave and shivered, suddenly aware of the freezing chill in the air. "Congratulations," said Gideon Cade, his voice just as frigid. "You've got what you brought me here for." She looked at him blankly. He nodded after Jack and her father, buckling his belt. "You won't be marrying that poor fool in the morning, or ever. Pity you hadn't the stomach just to tell him, without using me."

"Do you honestly believe I planned for this to happen?" Tess cried. "Jesus in heaven, what kind of girl do you think I am?"

Cade pulled on his jacket, then leaned down to step into his boots. Something glinted on the blanket by his heel in the dim firelight. He picked it up, examined it briefly, and then tossed it toward her. The gold chain, its dainty links snapped in pieces. Tess let it fall unheeded into the fire, searching his face for some trace of the warmth they had shared, but finding none there. "I think tonight's escapade established exactly what sort of girl you are," he told her, "not that there was ever really any doubt. Jack summed it up rather nicely." Boots laced and tied, he started for the entrance to the cave, then looked back. "The next time you need a gull, though, let me know. It's been quite entertaining. Good night, Mistress Jericho."

II

6

"Jack!" Tess cried as loud as she could, waving as she ran toward the north field, where he and Mungo were hoeing. The effort to gain his attention succeeded; he put his back to her very deliberately and dug the hoe into the rocky earth with un-Shropshire-like energy. "Jack!" she shouted again, then cursed as he went on hoeing. Long legs flying, she ran closer to the field, so that Mungo, who was slightly deaf, could hear what she was saying. "Mungo, tell him Dad needs him right away in the stables! The pony's taken sick!"

Jack said something to Mungo, who leaned on his hoe and called back to Tess, "He says he's busy!"

"Jack, it's important! Oh, damn you!" she fumed as he put his back to her again. How could he be so childish, carrying on this ridiculous act of not speaking to her for four entire months? What had he got to complain about, anyway? He'd married Millie Fish, hadn't he? And gossip said he'd already got her with child. She ran closer still. "Mungo, tell him the pony's in trouble. Dad needs his help; he can't see to her proper with his arm still in a sling."

Again Jack and Mungo held a brief colloquy. "He says," Mungo bellowed, " 'tain't his fault yer dad's arm's broke!"

"Well, it's not mine either!"

That provoked Jack into direct speech. "The hell it's not! If ye hadn't been doin' . . . wot ye was doin' up there that night, he'd never have stumbled comin' down from the cliffs!"

Tess counted silently to ten, thinking of the suffering pony. "All right, it is my fault. Now, please, will you come?"

"Tell her I've got to finish the hoeing," Jack ordered Mungo.

That was a bit much even for the old man. "Come on, Jack. How much difference can a mite o' hoein' make to crops like these?" He flung his arm toward the weak, stunted stalks of oats that bent toward the rock-strewn soil. "Wot with the weather we've had this summer, this field's a goner anyway."

"Aye, 'n' whose fault's that?" cried Jack.

"Oh, honestly," said Tess. "You can hardly blame Gideon Cade for the weather!"

"I'll do as I danged well please!" he shouted back at her.

Tess let out an exasperated sigh. "Dad wouldn't ask unless the pony was really in trouble, Jack. I'm not asking for me. I'm asking for him."

"Jack . . ." Mungo began.

He threw down his hoe. "Oh, all right! But tell Jezebel there I'll not walk to the stables with her."

"He says—" Mungo called.

"Never mind, I heard him. You go ahead, Jack, and hurry, please!" She rolled her eyes toward heaven as, at long last, Jack set off at a slow trot.

Mungo came stumping toward her over the rocky ground. "Got a lot on his mind right now, Jack has," he offered in explanation. "His Millie's with child, ye know."

"Yes, Mungo, I *do* know, thank you. You're only the fifteenth person to share that happy news with me in the past two days. And just when I thought everyone in Windber-on-Clun had stopped speaking to me!" Tess said airily. "Imagine my relief."

"Aye, well. Just tryin' to be helpful," the old man told her, edging away.

"I'm sure," said Tess, and stuck out her tongue at his back as she headed for the stables in Jack's wake.

If there had been times before that night in June when she felt like a leper, these days she might well have carried the plague. Girls who'd once been her friends avoided coming near her; she had the feeling their mothers used her as an example of what would happen if their daughters didn't behave. As for the menfolk of Windber-on-Clun, except for two who'd propositioned her—one even offering her money—they'd been no more forthcoming. What was it, she wondered, that made it permissible for a husband and father to suggest she meet him in the stables some night for the grand sum of two shillings—not to mention for Jack to have beaten and raped her—but unforgivable sin for her to get carried away by dandelion wine and the heat of the moment and make love to Gideon Cade?

"Making love" wasn't really the right term for what had gone on between them, of course. Especially considering that his lordship, just like his tenants, had gone out of his way to avoid her ever since. What with Ben speaking to her only when he absolutely had to, if not for Job and Linzy, she reflected, her voice might have withered away from disuse.

I should never have stayed, she thought for the thousandth time since it had happened. I ought just to have packed up my bags and left the next day, gone to London and then to the New World. But how could she, when she'd no sooner left the cave than she heard Ben howling with pain? Blind in his wrath and disillusionment, he'd walked into a ditch and broken his arm in three places. It was months before he'd been able to handle the horses again, or look after himself.

And so she did stay, enduring his silence, abiding his reproachful eyes. It was a penance, she decided, the price she owed and would pay for disappointing him. In time he would forgive her. If not—well, the general opinion seemed to be that his scorn was no more than she deserved for the sin she'd committed. Who was she to rail against the collective wisdom of Windber-on-Clun?

There was one more consideration, of course; once her father and her betrothed had stumbled into that cave, there was no longer any question of her marrying Jack. But she would not admit even to herself that that had figured into her decision to stay in the village, for to do so implied that what Gideon Cade had said to her there might be true—that she had made love to him in hopes Jack would find out somehow.

Made love . . . There she went again, using that absurdly inappropriate term. There had been more "love," skewed though it was, in Jack's rape of her than in what Cade had done. What was it he'd said afterward, with his blue eyes like ice? "It's been quite entertaining." And no doubt it had been, for a cheat and a rogue such as he. Her cheeks burned as she recalled the way she'd let him touch her, the eagerness with which she'd returned his embraces. Ben was right: she was her mother's daughter. The difference was that she'd learned her weakness, and she did not intend to give herself to any man ever again. Full of resolve, she hurried back to the stables to help.

"Where the devil have you been?" her father demanded as she entered the birthing room, where he'd secluded the ailing pony. "Never mind," he went on before she could answer, and she knew from his tone that the trouble had worsened in the brief moments she'd been away. The pony was still less than halfway through her eleven-month gestation; that morning, while cleaning her stall, Tess had noticed fresh blood and pus on the straw. "Come and hold her head here, and see if you can calm her down."

"Is she losing the colt?" Tess asked, hugging the wide-eyed pony's withers, stroking her nose.

"That's up to Jehovah, ain't it?" Ben stumped around to peer at the pony's backside, his arm cradled in its linen sling. "Though I must say 'tis danged peculiar if she is."

"Why is that?" Jack wanted to know.

"Most times a mare will miscarry in the first four months or not at all," Tess told him.

"Aye," Ben grunted, poking gently at the pony's swollen belly. "When I get them this far, it's usually clear skies from here."

"It would be all of a piece with everything else that's gone on this summer," Jack said bitterly.

Ben looked up from his ministrations, head cocked to one side. "I don't see what you've got to complain of, laddie. A pretty new wife, a new house, and soon a new baby—"

" 'Tis not just myself that I'm thinking of. 'Tis the predicament we'll all be in soon, thanks to Gideon Cade. Have ye seen the crops in the fields? They're all stunted and twisted."

"The weather's been bad," Tess said patiently. "It's got naught to do with who's living in the big house."

Jack's expression turned most unpleasant. "Naturally, ye would defend him."

"I'm not defending anyone." Tess's green eyes flashed. "I just don't happen to believe that Gideon Cade can control the weather."

"Maybe not." Jack sneered. "But he sure knows how to make the most of a storm."

"Go to hell, Jack Brady," she spat back.

"Both of you, shut up!" Ben ordered tersely. "Jack, go and fetch his lordship."

"I'm damned if I will."

"Do as I say, lad, and run! She's losing the colt." Jack still didn't budge. Ben shoved him out of the stall. "Go on, then, or by Jehovah I'll have your hide!"

"Thanks, Dad," Tess said quietly when Jack had gone.

"For what?"

"For sending him instead of me."

"Don't think I was trying to spare your feelings," he told her coldly. "It's just that I need you here right now more than I need him. The colt's already dead, but I'll be danged if I'll have Cade blame me for losing the pony as well. Drat!" He spat on the bloodied straw. "I'd give my right hand right now to have a right hand."

Jack was back in two minutes, alone. "Well? Where is he?" Ben barked.

"I gave a message to Prince Oren."

"You might have waited to find out if he was coming!"

"Listen, I didn't ask to be here," Jack began, then stopped as the stable door opened and clicked closed again.

"Hello?" Gideon Cade called into the dim interior, and at the sound of his deep voice, Tess's stomach contracted in what she knew was hatred.

"Back here," Ben called back from the birthing room.

Footsteps, a faint scent of pungent spice on the air, and then Tess saw him again.

He was dressed like a prince, like a peer of the realm. He had on black satin breeches with high polished black boots, a black velvet doublet trimmed with gold buttons and braid, and a linen shirt, pale as new snow, that had layer upon layer of lacy ruffles at the cuffs and throat. Tess could not imagine any other man she knew wearing such an outfit without looking a bloody milksop, but somehow Cade carried it off; his dark angular face and the hard line of his jaw undercut the frippery so that one saw the man first and not the clothes. Ben, his good left hand plunged to the wrist in the panting pony's birth canal, looked his master up and down as he entered. "Sorry to interrupt your plans," he said caustically. "I'd no idea you were calling on the king and queen."

"What's that?" Cade saw the three of them staring at his clothing and waved a vague hand. "Lady Hardwick over near Stafford asked me to call tonight. I was just getting ready to send for Satan."

"Well, far be it from me to keep Her Ladyship waiting. Teresa, saddle his lordship's horse."

"No, no, don't be absurd. It's nothing that matters. Oren said the pony is ill. Will the colt be all right?"

"The colt's dead," Ben told him bluntly.

"Dead . . ." Cade moved to stroke the frightened pony's nose; Tess quickly stepped aside lest he accidentally touch her. "But just two days past you said everything was going so well!"

"And so it was, two days past. Dying don't take but a moment."

"Poor pretty lady, I'm sorry," Cade murmured to the pony, without a hint of self-consciousness. Then he looked back at Ben. "What will you do now?"

"You can see she's been bleeding. Ordinarily she'd go into labor, drop the colt, and that would be that. But there's some sort of obstruction . . ." Frowning, Ben groped inside the horse as best he could; she whinied frantically, trying to pull away, and Cade had to hang on to the bridle with both hands to keep her under control.

"I can't find it, not with only one arm. So Jack's going to have to bring out the colt."

"Why did you send for me?"

Tess saw the brief flash of contempt in her father's eyes. "We could lose the pony too, if aught goes awry. I just wanted you to know that. Now get on your way."

"No, I meant, is there something that I can do?"

"Aye, get the hell out," Jack muttered just below his breath.

Ben shook his head. "Nay, thank you," he told Cade, so obsequiously that the words came out rude instead. "Suppose I just stay out of your way over here, then, and watch."

"Suit yourself," Ben grunted. "Tess, hold her steady. Jack, come around here." He showed him how to ball up one fist and hold on to his forearm with the other. "Now, go on in there, lad, and tell me what you feel."

The pony bleated in fright as Jack reached up inside her. "Gor, it's all mucky with slime—"

"You'll have to go higher than that!" Ben told him sharply. "You should feel the caul, like a smooth silky sack, and through that the legs or the head . . ."

A thick yellow liquid streaked with crimson blood was seeping onto Jack's shirt and arms; his face had turned pale. "Gor, Ben, I can't tell what the hell I'm touchin'!"

"Hmph! Mind the midwife don't let you come near when Millie's time comes. Go on, lad, go on! Get right in there and grope about."

"It all feels the same to me. I can't tell what I'm doing!" As Jack's voice rose in consternation, the pony grew more agitated, snorting and pawing the ground in mounting terror.

"Hold on, lass," Ben cautioned Tess, keeping his own voice soothing and calm. "As for you, Jack, get a grip on yourself."

"I can't help it!" he screeched. The frantic pony bucked, yanking the lead right away from Tess, jerking free of Jack; his hands popped from the birth canal in a flood of tissue and gore. "Oh, Jesus!"

"Get . . . the . . . pony," Ben said, still feigning calm, but between gritted teeth. Though Tess reached for her, it was Cade who caught and held the horse, whispering quiet words as he wrapped one long arm over her withers and brought her under control. Jack had stumbled back against the side of the stall and was retching in long jagged gasps. Tess remembered the way she had vomited in this same stable after his assault on her, and was glad for the humiliating shame he was feeling now.

"Get out," Ben ordered him. "Go on, get out! You're doing me no good, and Jehovah knows you're not helping the pony!" His head still bowed, Jack staggered out of the stall. "You'll have to do it, Tess," Ben went on, circling round to take the bridle, "though heaven knows where you'll find the strength. At least you've the sense not to lose your dinner. Just take it slow and steady—"

"Let me try," offered Gideon Cade.

Ben's lip curled in a sneer. "Why? So you can show up that poor lad again?"

"So I can save the pony, you stupid old man," the lord of Windber-on-Clun said steadily.

Tess caught her breath. She'd never heard anyone call her father stupid before. She wasn't sure what she expected to happen: for Ben to take a swing at Cade, for lightning to strike, for the earth to open up under their feet. The last thing she would have considered was that Ben might agree. But oddly enough, he did. "Go ahead, then, if you like. Hold on, Teresa." He stood back, hugging his bad arm to his chest, clearly anticipating a repeat of the disaster of moments before.

Cade approached the pony slowly. By now she was foaming around the mouth, heaving at the belly; her dark eyes were rolling, feverishly bright. He began to murmur to her in some strange language, just as he'd talked to the horses on the night of the storm. "What tongue's that you're speaking?" Ben demanded.

"French," Cade told him. "One should always speak French to ladies and horses." And then, when Ben and Tess stared at him blankly, he flushed. "It's just an adage I learned at school."

"Hmph," said Ben. "I've been talking to horses for fifty years in plain English and doing just fine." The pony had calmed, though, at Cade's soft crooning tone; now he ran his hands over her coat, ignoring the blood and muck.

"You'll soil your fine suit for Lady Hardwick," Tess said spitefully, despising the unknown noblewoman for whom he'd dressed.

"She likes horses. She'll understand." He moved into place beside Ben, still stroking the pony. Likes horses . . . Tess pictured in her mind the dainty ladies who'd come to visit Lord Halifax with their husbands from time to time, the way they'd perched sidesaddle atop their mild little palfreys in outlandish riding outfits and hats. Likes horses! And little wonder, when she'd never in her life have to muck out a stable or even smell dung. "This way, Jericho?" Cade made a fist and gripped his forearm the way Jack had, and Ben nodded. "Ready, then?" he asked Tess, and for an instant their eyes met; she looked away first, nodding too. "Good girl, pretty girl, pretty lady," Cade murmured, this time in English, and then eased his hands up into the birth canal.

The pony tensed, ears back, nostrils flaring, but did not buck. Cade went on whispering endearments while Ben hissed, "What do you feel?"

"The caul, I think—there's a lovely pony!—and something inside it . . ."

"Well, what? Head? Buttocks?" Ben demanded.

"Legs. And then . . ." Again the pony went rigid as he reached higher. "Buttocks, I guess. It's surely not the head."

"Breech. The legs must be tearing her," Ben mumbled, more to himself than to Cade. "All right. Take hold of both the legs in your hand if you can. Very, very gently, now, or the bones will just crumble to bits; if that happens, we've lost her for sure. And give a little bitty tug, just to see if anything happens."

"Good girl," said Cade. "It's moving. I can feel it. It's moving toward me."

"Keep pulling, then. Can you get your other hand up to the buttocks?" Cade shifted, nodded tentatively. "All right. Go on. Keep pulling. Once the shoulders clear, it should slide out easily."

"You're doing a fine job of holding her, Mistress Jeri-

cho," Cade said out of the blue. Tess flushed with pleasure before she remembered how she hated him.

"Don't you worry about my Tess. She doesn't just like
horses. She knows 'em," Ben announced, proudly pointing up the difference between his daughter and the dilet-
tante Lady Hardwick.

"What a good horse you are! What a pretty pony—it's
coming more quickly now, just as you said. How could
you tell that the colt was dead?"

"I haven't been breeding horses for fifty years for
nothing." Ben had dropped his insouciant pose and had
his hand on Cade's upper arm, guiding him as to pace.
"Steady, now. That's it."

"What would make a colt die like that?"

"It's hard to say. I lost one a month earlier than this
because the mother had grazed on sheepbane. But I've
never had one go so far and just . . . here, now, you've
got it!" Tess craned her neck to see around the pony and
watched as the caul-wrapped fetus emerged in a gush of
fluids that drenched Cade from chest to toe. The pony
shook herself, letting loose another, lesser flood. Cade
didn't seem to notice, much less to care; he set the
opaque bundle down on the hay and cut the umbilical
cord according to Ben's orders. He was flushed with
pride at the job he had done.

"Take her to another stall, pet," Ben directed his
daughter, "and give her some water if she'll take it." As
she led the pony away, she glanced back and saw him
kneeling by the blue-white caul, pulling out his knife.
"And some tonic—that one with the comfrey and honey!"
he called after her. "Now, then, let's see if we can figure
out what went wrong here." Settling the pony in the next
stall, Tess heard a slicing sound as her father slit the caul
open, and then his swift intake of breath. "Great Jehovah
in heaven," he mumbled. "I've never seen anything like it
in all my life."

Curious, Tess left the pony with a bucket of water and
went back to see what had surprised him so.

"Dad?"

He shielded the caul with his body, waving her off.
"Go away, lass. Leave it be, now. 'Tis nothing. 'Tis

naught." But there were tears, huge crystalline tears, rolling down his face as he turned to Gideon Cade, who was staring at the bloody bundle on the stable floor. "Maybe now everyone will heed my warnings! Maybe now they'll believe who's come to dwell among us!"

"My God, Jericho, you can't blame this on me!"

"No? Who sent me to buy the pony? Who made me tie her and breed her to that devil horse?" Ben railed, waving his one good fist. "This is your doing! Satan's doing! Evil has come here; there's a terrible evil at work in Windber-on-Clun!"

"Dad, what is it? What's happened?" Tess demanded.

"Satan! The Old One himself!" Wild-eyed, Ben tore at his hair. "It's the Armageddon coming . . ."

She inched toward him cautiously. "Dad, don't get yourself all in a state."

"In a state?" He whirled on her, spittle flying from the edge of his mouth. "In a state! You, Jezebel, the devil's mistress, kneel down and thank Jehovah it's not you in such a state as that poor pony! That it's not you bearing such a cursed child!" Tess took a step forward, trying to move past him. He thrust her back, but not before she caught a clear glimpse of the thing he'd been guarding from her: a small fetal pony, perfect in all its miniature parts—except that it bore two heads.

7

The image of that monstrous colt haunted Tess; she could not stop thinking about it. Cade ordered the grotesque thing buried immediately, but it couldn't stay secret, especially not when Ben had set out straightaway for the Swan, needing something to calm his nerves. Cade's nerves hadn't needed any calming; once he'd seen to the burying, he'd returned to the big house, washed and changed into another set of fancy clothes, and set off for Lady Hardwick's, as cool as could be.

He hadn't come home that night, either. Tess knew, for she'd stayed in the stables, looking after the bereaved pony and thanking God she hadn't let Cade go through with his plan to set Linzy to the devil stallion's stud. When she wasn't thinking of the colt, she was imagining its owner, dressed like a king in black velvet and white lace as he danced with the woman he'd gone to see. She would be dark like him, Tess decided—tall and dark and elegant, dressed all in satin. And he'd speak to her only in French—for ladies and horses, he'd said. He'd used English to Tess, of course, and that showed what he thought of her.

Near dawn, with the pony sleeping soundly, she wandered outside. The sun was just rising above the White Moor, sending splinters of light driving through a heavy cover of clouds. One bright beam caught the side of the glasshouse and drew her there.

She'd seen Cade inside the sparkling structure each day as she went to the stables. He spent hours alone there, looking after the collection of plants he had, which grew lush and green. Sometimes when she knew he was out riding, Tess would press her nose up against the panes. Amidst the tangle of branches and leaves rising above the rows of terra-cotta pots on the tiled floor she could see oranges, no bigger than a pence-piece, but growing. There were even more exotic plants as well—twining vines laden with blue and white flowers, gray-green trees bearing fat black egg-shaped fruit—and tubs overflowing with columbine and snapdragons, sweet william and hollyhocks, and roses climbing toward the sky. "Strange sort of work for a man," her father sniffed, and Tess knew the rest of the villagers made sport of Cade for being fond of flowers. But she thought his glasshouse was a magical place, a sanctuary far removed from the real world of oats and hops and swine.

On the quiet dawn air she heard hoofbeats. Coming down the road from the White Moor toward the village, she saw the black stallion and his black-caped owner. Quickly she ran back into the stables. Let him at least realize she'd been staying up all night with his sick pony while he dallied and danced with bloody Lady Hardwick, she thought angrily.

He came through the doors leading Satan, and she left the pony's stall. "Do you want him rubbed down and fed?" she asked, heading toward the tack room.

"Good God, are you still here?" he asked in surprise.

"Someone had to look after the pony." She reached for Satan's reins, but he held on to them.

"I'll see to him. You must need some sleep." For an instant their hands touched before she snatched hers away, aghast at the way the fleeting contact had made her heart leap.

"Did you have a nice time?" she asked, hating that handsome black doublet, the furls of white lace at his throat.

"As a matter of fact, I did. How is the pony?"

"Surviving," Tess told him shortly. "Dad says she's done for breeding, though, from losing the colt."

"And you—are you done for breeding?"

"What in hell is that supposed to mean?"

He nodded at her stomach. "You've lost a child too."

She stared at him, astonished. "What child?"

"The one you were having that was why you had to marry that idiot Jack. Just as well, I suppose, since . . . It was Lord Halifax's, really, wasn't it? Or aren't you sure whose it was? Were there other possibilities of which I'm not aware?"

"You're mad," Tess said after a moment in which she tried to decide whether to run him through with a pitchfork or merely to laugh. "I wasn't having a baby."

His upper lip curled back on itself. "You forget. You told me you were, that night in the cave."

"I did no such thing."

"Christ, listen to you." He banged a fist against one of the stalls, making the horses nicker. "You'd as soon lie as breathe, wouldn't you? I remember exactly what you said. I asked if you were marrying Jack on the morrow, and you said, 'I have to.' "

Tess did laugh then, though without amusement. "Not because I was having a baby!"

"Why else would you have to?"

"That's none of your business, is it?" She started past him.

"I think it is, Mistress Jericho." He caught her by the wrist. She stopped, overwhelmed again by the memories his touch evoked, made breathless by the faint scent of warm spice that hung in the air. "After all, you used me to get out of that marriage. I spent most of the summer waiting for Ben to show up at the big house with a blunderbuss to force *me* to wed you."

"I'd sooner marry Job than you," she told him, trying to tug free of his hand.

He let go of her quite suddenly. "If you weren't pregnant, why did you say you had to marry Jack?"

"I don't owe you any explanations!" She stamped her foot in fury, then turned on her heel. "I don't owe you anything at all."

Again he stopped her, though this time his hand on her arm was less harsh. "But you weren't a virgin. You won't deny that."

"Leave me be!"

"I could tell that you weren't a virgin." Tess flushed,

remembering how Ben said he could tell the same thing the first time he slept with her mother; she'd forgotten all about that till now. Seeing her color rise, Cade smiled in ugly triumph. "Hell, from your performance that night I'm surprised you didn't get more than a chain out of old Halifax; you're worth at least a set of eardrops too. You've got a gift for lovemaking, Mistress Jericho." He pulled her close to him, lowering his head to touch his mouth to hers. "Mind you don't sell yourself too cheap— and to fools such as Jack."

Denying the sudden pounding of her blood, the flame he set loose in her heart, Tess ground her heel into the top of his boot and, as his grip abruptly loosened, backed away. "You're right," she said with deadly calm. "I wasn't a virgin. Shall I tell you why? The night after I had breakfast with you in the big house, Jack raped me here in the stables. He beat me and raped me, there on the floor." She pointed. "Facedown in the hay. My father let him get away with it. He said it was to teach me a lesson. To punish me for eating with you."

"Jesus." Gideon Cade had gone pale. "Jesus. You're jesting."

Tess shook her head. "No. That was the first time for me. The second was . . . the night of the storm. I've never been with child. And Lord knows I never slept with Lord Halifax. Now, if you're satisfied—"

"How in God's name could you have planned to marry a man who'd done such a thing?" he demanded. "And your father—Christ Almighty, what's the matter with him?"

"He loves me," Tess said simply. "And he told me that Jack loved me too. That that was why Jack did . . . what he did."

"He was wrong. That isn't love," Cade said passionately.

"Oh, and you know all about love, do you?" Green eyes flashing, Tess stalked past him and Satan. "Mind you close up the doors when you leave. I'm not about to chase after loose horses again."

The autumn harvest of the year 1670 surpassed all expectations. Everyone in Windber knew it would be bad. But not until the last acre of hay had been baled, the wheat scythed and threshed, the hops gathered, maize picked, rye and oats cropped, hogs slaughtered, cheese and pickles made, pears and cherries crocked, and all of it counted and weighed and put up and packed away in the barns and storehouses and noted down in Mort Brady's overseer's log, did the true results of Cade's initial experiments in agriculture become clear. "How does it look, Mort?" the villagers demanded, pushing close to him in the main barn on the final day of the gathering-in. "What's the story?" Mort paged through the logbook slowly, his expression inscrutable, oblivious of the jovial clamor. Only when he'd checked the figures twice did he look down at his friends and neighbors, shaking his head.

"The worst ever," he said.

No one spoke for a moment. Then, "Not worse than 1638, surely," old Sam protested dubiously.

"Oh, aye, it is," said Mort. "Nearly twice as bad."

Tess, standing next to her father, shivered. Every child in Windber-on-Clun grew up on horror tales of the '38 famine, when a spring without rain and summer without sun withered the crops in the fields. The cattle starved, Meg Mullen had told her, and then the weak and infirm, and then babes in arms. The villagers had boiled shoes for soup, and ate grass and tree bark. With the famine came plague, and one-third of the tenants had died.

"Sorcery," Ben declared. "Demonic sorcery. And it's all Cade's doing."

"Who said that?" Widow Jonas scanned the crowd, saw Ben, and snorted. "Ye did, I reckon. Well, tell me just one thing. Why the devil would Cade want to ruin us when it means he comes out the loser? He'll have no excess to sell at the market now. That means he'll make no profit."

"He's not after the things of this world," Ben countered. "He's after our souls."

The widow rolled her eyes. "I've never heard such twaddle in all my life."

"Hold on," said Mungo. " 'Twasn't Ben's idea to plant these here newfangled crops wot failed, was it? No, 'twas Cade's!"

"Aye, just like breedin' his devil horse to the pony," Jack put in, " 'n' see what came of that."

"Wot about that three-legged calf wot was born last year?" Widow Jonas demanded. "I didn't hear nobody blamin' that on Lord Halifax!"

"All I know," Millie cried, an arm shielding her burgeoning belly while she clung to Jack, "is that before Gideon Cade came here, everybody was happy! Nobody was scared! And now I'm afraid all the time!" Her outburst was greeted with sympathetic clucks from the women and a growing rumble of anger from the men.

"I remember thirty-eight," old Sam thundered, "and I've prayed every day for thirty-two years that I'd never see another such winter! Old women combin' through the snow for rat nests to have somethin' to eat, little babes witherin' in their cradles—" Millie let out a desolate moan.

"Aye, but if he lets us die, he won't have no one to work the fields for him, will he?" Widow Jonas tried to reason, but her querulous voice was lost in the growing commotion.

"No hops to brew beer!" Missus Backus shrilled. "We never ought to have let Lord Halifax go!"

"It's a bleedin' crime, what Cade's done to Windber," barked her husband. "A crime, I tell ye, 'n' we ought to make him pay!"

"A thousand years this village has been here," Meg Mullen declared, "and in less than twelve months he's run it into the ground!"

"Wot about that petition thing ye was talkin' about last spring, Ben?" someone shouted. His question was answered by a chorus of hoots: "It's too late for petitions now, ain't it?" "We don't need petitions!" "Stow yer bloody petitions!"

Ben pushed his way to the platform where Mort was sitting and leapt up beside him, waving his good hand for silence. Everyone hushed everyone else by poking and hissing, and then those sounds, too, died away. As Tess looked at her father, she saw in his eyes a strange sly flame of cunning, like some half-mad saint.

"Listen here," he began. "As Jehovah's my witness,

no one here has more cause to complain of Gideon Cade
than I do." There was a murmur of assent as everyone
turned to look at Tess. Damn you, Dad, she thought,
meeting her neighbors' curious glances as bravely as she
could. "Still, we're Englishmen, ain't we? And the hall-
mark of an Englishman is his sense of fair play." As I
live and breathe, Tess thought in amazement. Don't tell
me he's coming out on Cade's side!

"Aye, well, where's his lordship's sense of fair play?"
Tim Whitaker shouted.

"All I'm saying," Ben continued, unruffled, "is that
even Cade deserves a chance to explain—"

"Explain what?" Mungo bellowed.

"Explain how he intends to keep us fed this winter. So
I say we head over to the big house and ask him right
now!"

The prospect of action suited the tenants; they raised
up their pitchforks and scythes and cheered. Ben grabbed
the cattail torch that Mort had been using to read by and
waved it over his head. "Follow me!" Tess felt a premo-
nition of impending danger as the torchlight glinted in his
eyes, and wondered why; after all, his proposal was more
reasonable than she had expected. Despite her qualms, she
joined the stream of men and women as they left the
storehouse. To stay behind would serve no purpose;
besides, she was curious to hear what Cade would have to
say.

The crowd took on a raucous, brawling air as it crossed
the valley and started up the hill. More of the men
brought out torches, and the firelight glistened and gleamed
off their sweaty browned faces, made their pale shirts
stand out like ghosts in the dark. The night had turned
cold; as they marched and muttered and grumbled, their
breaths showed as small white clouds, and a thin crust of
rime-frost crackled under their boots. "We want Cade!"
Ben shouted, his voice carrying for miles in the quiet
night, and the whole host took up the cry, stamping their
feet as they walked, pounding their tools on the ground:
"We want Cade! We want Cade!" Those who'd been left
at home, too young or too old to help with the harvest,
poured out of their cottages, attracted by the tumult;

dogs barked and nipped at their heels, and the sheep bleated and milled in their pens.

"We want Cade! We want Cade!" The chant swelled as the tenants mounted the hill behind Ben and his torch. Tess, far in the rear with Job at her side, saw the Widow Jonas shake her head sadly. They passed the glasshouse, torchlight flaring on the darkened panes, and then marched over the frost-slicked grass to the drive.

"We want Cade! We want Cade!" Ben bounded up the portico stairs, flourishing his torch, while the others waited on the gravel below. "We want Cade!" he bellowed, and banged on the big brass doors in rhythm with the chant. Tess looked up toward the windows of the room Cade had called the librarium and saw the startled housemaids peering down at her. "We want Cade!" Ben thundered, battering the doors again.

"Aye, come out, ye bloody son of a bitch!" Mungo shouted, and the crowd roared its approval of his audacity.

"Here he comes!" Meg Mullen cried, seeing one of the bronze doors inch open, swinging her arms to get the chant going again. "We want Cade! We want Cade!" But the face that peeped out of the crack was Prince Oren's, bloodless and alarmed.

"Here, now, what's going on with all of you?" the butler asked.

"We've come to see Cade," Tess heard her father announce, "and we won't leave until we do!"

"You'll have a good long wait, then," Oren told him, "for he's gone off to Lady Hardwick's. And when he does that, he's usually gone for the night."

"Gone for the night!" Ben turned toward the villagers. "Do you hear that? Leaves us starving, he does, while he dallies with his fancy lady! Shame on him! Doesn't he know anything about being a lord? Doesn't he even know it's his responsibility to be here on the night we tally the harvest?"

"That's right!" Mungo cried. "He's supposed to be here! It's tradition!"

"It just goes to show," Ben went on. "He doesn't care! Cursed be the day he came to Windber-on-Clun!"

"For shame! Shame!" they shouted, and Sam's gruff

voice rose above the uproar: "He's a bleedin' varlet, that's wot he is!"

"I'll tell you one thing!" Ben shouted down from the porch. "If his lordship had to steal my daughter's virtue so no decent man will ever wed her, he might at least see that she's fed!" Color rising in her cheeks, Tess started to edge away from the indignant crowd, but found her progress halted by a hand that clamped onto her wrist.

"Where d'ye think ye're going?" Widow Jonas hissed, her black eyes bright in the torchlight. " 'Tis yer fault he's up there eggin' 'em on!"

"My fault!"

The old woman nodded. "How far d'ye reckon on lettin' things go before ye face up to wot ye've done?"

Tess yanked her arm free. "I don't know what you mean." The widow muttered something more, but she couldn't hear because of a sudden chorus of shouts that arose in response to something Ben said.

Prince Oren, realizing he himself wasn't the object of the villagers' wrath, came out onto the porch. " 'Tis a pity his lordship isn't here to listen to your grievances," he said with unctuous reasonableness, "though I daresay he'd only tell you all to go and have a pint on him. Oh, I forgot—he's never stood a pint for anyone, has he? Not like good old Lord Halifax."

It was the wrong thing to say. "He's never even stood us a pint!' Ben shouted, as though this were the ultimate outrage. "And now there won't be no more pints, nor loaves, nor porridge, nor bacon, not if he has his way!"

"For glory's sake, Ben!" Widow Jonas snapped. "Ye can't have it both ways! If there ain't enough ale, ye can't fault the man fer not buyin' ye drinks!"

But it was too late for reason. Ben's worn face glowed as though he were already drunk; his eyes burned with the fevered intensity of some Old Testament prophet delivering God's doom. Gor, what a preacher his father must have been, Tess thought in rapt admiration, if Dad learned this from watching him!

"If Gideon Cade cared what happened to us, would he be off cavorting with his wicked strumpet on this night of all nights?" Ben cried, and was answered with a resounding "No!" "If Gideon Cade were worthy to be called 'his lordship,' would he have left us alone on our harvest day?" "No!" roared the crowd. "If Gideon Cade . . ." Ben paused for breath, his whole body shaking. "If Gideon Cade has brought aught but misery and grief to any man, woman, or child in Windber-on-Clun, then by the Great Jehovah, let that person speak now!"

In the dead silence that followed this challenge, Tess saw the Widow Jonas look toward her as though issuing a challenge of her own. But her attention was riveted on her father. Wasn't it the truth, everything that he'd said? He'd been right about Cade from the start, from the very day Lord Halifax left, when he'd called the newcomer a thief and a scoundrel. He'd been right when he warned her to steer clear of him, and he was right now. She was sure of it, could feel it in the air that seemed to crackle with charged lightning, saw it on the faces of her neighbors, stark and bitter and betrayed.

Ben raised his torch high. "Well, I say it's time we paid him back for all the trouble he's caused us!"

Tess heard her own voice, loud and clear, among the roar of the mob: "Aye, let's pay him back!" "Let's give him wot's comin'!" The Widow Jonas was waving her hands, shouting, "Wait! Hold on!" but her cries were raindrops in a mighty flood. Prince Oren slunk back inside the big house and bolted the doors. Ben bounded down from the portico, stooped over, and scooped up a handful of stones from the gravel drive. "I say we destroy his glass Tower of Babel the same way he's destroyed our lives!"

The tenants cheered deliriously, gathering their own supplies of rocks and stones in aprons and pockets. Ben led the charge down the hill to the glasshouse, dropping his torch as he neared its walls. The rest of the mob ran after him, still shouting and whooping. But as they came within range of their target, an uneasy silence spread through their ranks, a tacit recognition of the dangers in the unprecedented act of rebellion their leader had suggested they commit. Tess, the front of her skirt filled with ammunition, paused with the others, remembering the sunny spring afternoon when she'd watched Mungo and Sam and the rest of the men fit the first of those shining panes into place.

Then Ben leaned back and let fly a rock, a big one. It smashed against a panel high in the roof, which shattered apart with a bright crystalline tang, ringing like a bell in the frosty night. The sound was a call to arms; within the space of a second a hundred more stones were flung toward the structure, and shards of thick glass showered down over the grassy hill.

Tess would never in her life forget what followed. Out from the splintered panes there billowed the most exquisite mingling of scents one could have imagined: a thousand shades of sweetness burst forth in the cold night air. Staggered by their impact as though by some physical force, she stopped in the act of hurling her stones and drank them in, breathed the magical unseen nectars cascading around her, wishing she could somehow capture and hold them in the folds of her gown. All around her the villagers pressed forward, shouting and screaming, tossing rocks and sticks, smashing the remnants of glass from the iron frames with their pitchforks and scythes. Their faces were no longer familiar to her; they were strangers, vandals intent only on the havoc they wreaked. She could not find her father among them; she saw, not Mort and Mungo and Sam and Jack, but hatred and fear and greed and the lust for war. And what made the violent scene all the more terrifying was the aura of orange blossom and eglantine and roses that bathed it, that washed the mad frenzy of destruction in nigh-unbearable beauty and grace.

In minutes the house of glass had been reduced to framework and fragments. The tenants charged through the mangled doors and stormed through the aisles, yanking down vines and branches, overturning benches, hurling terra-cotta pots to the ground. A bundle of gillyflowers, torn from its roots, landed by Tess's toes; even as she watched, the clove-scented petals, paler pink than a child's hand, curled in on themselves in a vain attempt to stave off the killing cold. In the midst of the crashing confusion she heard the sound of weeping: it was the Widow Jonas,

stooping to gather up scraps of tattered leaves and blossoms before she buried her face in her skirts.

All too soon there was nothing left to destroy; the
villagers scrabbled through the rubble, searching for anything that had escaped their eyes and hands, but the
carnage was complete. "I reckon that'll show the bastard," someone declared in great satisfaction, and the
crowd laughed and agreed. "Let's have some ale! To the
Swan!" another voice called. Thirstily euphoric, the men
swaggering, the women congratulating them on their courage, they trooped down the hill to the tavern, weapons
still held high.

This time Tess did not follow. There was a taste in her
mouth of milk gone coppery-sour; already the luscious
scents of the flowers had been swirled away by the rising
north wind. As quickly as the fragrance faded, so did the
blind hatred for Cade that her father's oratory had aroused
in her. The destruction of the glasshouse no longer seemed
brave and noble and defiant; in the chill moonlight she
saw it instead as an act of wanton savagery. She remembered how once, when she was a child, her father had
forbidden her some demanded pleasure, and how, to
spite him, she'd taken his razor and hacked off all her
long hair. Picking up one of the fragments of glass from
the ground, she stared at her moonlit reflection and saw
her face as it had looked then, in the cottage mirror:
shamed, bewildered, unable to comprehend why something that seemed so fine a revenge when she began it
should have left her so ugly and maimed.

'Tis yer fault he's up there eggin' 'em on, Widow Jonas
had said: *How far d'ye reckon on lettin' things go before
ye face up to wot ye've done?* She was only a mad old
woman, though; look at how she'd cried over the broken
plants that littered the ground. What had happened that
night wasn't Tess's fault. She hadn't begun it, and she
couldn't have stopped it. How would she have stopped
it? What could she have done?

Something clattered inside the ruins of the glasshouse.
Tess jumped, then saw it was only Job, nosing through
the rubble, searching for God alone knew what. She
whistled for him, long and loud, and he loped toward

her, ears swinging. "She was wrong, wasn't she?" Tess asked the dog. "It wasn't my fault, was it?" He stared up at her, his red-rimmed eyes sad as ever, and let out a mournful howl. "Oh, what would you know about it anyway?" she scoffed aloud. "Come on home. I need my sleep; I'd bet a shilling if I had it Dad will be at the tavern all night." And Gideon Cade would be at Lady Hardwick's, lying in the arms of his paramour while his orange trees withered and died.

"And do you know what, Job? I don't care if it was my fault," she told the gloomy hound, and aimed a kick at one of the squashed, mutilated branches that covered the ground.

8

Tess woke early the next day, while bitter cold still cloaked the cottage. Her father lay snoring on his cot, clothes strewn helter-skelter across the floor; she dressed hurriedly and restoked the dead fire, then heated her porridge, but he never stirred. Numb with sleep and chill, her thoughts on daily routine, she forgot all about the mayhem of the previous evening until she slipped through the door and saw, through shrouds of mist that clung to the hillside, the scattered wreckage of the glasshouse, its skeletal frame rising twisted and stark against the wintry sky.

The sight brought a hot flush to her cheeks. She turned her back on the grim reminder and hurried to the stables, immersing herself in mucking and grooming, as though by scouring the stalls and horses she could somehow scrub away the reality of what she and the rest of the villagers had done. So intent was she on her work that she did not hear the stable doors open; when she finally looked up, grimy and ripe with dung, and saw Gideon Cade standing silently before her, she had no idea how long he might have been there.

"What's become of the glasshouse?" he asked, his voice low and steady, but his blue eyes alight with a hard bright flame.

Tess's first instinct was to lie, to deny any knowledge of the matter, to say, like a cornered child, "What glasshouse?" But the look on his face—furious, yet at the same time pained and bewildered—shamed her into a halting confession. "It got torn down last night."

He nodded as though it were the answer he had expected. "Would you think it presumptuous of me to ask why?"

She gave a little shrug, poking with her shovel at a mound of manure. "The harvest was bad—the worst ever, Mort said. Everybody was angry."

"At the glasshouse?" he demanded, one black brow rising.

"Of course not. They were angry at you."

"And so you tore down the glasshouse, and killed my plants."

"Well, not quite all of us. Not Widow Jonas," Tess mumbled, squirming uncomfortably.

"Did you help?"

"Did I what?"

"Did you help to kill them?"

"You make it sound like somebody was murdered. They were only plants."

"They were living things—as alive as you or Linzy or Job. Did you help?"

"And what if I did?" she cried. "It's your own fault for not being here. But you couldn't be bothered, could you? Not even on the night of the harvest tally. One night out of the year that Lord Halifax always spent with his tenants, and you're off with her!"

He looked at her for a long moment. "Lord Halifax always was here for the harvest tally?"

"Well, of course he was! And if you'd been here when Dad marched us up to the big house to see you, you'd still have your precious damned plants!"

"Your *father* suggested you all come and see me last night?" he echoed incredulously.

"Aye, that's what I said," Tess told him with increasing impatience. "Is your hearing gone bad?"

"There's nothing wrong with my bloody hearing. Just what did the self-appointed prophet of Windber-on-Clun say when he discovered my absence, pray tell?"

"If by that you mean Dad, no more than the truth," Tess said heatedly.

"And what is the truth, Mistress Jericho, as Pilate once asked?"

"That you were off frolicking with your fancy-dance lady while you left us to tally the harvest! That you were lolling about in a bed of sin while we worried how we were to get through the winter!" Tess cried in rage. "That you'd be stuffing yourself on your glasshouse dainties come Candlemas, while old women scrounged for firewood and children ate shoe leather—what's so bloody damned funny?" He was doubled over against the doorjamb, clutching his sides, laughing so hard that his blue eyes were bright with tears.

"And so you tore down the glasshouse!" he gasped.

"You're damned right we did! Stop laughing!" She could have borne anything but this plain evidence of how little he cared for the village—how little he cared for her. She jabbed at him with the shovel; he grabbed it from her and pulled her into his arms. "Let me go!" She clawed at his face; he hugged her, dung stains and all, and smoothed down her hair with his hand. She could feel him shaking with laughter as he held her against him, and she felt something else as well: the hot sparks of desire that flared in her belly at his touch.

"Oh, Tess." She melted at the way he said her name, all resistance forgotten. He tilted her chin up and kissed her, swiftly and sweetly; if he'd reached for her bodice buttons at that moment, she'd have stripped naked before him and lain down with him in the straw.

But he stepped back, patting her behind like some fond uncle or brother, and tipped his riding hat to her. "Adieu, my heart!" He turned and strode toward the stable doors, whistling. Tess stared for a moment, the fire draining from her blood, and then ran after him.

"Where are you going?"

He shoved the doors open, and she saw Satan, still saddled and bridled, tied to the fence. "To London," Cade called over his shoulder, unhitching the big black stallion and mounting him with easy grace.

"London! For how long?"

He shrugged, settling into the saddle. "For as long as I like."

"But you can't go to London now!"

"Why the devil can't I?"

"Why . . . the bad harvest! There's not enough food, thanks to you!"

"If I'm the cause of all your troubles, I should think you'd be glad to see the last of me."

See the last of him. "You *will* be coming back, won't you?" she asked uncertainly.

"Why the devil should I?"

Tess stamped her foot, shielding the rising sun from her eyes. "You're the lord of this place, dammit all! You can't leave us high and dry!"

He gave sort of a wave, digging his heels into Satan. " 'Bye, now!"

She ran after the horse as it cantered away. "We'll all starve!"

"Oh, I doubt that."

"Wait! You can't just . . . Stop, damn you! What will we *do*?" she wailed.

"Ask your father!" he shouted back at her. "He's far more resourceful than I'll ever be!"

"They'll burn down the big house!" she screeched as his tall figure receded into the blinding sunlight. "They'll . . . they'll hang you in effigy!"

"Tell them to be my guests!"

"Oh!" Furious, helpless to stop him, Tess flung a handful of stones in the black stallion's wake. "Damn you! Damn you to hell!"

Cade's laughing voice floated back to her on a river of sunbeams: "And fare thee well to you too, Mistress Jericho!"

None of Tess's dire predictions of the tenants' behavior actually came true, once word of his lordship's departure spread; to the contrary, the residents of Windber-on-Clun seemed guiltily relieved to have been spared Cade's wrath. "Good riddance to bad trash," was what Ben said when his daughter told him of their encounter—without the part where he'd kissed her. "We'll be better off without him. Just you wait and see." The iron framework of the glasshouse still served as a silent rebuke to Tess, though, every time she passed it; she couldn't stop herself from wishing that when Cade asked her if she'd joined the mob in its destruction, she could have said no.

She was exercising Linzy in the corral a week later when she saw a strange sight: a coach, a fancy one, rumbling through the village and up the drive toward the big house. Holding tight to Linzy's bridle, she went to the fence and stared at the plumed hat and plum-colored livery of the driver as he steered the coach closer, wondering who might be riding inside. Just as the vehicle drew abreast of her, the driver reined his team of gray geldings to a stop and the panel window in the side of the coach slid back. "I say," called a voice so deep it might have been a man's, but with an undercurrent of whimsy that bespoke femininity, "is this Windber-on-Clun?"

"Aye, mum," Tess told the disembodied voice, "though if you're looking for his lordship, he isn't at home."

"Oh, I know that. I just had to see for myself. Chester, this is really too dreary, not being able to tell whom I'm talking to," the voice went on briskly. "Do hop down and stretch your legs and open up this door."

The coachman climbed out of his seat to do the voice's bidding. As the gilded door swung open, Tess caught her first glimpse of the occupant and blinked. It *was* a woman, she supposed, though a very old and wrinkly and small one—so small that she could scarcely see through the window from the coach seat—all bundled up in acres of luxe velvet and fur against the winter cold.

Out of the sea of wrappings and wrinkles, two ice-blue eyes looked back at her; then the creature smiled in delight. "Why, it must be Mistress Jericho, that does the horses! Well? Am I right?"

"Aye, mum," Tess said again, and dropped a small curtsy out of a general feeling that she ought to. "Though I don't know—"

"Giddy's told me all about you," the woman went on, still beaming. Then she winked. "Well, perhaps not all. That must be your pony—now what did he say you call her? Binny, is it, or Minnie?"

"Linzy. Her name is Linzy."

"Of course it is. Linzy! Well, my memory's not what it

used to be. Such a treat to meet you, dearie! And that would be the stable, there . . ." She pointed with a crabbed gold-and-gem-studded hand. "And that's your cottage, of course, yours and your father's, and the big house—my, it *is* big, isn't it?—and . . ." She paused, waving toward the hulking iron frame. "Oh, my. Yes. The glasshouse. Dear, dear, what a simply awful tragedy!" For a moment she appeared quite distraught; then she scanned the landscape again and heaved a happy sigh. "Such a clever man, Giddy—and such a gift for description! It all looks just exactly the way I expected it would."

"Excuse me," said Tess, "but who is Giddy?" She really wanted to ask who this strange woman was, but couldn't think of any way of phrasing that so it wouldn't sound rude.

"Ah!" the visitor cried with an absolutely girlish giggle. "There's the question, ain't it? Who and where and what is Gideon Cade?"

"You call him *Giddy*?" Tess echoed, wide-eyed.

"Only because he detests it," the woman said cheerfully. Her bright birdlike gaze darted again to the wreckage of the glasshouse, and her deep voice turned wistful. "Such a terrible pity . . . a hailstorm, he wrote me. Odd, isn't it? We've had perfectly chill dry weather over to Stafford for weeks; not so much as a drop of rain. Oh, well, 'twas the Lord's will, I suppose. Still, I won't deny I was looking forward to my little treat. Gillyflowers, that's what I was getting. Oh, I know most ladies would probably want something fancier—jasmine or peonies or roses— but if you ask me, there's nothing like gillyflowers to make the heart glad."

"Forgive me, milady," the coachman said gently, "but speaking of chills, you're going to catch one if we don't shut that door, and then Dr. Burton will blame me for letting you come out at all."

"Dear Chester." The old woman smiled beguilingly. "I know you're right, but . . . just another minute or two? We've come such a long way. And I am so enjoying my chat with Mistress Jericho."

"Perhaps you'd like to come down from the carriage and stroll around a bit?" Tess offered politely. "It's much warmer if you keep moving than if you're just sitting still."

The woman burst out laughing. "Bless you, dearie, I wish I could. But I haven't been able to walk for a good ten years!"

"Oh, dear God!" Tess covered her mouth with her hand, her face flooding crimson. "I'm terribly sorry."

"No need to be embarrassed, child, for something you'd no way of knowing. And as for being sorry—well, truth to tell, I get to feeling sorry for myself from time to time. But then when I do, I just remind myself: Emilia Hardwick, I say, you had sixty years of walking, and that's more than most people have living! And I can tell you one thing: I'd sooner be stuck in a chair than stuck in the grave!"

Hardwick . . . "Are you . . . Lady Hardwick?" Tess asked hesitantly.

"Why, of course I am, dearie!"

Tess hesitated a moment, then asked, "Have you got a daughter, perchance?" Or a granddaughter—that was more likely.

The septuagenarian shook her head. "It was the great cross of our lives, Albert and me, that we never had any children. Still, we were happy together." The bundled-up furs rose and fell with her sigh. "He used to bring me gillyflowers from the garden every day in summer, my Albert, and watch me braid them into my hair." Her lined face brightened slightly. "When I told Giddy that, he said he'd grow them for me in the glasshouse and bring me a bunch every week for free, even though he was going to make all the others pay!"

Tess looked at the bent iron framework up on the hill and then back at Lady Hardwick. "Do you mean he was going to sell what he grew in the glasshouse?"

"Well, what else would he go to all that trouble for? So long as he couldn't be certain how those new crops he was trying would do, he needed something to fall back on, or so he told me. He says it's quite mad to go on growing oats and wheat here. Something about the same crops all the time wearing out the soil." She, too, gazed at the ruins of the structure the villagers had christened Cade's Folly. "He'd have made a right ruddy fortune with those flowers, too, if you'll pardon my French. But there's no sense crying over spilt milk, is there?"

"Milady," the coachman said again, more firmly, "you are going to catch a chill."

"Oh, all right, Chester, don't be such a nag."

"If you'd like to go on up to the house," Tess suggested, "I'm sure the butler would fetch you something hot to drink—"

"What, that prig Prince Oren, you mean?" She laughed at Tess's surprise. "Your father named him that, Giddy tells me, and it suits him just to a tee. And speaking of your father, I would so like to meet him. Giddy says he's quite the most remarkable man he's ever known."

"*My* father?"

"Or, if you prefer," the coachman told his mistress politely, "I could dump you by the side of the road here and leave you to freeze to death; it might be even quicker."

"Oh, honestly, Chester." She stuck out her tongue at him, then appealed to Tess. "Isn't he dreadful? I don't know what I could have done to deserve such impossible servants. Do you know, once he—"

"I am closing the door now," Chester announced, and did so. "Sorry, mum," he told Tess, "but it really is for her own good."

Slightly muffled, Lady Hardwick's deep voice called from inside the carriage: "Good-bye! So lovely to meet you, Mistress Jericho!"

"Pleased to meet you too, I'm sure!" Tess called back, and then asked the driver, *sotto voce*, "Are you certain it wouldn't be best for her to stop on for a while at the big house?"

He grinned. "There's an inn outside Stover's Mill serves rum cream cakes she's been hankering after for months. I'm still not sure if it was them or his lordship's gillyflowers inspired this outing."

"Here, now!" Lady Hardwick was pounding on the inside of the door. "Are you two talking about me?"

"Naturally," said Chester.

"That's good. I'd hate to think folks were beginning to find me dull. Get a move on, you lazy loafer! Don't you know I've got a vital appointment at Stover's Mill?"

"With a plateful of cream cakes," sighed the driver, clambering back up to his seat. "Gi-yah!" He let out a piercing whistle, cracking his whip, and the geldings sprang forward, carrying the coach on its way. It circled around the front drive and came past Tess once more, with Chester tipping his high plumed hat. The last thing she heard as it rumbled by was Lady Hardwick shouting:

"Mind you don't tell Giddy I was out and about, young lady, or he'll have my ears!"

Ben had been in the stables repairing loose boards in Satan's vacant stall; he came forth now, hammer in hand, the nails in his apron pockets jingling, just in time to see the carriage tear through the village, scattering squawking chickens and bewildered sheep in its path. "Hmph!" he said, staring down into the valley. "What the devil was that?"

"That, Dad, was the Lady Emilia Hardwick," Tess told him, and patted Linzy's nose.

"Hmph!" he said even more loudly, and spat on the ground. "Cade's run out on her too, is that it? Come to track down her false lover, did she?"

"Not exactly."

Ben peered at her curiously. "Just what are you looking so pleased with yourself about, prithee? Don't tell me you think you're better-looking than she is."

"Not really. I'd say she's quite extraordinary-looking, considering she's more than seventy years old."

Her father smiled unpleasantly. "Chasing him down for her daughter, then."

"It would have to be a granddaughter, I imagine. And no. She hasn't got any children."

"You don't say. And I suppose she's a widow."

"As a matter of fact, she is. But what made you guess that?"

"Jehovah gave you a brain, Teresa!" he burst out. "Why can't you do him the favor to use it? A seventy-year-old widow without any dependents, and Gideon Cade paying court to her?" She looked at him blankly. "Dressed fancy, was she? A fine coach? Good horses?"

"Aye," Tess acknowledged, "really handsome gray geldings. But I still don't see—"

"Heaven help us, you don't, do you? Have I got to spell it out for you, are you such a babe in the woods as all that?"

"Spell what out?"

Ben made a growling sound low in his throat and hurled his hammer to the ground. "Well, she can't live much longer now, can she? And wouldn't it be like that bastard to slip 'twixt the marriage sheets just long enough to become her heir?"

"Oh, Dad." Tess's stomach churned over. "He wouldn't."

"Holy Jehovah in . . ." Speechless, he moved to throw the hammer again before realizing he already had. "How can you defend such a man, Teresa? He used you, seduced you, ruined the one chance you had to marry a good man, a decent man who loved you . . ." Was that what had happened? Tess wondered as her father raged on. Did Gideon Cade use her, or had she used him? *How far d'ye reckon on lettin' things go before ye face up to wot ye've done?*

She pictured the way Lady Hardwick's ancient face had brightened as she gloated over the prospect of her gillyflowers. God, could Cade really be so inhuman as her father believed? Or was he going out of his way to make a lonely old woman happy? What kind of man was he?

Ben was still blustering on. "It's all of a piece, ain't it?" he demanded. "Like trying to grow oranges in Shropshire. Like breeding ponies and stallions. Like having to ask if he ought to show up for his own harvest tally! I tell you, Teresa, so far as I'm concerned, I'd sooner starve to death than take a pork-and-gravy pie from the hand of that low-down, lying, cheating, two-faced, scurvy reprobate—and I'd see you starve too! Now, get that pony back in the stables; there's a dozen more waiting to stretch their legs where she came from!" He bent down to pick up his hammer and spilled nails all over the ground. "By the beard of the Great Jehovah, didn't I tell you to get that pony back to the stables?" he roared as she knelt to help him retrieve them. "Move!" Cowed by his temper, she led Linzy back to her stall.

Angel or devil? Tess wondered, as outside the stables her father went on calumniating the lord of Windber-on-Clun. She'd have given a lot more than she'd ever admit to Ben—she might even breed Linzy to Satan—to know the answer to Emilia Hardwick's question: "Who and where and what is Gideon Cade?"

9

The pinch had begun to be felt in Windber-on-Clun. Winter had come in earnest two weeks after Cade's departure for London—not a picturesque season of snowfall and sleighbells and diamond-bright icicles, but a real Shropshire winter, of mud and slush and bitter cold. The village children weren't pink-cheeked, and they didn't frolic in the hills, pelting one another with snowballs while their laughter rang out, for they hadn't got enough clothing or the warm boots such gaiety would have demanded; instead they huddled together by the hearths of their cottages, while their mothers wondered how many would live to see spring.

Mort Brady and Ben had taken charge of the food supply, calculating how much grain was available for each family; it was doled out every fortnight at first, but then Mort changed the schedule to weekly because no one could make the meager portion last. He and Ben had a long argument about whether to figure the allotments on the number of weeks until Easter or just until the beginning of Lent. Mort contended that something was bound to turn for the better by February, and anyway, surely his lordship would return or send gold before then. But Ben insisted they would be better off safe than sorry—and as for counting on help from Cade, well, he'd as soon count on dogs not to bark. Ben won. To ease the sting of his victory, he volunteered to lead hunting expeditions up into the Forest Clun. Almost every day, he and Jack and three or four others would take their bows and snares and Mort's big old blunderbuss and march off through the snow in search of deer or rabbit. They caught mostly crows. The big black birds were hard to pluck and harder to chew, even when they'd been boiled for an entire day. But they were food, all the same, and no one complained—or at least, complained very loud.

In such weather—gray, pinching, drear—and such circumstances, with the persistent wolf of hunger gnawing always at one's insides, even the simplest tasks seemed daunting. How Tess longed for a day that was sunny! Despite the cold, she'd have taken Linzy on a long ride high in the hills. But when it wasn't raining, it was sleeting, and when the sleet let up, the rain would start again, and besides, with her father off hunting, there was barely time enough to get the stalls mucked and the horses groomed and each taken on a few slick, muddy circuits of the corral.

The only kind thing Tess could say about the wretched winter was that it had a salutary effect on Ben's drinking habits. After a long day's hunting, he seemed to lack the energy to brave the hike to the tavern; most nights he just ate his supper and went to bed. The change was so pronounced that at first she was worried about him, and asked one night, when he came home, if there was something amiss. "Of course not!" he told her, pulling off his ice-crusted boots, blowing on his red hands to warm them. "It's just that we're all in the same pickle here, thanks to his such-and-such lordship, and we've all got to make sacrifices if we're to pull through. Good night, now." And he headed for his bed.

"Dad."

"Hmm? What is it?"

"You haven't had supper."

"Well, I know that, dang it! I was just testing you."

He looked tired and gaunt, but then, Tess supposed they all did. She saw Jack's wife, Millie, a week before Christmas and was shocked by her pallor, by the contrast between her hollow cheeks and big swollen belly. She mentioned her concern to the Widow Jonas at Sunday service.

The herb woman nodded. "That's how it happens when

ye're carrying a babe. The little one sucks all the nourishin' out of the mother to feed itself."

"Will the baby be all right?"

"Oh, my, yes, it'll be fine. It's Millie's to worry about. I've got some mugwort tonic might help her. I'll take it over right away."

Tess shook her head. "It's too cold for you to come out again. I'll stop by and take it to her."

Ben came up just then. "What are you two whispering about?"

"Teresa was sayin' how Millie looks ill. She's goin' to stop by my cottage and get some mugwort tonic for her," the widow told him.

"I'll do it," he offered.

Tess smiled. "We both will, how's that?"

But Ben shook his head. "You'd best go along home and see to that crow you're stewing."

"Don't be ridiculous. As if I didn't know all there is to know about cooking crow meat by now!"

"I'll go by myself," Ben insisted. "It's danged cold out. And you've been doing too much of late."

"Dad, that's just plain silly! I haven't been working any harder than you."

"I said I'll go, and I will!" he barked at her, so loudly that heads turned. He gave the widow his arm. "Come along, then. Enough of this shilly-shallying."

And so Tess went back to the cottage and saw to the crow stew. Two hours later the bird was as tender as it was going to get, and she'd set the table for their supper. She decided at the last minute to splurge with a bit of extra flour and a precious egg to make Ben's favorite dumplings, doughy-soft and fragrant with rosemary, and they were done too, but there wasn't any sign of her father. She swung the pot further from the fire and sat on her stool, not reading, not mending, not doing anything, reveling in the unexpected luxury of minutes to spare. But as more time went by without Ben's arrival, as the dumplings passed the point of perfection and turned gummy and gray, she began to grow impatient. Honestly, she thought, wasn't it just like him to disappear when she'd gone to the trouble of making something special just for him?

With Job at her side, she went to the door and peered down the hill toward the village. Beneath lowering skies the color of slate, a few snowflakes were falling; smoke curled from the chimneys of the cottages below. Perhaps he'd stopped for supper at Jack and Millie's, she thought, and instantly rejected the notion. With food as scarce as it was, nobody was inviting anyone to share meals these days.

She was about to close the door against the harsh wind when she saw him stumping over the little bridge that led from the upper village to the lower, bent nearly double as he fought the cold. "Christ Almighty, he hasn't even *been* to Jack's yet!" she exclaimed. "I swear, if he's been at the Swan all this time, I'll boil him alive. Go on, Job, and fetch him home." She nudged the hound outside, and he bounded off across the frozen fields, howling dolefully. Down in the valley, Ben raised his head at the sound; Tess shook her fist at him, and he waved a gloved hand as though acknowledging her ire. "Well, I should hope so," she said with a sniff, and slammed shut the door.

It still seemed to take him an awfully long time to make it to Jack's and back up the hill. When she finally heard Job scratching and snuffling to come in, she'd forgotten how much she enjoyed her hour or two of peace and was spoiling for an argument. "So glad you decided to drop by," she greeted Ben, her voice dripping sarcasm. "I'm sorry to have to report that your dinner is ruined."

He was breathing heavily, and his eyes were red-streaked and bleary; still he managed a small grin. "Didn't know . . . you could overcook crow," he puffed, shaking snow from his hat.

"For your information, while you were out gallivanting around all morning, I was making your favorite dumplings."

"Oh, Tess, you shouldn't!"

"You're right about that," she said darkly, "seeing as they've been ruined by now. What in blazes were you doing at the widow's for all that time?"

"Would you believe courting?"

Tess would have laughed if she weren't so cross. "No, I wouldn't!"

"Don't be angry, pet. She's an old woman living alone through this wretched winter, and seemed grateful for the company." As he shrugged off his coat, a small bottle slipped from the sleeve. He caught it in midair, turning and starting to tuck it away again, but Tess had seen it.

"What's that?" she demanded.

"Nothing." He bustled toward his cot. "You may think those dumplings are ruined, but they smell perfect to—"

"Dad, what is in that bottle?"

"I told you, nothing. What do you say we eat?"

"Is it whiskey? Don't tell me you're spending what little money we've got on spirits!"

"Of course it's not whiskey!" he said indignantly. "I've not had a drink in . . ." He paused, calculating. "Forty-six days."

"Aye, so I've noticed—and if you ask me, it's done wonders for you." He grunted something unintelligible. "But if it's not whiskey, what is it?"

"If you must know, a tonic."

"A tonic." Tess eyed the bottle curiously. "What sort of tonic?"

"For my arm. The one that got broken. It's a bit stiff in the mornings of late."

"Dad, why didn't you tell me?" She came up behind him and touched his shoulder. "I can make you hot compresses to put on it when you get home—and you ought to soak it in warm water and salt every night."

He drew away from her, setting the bottle on the shelf above his bed. "I didn't tell you because I knew you'd make a danged fuss, just like you're doing. It's a bit of stiffness, that's all. Now, can we please eat?" He bent down to unlace his boots; as he did, a small gasp escaped him, and he sat heavily on the cot.

"Dad?" Tess looked at him more closely; his brow was knit in tight furrows. "Dad, what's the matter?"

He shook his head as though to reassure her, but it was a long moment before he spoke. "Just a little cramp.

Must have come up the hill too quickly. Go on and put out the stew, pet."

"You haven't got a fever, have you?" If he hadn't been drinking, why should his blue eyes be so watery-bright? She reached her hand out to touch his forehead, but he pushed it away with a laugh.

"Don't be daft. Have you ever known me to be sick a day in my life—at least, when I was sober?" Tess shook her head. It was true; she hadn't. "All right, then, put out our supper! I'm half-starved, that's all that's wrong with me."

By the time she'd spooned out the dumplings and stew, he'd taken his place at the table. Tess, too, was famished after waiting so long for the meal; she attacked her portion eagerly while her father regaled her with tales of the previous week's hunting adventures and made extravagant compliments on the food. They each had six dumplings. Job sat by Ben's stool, begging. "You had best not be feeding your food to that dog," Tess warned, looking up from her plate long enough to see her father slip his hand under the table edge.

"What kind of idiot do you take me for?"

Ben had no sooner finished his meal than he took a long swig from the tonic bottle. "Fancy reading to me while I do up the dishes?" Tess asked, handing him the Bible before clearing the table.

"What would you like to hear?"

"I don't care, so long as it's cheerful." Tess whistled for Job and put the bowl of scraps she'd saved for him on the floor. Instead of attacking ravenously, as was his wont, the hound was almost standoffish. "Dad?"

"Hmm?" he asked absently, leafing through the pages.

"*Were* you feeding Job at the table?"

"Of course not! Here we are—how about St. Matthew? 'The kingdom of heaven is likened unto a man which sowed good seed in his field. But while men slept, his enemy came and sowed tares among the wheat, and went his way . . .' " As he read, Tess scrubbed the plates and spoons and stewpot, listening more to the cadences of her father's voice than to the Gospel, which she felt she'd heard a hundred thousand times.

" 'So the servants of the householder came and said unto their master, Sir, didst thou not sow good seed in thy field?' " Ben went on. " 'And he said unto them—' "

"Dad—"

"Don't interrupt, Teresa."

"Dad, this is important." The scripture had reminded Tess of something.

"More important than the Good Book? Surely it can wait until I finish." And he read on: " 'Let both grow together until the harvest: and in the time of the harvest I will say to the reapers, Gather ye together first the tares, and bind them in bundles to burn them: but gather the wheat into my barn.' Praise be to Jehovah."

"Praise be to Jehovah," Tess murmured dutifully.

"There's my good girl," Ben told her, and smiled. "Now, what's on your mind?"

"Do you remember, Dad, when we were talking after Lady Hardwick came by here, and you railing about Gideon Cade?"

"Seems to me I've done that more than once."

"Aye, but this time you were listing things he'd done, like tryin to grow oranges, and you said he'd had to ask if he ought to show up at his own harvest tally."

Ben looked at her blankly. "I never said any such thing."

"But you did! The parable about the harvest reminded me. You said—"

"I'm telling you, you're mistaken."

Tess would have argued it further, but her father's voice sounded suddenly weak. "Dad? Are you all right?"

He began to cough, and gestured for the tonic bottle. "Get me . . . get me . . ."

Tess fetched it for him, but his hand was trembling so violently that he couldn't grasp it. She held the bottle to his mouth; he swallowed some of the murky liquid and promptly regurgitated it, along with a thin stream of blood. "Jesus!" Tess cried, as frightened as she'd ever been in her life. "Jesus, Dad, what is wrong with you?"

"Touch of . . . indigestion."

"Don't lie to me, damn you!" Tess stared at the bottle. "My God, it's poison! That crazy old woman has given you poison! I'll kill her with my bare . . . Dad, don't *do* that!" He'd fallen over on the bed and was clasping his stomach while his eyes rolled back into his head. "Oh, God. Oh, Christ. Dad, what should I do?"

"Bring . . . the widow," he managed to gasp out.

"Are you gone crazy? She's the one did this to you!"

"Teresa." Even through the pain, she heard the urgency in his voice. "Do . . . as I say."

She began to cry. "Dad, I'm afraid. I don't want to leave you!" He was shaking all over now, curled in a tight ball, with sweat beading up on his neck and face.

"Fetch the widow, lass. I'm not going to die," he said as distinctly as the trembling allowed. Somewhat reassured, Tess tucked two blankets around him, grabbed her cloak, and flew out the door.

Widow Jonas came with her right away when Tess told her what had happened. She wouldn't speculate on Ben's condition until she'd seen him herself, despite Tess's frantic questions. When she got to the cottage, she felt his hands and head and neck, peered into his eyes, listened to him cough, examined his sputum, and probed his stomach and chest with her crabbed hands.

"Well, Benjamin," she said at last, "ye've given Teresa a fine scare. To pay ye back, I'm goin' to give ye somethin' that will take away the pain and let ye sleep for a long time—probably straight through till morning. All right?" He nodded weakly; she opened the satchel she'd brought and poked about inside until she found the little vial she was looking for. "A cup of water, Teresa, please."

Tess brought it and watched, not altogether trustfully, as the widow stirred in the vial's contents. "What is that?" she asked of the cloudy gray mixture that resulted.

"Wormwood and nightshade." She held the cup to Ben's mouth, and he drank. In a matter of minutes his tortured breathing turned even and steady; his clenched muscles slackened, and he drifted off to sleep.

"You've cured him!" Tess cried in delight, pulling the covers up to his grizzled chin.

But the widow only shook her head. "I've sent him off to sleep, that's all. Curin' him's beyond my power."

A cold sickly dread crept into Tess's belly. "What do you mean?"

"Just what I said," the old woman told her patiently. "He's beyond my powers to cure."

"But that's your job, curing people; that's what you do!" And then the full impact of what she'd said struck Tess. "Do you mean he's *dying*?" Widow Jonas nodded. "How can you know that?" Tess cried. "You've only just seen that he's sick; you can't possibly tell in that short a time what is wrong with him!"

"He's been coming to my cottage every day for the past month. Ever since he's been too ill to hunt."

"That can't be true! He would have told me!"

"If ye think that's so, girl, ye don't know your father so well as ye should," the widow said quietly.

Tess pondered that for a moment and had to admit the widow might be right. It would be just like Ben to keep such a secret, out of concern that he would worry her. She glanced at the sleeping man on the cot and wanted to burst into tears again. Instead she forced her voice to steadiness. "What's wrong with him, what has he got?"

"It's a fever from back when his arm broke that's settled down into his lungs. Haven't ye noticed he ain't been sleepin' well, or eatin'?"

"But he had half a dozen dumplings at supper today!" Then she remembered how Job had disdained *his* meal. "At least—I thought he did. And I have heard him coughing at night. But I thought it was a good sign, that it meant his body was cleaning itself out now that he's quit drinking."

"The only reason he's quit drinkin'," Widow Jonas said with grim humor, "is he can't keep the damned stuff down."

"He's sleeping well now," Tess pointed out, "on that medicine you just gave him. Why can't he just keep taking that?"

"He can, child, but it won't cure him. It only takes away the pain. He'd have to take it more and more often, and soon he'd be sleepin' like that night 'n' day, just lost in a dream world." Lost in *his* dream world, Tess thought, and shuddered, thinking of the hundreds of mornings when he'd wakened her with his nightmares of the Armageddon. Was he being tormented by those visions even now; was that what death would be like for him?

"There must be something more you can do!" she said in desperation.

"Not I. He needs the bone broken again 'n' reset, 'n' that's somethin' I don't know how to. Ye'd need a surgeon from the city, from Shrewsbury or Stafford."

Tess sighed with relief. "Why didn't you say so? I'll just go and fetch one! You can stay here and look after Dad until I get back. And I'll stop by and ask Jack to feed the horses; he shouldn't mind if it's for Dad."

"Aren't ye forgettin' somethin', Teresa?"

She paused on her way to the door. "I don't see what."

Widow Jonas rubbed her thumb and forefinger together. "Ye'll find no surgeon willin' to come way out here without first gettin' paid."

"Well, he'll just have to! I'll explain it's my dad that's sick, that we'll pay when we can."

"The world don't work that way, child," Widow Jonas said gently. "Ye can't expect strangers to come to yer aid the way neighbors do."

"Damn!" Tess thought longingly of the gold chain Lord Halifax had given her, that she'd lost on the night of the storm. Thinking of that gave her another idea. "I'll go to Cade," she decided. "I'll get money for the surgeon from him."

The widow sighed. "If ye want to know the truth, I think yer father didn't want ye to know he was sick because he was afraid ye'd do that."

"But if I don't bring a surgeon, he'll die!"

"And he'd sooner die than have to ask Gideon Cade for charity."

"It's not charity," Tess said stubbornly. "He's the lord! He owes us. He's supposed to look after us, isn't that so?" Widow Jonas didn't answer. "I say he is! And I'm going to see that he does!" Less belligerently, she posed another question: "If, that is, you'll very kindly look after Ben. How long do you think it takes to get to London and back?"

"At least three days each way. I'll be glad to look after yer father, child. But London's a mighty big city. How d'ye reckon on finding his lordship once ye get there?"

"Oren must know some way he can be reached. I'll stop at the big house and ask."

"Ye're not leavin' now! Why, 'twill be dark in an hour," the widow protested.

"There's no time to lose," Tess told her, scrambling about the cottage for her warmest clothes, layering shirts and skirts and stockings one atop the next, "not if we're to save Dad. What are you staring at?"

"Nothin'," said Widow Jonas. But had Tess only known it, her cheeks were flushed scarlet, and her green eyes sparkled for the first time in months and months. "Lookin' forward to seein' his lordship again, are ye?"

Tess stuffed a heel of bread and some cheese into her saddlepack. "What, are you mad? I detest the man."

Widow Jonas nodded thoughtfully. "Aye, of course ye do."

Tess kissed her sleeping father and then, on impulse, the widow too. "Take good care of him, won't you? I'll be back the minute I can."

"Ye take care of yerself," the old woman told her. "And mind yer step in the big city!" She wagged her head. "I hear it's a strange world out there."

10

Tess looked down at the map of London the guard at the city gate had drawn for her. He hadn't wanted to let her through when she admitted that she hadn't any money. But he'd been ever so nice once she explained she wasn't going to stay. It was beggars they were trying to keep out, she supposed, like the ragtag boy she'd passed at that last corner. Skinny as a rail, he was, and as dirty as though he'd mucked stables all day. So far she didn't think much of the big city; unless you were the sort who frequented establishments like the one before her, it seemed a harsh, lonely place.

The establishment before her was the Peacock Inn, according to the guard's map, and yet it hadn't got a sign out in front of it. Who ever heard of an inn without a sign? Tess thought crossly, not at all sure she'd got the right place. It seemed far too grand for the likes of Gideon Cade to be staying there, anyway. She wheeled Linzy around and rode back to the beggar-boy she'd passed moments before.

"Thought better of it, did ya?" he cried, stretching out his thin hand. "I knew ya 'ad a kindly look about ya! Jest a farthin' fer a poor starvin' lad—"

"If I had a farthing, I'd give it to you," Tess told him ruefully. "But I've got no money."

"Well, to 'ell with ya, then!" He stuck out his tongue and ran after a carriage that was clattering past. "Alms, good sir, fer a poor starvin' lad! Won't ya take pity on me, good sir?" The carriage window snapped open, and Tess saw the boy's eyes light up as a few coins showered

161

onto the cobblestones. "God bless 'n' keep ya, kind sir!" he shouted as he scrambled to get them. "Aye, keep ya rich 'n' me poor, ya stingy bastard—nothin' but pennies! 'Ey!" He let out a string of vile curses and kicked Linzy's knee as Tess rode closer. "Beg yar own bloody supper!"

"I don't want your money. I just need information."

"Hmph." The last of the coins tucked away in the recesses of the rags he wore, he glowered at her. "Wot'll ya give me fer it?"

"It won't cost you anything to answer a question!"

"This 'ere is London, lady. Ya don't get somethin' fer nothin' 'ere."

Despite the cold, despite her aching muscles and empty stomach, Tess couldn't help laughing. "How can you say that when I just saw you beg those pennies? You didn't give that man in the carriage anything back!"

"I surely did. I gave 'im me blessing," the urchin said archly.

"Well, I'll give you *my* blessing if you'll answer my question. And I'll wager mine's worth at least as much as yours."

The boy giggled. "I reckon ya're right about that. Go on, then."

"That place back there . . ." Tess pointed toward the sign. "That's the Peacock Inn?"

"That's wot they tells me."

She eyed the big handsome stone building, then looked back at him. "What sort of place is it?"

He shook his head, grinning cockily. "One question, ya said. That's two."

Bloody little bilker, Tess thought, and stuck her tongue out at him. "I'll give you another blessing."

He giggled again, delighted by her reprise of his rude gesture. "Gamblin' 'all," he said succinctly. "That's why I begs out 'ere. The winners is generous—most o' the time."

"A gambling hall . . ." She'd thought the place had a seedy air to it, she decided belatedly, despite its grandeur, the marble staircase and bronze doors and broad leaded windows lining the street. And wasn't it just like

Gideon Cade to tell Oren this was where he could be reached in an emergency? "I suppose they play cards."

The boy shrugged. "Play cards 'n' throw dice 'n' such, I reckon. I never been inside. But it draws all the swells. One time I seen the king's own carriage leavin'."

"Oh, I'm sure," Tess murmured.

He thrust out his chin. "Ya doesn't 'ave to believe me, I don't give a cat's bloody damn. But it's true." Head cocked to one side, he looked her up and down with open curiosity. "Why're ya askin'?"

Tess realized that, what with her travel-stained clothing and three days of grime from the road, she didn't look any better off than he. "There's . . . someone I know is in there," she said haltingly.

"Oh, I'm sure," said the boy, in such perfect imitation that Tess burst out laughing.

"Thank you for the information. I wish I had a penny to give you."

"Aye, well, ya know wot they say. If wishes was pennies, God wouldn'ta 'ad to make beggars. Blimey!" Another carriage was turning out of the yard of the Peacock Inn; he gave Tess a cheery wave and chased after its rumbling wake.

Tess sat for a moment staring at the elegant inn, watching the servants in the yard—she assumed they were servants, since they were all dressed alike in blood-red livery—scurry to and fro, trying not to think what her father would say if he could see her now. A gambling hall would be near if not at the top of any list Ben made of dens of iniquity. He abhorred gambling; when Tess was a child he'd never let her so much as join in a game of marbles. But what the hell, she thought suddenly. He'd be furious anyway that she'd come looking for his lordship in London. And it seemed the height of unfairness that Ben should lie dying while Cade frivoled his money away in this big fancy palace. Spurred on by that thought, she dug her heels into Linzy and rode up to the gates.

The servant stationed there barely glanced at her before reciting, "Applicants for employment around the back."

"But I don't—"

"Around the back," he repeated in the same flat tone, gesturing toward the alley that ran beside the inn.

"You don't understand. I am looking for—"

"Applicants for employment around the back." He reminded Tess of a magpie Meg Mullen once kept in a cage, which she'd taught to say, "Hello, lady!" but nothing more.

"If you'll just," Tess began, but the servant had slapped Linzy's withers and sent her cantering toward the alley. Since further protest didn't seem likely to yield any different result, she rode around to the back.

In the paved enclosure in which she found herself, a boy in red came running to take Linzy's reins. "Could you possibly be so kind as to feed and water her?" Tess asked hesitantly.

He gave her a withering look. "Wot the bloody 'ell d'ya think I'm 'ere fer?" Not until she was halfway across the yard to the inn's back door did it occur to her that she'd certainly be expected to pay for the service when she came out. Oh, well, she told herself, she'd just ask an extra penny or two from Gideon Cade.

The back doors of the inn were standing open. Tess peeked inside and saw a kitchen, enormous, brick-lined, bustling with women in crisp white aprons and caps. The smells of baking bread and roasting meat were so headily delicious that she nearly fell to her knees; it seemed weeks since she'd had her last meal. She was about to snitch a gold-crusted roll from a tray set to cool by the doors when one of the women saw her. "Wot d'ya want, then?" she barked.

"I—I've come to see a man who's here."

To a soul, the serving women turned and stared at her, their faces stamped with curious sympathy. The one who'd approached her seemed to soften visibly. "Wait 'ere," she said in a low voice. "I'll fetch Madame right away." Then she hurried off. Famished, Tess looked at the rolls again.

"Go on, luv," the nearest scullion whispered. "I've 'ad three meself, 'aven't I? I know jest wot ya're goin' through." Well, if she'd had three of the rolls, Tess thought, it surely couldn't hurt for her to take one. She reached toward the tray just as the woman who'd left reappeared, preceded by the most beautiful lady Tess had ever seen.

She had snow-white skin and thick auburn hair piled high on her head, wide blue eyes and a cherry-red mouth, and she wore a shimmering sky-blue gown trimmed with ribbons and lace. It was impossible to guess her age; from her flawless complexion she might have been twenty, but there was a sort of world-weariness in her gaze that bespoke many years of experience.

"How do you do," she said in a musical voice tinged with some accent that was neither Shropshire nor London nor anything else Tess had heard before. "You are looking for someone?"

Tess bobbed in a nervous curtsy. "For Gideon Cade. I was told I could find him here."

The woman pursed her red lips. "And why do you look for him?"

Tess's gaze dropped to the floor. "It's . . . personal. I'd rather not say."

"Oh, Gideon." The woman sighed, then let out a string of words in a foreign language, like the one Cade spoke to the horses. It went on for some time, accompanied by gestures of the woman's long-nailed hands and an occasional rolling of her fine eyes. At last she wound down, sighed once more, and told Tess in accented English, "Come, then. I will find a place . . ." She beckoned her on through the kitchens; they were followed by a low buzz of comment from the scullery maids.

Tess trailed after her down a long, long hall to a stairway made of rich dark wood, which was lined with pictures of women wearing shockingly little. At the top was a carved wooden door; her guide pushed it open and crooked her finger at Tess. "Come quick." Tess followed her through the doorway and gasped. They were in a gallery that lined a room ten, nay, a hundred times bigger than any she'd ever seen. There were doors all around the gallery, and columns with rich red velvet hangings, and a railing of that rich dark wood trimmed with gold. The floor far below was dotted with gold-colored tables and chairs; men in gorgeous clothes sat or stood about, playing cards or drinking from gleaming glasses that were offered on trays by beautiful languid women all dressed in the most wonderful gowns imaginable. The air hummed with laughter and low conversations, with the tinkle of glasses raised in toasts and the lustrous jangle of coins falling into piles.

"I said quick!" the blue-eyed woman chided, pulling Tess along by the elbow.

"I'm sorry," she said apologetically. "It's just that I've never seen anyplace so grand!"

The woman seemed pleased. "You like my little *établissement?*"

"When the boy outside told me King Charles came here," Tess admitted, awestruck, "I didn't think he was telling the truth. But I believe him now!"

Her guide laughed, a gay, lilting sound. "He comes from time to time, your King Charles. But we do not encourage him."

"Why not?"

"Because," she said matter-of-factly, "he is not good for his debts." Her gaze turned thoughtful. "Gideon, though, he always pays his." She stopped in front of one of the doors and rapped on it lightly. "Occupied!" a female voice called cheerily.

"Pardon, chérie!" the woman called back, and led Tess further along. At the next door the same thing happened, but at the third, no one answered. Tess's guide nodded in satisfaction and pulled her inside.

Tess didn't know exactly what sort of room the one in which she found herself was supposed to be. It had a bed in it, a big one with a blue satin canopy, but it was much too spacious to be only a bedroom. There was a table with two enormous upholstered chairs pulled up to it as well, *and* two more chairs, with huge plump cushions, in front of a bookcase, *and* a round, polished copper tub sitting up on feet, with room enough for most of Windber, it seemed. Not to mention the thick, cushiony rug on the floor, patterned with roses, and a glass-doored cabinet that held goblets and bottles, and pillows lying everywhere, on the bed and chairs and in the windowseats and even on the carpet. The foreign woman went about tidying shelves and straightening the draperies for a moment or two; then she turned to Tess and sighed.

"We have a saying in my country: without a partner, one cannot do the dance. I do not assume that you are without fault here, you understand?" Tess, light-headed from hunger and the strange surroundings, nodded, anxious to be polite. The woman's stern expression softened; she smiled, a warm, wonderful smile. "Still, neither do I assume he is innocent, either. I am, you say, neutral. Under the circumstances . . ." She reached out and opened Tess's cloak, made a face, shook her head. "I think it only fair to even the odds. I will send Charmian to you with water to bathe, and a gown. *Eh bien?*"

"I don't know what that means—*eh bien*," Tess admitted, blushing.

"It means, 'all right?' "

"Oh. Well . . . where is Gideon? Is he here?"

"We talk again after you bathe."

"But—"

"Enjoy!" The woman went out, leaving Tess alone.

For a moment she just stood, feeling rather dazed; then she stretched her aching legs and went to a window. It looked out on the rear yard; she could see the boy grooming Linzy—and doing, she had to admit, an excellent job. With that worry gone, she peered about for something else to alleviate her nervousness. Wishing she'd had time to swipe that roll, she wandered over to the bookcase, pulled down a slim volume, opened it, and then slammed it shut. What in God's name . . . ? Peeking back at the door to make sure it was closed, she looked again. She hadn't been mistaken. The book was full of sketches of men and women, stark naked, in the most amazing positions one could imagine: lying one atop the other, sitting in each other's laps, curling their legs about each other's necks, while they smiled and kissed and stroked each other's private parts.

Shocked, she stuck the book back on the shelf and pulled down another. In this one the pictures were colored, and the man and woman had strange slanting eyes, but they were doing much the same things. On one page the man had his head between the woman's legs and seemed to be kissing her there; on another the woman knelt down in front of her partner and put her tongue to his manhood while he grinned and toyed with her hair. Thinking that surely all of the books couldn't possibly be filled with such stuff, she looked in another, and then another. Some were mostly words, some only pictures, but they all had to do with making love. " 'In the third tantra,' " she read from one in a whisper, her color rising again, " 'the goal of ecstasy is reached through concentration on mutual stimulation of the male and female organs, using only the feathers of a snow-white dove.' " There was a sketch to go with the text, of a man lying flat on his back, his member sticking upright, while a woman leaned over him and plied a long feather to his groin.

With the book in her hands, Tess turned and stared at the furnishings of the room, the overstuffed chairs and big bed and copper tub and plump pillows, and it dawned on her that everything there was meant for the same purpose shown in the books. "It's all for lovemaking," she murmured. "It's a bloody brothel, that's what it is!"

There wasn't any such place in Windber-on-Clun, of course, but there was one in Shrewsbury; Tess had heard the priest at Sunday services warn of the dangers of going there. And a few years back, when Tim Whitaker was getting married and a whole gaggle of the village menfolk were gone for a whole night with him just before the wedding, Meg Mullen had gossiped that it was a whorehouse in Stafford they took Tim to.

Still, Tess had never dreamed she'd see the inside of such a place! Just standing there made her feel all funny, shamed and repelled and yet excited too. She was about to examine another book when she heard a knock at the door, and a soft voice called, *"Mam'selle?"*

"There's only me here," Tess called back hesitantly, shoving the book back onto the shelf.

"Oui, mam'selle," said the small smiling girl who looked in, "it is you I look for."

"Oh." The girl started to carry in buckets of water she had lined up in the hallway. "Here, let me help you with that!"

"Merci, mam'selle." Together they poured the buckets

into the big round tub. *"Eh voilà,"* she went on, opening a cupboard behind the tub, waving her hand at the contents. *"C'est tout ici, ce que vous voudrais. Je reuiens à bientôt!"* Waving, she turned to leave.

"Wait!" Tess cried. "Can you tell me, please, what sort of place this is that I'm in? And where is the man that I came to see? What is going on?"

The girl looked at her apologetically. *"Pardon, mam'selle. My English—it is not good, yes? You wash now, yes?"* And before Tess could say any more, she ducked out again.

Tess sighed and dangled her fingers in the bathwater, testing the temperature out of habit. It was just the way she liked it, hot enough nearly to sting. What was that peculiar saying the Widow Jonas used? "When in Rome, do as the Romans do." Though she very much doubted the appropriateness of following such advice here, the thought of a bath was irresistible to her sore muscles and aching back. From the cupboard she took a piece of sweet-smelling lavender soap and a big fluffy towel; then she peeled off her clothes and climbed into the tub.

She had finished lathering and rinsing and was simply soaking, feeling much better, though still ravenously hungry, when the little maid knocked on the door again and popped in bearing an armful of satin just the gray-green color of the first willow leaves in spring. *"Ah, mam'selle,"* she cried, *"vous êtes très belle sans toute l'ordure, n'est-ce pas? Voilà, votre robe."* She laid the satin out on the bed and gathered up Tess's discarded clothes from the floor, unable to keep from wrinkling her nose. *"Et puis—"*

"Hold on," said Tess, rising out of the tub. "Where are you going with them?"

"Au fourneau, certainement," the girl said agreeably, ducking back through the door.

"Oh, well, then, so long as you're taking them to the four-no." Tess couldn't help laughing as, alone again, she tried to make the same sounds the girl had, and felt them tickle her nose. She rubbed herself dry with the towel, combed through her damp curls as well as she could with her fingers, and went to examine the garments that lay on the bed.

"Oh, my!" It wasn't even the magnificent gown that first caught her eye, but the underclothes lying beside it: embroidered drawers made of lawn so sheer they were nearly invisible, a lacy chemise that fastened with rose-colored ribbons, and pettiskirts sewn from layer upon layer of green taffeta crisp as lettuce leaves. "I couldn't possibly put these on," she murmured aloud. "They're grand enough for a duchess!" But their silky splendor was impossible to resist. "I'll just try them on ever so quickly," she told herself, "and then ask for my old things back."

Putting them on was like slipping into someone else's skin; she felt more foreign than the maid as she pondered her reflection in the full-length mirror that hung on the wall. "I suppose it couldn't hurt just to try the dress too," she murmured, entranced by the way the pettiskirts crackled as she turned from side to side. But it wasn't exactly a dress, she discovered as she slipped her arms into the wide satin sleeves and tried to figure out how to fasten the buttons of the bodice. At least, she couldn't imagine wearing it in front of anyone else. The neckline in front plunged all the way to her waist, revealing the ribbon laces of the chemise beneath the swell of her breasts, and when she took a step away from the bed, the willow-green skirts parted to show the petticoats from her ankle to her thigh.

There had been some sort of mistake, she thought, even as she couldn't help but admire the way the cool green satin brought out the color of her eyes, and the rose ribbons matched the becoming rose blush on her cheeks. Something her father had told her about her mother came back to her as she looked in that mirror: *Everything she wore on her was brand-new and fine . . . all lace and silks and velvet she was.*

Her mother would have felt right at home in these clothes, in this place. But Tess didn't. Ben was wrong; she wasn't her mother's daughter. She was his, and she'd come here for one reason only: to save his life. She heard the door open and turned from the mirror, ready to tell the maid she wanted her own clothes back, then heard the voice of Gideon Cade, deep and low but unmistakably angry:

"What the devil sort of hoax is this?"

Their eyes met across the room. He froze in the doorway, his hand on the knob, the shock of recognition stark on his face. "Tess," he said hoarsely. She couldn't move either. God, how had she forgotten how handsome he was, with his black hair and eyes like the October sky? Just the sight of him made her heart pound, sent the blood rushing straight to her head.

Even as she stared at him, his uncertain expression changed, the clear blue of his eyes turning gray and clouded, and he laughed, slamming shut the door. "Christ, you just don't give up, do you?" he demanded. "Do you honestly expect me to believe you've just now discovered you're with child from that little contretemps last summer? Or is it some sort of immaculate conception thanks to our farewell kiss in the stables? Who's the lucky fellow this time, Mistress Jericho, whose folly you would pin on me?"

"I'm not—"

He paced across the room to the window and then back again. "Ever since Suzette sent a message that some poor wronged waif had shown up on her doorstep accusing me of having got her in the family way, I've been racking my brain as to who it could be. It never occurred to me it might be you."

"But—"

"I suppose you begged those clothes from Suzette too." He leaned toward her and away. "*And* perfume. Lavender seems a bit wholesome under the circumstances. I'd have thought you'd go for something more exotic—ambergris, or musk."

"It's soap, not perfume," Tess began indignantly. "And—"

"Your timing is off, I see," he went on, perusing her from head to toe with frosty blue eyes. "Your hair's not even dry. But perhaps you didn't know I could ride so fast when my honor's been impugned. My dear girl, it simply won't do for you to run about making these accusations every time you get into trouble with one of your homespun swains. I—"

"Would you kindly shut up and let me say something?" Tess demanded, her voice cold with fury.

He shrugged off his long cloak and sprawled onto one of the oversize chairs. "You have my undivided attention, Mistress Jericho." Then he pulled out a pocketknife and began to clean his fingernails.

"For your information, I'm *not* with child—and I'm bloody damned tired of you insinuating I am!"

"And you didn't tell Suzette you were," he said, blandly skeptical.

"I most certainly didn't."

"Then where in the world do you suppose she came up with the notion?"

"I suppose," Tess said very coolly, "she's accustomed to girls turning up here and accusing you of fathering their children."

He stared at her in surprised silence, then burst out laughing. "Touché! By God, I've missed you, Tess Jericho!"

Tess bit her lip. He'd put into words exactly what she was feeling; even as they'd sparred with one another, traded angry words, all she could think was: How splendid it is to see him again.

"Are you hungry?" he asked out of the blue.

"Am I what?"

"Hungry. You know." He made chewing motions. "You've summoned me away from my supper."

"Oh! I'm very sorry."

"Don't be. Whatever is cooking downstairs smells much better than what I was having. Suppose I go and ask for a tray." Before Tess could answer, he bounded up from the chair and vanished through the door.

Tess would have stopped him, but by now she was faint with hunger. Besides, she was glad for a few moments' space in which to compose herself. She hadn't expected to be made breathless by the sight of him, hadn't reckoned on the flood of longing his smile would unleash in her soul. You came here for a purpose, she reminded herself—to save Dad. Just ask for the money and be on your way.

Still, she couldn't keep her heart from leaping when he came back carrying a high-piled tray. He kicked the door shut behind him, then paused. "I'm sorry for those things I said," he told her softly. "I had a word with Suzette. The kitchen maid just assumed, when you showed up all bedraggled, asking for a gentleman—"

"It's all right," she said, suddenly shy. "I suppose I did look wretched."

"You look beautiful now." Tess stood, tongue-tied. He set the tray down. "Beautiful but famished. Shall we eat?"

Tess took her place at the table as he began to carve the crisp brown roasted chicken and served up sauce and peas and the heavenly rolls that she'd glimpsed in the kitchens. "I don't suppose you had a chance to examine Suzette's library, did you?" he asked, nodding toward the bookcase.

"No. No, I didn't."

"Ah. I only ask because I noticed some of the volumes were disarranged." His eyebrow was cocked; Tess knew he knew perfectly well that she'd lied. "It's one of the most comprehensive collections in Europe."

Tess swallowed a bite of the delectable chicken and said primly, "I can't think why anyone would want to collect such filth"—then realized she'd given herself away.

He laughed outright. "So you did look! Do you really think it's filth, or is that just your father talking? Here." He reached back and pulled out a volume, opened it, and held it out for her to see. "Look at this."

"I don't care to." But Tess couldn't resist peeking at the page. It showed a young couple lying naked in a garden, arms and legs entwined.

"Do you think that is lewd and disgusting?" Cade asked.

"What, lolling about in broad daylight without any clothes on? I certainly do."

"Even your father would have trouble finding fault with that illustration, I'm afraid. It's of Adam and Eve."

"Who it's of isn't the point," Tess said after a pause. "What sort of person would look at such stuff?"

"Suzette bought most of her collection from King Charles a few years back, when he was strapped for cash."

"You're jesting," said Tess, a roll halfway to her mouth.

"God's truth."

She set the roll down. "This is a brothel, isn't it?" He nodded. "Do you live here?"

"No. But Suzette always knows where I can be found."

"Is she your mistress?"

"Suzette?" He laughed. "No." Then he stopped, though Tess could tell there had been something more he was going to say. The silence stretched as Tess ate hungrily.

When she'd finished off her chicken, she glanced up to find him watching her, his own plate scarcely touched. Thinking she must have sauce on her chin, she rubbed it with her napkin, and saw him smile.

"She told me the king comes here," she offered, wanting to say something, anything, so he'd stop staring at her so strangely. "Have you ever met him?"

He found that amusing too. "No. I'm sure Suzette could arrange to introduce you to him, though, if you'd like."

"What, me meet the king?"

"Why not? He's quite the connoisseur of beautiful women. He might make you his mistress."

"You mustn't say such things," Tess told him, scandalized. "I'm sure the king wouldn't be unfaithful to Queen Catherine."

A corner of his mouth twitched. "Of course. Forgive me. No doubt he only comes here to play cards. Tell me, are men never unfaithful to their wives back in Windber-on-Clun?"

"Well, it's rather difficult, with the way everybody knows everybody's business."

"Quite so. Would you like some wine?"

Tess wrinkled her nose as she pushed her empty plate away. "I don't care for wine. That is—I've had it only once. The Widow Jonas' dandelion wine." On the night before she was to marry Jack . . .

"I think you'll like this." He went to a sideboard,

fetched a decanter and two gleaming goblets. She followed him with her eyes, taking pleasure in the way he moved: like a fine stallion, like Satan, with no wasted motion, fluid and lean. Something her father once told her ran through her mind: *If Jehovah hadn't made horses, how different my life might have been.* And mine, she thought, if he hadn't made Gideon Cade.

It was long past time she brought up the matter of her father. And yet she hesitated, caught up in the pretty fantasy of the moment: the splendid room, her fine clothes, the admiration that shone in his gaze. He was treating her differently than he had back in Windber, like a lady, a queen. She sipped the bit of wine he poured for her; red as a jewel, it was heady and rich and strong. "Oh, my," she said breathlessly.

He smiled at her awed surprise. "Didn't I tell you so? It's called claret."

"Claret. I shall have to remember that." Then she laughed. "Though I don't know why. I will likely never taste it again."

"Then you had better have more. The Chinese say there is nothing sadder than a pleasure known only once." His blue eyes were burning as he reached to fill her glass. When he handed it to her, their fingers met, and she felt his touch on her like a fiery brand. A pleasure known once . . . She shivered, transported back to that night in the cave, saw his eyes darken, and knew he was there with her. His hand closed on her wrist. The goblet clicked against the tabletop, the wine inside it tilting like a moon-drawn tide. I am drowning, thought Tess, drowning in a flow of need and memory, in a sea of fire. He bent down and put his mouth to hers, and she was lost; the waters closed over her head. Claret spilled to the floor, dark as blood, as he carried her to the bed.

"Is it what you want? Tell me, Tess."

She was already reaching for the buttons of his shirt. "Yes. God, yes."

He laid her down amidst the soft feathers and fell on her, tearing the gown from her shoulders, stripping the bodice to her waist. The thin chemise gave way before his greedy hands; hers were just as greedy, running over his chest, the taut length of his belly, finding the buckle of his belt and fumbling to undo it while he stroked her breasts and kissed her hungrily.

They didn't speak; there was no need for words when their bodies spoke for them, arching and aching to meet one another, to melt, to merge. When he entered her, Tess felt flames ripple through her; she clung to him as he thrust deeper, his manhood filling her completely. He was all heat and wild urgency, she the sole coolness to quench him, and he plunged down into her over and over again.

Let this never end, Tess prayed. And then: God, let this end now—as the pleasure turned too fierce to bear, threatening to consume her. She thought she would die of joy, fly straight to heaven on wings of flame. Above her he groaned, head thrown back, chest heaving with each hard, hot thrust, and she rose up to meet him, pulled him down to her, welcomed him in.

His groin muscles tightened against her; the swift rhythm of their joining became quicker still, until all limits—his hand, hers, theirs, hair, hearts—stretched and blurred. They became each other, and then something more, the sum of two souls, freed of earth, soaring, shining. "Oh," Tess cried in wonder, "oh . . ." He answered the cry with her name; his seed exploded inside her, and together they tumbled headlong over the edge of that blinding brightness into the night.

11

Tess opened her eyes to twilight the color of plums and the sight of Gideon Cade stretched out beside her, wearing only his breeches, calmly sipping claret. She sat up on the bed, saw she hadn't any clothes on, and grabbed for the coverlet. "Welcome back," Cade said, and offered her the glass of wine.

"What happened?" she asked, dazed and drowsy.

His eyebrow arched. "Are you claiming not to remember?"

She blushed. "I remember *that*. I meant afterward."

"Ah. You fell asleep. I couldn't decide whether I'd bored you or if you were exhausted." He grinned. "I chose to believe you were tired."

"You didn't bore me," she said shyly, clutching the blanket as she pushed back her hair. "How long was I asleep?"

"Nearly twelve hours."

"Twelve hours?" She stared at him, then at the window. "But night's just falling!"

"Wrong. Dawn's just breaking." He leaned over to kiss her, but she was already climbing down from the bed.

"God, I've got to get back!"

"Back where?"

"Why, to Windber. What the devil did that girl do with my clothes?"

"What do you mean, you've got to get back to Windber? Not that I'm not flattered, but isn't this rather a long way to come to spend just one night?"

"No, you see, because I needed the money. Oh, where on earth are my boots?"

"The money." There was something terrible in his voice. Tess turned to him, suddenly realizing they hadn't discussed that as yet.

"Aye," she began, "you see—"

"I do see. I see very well."

"No, you don't understand. I needed money, and—"

"And you thought the easiest way to get it was to come after me and play whore."

Tess stared at him in shock. "That's a horrid thing to say! It wasn't that way at all!"

"No?" He'd gotten up from the bed and was pulling on his belt and shirt. "I suppose when you saw me again you were just so overwhelmed that you couldn't keep from spreading your legs. Or was the claret so strong that one sip turned your knees to jelly?"

"If you'd just listen—"

"Oh, no, Tess Jericho. I'm through with listening, and I'm through with you." He unfastened his purse from his belt and flung it at her; it fell at her feet. "There you go. Take it. It's all the money I've got in the world."

"But—"

"Go on, you earned it! And if you ever need more, mind you come back here to earn it. I'll be sure and put in a word for you with Suzette." He grabbed his boots and stalked toward the door. "Jack was right—you are a whore. But at least you're a good one."

"But I need the money for—" The door slammed on her words, wood quivering. "For my father!" she finished, though she knew he couldn't hear her. "I never meant . . . I didn't . . . Oh, damn you to hell!" She ran to the door and flung it open, but he'd already vanished. With nothing on but the blanket, she couldn't go after him. She turned back to the room and saw the little maid standing in the hallway, staring at her with wide eyes. "I need my clothes, please," she told her.

"But, *mam'selle*—"

"I need my clothes!"

"I bring Madame," the maid murmured, starting away.

Tess caught her arm. "I don't want Madame, dammit! I just want my clothes. I want . . ." She drew in her breath as her tears spilled over. "I want to go home!"

The maid's brown eyes were filled with sympathy. *"Eh bien,"* she said softly, pushing Tess back toward the room. "You wait here."

Tess stumbled into the chamber, averting her gaze from the huge bed with its disarrayed linens, the fancy gown and underclothes strewn over the floor. Then she saw the purse he'd flung at her and snatched it up. Its hefty weight surprised and angered her; it must have held five, ten pounds.

Who cared what Gideon Cade thought of her? She'd got the money for her father, and that was what mattered. Cade had shown the sort of man he was when he walked out on Windber-on-Clun. And once she went back there, she'd never, ever have to see him again.

The maid popped into the room, arms piled with clothing. *"Voilá, mam'selle."* She showed her bundle to Tess: wool smock, skirt, stockings, a thick budge cloak.

"These aren't mine," Tess said impatiently.

"Non, mam'selle. You see, I burn yours."

"You *what?"*

The little foreigner shrugged nervously. "They were so dirty . . ." She made a face. "I did not know how to make them clean."

"Well, whose clothes are these?"

"Mine, *mam'selle,"* she said with a tiny curtsy.

"Oh, for glory's sake! I can't take your clothes!"

The maid thrust them at her. "But you must! It is my fault; if Madame finds out, she will be angry!"

Tess hesitated. Time was wasting. And she could hardly ride back to Windber wrapped in a blanket. "All right, then. But you must let me pay you for them." She went to open Cade's purse.

"Non, absolument!" the maid insisted, shaking her head.

"Charmian!" a voice called from the hallway—Suzette, sounding cross. "Where have you got to?"

Casting Tess a pleading look, putting her finger to her lips, the maid slipped out again.

Well, thought Tess, and everyone in Windber always

says foreigners are so horrid! She dressed as quickly as she could. The clothes were a good deal too short, but they were soft and warm and far finer than the ones Tess had worn from home. She still didn't feel right taking them without paying. I'll give extra to the stableboy when I pay for Linzy's board, she decided, and ask him to pass it on to her.

She peeked out into the hallway and saw an enormous fat man in black velvet kissing a pretty blond woman farewell in front of one of the doorways. She ducked back into the room; when she looked again a moment later the man was gone, though the woman still stood in the doorway, rubbing her mouth with a lace handkerchief.

"Excuse me," Tess said hesitantly, "but is there a back stair out of here?"

"Ooh, competition!" The woman smiled, eyeing Tess's fiery hair. "Just starting, are you?"

"Just leaving, actually."

"Oh? Well, there's only one stairway, ducky, to keep the clientele from going without paying. Two doors down." She frowned at the handkerchief. "I can't stand that man; he drools like a dog."

"Thank you," Tess said, suppressing a shudder as she made her escape.

She retraced her steps down the stairs and along the paneled hallway. Neither the maid nor Suzette was in sight. With all the hurly-burly in the kitchens, it was an easy matter to slip out to the yards again. There was snow in the air, Tess thought, her spirits rising as she crossed the cobbles to the stable. Soon she'd leave this dreadful place behind and head for home again.

"The silver pony," she told the boy who answered her knock at the stable doors. A moment later he led Linzy forth, saddled and bridled. Tess threw her arms around the pony's neck, feeling as though she hadn't seen her in years. "You did a beautiful job of grooming her," she told the boy. "Thanks ever so much."

He blushed to the roots of his straw-colored hair. "She's a pip, she is, mum. I enjoyed it." He cleared his throat. "There's still a matter of sixpence due, though, for stablin' 'n' board."

"Oh, of course." Tess pulled out Cade's purse. "And I wonder if you might do me a favor. The little foreign maid with the dark eyes—"

"Charmian."

"Aye." Feeling generous, Tess pulled out five shillings. "Could you give the rest of this to her—and take an extra twopence for yourself." She thrust the coins into his hand and climbed eagerly into the saddle.

The boy stood, still holding the bridle. "Wot's this, then, some sort o' joke?"

Tess laughed. "No joke, lad. Just my way of saying thanks."

"Aye, well, I can do without suchlike thanks, can't I?" he spat, and flung the coins into a heap of muck-mottled straw.

"Why—" She stared at him. "What do you mean?"

"Take me for a fool, d'ya, tryin' to pay me in lead?"

"Lead?" Incredulous, Tess yanked open the purse again and poured a stream of coins into her fist. They were the same size and shape as shillings, she saw now, but their color was a dull ugly gray. "Oh, God. It can't be. Jesus in heaven . . ." She tore through the slugs to the bottom of the purse, but they were all the same; not so much of a farthing of it was real.

"I'm sorry, mum," the stableboy said awkwardly, realizing she'd offered him the coins in good faith. "I seen tricks like that before. Lots o' men wot come here, gamblers, connivers, they'll fill their purses up with them lead coins to make themselves look better off than they is. Ya'd best take that purse straight back to wotever swindler gave it to ya."

"But I can't do that!" Tess stared at the coins, stunned, disbelieving. All the money I've got in the world, Gideon Cade had said. No wonder he'd given the purse to her so readily.

"Mum?" The stableboy looked at her uncertainly as she began laughing. "Mum, are ya all right?" Tess tried to answer, but she couldn't stop laughing even as tears rolled down her face. "I'd best go and get Madame," he said uncertainly.

"No!" Tess gasped in breath. "No! No, I'm perfectly fine." Her laughter threatened to erupt again. A whore and a swindler—Christ, what a well-suited pair. "But you'll have to forgive me that sixpence. I've got to get home to my father. You see . . ." She giggled hysterically. "You see, he's dying."

"Mum—"

"Don't worry about me!" Tess waved gaily, digging her heels into Linzy. "I'm perfectly fine!"

She had nothing but time for the next three days, as she retraced her long ride through the chill, colorless countryside. Time to think what might have happened had she never burst in on Gideon Cade as he stepped from his bath one spring morning . . . what might have been if the black stallion and Linzy hadn't escaped from the stables one hot summer's night. Time to reflect that if Gideon Cade had never come to Windber-on-Clun, she might be sitting by the hearth in a cottage with Jack, sewing scraps into a bunting for a baby that could have been hers, with Ben safe at her side. And instead . . .

Instead she'd given herself to Cade again—and this time with no excuses. God, Ben had been right: it was her mother's blood, wicked and wanton, that ran in her veins. And as punishment for what she'd done, her father would die.

If Jehovah had never made horses . . .

If only he'd never made Gideon Cade.

Her shame was only heightened when all along the way folk went out of their way to be merry and giving. Christmas was nearly at hand, and her countrymen took care to see that she and Linzy were fed and had a warm place to sleep, perhaps thinking of another woman, long ago, for whom there had been no room at an inn. She bore their kindness in silence, certain that had they known the awful things she'd done, they'd have pilloried her for a magdalen.

It was near dusk on Christmas Eve when she crossed the White Moor through the Forest Clun and looked down on her village again. There was a sprinkling of frost on the ground, and the gray sky hinted of more to come. "We're almost home," she whispered to Linzy, and heard

her voice crack on that last word. "Good girl, come on."
The snow began to fall as they rode down out of the hills.

The dinner hour was near, for the road and fields were
deserted. Smoke curled from every chimney—every chimney, Tess saw then, her heart stitching up in her chest,
except one. Halfway up the road to the big house, close
by the stables, stood a single cottage with no fire lit in the
hearth.

"Oh, God," she whispered. "Oh, God, no, don't let
me be too late!" She spurred the weary pony on, saying
frantic prayers: "Please, Dad, please, still be alive! Hang
on, Dad, I'm coming!" The instant she passed the well
she flung herself from the saddle and skidded over the
frozen turf to the cottage door. "Dad! Dad, it's me! I've
come home!" But the room inside was pitch dark, and
colder than her heart, which had turned to ice.

"Dad!" she screamed, fumbling for the table, a candle,
flint with which to light it. "Dad, where are you?" In the
candle's flickering glow she saw his neatly made-up cot,
and the sight of those downturned blankets sliced her like
a knife.

He was dead. She was too late. She'd missed him.
She'd gone off on a wild-goose chase and left him to
suffer and die—perhaps at some moment when Cade had
been thrusting inside her or kissing her breasts. "Oh,
God, Dad, I'm sorry," she cried, collapsing onto his
empty bed. "Dad, Dad, I loved you so much. Please,
Dad, forgive me . . ." The desolation that filled her was
unbearable; she wanted to die herself.

"Who's there?" a voice called from the doorway. Tess
raised her stricken gaze and saw Mungo peering at her in
the candlelight. "Is that ye, Teresa?"

She nodded bleakly, tears streaming down her face.
"Where is he, Mungo? Where have they taken my father?" They couldn't have buried him already, not with
the ground frozen hard.

He took an uncertain step toward her. "Here, are ye
all right?"

"I never even told him how much I loved him, Mungo,"
she whispered. That was what hurt most of all.

"Ye might go tell him now."

She struggled to her feet. "Aye, that's what I'll do. Where have they got him laid out?"

"Laid out?" The old man blinked. "Bless me, I don't think even Ben Jericho could be laid out already, girl; the festivities is only just begun." He turned back to the door. "Best hurry or ye'll miss yer share o' the goodies! There's puddin', ye know, 'n' sugarplums 'n' roast chestnuts, 'n' Backus roasted up a whole pig!"

"You needn't sound so eager, Mungo, for God's sake," Tess told him, appalled that all he could think of was the funeral supper. "I thought my father was your friend!"

"Aye, and so he always will be, girl. Say, did ye say 'was'? Ye sound as though the poor man's dead!"

Tess stared at him. "Why . . . isn't he?"

"Not the last I looked." Then he scratched his bald head. "Wait, now, didn't the widow tell me ye'd gone off somewheres? Then ye wouldn't have heard . . ."

"Heard what, for God's sake?"

"Why, his lordship's sent a great packet of gold to us all for Christmas! It must o' got here . . ." He paused, thinking. "Aye, just a week ago. Saturday." Saturday . . . the day after she'd left for London, Tess realized. "Jack rode over to Stafford," Mungo went on, " 'n' fetched a surgeon for yer father that same afternoon. The fellow came 'n' bled him 'n' set up his arm 'n' I don't know wot all. But he's been up 'n' about for the last four days."

"Dad's all right?" Tess asked in disbelief.

"Aye, fit as a fiddle, wot d'ye think I'm tellin' ye? Now ye'll have to excuse me or I'll miss that puddin'." He left the cottage, licking his chops.

Tess followed him, and beneath the winter sky whirled about in a dance of wild exultation. Her father was saved—and his lordship had sent money! A great packet of gold he had sent them! God forgive me for misjudging him, she thought as hope and joy flooded into her heart once more. God forgive us all! No wonder he had naught but lead in his purse; he sent all his gold here!

"Merry Christmas, Mungo!" she cried, and kissed the startled man on both cheeks. "Merry, merry Christmas— and God bless Gideon Cade!"

"Gideon Cade?" He pulled away from her embrace. "Wot, girl, are ye daft? Why would ye bless him?"

She looked at him, uncomprehending. "But you said his lordship sent gold!"

"Aye, so I did, but I never meant Cade!" He spat the name out with undisguised disgust. "No, girl, 'twas Lord Halifax! He sent it us for a Christmas gift, may his name be praised forever. Sent it by special courier, he did, all the way from the colonies!"

III

12

Gideon Cade came back to Windber-on-Clun in late winter. It was Passiontide, still a fortnight before Easter, which fell early that year. Not even the snowdrops had bloomed yet, but the witch-hazel tree by the big house held sulfur-yellow flowers curled tight to its leafless branches. When the wind swept down the hill, Tess could catch their fragrance, elusive and haunting, and knew the time drew near when the season would change. For now, though, the earth was still frozen, hard as Sheffield steel beneath its varnish of hoarfrost. That was what made the wheels of the wagon rumble like midsummer thunder on the day Cade returned.

Tess was in the stables with her father, rubbing neat's-foot oil into an endless succession of worn leather thongs and bridles, when she heard the far-off clatter. "What do you reckon that is?" she asked, dipping her rag into the pot of grease. Ben raised his head for a moment and listened.

"Gabriel's trumpet?"

Tess looked to make sure he was smiling before she laughed. "If it is, God ought to have let him practice before the big day!"

His grin broadened. "Aye, well, you know how sour Sam always sounds when he first tunes up his fiddle for playing. It's hard to hold on to your nerves when you're put on the spot." They beamed at one another, quietly relishing the renewed affection sprung up between them since Tess's journey to London. Though Ben hadn't approved of her seeking out Cade, he was touched by the

189

lengths she'd been willing to go to for his sake. And since, as Tess told him, she never did find his lordship there in the city, there was no harm done.

The thunder wasn't going away; on the contrary, it kept getting louder. "Do get up and see what that is, Dad," Tess urged. "I can't keep my mind on my work when there's a mystery about."

"Curiosity killed the cat, so they tell me," he grumbled, but he left the tack room and went to the stable doors. "I'll be damned," he said a moment later. It was the first time Tess had ever heard him use actual profanity.

"What is it?" she demanded in astonishment, jumping up from her stool. For answer he pointed down the hillside to the road from the village, where a wagon drawn by four heavy-hoofed draft horses was inching up its length. There wasn't any mistaking the identity of the tall black-caped driver in the cocked hat, even from that distance: the square set of his broad shoulders and the assurance with which his gloved hands steered the course of the cart's heavy load made it perfectly clear.

"I never thought I'd see the day when he'd dare show his face here again," said Ben, and his voice held a faint trace of grudging awe at Cade's audacity.

Tess did not, could not, answer. At the sight of Cade she'd been swept by such a flood of contrary emotions that her knees went weak; she had to cling to the door-jamb lest Ben should see. Shame and hatred, fear and fury, disbelief and a hard, piercing longing engulfed her, and like the undercurrent of a storm-swelled ocean, the longing threatened to sweep all the others away. "Look at him," Ben muttered, irked past awe by his lordship's insouciant elegance even acting the drover. And: Aye, look at him, Tess's battered heart cried in ecstasy.

They weren't the only ones to hear the clatter. Down in the village, men and women filled doorways and windows, unheedful of the cold, and stared after the cart. Backus had been chopping firewood out behind the Swan Tavern; he still stood with the ax raised over his head, a sorcery-struck statue, and watched the slow progress of the wagon's sagging rear axle as it climbed the hill. "What the devil do you reckon he's hauling up here?" Ben wondered aloud. From the cottages below, there emerged an ad hoc examining committee made up of Mungo, Robbie, Sam, and Jack, who were evidently wondering the same thing. The wagon moved so slowly that they could easily have overtaken it, but they hung back, walking instead in its wake like some bewildered funeral cortege.

"High time I found out what this is all about!" Ben declared, tossing his oil rag aside and starting out to join the mourners.

"Dad, wait!" Tess grabbed the back of his jacket; he turned to her questioningly. "It's . . . it's not really any of our business why he's here, is it?"

He looked at her as though she had just posited that the Fall of *Man* had all been some silly mistake. "None of our *business*?"

"Well, why don't we finish up these harnesses first?" God, she'd never in her life dreamed that he'd come back.

"Correct me if I'm wrong, lass, but wasn't it you said not two minutes ago you couldn't work with a mystery going on around you? If why he's returned is not a mystery, then I'm pickled eggs!"

Tess felt her color rise as she realized how unlikely her protest must seem. But the thought of her father trotting out there to hear what Cade would have to say about her visit to London was unbearable. "I shouldn't think you'd consider anything about that scoundrel a mystery by now," she said desperately.

"I'd say the mysteries around here are growing by leaps and bounds." Ben's expression warned her not to press the matter any further. She trailed after him toward the road. If Gideon Cade was going to accuse her of whoring, she'd at least make him do so while she was there.

He'd drawn the team up at the edge of the manor's drive; now he climbed from the cart seat as Ben approached him. "Jericho." He nodded with perfect equanimity. "Good to see you again."

The civil greeting caught Ben off-guard; Tess watched him bite off whatever insult he'd had on his tongue and hesitate, while the rest of the men ranged themselves warily behind him. "Your lordship," Ben said finally, not knowing how else to address him. "Had a fine warm winter there in the city, did you?"

"Not exactly." His frigid gaze passed right over Tess. "Mungo. Robbie. Sam. Jack, how's that pretty wife of yours?"

Put out of kilter like the rest by Cade's genial politeness, Jack grunted one word: "Expecting."

"Is she! Congratulations. All going well, I hope?"

"Well enough." Jack was regaining his nerve. "No bloody thanks to ye. If ye'd had yer way, she'd be starved to death with the rest of us by now."

Cade looked him up and down. "You seem sufficiently fed."

Old Sam puffed out his chest. "That's on account o' Lord Halifax, God bless 'n' keep him. Sent us twenty quid at Christmastide, he did, all the way from the New World. It's all we had to keep body 'n' soul knit together— 'specially poor Ben. Dreadful sick, our Ben was."

Something glimmered behind Cade's blue eyes. "Sick at Christmastide, were you?" he demanded of Ben. "That would be just about the time your daughter came looking for me, I heard."

"But didn't find you, caught up in whatever wickedness you were," Ben spat. Tangled in the web of her lie, Tess waited for her doom.

Cade's cold gaze flickered over her briefly. Then, "No. What a pity," he said.

"Ye've a bloody nerve showin' yer face around here," Mungo told the lord, whiskers quivering. Tess gasped as Cade raised his crop against the harmless old man.

"And you've a bloody nerve talking to me that way," he answered, such venom in his voice that even Ben was cowed. "You, Brady." He turned the whip to Jack. "Get whatever able-bodied men there may be in this stinkhole and unload the cart."

Bristling, Ben moved toward the wagon. "Go on, Jack. I'll untie the wrappings."

"No," said Cade.

"Listen," Ben said angrily, "I may have been sick, but I'm as able-bodied now as any soul in Windber."

"You'll do as I tell you, Jericho. I need you to go through the stables and find me a mount." For the first time, Tess realized he hadn't brought the huge black stallion back with him.

"Why . . . where's that devil horse of yours?" asked Ben, noticing the same thing.

"Dead," Cade said shortly, stalking toward the stables. "Let's go."

Ben started after him. Sam, who'd been pawing at the ropes and padding in the wagon, whistled him over with a secretive hiss: "Whist! Look here!" Ben threw a quick glance at Cade's back, then circled round to his old friend, followed by the rest of the men. Tess craned to see as Sam pulled the wadded padding aside.

"Crikey," Mungo whispered.

"I don't believe it," Jack muttered.

"He's a right ruddy madman," Robbie declared.

"Ye don't reckon he's plannin' on doin' wot it looks like he's plannin' on doin'—do ye?" Sam asked, scratching his head.

Ben stared for a long moment at the tall glass panes Sam's exploration had revealed. Then he stepped back from the wagon, nearly bowling Tess over. As she moved out of his way, she saw the most curious expression on his face. It took her several seconds to recognize that look, for he was trying to mask it as best he could. But there it was, and he couldn't hide it completely: admiration for Gideon Cade.

"He's rebuilding that danged glasshouse of his," he said, and nearly caught himself laughing. "I'll be danged. The stubborn son of a bitch!"

That wasn't all Cade was planning on doing. Over the next weeks a steady stream of carts and wagons toiled into Windber, bearing sacks of seeds for planting, bricks and mortar for new outbuildings, tools for the field hands, boxes that the housemaids said were full of books and furnishings. Wild rumors circulated as to where he'd got the money to pay for it all: that he'd robbed a London bank, that he'd murdered someone, that he'd mortgaged the land. The tenants whispered and gossiped as they scurried to do his bidding, while Cade rode between field and hill and the big house overseeing their work from the back of the big bay mare Ben chose for him. She was the brawniest beast in the stables, but compared to the memory of Satan, she seemed a dwarf.

As for Tess, Gideon Cade utterly ignored her. Better that than to have him tell Dad what went on in London, she told herself, denying the pang of pain in her heart when he looked through her as though she didn't exist. It was plain enough from his actions what she meant to him: absolutely nothing. And that, thought Tess, is exactly what he means to me.

One evening at the end of March, Ben came home to the cottage with a leather pouch in one hand and an odd-shaped bit of fired white clay in the other. "What's that, then?" Tess asked as he laid them on the table beside his plate.

"Something Cade's got us planting over on the south acreage."

"He's got you planting *clay*?"

"Of course not!" Ben snorted. "He's planting this stuff here." Opening the pouch, he shook a small pile of dark brown threads onto the tabletop. "Tobacco, it's called. Comes from the New World."

Curious, Tess wet her finger and touched it to the threads, then tasted them. "Blech!" she cried, spitting them back out into her hand.

"You're not supposed to eat it, lass!"

"Then what the devil good is it?"

"You smoke it. Like so." Ben jammed a pinch of the stuff into the rounded end of the clay contraption, grabbed a brand from the hearth, and held it to the threads until they began to smolder. Then, while Tess watched in amazement, he sucked at the opposite end of the clay stalk, his cheeks going hollow, took the stalk from his mouth, and breathed a thick cloud of odoriferous gray fog back out into the air.

"Well, I never," said Tess.

Her father took another long suck at the stalk and

exhaled, with a sigh of pure bliss. "Oh, I did," he told her. "Back when I was working for the great lord in London. He liked nothing better than a pipe and a bit of whiskey at the end of the day. Of course, it was a rare thing for me to get hold of the stuff; it cost a right ruddy fortune."

"Why would you want to get hold of it?" she asked, holding her nose against another billow of smoke.

"Why, it's relaxing for a man to have his pipe. Not to mention it strengthens the heart and the lungs."

"Oh, does it really?"

"That's what my lord used to say." He leaned back in his chair, one hand scratching Job's head, the other clutching his pipe, the picture of contentment. "Cade says if the crop takes, I'm welcome to all I can smoke. This here . . ." He patted the pouch. "This is just a wee gift, to show the rest of the tenants what we're growing it for."

"Since when do you take gifts from Gideon Cade?"

The threads in the pipe bowl had burned out; Ben knocked them into the fire and began the whole process again. "Do you know," he mused, "I've been thinking I misjudged that man."

"You *what*?"

"Well, lass, you must admit, 'twas a hard row he set himself to hoeing when he came here to be lord of a bunch of strangers, and not knowing anything about what he was doing. After last harvest, I reckon most men would've just up and quit, sold out and been rid of us. But Cade's no quitter; you've got to give the man that."

"For God's sake, Dad." Tess grabbed his plate and took it to the stewpot. "Look at yourself! You're worse than a child. The man gives you a present, and all of a sudden he's your bosom friend." She set the plate back on the table so hard that it cracked.

"I didn't say that," Ben told her mildly, puffing away. "But it only makes sense what he says about trying new crops. This land's worn out for oats and wheat, and wasn't that good to begin with. 'Course, as he says, some stuff's bound to fail, but that's always the way when you try something new."

"What's this," Tess demanded, "the gospel according to Gideon Cade?"

"I should think you'd be glad to see me admit I can change my mind."

"Aye, so I would be, but not about him."

Ben knocked out his pipe and refilled it. "Didn't know you cared so much about the man, Teresa."

"I *don't* care about him." She filled her own plate and sat across from him.

"You're sure of that, are you?"

"Christ, Dad, I just said so! He means nothing to me."

He sucked in smoke. "You know, lass, there's some folk say you did find him on that trip to London. That he bought you those clothes you came home in."

"I told you where I got them. A man splashed me with his carriage and insisted on buying—"

"I know what you told me. I'm just telling you what folks say."

"Dad, I haven't even spoken to the man in two months!"

"So folks have noticed. They say you had a falling-out with him. A lovers' spat."

"For God's sake, Dad, he's not my lover! Didn't you always tell me not to listen to gossip? Now, put out that damned thing and eat."

Ben obediently emptied the pipe and did not refill it. "Well, if you're sure you don't care for the man—"

"I don't! So why don't we stop talking about him?"

"Fair enough," said Ben. "By the by, Tim Whitaker came to me yesterday. He's got a cousin over to Stafford, an older fellow, whose wife died this winter."

"Fascinating," Tess muttered.

"His name's Ballard, John Ballard. He's been left with five children, poor soul. Tim says he's near at wits' end."

Tess looked up from her stew, suddenly wary. "So?"

"He's looking for a wife," he told her. "Tim says he wouldn't mind so much if . . . Well, he's a widower, like I told you."

"Wouldn't mind so much if what?" asked Tess, her voice brittle.

"If you want to make me spell it out for you, I will. Wouldn't mind so much if she was used goods."

"Jesus, Dad!" Tess dropped her spoon with a clatter, blushing violently.

"Hear me out, Teresa, and don't go getting your back up! It's time you faced facts. You aren't getting any younger."

"I'm only eighteen!"

"You'll be nineteen come August, and twenty after that. Lass, there's no one hereabouts for you to marry! It's high time you were wedded and starting a family, or you'll wake up some morning and find your life wasted away."

Tess's hands had gone clammy. "What do you mean, there's no one for me to wed here? If I'm to be stuck with some old man, why not Mungo or Sam? At least they're not strangers."

Her father coughed, an odd, delicate sound. "Nay. They know you only too well."

"What's that supposed to mean?"

"This isn't easy for me, lass. But the fact is, no one in Windber will wed you for fear the children you have might be his."

"His? *Whose*?" But Tess knew perfectly well. "Oh, damn! Damn it all, that's not fair!"

"Maybe you should have thought of that before you went sinning with him up in that cave."

"So I made a mistake—one mistake! Am I to spend my whole life paying for it?" Tess demanded angrily, and tossed her head. "If no one here will have me, then I just won't marry! I'd still have you and Job and Linzy."

"Don't be a fool," Ben said with harsh abruptness. "Whatever else you learned this past year, you must know I won't be around forever. And that horse and hound are poor substitutes for the grandchildren I yearn to have someday. Tim says Ballard's a good man."

"But I can't leave Windber!"

"Why not?"

"Because you're here!"

"Tim says Ballard would have me with you."

"Oh, Tim says, Tim says! This is our home, Dad! We wouldn't be happy anyplace else."

"Are we happy here?" Ben asked wistfully.

"A damned sight happier than we'd be living with a stranger and his five bloody children!"

"How do you know that, Tess? Whatever happened to your thirst for adventure? I used to think I'd never be able to keep you in Windber-on-Clun."

"Aye, well, things have changed."

"There's only one thing I see that's changed," said her father, "and that's the second coming of Gideon Cade. So unless you're lying when you say you don't care about him—"

"Would you like me to swear on the Bible?" His eyes went toward it, and Tess threw up her hands. "Oh, for God's sake, Dad!"

"Then I've made up my mind. I'm going to ask Cade for permission to ride to Stafford tomorrow. I'll have a talk with Tim's cousin, and if I like him, I'll offer your hand."

"You wouldn't," said Tess.

"That's how it's going to be." His gaze, knowing and defiant, met his daughter's.

"You can't make me wed him," said Tess, equally defiant.

"We'll see, lass. We'll see."

13

True to his word, Ben rode one of the bays to the big house first thing in the morning. Tess watched from the cottage doorway as he hitched the horse at the portico and knocked at the front doors. She saw Oren open to him and, after a moment's discussion, let him inside.

She waited, imagining her father climbing the stairs to the librarium, finding his lordship at breakfast, standing ill-at-ease before him, hat in his work-roughened hands, as he explained the mission to Stafford that would win his disgraced daughter a husband at last.

She imagined, too, how Cade might answer. As she stood and watched the closed doors, she found herself hoping, even expecting, that they would fly open, that he would come running down the hill to the cottage and sweep her into his arms. He would kiss her, tell her he'd turned down her father's request because he wanted to wed her, that he loved her with all his heart and would until the end of time. She was so engrossed in this scene that it came as a genuine shock when the doors did open to reveal her father, who got back on the bay and rode off toward Stafford town.

In the clear, bright morning air, with the sweet scent of apple blossoms borne on a soft wind, Tess stared at the bouncing rump of the bay and knew once and for all that her life was over before it had ever really begun. She'd be marrying this widower, moving to Stafford to look after his household and children, and the chances were that once she did she'd never even see Gideon Cade again.

Still, it wasn't because she was in love with Cade that she felt so bleakly empty, she told herself. It was just that she was sure no one else—and certainly not some gray-bearded widower worn down by a passel of motherless children—would ever be able to make her feel the impossible ecstasy he had when she lay in his arms.

Furious with herself, with her father, with Cade, with the world at large, she pulled a jacket on over her hand-me-down breeches and shirt and marched out to the stables to do the mucking, with Job, a fittingly gloomy companion, dogging her heels.

Not until late afternoon did she find time for Linzy. She whistled her in from the pasture; as the silver pony galloped toward her, mane tossing, tail flying, she felt a pang of regret. "Do you know, pretty lady," she whispered as she saddled her up, "I almost wish I'd let his lordship breed you to Satan. Not with the ropes, mind you, but just the two of you running wild together, the way you did the night you got loose from the stables, the night of the storm." Cade's smoky blue eyes in the firelight . . . the touch of his mouth at her breast . . .

She sighed and scratched the pony's forelock. "But perhaps it's better you didn't. After all, I might want to breed you to another horse someday." She left the rest of the thought unspoken: And I shouldn't want you spoiled for that because you'd once had the best.

She started riding southward, past the village, intending to have a look at the tobacco crop her father had been following with such interest. But when she glimpsed Jack hoeing there, that project lost its appeal; instead, she headed into the woods and circled back toward the hills. Though she wasn't aware she had a conscious destination, somehow she wasn't surprised when she found herself nearing the cavern high in the cliffs.

She dismounted, tying Linzy to a tree where there was a patch of new green grass to nibble, and approached the cave on foot, loath to disturb the whispering silence of the surrounding wood. The rocks that had once blocked the hidden entrance still lay strewn across the ground where she and Cade had tumbled them on the night of the storm. She hadn't been back there since, and she was sure Jack didn't come to their childhood hideaway any-more. The ferns around the stones were furled in tight fuzzy croziers, and the moss grew thick and lush, more plush beneath her boots than the carpets in Suzette's gambling hall.

This was where it had all begun, the long downward spiral of griefs and deceptions. Or had it started even before that night of lightning and longing, perhaps in the stables, the first time she ever saw Gideon Cade? Tess leaned against a beech tree and closed her eyes, picturing that initial encounter, the way he'd knocked dung from his hat and cursed her roundly. He'd thought her a boy . . . She bit her lip, remembering that mistake. And then he'd blocked the gate to the stall, lounging against the jamb, half-smiling, looking her up and down with those strange blue eyes unlike any she'd ever seen before . . . Oh, God, what was the sense of pretending? She had been in love with him from that moment, wildly in love with his differentness, his exotic looks and alien manner, with the unspoken promise of dangerous excitement that lay in the taut curve of his mouth and the arch of his brow. Her fall from grace had been assured in that instant, as irrevocably and inevitably as Eve's.

There, she'd admitted it: she was in love with him. And what good would it do her, now that her father had mapped out her future with some antique Stafford widower? Cade had acquiesced in that future, she reminded herself, tears stinging her clenched eyes. If he'd shared her feelings at all, if he'd even wanted to keep her close by as his occasional lover, he would have told Ben to tend to his stables and just stay home. No, he'd made it clear enough; he didn't care about her at all. If only she could turn back time, return to before she ever knew him, when her yearnings were shapeless and dim, before she learned that the cause of her unhappiness had a face and a name.

Leaves rustled, and a twig broke somewhere nearby. Tess opened her eyes and saw Gideon Cade emerging from the cavern, hunched low to fit, his black hair tangled by the wind. As he straightened to his full height, he saw her as well, dark face registering his surprise. Tess had the impression it was not an emotion he was fond of displaying, for it was replaced at once with frosty indifference. "Well," he said. "You."

Tess had the dreadful feeling that he might be able to tell just by looking at her what she'd been thinking about; she began talking, hoping to fend off any such insight. "What were you doing in there?" She nodded toward the cave.

"I lost something here last summer. The night Satan broke free." He touched the throat of his shirt. "A cravat stick."

"And just realized it now?"

"It wasn't my favorite one. What are you doing here?"

"I was just riding." She gestured toward Linzy. "And I got tired. So I stopped. You didn't bring a horse, did you? How did you get up here?"

"I walked."

"Is the bay Dad picked out so awful?"

"Not awful, no. But Satan spoiled me."

Tess nodded. "He was the most splendid horse I've ever seen. You ought to buy yourself another."

"I don't find it so easy to simply replace something that I've lost," he told her, his jaw very tight.

"I didn't mean it would be easy." For some reason, Tess found she was blushing. "But it's got to be done. You can't go on walking for the rest of your life."

"I don't intend to. Set your mind at rest." There was a harshness, an edge of brutality to his voice that she'd never heard there before; it made her inch away.

"I had better be going. Did you find your cravat pin?"

"No."

She turned to mount Linzy. "Well. I'm sorry for the loss, I'm sure."

His strained voice stopped her with her boot halfway to the stirrup. "Why didn't you tell me that your father was ill?"

Not looking at him, hand clenched on the saddlehorn: "What do you mean?"

"When you came to me in London." The words burst from him, bitter, accusing, floodwaters through a dam. "Why didn't you just tell me? Did you think me such a monster that you had to buy my help with your body like a common whore?"

"I meant to tell you. I *tried* to tell you, but . . ."

"But what? You thought you'd make sure first I wouldn't turn you down by sleeping with me?"

"But you kept interrupting," Tess cried angrily as she turned to face him, "the same way you are now! You are always assuming you know everything, just as you assumed I was having a baby! Maybe if once in a while you'd listen—"

"We sat in that room for two hours," he said, his voice barely controlled, "we ate, we drank, we traded jests, and you never said a word to me about Ben being ill. So why don't you tell me what you were thinking?" He crossed his arms over his chest. "Go on. I'm listening now."

"I don't know what I was thinking! I was hungry and tired . . ." Tess squeezed her eyes shut, remembering what it had been like to be dressed in fine satins and silk in that handsome room. To see the admiration in his gaze, have him look at her as though she were the most beautiful creature in all the world and want to prolong the moment. "I was thinking . . . how good it was to see you again."

"The time's long past when I might have believed that."

She looked up at him, hands balled into fists. "Then I don't know what else to tell you, because it's God's truth."

"Oh, come on, Tess. The truth is, you used me that night in the cave to keep from marrying Jack, and you were trying to use me again. Christ, I pity that poor Stafford widower, married to the likes of you."

His words cut her like knives. So cruel his dark face was against the green trees, so hard and cold. "And I pity you," she cried, "a no-good crook, a swindler who fills up your purse with lead just so you'll look like somebody! You don't give a damn about any of us. I wish to hell you'd never come to Windber. I wish you were dead!"

He shrugged and smiled tautly. "Cheer up, Mistress

Jericho. That's one wish you can be sure will come true someday." Then he stalked past her toward the hill.

From the village below them the church bell pealed out, like a seal on their parting. Tess buried her face in Linzy's silky coat, sobbing as the mournful toll rang through the forest again and again. When Cade grabbed her arm and pulled her around to face him, her heart stopped beating; for one wild moment she imagined he had come to apologize, beg her to forgive him—

"What the hell does that bell mean?" he barked.

Disappointment, sour as vinegar, tartened her tongue. "It tolls the hour. What the hell did you think?"

"It's rung nine strokes already; would you have me believe it is nine o'clock?"

"Of course it's not . . ." Tess felt her mouth go dry. "Fire," she whispered as the bell's meaning struck her. "It means there's a fire."

Without even asking Tess's permission, he leapt atop Linzy, yanked Tess up behind him, and dug his heels into the pony's withers, urging her through the trees.

They could see nothing but the forest around them till they cleared the ridge below the cliffs; then all they could see was the smoke, great billowing gray clouds of it filling the dusk-violet sky. The bell was still tolling, and now they could hear shouting as well, as the tenants roused to the danger in their midst. "Where is it? Can you tell?" Cade demanded.

"No. There's too much smoke." Even as she spoke, though, wind swished through the valley, lifting the heavy gray veil, and for an instant she saw a heart of red-gold flame. "Oh, dear God . . ."

"What?"

"I think it's the stables."

Tess wouldn't have believed he could coax any more speed from Linzy, burdened with both their weights as she was, but he made her move faster, not with a whip or blows, but just by communicating his own urgency. When they reached the road, she was proud to find that their master's absence hadn't caused the tenants to panic. Mort and Jack had already organized a line of men to draw buckets from the well by the cottage and hurl water on the blaze that had engulfed the stables' old wooden walls.

"Jack!" Cade jumped down from the pony and ran toward the fire; he had to bellow to be heard above the crackling flames. "Where are the horses?"

Soot-stained, already soaked, Jack threw another bucket of water against the side wall, barely glancing up. "Still in there, sir. I'm sorry. We tried to get in to save them, but the smoke and the heat were too much."

Tess shivered, clinging to Linzy's mane, as through the roar of the conflagration she heard the animals screaming, high-pitched, terrified. The pony heard it too, and went white-eyed, bucking and bolting. "Meg!" Tess leapt down and handed the reins to the woman who'd come out to watch the disaster. "Take her and tie her someplace safe—up at the big house, or down by the tavern. I've got to go in there."

"Ye're mad, girl! 'Tis hell itself in those stables!"

"Just do as I say, Meg! I can't stand here and let them die!"

"I'll take the pony, Teresa." That was Widow Jonas, calm-eyed in the midst of the wild upheaval. "Just ye be careful."

Already stripping off her jacket and tucking her loose hair into her shirt, Tess nodded over her shoulder. "Don't worry. I will." As she approached the flames, she thought how glad she was Ben wasn't there, so he wouldn't kill himself trying to save the horses—and so he couldn't be blamed for the blaze.

Cade had dipped his jacket into a bucket; with it pressed to his face, he was trying to kick the stable doors open. "Did you lock these?" he bellowed at Tess as she came up beside him.

"Of course not!"

He kicked the burning wood again, sending up a hail of blood-red sparks. "Something must have fallen across them from inside . . ." With a sudden crash, they burst open to reveal a blinding inferno so bright that Tess had to shield her eyes as she stepped toward it. Cade caught her arm. "Where the devil do you think you're going?"

"To get the horses."

"The hell you are. Stay right here."

"But you'll need help! They know me better than they know you," she tried to argue.

"I'll go first. If I need you, I'll tell you." He pushed her back from the doorway. "Stay here! Mungo, hold on to her for me."

"Aye, yer lordship!"

Tess shook him off. "I'm not a bloody baby!"

"Then prove it," Cade roared, "and do as you're told!"

Holding the jacket over his head, he plunged through the doors and into the fiery madness. Right behind him, a rafter came crashing to the ground in a jumble of charred wood and flames. "Jesus!" Tess cried, jumping backward, smacking into somebody's chest—Jack. "Get back to the buckets!" she told him frantically. "You've got to put out the fire!"

"It's too late. It's hopeless." For the first time since he'd found her with Cade in the cave, there was something like sympathy for her in his hazel eyes.

"It can't be too late." But even as she spoke, Tess realized the horses had long since stopped screaming. There was a wrenching stench of burnt hair and meat in the acrid air. "Oh, God. Oh, no, please, no," she whispered. "All my beautiful babies . . ." Jack put his arm around her, squeezing her shoulders, as Mungo shouted into the furnace that had been the stables:

"Yer lordship! It's no use, ye'd best get the hell out o' there!" With Tess and Jack at his side, he tried to peer past the flames. "D'ye hear me, yer lordship?" Their buckets abandoned, the rest of the tenants crowded around. "Yer lordship!"

"Gor, he's a goner," Meg Mullen announced, her cheeks bright with heat.

"I'd best go in and find him," Jack said worriedly.

"Wot, are ye daft, man?" That was Backus, who'd been hanging well back from the blaze. "He's brought us nothing but trouble! I say let him burn."

"Aye, let him!" his wife echoed, her face pinched and cruel. "It's no more than he deserves."

"Hold on, there," Robbie protested. "Ye can't mean to let the man burn to death!"

"Why not? Why should Jack risk his life?" Missus Backus snapped. "D'ye think his bloody lordship would risk his for Jack?"

"All the same . . ." Jack frowned and wrapped his shirt over his head.

"Jack, for God's sake!" Millie ran toward him from the back of the throng, hands on her huge belly. "Don't! Wot about me, wot about our child?"

"Look there." The Widow Jonas' voice, clear and bell-like, cut through the hubbub as she pointed straight into the blaze. "He's coming."

"Just our bloody luck," Backus grumbled.

"Wot's that he's carrying?" Tim Whitaker wondered aloud, as Cade stumbled toward them through the flames.

"Must be a colt," said Mungo, "from the size of it."

There aren't any colts, Tess realized, and said it aloud just as the lord of Windber-on-Clun burst forth from the ruined stables, gasping for breath, a blanket-wrapped bundle cradled in his arms and a ragged, sooty hound dog close at his heels.

"Job?" Tess blinked as the hound bounded toward her, long ears singed bare. "What in heaven's name . . . ?"

"Stand back, everybody," Sam warned, "the roof's cavin' in!" Just then it did, with a thunderous, rumbling, shattering blast like the end of the world.

"Tess!" Cade was searching for her above the heads of the crowd. "Tess, come quickly! Over here!" As she moved toward him she felt the Widow Jonas touch her arm, a brief, wordless caress. I never knew she cared so much about horses, Tess thought, and then, seeing the blanket fall back from Cade's bundle, began to scream:

"Dad, Dad, Dad, Dad . . ."

Ben Jericho's eyes, glazed, unseeing, stared out from a face scorched by horror, branded by death. But his mouth moved, just barely: "Teresa . . ."

"I'm here, Dad." Fighting back a swell of nausea as she smelled his burnt flesh, she leaned her head close. "Dad. I'm here."

His charred, swollen lips moved again. "What did he

say?" Missus Backus demanded, trying to push closer to him. "Could ye hear wot he said? It's important, a man's dyin' words—"

"Shut up, you old cow," Mungo told her, and yanked her back. "Who says he's dyin'?"

"Why, you've only got to look at the poor maimed—Oh!" The tavernkeeper's wife stared, shocked by Sam's stinging slap of her cheek.

"Shut up!" he snapped, echoing Mungo. "Everybody stand back, give them room!"

But Tess had already caught her father's mumbled message, though she could have guessed it from the bleak, blind terror in his eyes. "Armageddon," that was what he'd whispered. "The Judgment Day."

14

Against all odds, Ben didn't die then and there. He was still breathing, ever so barely, as Cade carried him to the big house, insisting that a feather bed and linen sheets would be less likely to abrade what remained of his skin than wool blankets on the cottage cot. Tess trailed after them, listening mutely to the stream of orders Cade issued as he climbed the hill past the glasshouse. Jack was to ride Linzy to Stafford to fetch the best surgeon there, and take Cade's purse to pay him to come right away; Cade made him repeat the instructions five times before he left. Widow Jonas was to bring whatever ointments and lotions she had made up that might serve to treat burns. Oren was to see that the housemaids boiled all the bedding and let it dry outside as soon as the smoke cleared away. Missus Wallace was to make beef broth with plenty of marrow and parsley for Ben, and while that was cooking, a pot of strong coffee for Cade. On and on he went, scarcely pausing between directions, and all the while holding Ben more gently than a hen broods eggs.

No one questioned or interrupted him until, inside the big house, he started toward the staircase Tess had once climbed to find him in his bath. Then Prince Oren murmured, "Not your own rooms, surely!"

"Where the devil else would you have me take him?" Cade snapped, heading for the second story. "Go and look to that laundry, you bloody prig!" Seeing Tess standing uncertainly at the foot of the stairs, he nodded to her. "Mistress Jericho. Tess. Come this way."

Dazed, moving as though through water, she followed him to the upper hall and through a doorway. Inside was a sitting room furnished with comfortable chairs and a woven blue rug. Beyond that was his sleeping chamber, with a big square oak bed placed between two wide windows hung with indigo draperies.

"Can you pull back the bedclothes?" he asked.

When no one moved to his bidding, Tess realized he must mean her. Still moving clumsily, thickly, she tugged at the coverlet with both hands. It didn't move; her hands were useless and weak. "Never mind," he said. "Go in the other room and sit down."

"I've got to help."

"You won't help your father or me by fainting. Sit down."

Tess wanted to protest again, but Widow Jonas had come in behind her and led her to a chair, then pulled back the covers on the bed. Cade laid Ben down and stood by the widow's side. They were speaking in low voices. Tess tried to hear them, but the effort was too much; the words seemed to wash over her head. Everything around her smelled of smoke, of death; the stench clung to her hands and hair. She forced herself to concentrate on breathing, in and out, in and out, while her heart sang a desperate prayer:

"Let him live, God. Please. I'll do anything, just let him live. I'll even marry Tim's cousin, God, I don't care!" Then the horror overwhelmed her, and she closed her eyes and escaped into unconsciousness.

"Tess? Can you hear me?"

She opened her eyes and saw Gideon Cade standing above her, looking haggard and grim. The memory of the fire came flooding back into her mind, and she began to cry, pushing up from the chair. "He's dead, isn't he? I know he's dead—"

"No, Tess. He's alive. He's resting. Drink some of this." He held a cup to her mouth, and she tasted coffee, bracingly strong.

"Where is the doctor?" she whispered.

"Already come and gone. Take some more of this."

"I don't want any more. What did the doctor say?"

"I won't tell you till you finish your coffee."

Tess looked and saw that he was smiling. Surely he wouldn't be smiling if Ben was dying. Reassured, she drained the cup, grimacing at its taste. "Now will you tell me?"

"Do you want to go wash?"

"I want to know what the doctor said!" He sighed, squatting down by her chair, and Tess's heart sank. "It was bad news, then."

"The doctor wasn't much help, Tess. He said there wasn't anything he could do."

"Oh, God—"

"But Rachel thinks he might recover," he went on hastily. "She said we must keep the burns very clean—"

"Rachel? Who is Rachel?"

"The widow. Missus Jonas."

"Oh." How odd that he should know her proper name. Tess had never heard anyone else call her that.

"She's making up an ointment for Ben's burns. She really is one of the most remarkable people I have ever met."

"Widow Jonas?" Tess echoed, wondering if they meant the same woman. "Our Widow Jonas?"

He nodded, bemused. "She midwifes too, she tells me. And it's astonishing how much she knows about the plants around here. Windber's lucky to have her."

The widow and her herb potions were such a part of village life that Tess had never given them a second thought. Tess would never have put her on a par with a real doctor, like the one from Stafford. And yet Cade was willing to take her word over the doctor's. "I suppose she is good at what she does," she acknowledged. "Can I see him now?"

"It's not a pretty sight," he warned her. "His hands and face and chest were burned pretty badly."

"I don't care. I'm not afraid."

"All right, then." He got up and opened the bedchamber door.

The indigo draperies had been drawn, so she couldn't tell if it was night or day. An oil lamp flickered at the bedside. The linens were bleached white; against their pallor Ben's face was the color of copper-beech leaves. "Oh," Tess whispered, and swallowed hard, seeing his arms and hands. "Oh, God . . ."

"Rachel gave him something to help him sleep. He's not in any pain now."

Tess moved gingerly toward the bed. "Poor Dad." She kissed his forehead ever so gently. "Took your lashes and eyebrows straight off you, it did. Makes you look like a great huge baby. You won't much like that." His breathing was faint but steady, she noted, and the pulse at his throat moved steadily too.

"He was all the way in the back, by the hay bales," Cade said from the other side of the bed. "I'd never have known he was there if Job hadn't kept howling. The flames were all around them, but he wouldn't leave his master's side."

"He was supposed to be in Stafford until tomorrow! Why did he come back, did he say?"

"He wasn't really coherent. All that smoke—and he'd got a gash on the back of his neck. Rachel's dressed that too."

Tess scraped a bit of blood from the headboard with her fingernail. "What an awful mess he's made of your sheets—of your whole house. I'll take him back to the cottage as soon as I can."

"There's no need for that. I'm glad to have him here."

Tess's back stiffened. "Amuses you, does he? A country buffoon?"

"Not at all. I admire him for the same reasons I admire Rachel."

"And why is that?"

"They're both very good at what they do."

"He is good with horses, isn't he?" Tess said fondly.

"With the horses? Oh, aye. That too."

Tess blinked. "Why . . . what else does he do?"

"He's a father to you."

"Oh, well." She laughed. "How hard is that, anyway? Do you know, just last night he was telling me that he respected you."

"He didn't really say that." So dubious he sounded, and yet so pleased.

"Oh, aye, he did."

"Well." The lord of Windber-on-Clun was grinning like a boy. "I'm sure I don't know why he would. You've seen he's all right. Now, how about that bath?"

"I don't like to leave him—"

"Rachel said she'd sit with him while you cleaned up and changed."

"Then I had better go home."

"I had your clothes brought up here. And there's a tub already drawn right down the hall. I believe you know which room."

Tess could feel her cheeks flooding red. "I couldn't possibly."

"Why not?"

"Why, because . . . What would people say?"

He kept his face straight, with a struggle. "Mistress Jericho, please. There's sufficient excuse that I doubt even Meg Mullen's tongue will wag if you stay. And look, here's Rachel." The Widow Jonas had just entered the sitting room from the corridor. "You'll be our chaperon, won't you, Rachel?"

"Of course," the old woman said with perfect equanimity. "Go and bathe, Teresa, for the love of heaven. Ye stink."

Tess almost laughed, she was so giddy with relief. "Well, if everyone insists . . ." She started for the hallway, with Cade so close behind her that she bumped into him when she whirled around. "I forgot to ask about Job. Is he all right too?"

"Aye. And he's already had his bath." Gideon Cade reached down and brushed a strand of sooty hair from her eyes, his touch as gentle as spring rain. Then he pushed her toward the hall. "Go on and get yours. Rachel's quite right. You do stink."

"So do you," Tess said, and smiled.

That was how she came to stay in the big house. At first, frantic with fear for her father, she stuck like a burr to his bedside. But after the first few days Widow Jonas insisted on spelling her at night, and she gave in out of sheer exhaustion. Ben was so full of potion for the pain that he never woke up anyway. Tess slept in a bedchamber next to the sickroom, so she could be summoned quickly if anything happened. She didn't know where Cade was sleeping since he'd given his room to her father, and she rarely saw him—only in the mornings and evenings, when he came by to ask after Ben.

After a week had passed, the widow adjusted the strength of the potion. Ben's sleep became less deathlike; sometimes he stretched and groaned, though he still didn't respond to Tess's voice. On one of his nightly visits, Cade reminded her about Linzy.

"I've had her out in the pasture, but the fact is, she wants riding," he told her. "Not to mention that she looks glum. She misses you terribly."

"Poor girl." Tess kept her voice low, her chair hiked up to Ben's bed. "I wish I could take her up to the hills."

"Why don't you?"

"I can't leave Dad."

"An hour or so every afternoon wouldn't hurt."

Tess thought about it. "I suppose I could ask Meg or Lizzie or someone to come by."

"I'd stay with him," the lord offered.

"That's very kind," she told him. "But I know you've got enough on your plate, what with spring planting and the glasshouse—not to mention getting the fire cleaned up." She'd watched from the window that afternoon as Jack led a team of tenants in clearing the charred timbers of the stables away.

"I'd enjoy the break in routine. I mean it," he insisted, seeing her dubious expression. "It would give me a chance to catch up on some reading."

Tess remained unconvinced. "You've already done too much for Dad."

"It's no more than I'd do for any other man who nearly got himself killed trying to protect my property. What's wrong?" he asked then, seeing her crimson blush. Tess couldn't answer; she was still haunted by the question of why her father had been in the stables at all when she'd last seen him riding off to Stafford, still terrified that he might have been the cause of the fire.

Gideon Cade, standing over her, his eyes sky blue in the lamplight, touched her shoulder for an instant. "It couldn't have been his fault."

She looked at him, stricken. "How can you be sure? He might have been smoking—"

"No. He'd never in his life do anything that could have hurt those horses. You know that, don't you?" She didn't answer at first, and he asked again. She nodded uncertainly. "Good. Then you also know he'd want you to exercise Linzy. So it's all settled. I'll be back here to relieve you tomorrow at two."

He showed up on the hour, a book in his hand, and when Tess tried to renege, he refused to let her: "Go! Linzy needs you too. Don't fret, for God's sake; you're like some old mother hen."

"If something happens—"

"Nothing will happen! Go on, get out of here. That's an order." He closed the door in her face. Tess hesitated, knocked, and heard him roar: "Go *away*!" Smiling despite herself, she went riding—once around the corral. She was back within ten minutes—hardly enough time, Cade complained, for him to find his page. But he came back the next day, and the next, and each time Tess stayed away a little bit longer, and even began to enjoy riding again.

The first of May was a glorious day, warm and sun-drenched, all green grass and blue sky, and for once Tess didn't need any coaxing to leave Ben; by now she knew Cade would look after him properly. She rode all round the village, checking the progress of the crops, admiring the blossoms in the glasshouse, greeting the neighbors and reporting on her father's progress: the burn wounds were starting to heal over with new skin, though he still hadn't spoken and seemed in a great deal of pain. She was going to start back, but the White Moor beckoned, and she galloped up and then back down quickly, with Job, looking nearly cheerful for once, running at Linzy's side. Much as she relished the outing, she felt guilty by the time she returned to the big house, and even guiltier when she got to the sickroom and saw Cade's face. "Some-

thing's wrong, isn't it?" she guessed immediately. "What
is it?"

Her father was lying in much the same position as
when she'd left him, though the bedclothes seemed more
disheveled. "He's calmed down now," Cade told her,
"but before, when I opened the draperies to let in some
sun, he was talking."

"Talking!" Relief coursed through Tess. "Why, that's
wonderful news!"

"You don't know yet what he was saying. It was crazy
stuff about men on horses, and some sort of woman
monster with horns, and the world on fire—" He stopped;
Tess was laughing. "You think it's *funny*?"

She pulled her face straight. "No, no. Of course not!
But it is proof he's getting well. That's Dad's bad dream,
you see, of the end of the world. The Apocalypse. He
used to get it all the time when he'd had too much to
drink. That potion must be bringing it back to him, poor
thing." She ran her hand over the bandages binding his
forehead.

"Odd," Cade mused, staring down at the sleeping man.
"I wouldn't think your father had much reason to fear
the Judgment Day."

"His father was a preacher. I guess it's just bred in
him. And besides, we've all got our secrets." Tess chewed
her lip. "I've meant to thank you for not telling Dad
mine. About London, I mean." Images of their time
together there crowded her memory. Above the strong
smells of the sickroom, lotions and liniments and oils, she
had caught his scent, warm spice and soap, that always
made her heart beat fast. She moved to the foot of the
bed, straightening the linens to hide her trembling hands.

"He cares for you so much. I saw no reason to hurt
him," he said quietly. "Besides—"

He never finished what he meant to say. At that moment, through the open window, came a woman's voice,
bright and cheery, crying, "Yoo-hoo! Giddy! Come out
here, dear, I've a surprise for you!"

"Emilia?" Cade went to one window, Tess to the other.
She remembered the fancy carriage she saw below, and
the driver in the plum-colored suit, and the old woman,

wrinkly and small, who was peering through the open coach door: Lady Hardwick. "What the devil are you doing here?" Cade called down to her with feigned crossness. "Chester, how dare you let her come all this way?"

The purple-coated driver tipped his plumed hat. "Very nice to see you again too, your lordship."

Cade laughed. "It's beyond me why you put up with such saucy servants, Emilia!"

"It's beyond me how they put up with *me*! Who's that in the other window, Giddy?" The woman squinted up at Tess. "Oh, my, I never could mistake that hair. How do you do, Mistress Jericho? Do you suppose you might come down here, both of you? I am getting the most frightful crick in my neck staring up at you."

"B-both of us?" Tess echoed.

"Certainly, my dear. My little surprise concerns you too."

"We'd best do as she says, Tess. She's a very terror when she's crossed," Cade warned with a wink, and then shouted out the window again: "Hold tight, Emilia, we're on our way!"

Cade emerged onto the portico with Tess trailing shyly behind him. "Help me get your mistress out of that carriage, Chester," he called to the coachman, "and I'll carry you down to the glasshouse, Emilia, and show you your gillyflowers. Sorry they're not in bloom yet, but they're coming along most—"

"Oh, shut up, Giddy." Lady Hardwick poked Chester with a fan as he tried to obey. "You're always taking charge. Well, I simply won't have it today. I've already been driven all around your glasshouse three times, *and* had a look at those new stables you're building. Mistress Jericho, Giddy wrote to me that your father was hurt in the fire. I'm so very sorry. How is he?"

"He's better, thank you," said Tess, quite disarmed by the woman's breezy charm. "He even spoke today, for the first time since it happened."

"Did he? How splendid! It's a red-letter day all around." Lady Hardwick's clear blue eyes sparkled with glee. "I saw your Linzy, too, dear, out in the pasture as we drove by. I'm so glad she was spared. Still, it's quite dreadful, isn't it, to think of all the others dying? There have been nights I woke up from dreaming about it, and I declare, I was all a-shake."

"Well, you're not to dream about it anymore," Cade said sternly. "It's over and done with, and we've just got to go on as best we can."

"Aye, but how, that's the question!" Draped in bright patterned shawls, her ladyship leaned forward on the coach seat. "How can you go on when the only horse left you is Linzy? And that, my friends, brings us to my surprise!" She groped amongst her cushions, produced a handbell, and rang it sharply three times.

From around the far side of the big house appeared a plum-liveried horseman, sweaty and straining as he held to the reins. "*Voilà!*" Lady Hardwick cried, waving an arm as he made his way toward them.

"Aye, voy-la and bloody welcome," the horseman grunted, leaping down from the saddle at the earliest possible opportunity and tossing Cade the reins. "Don't know how ye ever handled this load of horseflesh, guv'nor, for I'm well rid!"

Lady Hardwick beamed. "There, you see, Gideon? I've bought Satan back for you!"

Stunned, unmoving, Cade stared at the huge black stallion. The horse stared back at him with wide velvet eyes, then let out a soft low whinny, ducking his heavy head, nuzzling his master's sleeve. Cade reached out and stroked his muzzle, and the horse nickered and pressed up to him, docile as a lamb, a lapdog craving a treat. Tess heard the lord of Windber-on-Clun let out his breath in a sigh.

"Emilia. You shouldn't have."

"Well, why not?"

Tess was so busy staring at the stallion herself that she scarcely caught the excruciated glance Cade cast her way before lowering his voice: "The expense . . ."

"Oh, hang the expense!" she cried gaily, taking no notice at all of his embarrassment. "What's money for if not to bring a bit of joy to the people we love? And when it comes to that, that fool Buckingham was as well rid of him as poor Chauncey here." She gestured toward the servant who'd so willingly relinquished the reins. "Why, Sebastian—you've never met my grandnephew Sebastian, have you? It was he who wrote to me that the Duke of Buckingham had a new horse, a huge black devil named Satan. I knew right away that it had to be yours, though I couldn't imagine why you would have sold him. Anyway, Sebastian says Buckingham got thrown the first five times he tried to get on the poor creature. No, Giddy, that horse was meant to stay right here with you! And I sincerely hope that the next time you find yourself short on cash you'll just come to me instead of doing something so rash."

Tess tore her gaze from the resurrected stallion to consider his master, who was—there was no other word for it—blushing, even as he caressed Satan's satiny nose, ran his hand over that ebony mane. "Emilia, I don't know what to say."

"Well, say thank you, hang it!"

"Thank you. But I can't let you do this. I'll want to pay you back."

"I won't hear of it. No, if you want to repay me, you might give me one of the colts."

"The colts?" asked Cade, still looking dazed.

"Aye, one of the colts you'll get when you breed her with Linzy! I can hardly wait to see what they'll be like, can you, Mistress Jericho?"

"Mistress Jericho decided a long time ago," Cade put in before Tess could answer, "that she didn't want—"

"That I didn't want Linzy bred to anyone," Tess interrupted him in turn, "if it couldn't be Satan." The grateful expression on Cade's dark face as he turned to her was so poignant that she wanted to cry. Instead she added, "And if I've anything to say about it, the first colt is yours, Lady Hardwick."

"Well, that's that," the noblewoman said briskly. "Now, if you'll excuse us, I've an extremely important bit of business to attend to in Stover's Mill, and I must be going."

"Rum cream cakes," the grinning coachman mouthed at Tess. Then he shut the carriage door and climbed up to the driver's box, with Chauncey close behind him.

"But you can't just run off!" Cade protested through the coach window. "Come in and sit for a while. Or at least let me show you the glasshouse!"

"No, thank you kindly; there simply isn't time. But do come and visit soon, Giddy. You know I'm much more comfortable in my own home, amongst my own things. Give my best to your father, Mistress Jericho. And mind you look after Satan, Giddy. I want my colt, come next spring!" With a jangle of her handbell, she set the carriage in motion, rolling back down the drive.

The clatter of wheels died away slowly. Satan whinnied and stamped, eyeing his master expectantly. From the pasture came an answering whinny: Linzy, silver tail swishing, welcoming home an old friend. Gideon Cade stood looking down at the pebbles under his feet.

"You should take him riding," Tess said softly. "I'll wager he missed you." Cade said nothing. She stroked the stallion's silky black flank. "Well, that's what I'd do if I were you, anyway. I'll go see about Dad." She gave the horse a final pat and hurried back inside.

Ben was sleeping soundly. Tess went to the window and looked down on the drive. Master and stallion were gone. Instinct drew her gaze to the White Moor, and she saw them there: a long-legged black spot against the pale earth and blue sky, going hell for leather, riding higher and higher into those beckoning hills.

15

"Anyway, Dad, there's the long and the short of it. God alone knows why he told us Satan was dead, for there that big black brute was, just as bold as day. And wasn't he looking glad to be back here at home—Satan, I mean, not his lordship. I'm going to give you just a bit more of this, now. Ready?" Into Ben's open mouth Tess poured barley-sugar water from the bowl of a spoon, then tipped his chin back so the sweet liquid would run down his throat. "Doesn't taste too bad, does it?" Her father's eyes were closed, and there was no indication that he heard or understood her, but she liked talking while she fed him; it reminded her of the conversations they used to have while they ate supper together in the cottage in days gone by.

"And one spoonful more. Rachel says . . ." She laughed, slipping the spoon between his lips. "That's what his lordship calls Widow Jonas, you know; now he's got me in the habit of it. Anyway, she says the most important thing we can do right now is keep you fed so as to keep up your strength." Behind her shoulder, the door to the bedchamber opened. "Well, speak of the devil, here she comes now!" she went on, not turning as she wiped Ben's chin. "Did you hear the news, Rachel? His lordship's horse wasn't dead after all; he'd just gone and sold it. Lady Hardwick bought it back for him and brought it round this afternoon, can you imagine that?"

"Rachel's on her way up. She had something to do in the kitchens."

Tess dropped the spoon, dribbling barley-sugar water

down the bib Ben wore. "Oh, Lord, sir, I'm sorry. You must think me an awful gossip."

Gideon Cade seemed to take no notice of her chagrin. "I stopped by to ask: if you haven't had your supper yet, I thought you might do me the favor of dining with me."

She gazed at him as he stood in the doorway. He'd come straight from riding; his shirt was unbuttoned at the throat, so she could see the curling black hairs on his chest through the linen. His breeches sat low on his hips above boots caked with mud. He smelled of leather and horseflesh, her favorite smells in all the world except for that spice scent he bore beneath. "That's very kind of you, sir," she said finally, "but I don't think it's such a wise idea."

"Why not?"

Why not? Because I'm afraid, Tess thought, afraid to be alone with you. Because the last time we supped together was in London, and just look where that led! She turned back to her father, unwilling to let her gaze linger too long on Cade's long hard body, those strong arms, his dark handsome face. "You know how people talk," was all she said.

"You told me they'd talk anyway if you stayed here. Don't you think we might as well give them something to talk about?" He must have seen the sudden tensing of her muscles, for, "I only meant that as a jest," he added quickly. "Don't you get tired of eating alone? God knows I do." The words were jocular enough, but there was truthfulness in his tone.

"I have my tray here with Dad; I don't eat alone."

"Well, I do, and I'm fair sick to death of it," he said with unaccustomed vehemence. "It's enough to make one understand why some men w . . ." He stopped, then finished: ". . . wind up talking to themselves." Why some men wed—Tess was almost sure that was what he'd started to say. He rushed on. "It's nothing fancy on the menu, mind you. But there are strawberries in cream for a sweet. I found a whole passel of them growing over in that patch by the White Moor today."

"And you picked them?" Tess couldn't help smiling at

the image of him cradling wild strawberries while he rode home on that black war-horse of his.

"I'm very fond of strawberries," he said rather defensively, and Tess felt love for him deep inside her, thick and hard as bone. "Will you, then?" he pressed, sensing her about to give way. "In the librarium, as soon as Rachel comes? I am starved." Then he frowned, looking down at his clothes. "Though I suppose for your sake I should bathe and—"

"It doesn't matter. You forget, I've lived all my life with the smell of the stables." On the bed by her stool, Ben suddenly stirred, plucking at the linens with his bandaged hands.

"Who's there?" he whispered, his voice so hoarse with disuse that Tess had to lean close to distinguish the words. "Who is it? Who's there?"

"Oh, Dad!" Tears sprang to Tess's eyes. "Oh, Dad, it's so fine to hear you talk again!"

"Who's *there*?" His eyes were closed; she realized that he couldn't see.

"It's me, Dad, Tess. And his lordship."

"Prince Oren?"

Tess glanced at Cade, embarrassed. "No, Dad. Not Oren. It's Lord Cade."

"Oren?" he said again, querulously.

"No, Dad, it's Lord Cade. Gideon Cade, who saved your life," Tess told him.

"Don't push him," Cade said quietly. "It's just the drugs Rachel gives him. He's still a bit muddled, I'd guess."

"But he's talking, just as you said!" Up to that moment, Tess had never admitted even to herself her fear that Ben might not recover. "He's going to be all right!"

"Why, of course he is," said Rachel, coming through the door. "Didn't I tell ye he would?"

"I know, but . . ." Tess beamed at her, then bent to kiss her father's forehead. "Oh, Dad, I love you so!"

Her words calmed Ben as if they were magic; he stopped pawing the bedclothes and lay still, his breathing quiet and even. "He'll sleep now," Rachel said crisply. "Ye two had best go have yer supper. Oren's layin' it out in that librarium.''

"Laying it out already?" Tess arched her own left eyebrow at Cade. He was so sure of himself!

He grinned back at her. "Shall we, before it gets cold?"

The room looked different from the last time she'd been there, when they'd shared breakfast. The shelves on the walls were filled with books. "Nothing so interesting as the ones at the Peacock, I'm afraid," he said, seeing her looking at them. "They're mostly works on horticulture and husbandry." Oren poured them wine, and then Cade dismissed the butler, serving the food himself: spring lamb, peas, a salad of dandelion greens. He raised his glass to her across the table. "Shall we drink to your father's recovery?"

The crystal glasses pinged as she touched hers to his. "And to the recovery of Satan," she said softly. "Why did you sell him?"

He shrugged, taking a bite of lamb. "The Duke of Buckingham saw him in the stables at the Peacock and offered a sum for him that only a fool would refuse. He seems to have more money than he knows what to do with."

"And you didn't have any, did you?"

"This lamb's quite good. You should try it."

"Lady Hardwick told me you'd planned to sell what you grew in the glasshouse. Once we tore it down, you didn't have any money and you had to sell Satan, is that it?"

"Emilia talks too much. When did she tell you that?"

"She came by right after the harvest tally. Only she said you wrote to her the glasshouse got hit by a hailstorm."

"It's no easy thing to admit that one's tenants have rioted against you. Nor, for that matter, that you haven't got any money. Won't you please try this lamb?"

Tess did so. "Delicious. Do you know what else Lady Hardwick told me? That you were a great mystery. No one knows who you are, where you came from."

"That's sheer foolishness. I came from London. Peas are one of my favorite foods; do you like them?"

Tess leaned her chin on her hand, head cocked to one side. "You *could* just tell me to mind my own business, you know."

"I like hearing your voice. Speaking of which, do you think you might call me Gideon, just when we're alone together like this?"

"We're never going to be alone together like this again. This is the result of a temporary lapse of reason on my part. I like peas too."

"Call me Gideon."

"I won't."

"Please. Just once."

She sighed. "Gideon."

He grinned. "It's a name your father would approve of, I think. Old Testament and all that."

"What would a rogue like you know about the Bible? Anyway, you are changing the subject again."

"I didn't know there was a subject."

"Well, there is. Where you came from."

" 'Oh, my Lord,' " he quoted from the story of Gideon, in the Book of Judges, " 'wherewith shall I save Israel? Behold, my family is poor in Manasseh, and I am the least in my father's house.' "

Tess shook her head at him, red-gold curls flying. "Is that supposed to be an answer? Why did you steal Windber from Lord Halifax?"

"I didn't steal anything."

"I beg your pardon. Go to court to win us, I mean. Such a godforsaken place as this!"

"It seemed as good a place as any. Why did your father settle here?"

Her green gaze widened. "What do you know about that?"

"Nothing at all, except that he's clearly not from hereabouts."

"How can you tell?"

"He talks differently. So do you. And he's got a different view of the world, hasn't he? More of an iconoclast."

"I don't know what that means," Tess admitted, blushing.

"Then it's good you asked me. It means he's willing to

work to change things to his liking. That he's not content just to make do."

Through the open window came the trumpet of a stallion, mighty and triumphant. Cade put his napkin down and went to look out; Tess came to his side. In a flood of pale moonlight, in the pasture at the foot of the hill, Satan and Linzy were coupled together, black and silver moving in a single graceful, thrusting mass.

"I took you at your word, what you told Emilia this afternoon," said Gideon Cade, staring out at the horses. "I was afraid you might change your mind otherwise. But no ropes. It was Linzy's choice this time."

Stallion and pony pranced, danced, ecstatic, in moonlight. "When you made love to me," Tess whispered, "were you just making do?"

"Never."

The swift fierceness of the answer took her by surprise. She leaned both hands upon the windowsill, faint with his nearness, his scent, desire coiling in her belly.

The horses in the pasture plunged and reared. Cade's fingers fluttered, birdlike, against her wrist and then circled it, pulling her toward him. "Tess . . ."

God, how had she ever lived so long without his touch?

As he seized her, she melted against him, body aching to fuse with his. He tore the pins from her hair, letting the fiery curls cascade over his hands while he pushed her smock from her shoulders and buried his face against her cool white flesh. "Tess, Tess." He had raised her into the air, into the shimmering moonlight, and crushed her to his loins so that she felt his manhood, hard and throbbing, press at her thighs.

One arm at her waist, he pushed her back into the deep windowsill, until she felt the chill glass at her shoulders. With his free hand he was scrabbling at her bodice strings, tugging them open so that he could reach her breasts. When his long fingers found her nipple, it was already taut and swollen; he sighed and shuddered and bent down to take it into his mouth, savoring her taste.

Head thrown back, hands clutching his shoulders, Tess parted her knees so that he stood between them, so that his manhood thrust at the gentle swell of her mound of

Venus. Groaning, he ground his hips against her while he sucked at her breast. She brought her legs up around his waist, drawing him even closer. He caught up her skirts, hiking them over her knees, running his hands over her thighs before he yanked open his belt and unbuttoned his breeches. His mouth covered hers; she heard his breath, wild and panting, as he pulled her drawers aside and thrust his manhood deep inside her, as far as it would go.

"Oh, Tess. Oh, Christ." There on the windowsill he drove into her again, hands clutching her buttocks beneath the tangle of her skirts.

"Yes," she whispered, clinging to him, meeting his thrust with a shivering sigh. "Yes, yes . . ."

His passion was cresting at a feverish pitch even as hers matched it; they were riding a wave so maddening-hot that all skill and finesse were forgotten, leaving only need. Feral as the horses, they bucked and thrust and came together in a blaze of fire more blinding than sun and stars and moon all merged into one. Then, as the afterglow pulsed through them and receded, they held each other tightly and gasped for breath.

He caught his first, raising his head, black hair in sweat-damp curls against his throat as he whispered hoarsely, "I'm sorry . . ."

"Are you?" Tess looked straight at him, her white breasts rising and falling above her disheveled smock.

He laughed, his member still hard inside her. "All right, I'm not. Yes, I am too. Because you deserve more than that, more time taken, more care."

"Sometimes, perhaps." She smiled, her green gaze sidelong beneath long sweeps of dark lashes. "And sometimes not. It's no insult, surely, to be wanted so."

"And . . . to want?" His sky-blue eyes challenged her to admit it. When she nodded, he kissed her, mouth against mouth, and cupped her breast in his hand. Within her sheath his manhood swelled and hardened; when he moved to withdraw from her, she sighed and followed with her hips, not letting him go.

"Oren will be coming back with those strawberries at any minute," he reminded her, even as his hands slipped to her hips again, lifting her against him. "He talked before, and he'll likely talk again."

"Let him say what he will." Tess twined her fingers through his black hair, pulling his head toward hers. For there in the moonlight, with her body wrapped around his, she had made her decision, irrevocable and sure: there could be no other man for her, ever. She would have him, come what may.

"Gideon," she said, and laughed, hands running over his smooth hard buttocks before she tilted back on the sill, opening herself to him like a full-blown rose. "Gideon . . ." He groaned his startled pleasure, caution forgotten in a rush of erotic sensation, and fell on her, hungry with need once more.

From that night on, Gideon slept in Tess's bed, and she slept curled against him. Each evening they supped together; each afternoon they rode Linzy and Satan into the hills. They made love in the cave, and under the broad canopies of trees, and in the tall grass of meadows; they made love in the streams that fed the River Clun, and on the hard-packed earth of the moors, cushioned only by lichen, and in the maize fields, while the tender green shoots waved above their heads and the songs of the men in the next acre over mingled with their cries.

Tongues wagged. Isolated as she was in the big house, Tess rarely heard them, but she saw the new way Oren looked at her, scornful yet lascivious, and knew that the women in the village avoided her assiduously. Once, going to Rachel's cottage for some herbs for an ointment, she saw Millie Brady sitting on her doorstep, dandling her newborn son. When Tess crossed the road to congratulate her, she tucked the boy behind her as though to shield him from some pernicious wind. Uncomprehending at first, Tess complimented her on the boy's bonny appearance. Smiling tightly, Millie accepted the compliment with a nod, then said venomously, "Aye, isn't he fine? And bears his father's name to boot—which is more'n yers will, ye slut."

Tess laughed and walked on. She didn't care. Why should she? She had her man, and he loved her. Oh, he might not say as much, not in so many words, but she knew it was so. She knew from the way he tore her clothes off when they were alone together, and shuddered and cried her name when passion boiled his blood. She could tell by how his hard blue eyes softened as he looked at her across the supper table each evening, and the way his hands would seek her, anxious and vexed, in the night as he slept.

Ben was healing; with every passing week his sores grew smaller, the new pink skin greater. He was talking more, too, though he still seemed to get Gideon confused with Oren for some reason.

Rachel seemed untroubled by any gossip she heard, and willingly watched Ben at night, though she could have had little doubt of where Tess was sleeping. And Gideon Cade loved her. How could any jealous old Millie Brady have disturbed Tess's utter happiness?

She and Gideon were in the glasshouse when he told her he was leaving. She spent time with him there in the evenings, watching him prune and pinch and primp the hundreds of plants he'd grown from seed or sent for from London to replace those that had been killed when the first glasshouse was torn down. She loved to see how gently his huge hands could move, severing a yellowed leaf or training a soft tendril to climb on twine. Sometimes they talked while he worked, but mostly they shared a companionable silence, with Gideon's lamp casting shadows as the sky overhead filled with stars.

"Mmm! What's that wonderful smell?" she asked on this night, as he opened the door onto some heavenly new sweetness.

He sniffed, then said, "Heliotrope. A kind of borage I'm trying. Do you like it?"

"It smells good enough to eat."

Gideon laughed. "The man I got the seeds from swore it smelled just like cherry pie."

"So it does!" Tess took a deeper whiff of the small purple flowers. "I think that's the best-smelling thing you've got in here."

"Just wait until the night jasmine blossoms."

"What does night jasmine smell like?"

"Like you." He stroked her gown between her legs. "Down here. The sweetest smell in all the world." Then he sighed and kissed her. "I am going away."

"Away! Away *where*?"

"London. Don't be cross, Tess."

Sure of her hold on him, she leaned close so that her breasts brushed his chest, and kissed him. "I won't, so long as you take me."

He groaned as her taut flesh pressed against him. "I can't."

Still teasing, still confident he could not mean that, she slid her fingers down his chest to his breeches buttons. "Why not?" she whispered, and began to stroke him, her touch by now so practiced that blood surged to fill his rod immediately. He laughed and thrust her hand away.

"*That* is why not, you saucy thing."

Tess pursed her mouth in displeasure. "I thought you liked me to touch you."

"Oh, I do." She smiled, reaching for him again, and again he pushed her back. "But when you touch me, I can think of nothing but you."

"I don't want you to think of anything but me."

"I'm afraid I must. I need money."

"But why? The crops are doing well," she protested. "Everything is doing well! Just last week Jack's dad sold the first lot of green peas over to Stafford and got two shillings, sixpence the bushel!"

"How do you know what he got for them?" he asked, half-annoyed, half-amused.

"Everyone knows everything about everything here in Windber-on-Clun. So you made nearly ten pounds!"

"Ten pounds isn't much of a cushion to sit on, Teresa. What if the summer rains come again? Or a drought? Do you want to go through another winter like that last one?"

"Well, then, why can't you take me with you?"

He laughed, chucking her outthrust chin. "Haven't I just told you? You're a dreadful distraction, Tess Jericho; when you're near me, all I can think of is getting you naked and into my arms. How would I ever get so far as to play a hand of cards, much less win one, knowing you were waiting for me?"

She stared at him, aghast. "Do you mean you are going to gamble with the profit from the peas?"

"How else would a no-good cowardly rogue make money?"

It took her a moment to realize he was only joking about being a rogue. "But what if you lose?"

"I won't," he said confidently. "I never do."

"But you could!" she objected. "If you need money, why don't you ask Lady Hardwick for it? She said—"

"I know what she said." Now there was irritation in his voice. "But I'm not in the habit of taking money from women. I prefer to earn what I need."

"It's a strange way of earning, I'd say—sitting in a little gold chair while a tart in a low-cut gown fetches you wine and tobacco," Tess said spitefully. "That's where you'll be going, isn't it? To the Peacock Inn?"

"Is that what this is all about? Mistress Jericho, are you jealous?" His eyebrow inched up, and his wide mouth twitched at one corner.

"Don't you laugh at me, damn you!"

Quickly he pulled his face straight. "I'm sorry. If it makes you feel any better, I can't afford the stakes at the Peacock. I don't gamble there."

"No—you just make love to the proprietress!"

"Suzette and I are . . . old friends."

"Oh, really? I must say, you pick a fine sort of women for friends."

"Mind what you say about Suzette." His voice had a sudden sharp edge. "You know nothing about her."

I know all I want to, Tess was about to say, but then bit the words off. Lord, listen to yourself, she thought; you sound as shrewish as Missus Backus. She'd always hated women who harped at their men; it seemed the quickest means she knew to drive them away.

"Tess," he said more gently, "don't you know what you mean to me? How lonely I was before I found you?"

Tess looked at him there in the sweet-scented half-darkness, and it was as though she saw him, truly saw him, for the first time. Beneath the dark good looks, those cool blue eyes, there lurked a man whose life was solitary, sad. How little I know about him, she realized with a start, of his family, his life before he came here, his innermost thoughts. What was it he'd said to her the night he asked her to sup with him? *Don't you get tired of eating alone? God knows I do.*

But this moment of insight wasn't enough to make her give in with grace. "Go on. Go to her, then," she said spitefully. "Go and don't come back for months and months, just like the last time. You don't care about me, about any of us here. It will serve you right if we tear your bloody glasshouse down again."

Something gleamed far back in those blue eyes. "Do you know why I wasn't here that night, Tess—the night you tore the glasshouse down? Because I asked your father whether I should be, and he said no. He said it wasn't the custom for the lord of the manor to be present at the harvest tally, that the tenants would resent it if I came. So I went to Lady Hardwick's."

"Ooh, that's a low thing, Gideon Cade," Tess cried, hands balled into fists, "to tell such a lie about a man when he's lying unconscious and can't defend himself!" But even as she rebuked him, she pictured her father as he'd railed against the new lord long months ago, after Lady Hardwick's first visit, and remembered what he'd said: *It's all of a piece . . . like having to ask if he ought to show up for his own harvest tally!* Ben had denied he ever said any such thing when she asked him about it. But she knew then, just as she knew now, that he had.

"That can't be! It would mean—" She broke off as the full impact struck her. It would mean Ben had led the tenants up to the big house that night already knowing Cade wouldn't be there. That he'd planned the uprising on purpose, charted every step right to the rocks they'd use to bring Cade's Folly down. "Oh, Dad," she breathed, the breach of a lifetime's confidence constricting her heart.

"It's hard, isn't it," the lord of Windber-on-Clun said quietly, "when we realize for the first time that a parent isn't all we thought he was?"

"Even if that's true, what you said," Tess shot back,

green eyes flashing, "it wouldn't stop me from loving him."

"I wouldn't want it to. The part of you that loves him so fiercely is the part that I . . ."

He stopped. It didn't matter; Tess knew what he'd started to say. *The part that I love.* Maybe he couldn't speak it, couldn't finish yet, but he would someday.

Shining with her newfound knowledge, she put her hands on his chest and smiled. "Go to London," she said again, only this time she meant it. His heart beat beneath her hand. "But mind you don't stay away so long this time."

His breath came ragged and fast. "Oh, Tess. A week, no longer. I swear it."

"A week's scarce enough time to get to London," she scoffed, "much less win a fortune at cards."

His mouth brushed her ear. "I'll ride like the devil and play like the devil," he promised, "to get back to you, Tess Jericho."

16

Tess couldn't believe how she missed him. Oh, she'd expected to be lonely at night, when she lay by herself in the big bed she'd grown used to sharing, her body aching for the touch of his mouth and hands. But she hadn't known that thoughts of him would occupy all her waking hours, that while she nursed her father, exercised Linzy, ate, washed, dressed, she would find herself waiting for his voice, turning in hopes she'd see him, wanting his company with a steadiness as deep and instinctive as drawing in breath.

It didn't help that she had no one to talk to about him. Ben was still lost in a haze between sleeping and waking, but she didn't dare speak to him of Gideon; Rachel said there was no way of telling how much he heard. She couldn't bring herself to discuss her feelings with the widow, either. Though the woman had to be aware of the affair going on under her nose, she never mentioned it to Tess. That left Prince Oren—hardly the sort with whom one would share secrets—and the rest of the house staff, which seemed to be under instructions from the butler to ignore Tess as much as possible, and Job and Linzy, who were good enough listeners but had little to say.

Rachel would take Tess's place by Ben's bed every afternoon so she could go riding, but even that couldn't take her mind off Gideon. Once, as she headed back to the big house from a trip up and down the White Moor, she reined Linzy in outside the propped-open door of the Swan. Gusts of laughter and loud talk greeted her: she could hear Sam, and Robbie, and Mort Brady. Even

Missus Backus' shrill voice had a certain nostalgic charm for Tess. It seemed like years since she'd been inside. I ought to pop in and let them know how well Dad's doing, she thought, and dismounted, hitching Linzy to a post by the door.

"Where d'ye think ye're goin'?"

Tess stopped just short of the door, turning to see Meg Mullen approaching. "I just wanted to tell you all, my dad's doing fine."

"Is he, now?" The woman's nose, thin and long as a shrew's, seemed to twitch as she looked Tess over. "Reckon that means he's still delirious."

"Why would you say that?"

"If he'd come to his senses," Meg hissed, "he'd have heard the news, and it'd kill him straight off."

"What news?" Tess asked, appalled.

"Wot news? Wot news? Ooh, you're cool, ain't ye? Aye, butter wouldn't melt on yer tongue!" She shot Tess a look rife with scorn. "The news his only daughter's prowlin' about the big house like a she-cat in heat, that's wot news!"

Tess flushed. "That's not true!"

"Oh, ain't it? What's wrong, missy-miss? Now yer light-o'-love's left ye, are ye comin' down here to steal honest women's husbands?"

"He hasn't left me!" she cried, and then, realizing the admission implicit in her denial, flushed even more. "And if you mean his lordship, he's not my . . . he's not what you called him."

"Oh, aye, aye." Meg cackled. "And roses ain't red. If ye'd a shred of common decency, ye'd be ashamed to show yer face round here. 'Tis the most brazen thing I've ever heard of in all my born days—carryin' on like that with your poor dad lyin' there on his death-bed."

"Dad isn't dying! He's going to be just fine, thanks to Gideon."

"So it's Gideon now, is it?" Tess hadn't imagined a human face could look as bitterly twisted as Meg Mullen's did. "Well, I reckon it should be, what with ye doin' yer shameless acts all over God's creation, right in plain sight where anybody might see ye!" Tess colored again.

Someone had been spying on them—or had they been seen the night of the full moon through the librarium window? Her own reaction infuriated her even more than Meg's tirade. The woman was making what she shared with Gideon seem tawdry and dirty, when it wasn't like that at all!

"Now, listen here," she said angrily. "Gideon Cade is a good man, a hardworking man who's trying his best to help everybody here in Windber-on-Clun. And the last thing he needs is for busybodies like you to fault him for matters that are none of your business!" She paused for breath, and in the pause Meg broke in, with a smile that was even more hideous than her scowls before:

"Oh, no one's blamin' him." Whatever Tess had meant to say slipped her mind completely; she stared. "Well, why should we?" Meg went on. "Ye can't fault a man for taking from a plate when it's waved right under his nose. No, ye fault the one wot's doin' the wavin'—'n' that means ye, missy-miss! I just thank God yer poor dad's too far gone to see the spectacle ye're pleased to make of yerself, not to mention yer poor sainted mother. Get on with ye now, and leave decent God-fearing folk to drink their ale in peace!" And she stormed into the tavern, where she was greeted by thunderous applause from the regulars—who, Tess realized belatedly, must have heard every word of the exchange.

She hesitated for a moment, torn between confronting the rest of her neighbors and just moving on, when out of the cool darkness inside the tavern she heard the voice of Missus Backus, sounding a hundred times more vituperative even than Meg as she cried, "Just let that harlot show her face in here; we'll teach her, won't we?"

"Wot'll we do?" asked Robbie.

"Why, we'll shave her head, like they used to do back in the old days to whores such as she!" This proposal was greeted by more cheers, so enthusiastic that they left Tess with little doubt her neighbors would carry it out if they were given the chance. Nervously patting her red-gold curls, she untied Linzy and started to ride off. Sam's gruff voice carried halfway up the street through the open door:

"Here, Backus, set up a round to his lordship. That man's a right ruddy genius, ye know. I never in my life seen finer crops than them we've got this year!"

That was all Tess heard before she moved out of earshot, but it was enough to make her wonder anew why it was that, just as when she'd been raped by Jack, she was getting the blame for what happened, and the man was getting nothing but praise.

That night, restless and sleepless, Tess paced back and forth in her room, avoiding climbing into her empty bed. She'd already offered to spend the night with Ben in Rachel's place, but the herb woman declined politely and firmly, insisting that Tess needed her rest. When that failed, she took a bath in the tiled room down the hallway, hoping warm water might lull away her loneliness. It didn't work. Oren was so unpleasant about heating the water tank in the kitchens below that the bath was chilly, and Tess's disinclination to linger was only strengthened by the memory of how she'd burst in on Gideon there and seen him naked. The picture rose up in her mind, so clear and real that the muscles in her belly tightened and her nipples turned hard. "This isn't getting me anywhere," she muttered, and dried herself off and went to her room.

Where was he tonight? At the Peacock, gambling? At the Peacock, with Suzette in a low-cut blue gown fetching him wine and feeding him choice tidbits? She pushed that vision, too, from her mind. She wished he'd never gone, that he'd taken her with him, that, like the London alehouse-keepers her father once told her about, who made all their customers check their weapons at the door, she could have had him leave his manhood behind. What if she was mistaken in believing he'd come back? What was she to him, really, but a pliant mistress? He could find plenty of women in London even if he didn't go to see Suzette.

The room had grown too small for her pacing; she went into the hallway. He loved her, though, she was sure of it. At least, he was beginning to, just a little. Then again, maybe he didn't. Oh, God, she thought, turning and starting in the opposite direction, she was going to drive herself mad. If only she didn't miss him so much! Abruptly she stopped pacing at his study. Was it her imagination, or could she catch his scent from within? She pushed open the door and smiled, breathing deeply. She'd been right. The whole room smelled of leather and spice.

In the moonlight that crept through the open draperies she saw a lamp on the desk. She went and lit it, then closed the door behind her, sealing herself in.

For a long time she just walked in the room, touching things she passed—a mud-stained jacket flung over a chair, a bootjack, the books on the shelves—thinking with pleasure: He wore this . . . his hands have held these. After a while she sat at his desk, her bare feet tracing two grooves that his heels had worn in the floorboards beneath. The long hollows made her realize how many hours he must have spent there, feet rubbing anxiously back and forth, in his first months at Windber-on-Clun, when everyone had been so horrid to him.

His pen sat on its stand, a fine lofty white feather. She ran her fingers along the vane, giggling to see it spring back into place. Beside it lay a stack of small scraps of paper; she leafed through them slowly. Notes he'd written to himself, some cryptic, some straightforward: "Chicken dung," one read, and another, "How about artichokes?" Still another was a reminder that Lady Hardwick's birthday was in July: "Send gillyflowers," it said, with a brief query at the bottom: "When is Tess's?" She smiled, considering adding on the answer, but thought she'd better not.

When she'd gone through the notes, she opened the top drawer of his desk. Inside lay stacks of his cream-colored writing paper, sticks of sealing wax, and his signet, a plain round C. Not so handsome as Lord Halifax's splendid curlicued H that he used to stamp papers with, Tess thought curiously.

The second drawer was stuffed with sheets of paper on which he'd drawn plans for buildings. There was the glasshouse, all marked with arrows and measurements to show how it fitted together, and the new stables, and another structure too. "A manor house," Tess said aloud, examining the sketches. Only these weren't finished; they looked as though he'd just been jotting down ideas.

In the third drawer were piles of letters. Tess shoved it closed, not wanting to read his private correspondence. The last drawer was full of documents, official-looking sheets of heavy oyster-white vellum written in Latin. From the bit of that language she'd learned from her father, she gathered they had something to do with the transfer of the estate. All the way at the bottom of the pile was a document with the name "Suzette Marie-Louise de la Mare" penned across it in gorgeous script. There was another name on it too—James Anthony George Trelawny. Tess looked at the paper more closely. She knew what it was; she'd seen others like it in the big book at St. Jude's Church, where the business of the village was recorded. A marriage certificate.

She was about to pull it out of the drawer when the door opened behind her. "I noticed the light," Prince Oren said as she whirled around. "And since this is his lordship's *private* study, I took it on myself to investigate. Are you looking for something in particular, or just spying?"

He really was a nasty man, Tess thought as she shook her head and shut the drawer. "No. I just came in because I missed him. Because this room reminds me of him."

"I'm sure."

Tess laughed. "I don't suppose you would understand that. I doubt you've ever been in love."

"If I ever did fall in love, it wouldn't be with someone above my station," he said cuttingly.

Tess got up from the chair. The spell of the room was broken; instead of smelling like Gideon, it stank of the butler, of oily pomade.

"Nor with someone beneath you, either, I suppose," she said sweetly, "which leaves only female butlers. And since I've never heard of one of those, that explains why you're a dried-up old bachelor, doesn't it? Good night." She swept past him and out the door. At her back she heard him mutter something that sounded like the word "whore." She ignored it and went back to her room whistling cheerfully. Nothing could damp the rise of her spirits that had come when she learned that Suzette, her auburn-haired nemesis, was already married. Now she was certain that if she could just be patient, Gideon Cade would wed her eventually.

Ben woke up the next day.

Tess was sitting by his bed, taking up the hem of a skirt she'd made from a length of deep green serge that Rachel had presented to her, insisting she'd never use it. After some protest, Tess had taken it; she would be glad to have something new to wear for Gideon when he came home. She was concentrating hard on keeping the stitches small and straight—needlework had never been her strong suit—when she heard her father say, "The time—what's the time?"

She didn't even look up from her sewing; over the past two months she'd grown used to his unconscious ramblings, the snatches of conversations from his dreams that he mumbled aloud. "Hush, Dad," she said in the same soothing tones she used to talk to Linzy, and then licked her thread.

"Dang it, lass, I asked you a simple question," he snapped, "and I expect to get a civil answer! What time is it?"

Tess's new skirt slid from her lap to the floor as she stared at him and saw his blue eyes were wide open. "Dad?"

"Well, who the devil else would it be?" he asked crankily. "Are you going to tell me the time or not?" He went to push his hair from his eyes and blinked at the bandages wrapped round his hands. "What's this here?"

Tess rose from her stool and backed away from the bed toward the sitting-room door. "Rachel!" she called, her voice so faint and shaken that she had to shout once more: "Rachel, come here!"

"What about the time?" Ben demanded.

"I don't know, Dad! One o'clock or half-past or something. Rachel, please come quick!" she cried again.

"Afternoon or nighttime?"

"Jesus, Dad, what does it matter? Rachel!" At last Tess saw the herb woman hurrying toward her. "See what's happened!" She pointed to Ben.

He was trying vainly to pull the covers up around him. "Get her out of here! Can't a man have a bit of peace in his own danged cottage without nosy neighbors poking their heads in?" Then he noticed the canopy over his head, and his eyes turned suspicious. "Say, where am I, anyway?"

Unlike Tess, Rachel didn't seem one whit surprised by this sudden resurrection. "Hello, Ben," she said calmly. "You're in the big house. How d'ye feel?"

"Sticky," he announced with a grimace. "I feel all sticky. Like someone's rubbed me with honey."

"Someone has," the herb woman told him. "Twice a day for the past nine weeks. How many fingers am I holding up?"

Ben snorted. "What, are you daft? Three. What's all this nonsense about honey?"

"Dad, don't you remember—?" Tess began, but Rachel silenced her with a wave of her hand.

"Ben, what's the last thing ye remember?"

"Your asking me how many fingers you were holding up. Look here, Tess, what's going on?"

"Before that, Ben," Rachel went on. "Before ye woke up just now and saw Teresa. Tell me what ye remember."

"Is this some sort of game?" he asked. Both women shook their heads. "Well, then, have I been drinking?"

"Just try, Dad," Tess urged. "Tell us what you remember."

He paused, started to speak, stopped. Tess watched anxiously as his clear gaze seemed to cloud over. "I must have tied on a good one," he said finally, looking shamed. "What's happened to me? I can't remember anything at all."

"Oh, Dad." Tess went to the bedside. "You've got to remember. You—"

"Ye was goin' to Stafford," Rachel broke in, "to see Tim's cousin."

"Was I?" He pondered that for a moment. "Well . . . maybe I was."

"But you never made it there," Tess started to remind him. "You came back, and—" Now she stopped, for the widow had put a warning hand on her shoulder.

"Don't rush it," she said in a low voice. "It will come back to him. All in good time."

Ben heard the last word and seized on it. "Aye, the time! That's just what I was trying to find out, only Tess won't tell me."

"Half-past one in the afternoon," Rachel said.

"There! Half-past one!" He looked at Tess in triumph. Then his eyes closed, and he began to snore.

Tess pulled Rachel into the sitting room. "What's wrong with him? Has he gone crazy?"

"He's had a frightful shock, Teresa. The mind's a right peculiar thing, ye know. Sometimes when it can't bear thinkin' about somethin', it just closes up and pretends like it never went on."

Tess pondered that for a moment. "He'll get his memory back eventually, though—won't he?"

"Most likely," said the widow. "But ye've got to be patient with him. It's just like a horse that's been sickly; ye wouldn't expect it to get up 'n' gallop straight off, would ye? No, ye'd let it start slow. Now, he's bound to ask questions, 'n' when he does, ye 'n' I will answer 'em. But there's some questions only he can answer. We'll just wait and see."

He woke again later that afternoon and called for his pipe. "Oh, Dad, you can't mean it!" Tess said, dismayed.

He glared at her from the bed. "Why shouldn't a man enjoy his pipe when he's feeling sickly?"

"I should think smoking a pipe is the last thing you'd want in the world, after . . ." Tess stopped, thinking of the widow's cautions.

"After what?"

"Nothing," said Tess, and went to the cottage to fetch it for him.

But when she put a taper to the packed bowl he held in his mouth, his eyes turned distant again, and he gestured for her to take it away. "What are these bandages for?" he asked, contemplating his hands.

"Burns," she told him.

"How did I get burned?"

"There was a fire."

"Where?"

How can you have forgoten? Tess wanted to cry, but instead said simply, "The stables."

"The stables . . ." He shook his head, uncomprehending. "Was anyone hurt?"

"Only you."

He lay back on the pillows, closing his eyes, but a moment later he looked up again. "The horses?"

"We've still got Linzy. And Satan too. Lady Hardwick brought him back," she said brightly. "How about another try at that pipe?"

"Just Linzy? Where are the rest?"

Tess couldn't bring herself to say it, but he must have read it in her eyes. "Jehovah in heaven," he whispered, and turned his face to the wall.

That was how it went for the next few days. When Ben slept, there were no more incoherent ramblings. While he was awake, he asked Tess and Rachel questions: How had the fire started? What was in the ointment they spread on his face and hands? Who'd spotted the blaze? Why hadn't someone saved the danged horses? It was in answering this last one that Tess told him Gideon Cade had saved his life at the risk of his own.

"Did he?" She watched as he digested that information, saw he looked pleased. "The lord himself, was it? Well, no one can fault the man's courage. Didn't I tell you I respected him?"

"It was his own suggestion, too, to bring you here to the big house," Tess said eagerly, delighted by this proof of her father's approval.

"Was it, now?"

"Aye. And do you know what Gideon told me?"

She knew at once she'd misspoken; Ben's gaze was as sharp as ever. "Gideon, is it? Since when do you call his lordship by his Christian name?"

Tess forced a laugh, reaching for his broth bowl to hide her fluster. "Oh, I don't. Not to him, I mean. I've just got in the habit since . . . well, you know. Since I've been staying here."

"Hmph," Ben Jericho said. "And just why is it you are staying here?"

"Why, to look after you." She held out the spoon to him. He took the broth and swallowed, his eyes never leaving her face.

"What did his lordship tell you?"

"I beg your pardon?"

"You said: did I know what he told you."

"Oh." Tess fed him yet another spoonful of broth. "It was just . . . that he respected you too."

"He'd best hope he does," said Ben, his voice thoughtful indeed.

17

Now that her father was conscious again, Tess faced a new problem. From time to time his friends had been stopping by, asking to see him. Rachel had taken the matter out of her hands so far, declaring bluntly that Ben was too sick for visitors. But now there wasn't any reason why Sam and Robbie and Mungo shouldn't come—except for Tess's reluctance. She was sure they'd tell tales about her and Gideon. Even if Ben's best friends were too kind to distress him with gossip, once she let them come, how was she to put off Meg Mullen or anyone else? She had a sense that the cat was out of the bag for good now, and wasn't about to be put back in.

Still, on the sixth day after Gideon's departure, when Rachel told her Mungo had renewed his requests to drop by on the morrow and that she thought it would be good for Ben, Tess found she'd run out of excuses. "But let them come in the morning," she argued, "so he won't get tired." At least that way she'd be present; if Ben's mates wanted to tell her father she was sleeping with the lord, they'd have to do it with her looking them in the eye.

The next day dawned overcast and gloomy. As Tess brought Ben his breakfast, he grinned, head turned to the windows that were glazed with a hard steady rain. "Good for the crops, eh?"

"Aye, I suppose so." But Tess's spirits sank lower with each weighty drop that skittered down the panes. Gideon might have promised to return that day, but anyone riding in such weather risked catching the ague, not to mention falling and breaking his neck. She wouldn't want

him to take any chances, even to keep his word to her.
And yet . . .

"Are you going to feed me that porridge or not?"

"What?" Tess started from her reverie to find him
hungrily eyeing the bowl that she held. "Oh. Sorry, Dad.
Here."

He swallowed a mouthful and smiled. "That's all right,
pet. Rainy days were made for dreaming, weren't they?
My, that's good gruel."

By noon Tess had to face the fact that the rain showed
no sign of abating. Mungo and Sam braved the downpour
to be admitted to the sickroom by a pained-looking Oren.
Tess's stomach churned as she saw them; they nodded to
her and stood by the bed, stiff and awkward, their muddy
boots making puddles on the rug. Ben felt no shyness.
He beamed in delight, expansive as some Eastern pasha
as he greeted them from his nest of pillows and bandages: "Mungo! Sam! Good to see you again—and both
as ugly as ever. Tess, bring chairs for my friends. Both of
you, sit down!"

"How're ye feelin', Ben?" Mungo asked when they'd
both perched on the very edges of the chairs Tess fetched
them.

"Why, fit as a fiddle! 'Course, between Rachel and
Tess, I've had the best care in the world. Oh, except that
they won't let me drink ale. I don't suppose either of you
happened to sneak me in a pint?" He laughed as they
exchanged uncertain glances. "There, I'm just jesting!
I'm more starved for news than for drink. What's going
on in Windber? What's the gossip about?"

There was a brief uncomfortable silence. Then, "Millie
Brady had her baby," Sam offered.

"Did she? Girl or boy, was it?"

"Boy," Sam told him. "They've named him Thomas.
For Jack's granddad, ye know."

"You don't say. I thought maybe they'd call it Andrew
if 'twas a boy. For Lord Halifax."

Mungo grunted. "More likely they'd name it Gideon
these days."

"How's that, Mungo?"

"Why, his lordship's come up quite a bit in estimation

lately. Crops is all growin' like topsy. 'N' he's a right hard worker, he is."

"Got some bright ideas, too," Sam put in. "Odd, mind ye, but bright."

Tess watched as her father nodded in satisfaction, leaning back on his pillowed throne. "He'll be the best thing ever happened to this village," he announced. "I've known it from the first moment I clapped eyes on him. These are new times we live in, my friends! And it takes a new sort of lord to keep up with the times. Don't you agree?"

Sam blinked. "Ye used to say he was the devil."

Ben laughed. "You don't really think I believed that, do you? Faith, I was just having you on! The devil—why, the man's a ruddy prince! Didn't he risk his own life to save me from that fire? And didn't he take me into his own house in my time of need—aye, take me into his very own bed? Not to mention Tess."

"Tess?" Sam said quickly—too quickly. She flushed, feeling his gaze slant toward her, and Mungo's as well.

"Aye, he's put her up too! Why, we're both living here like a couple of nabobs, aren't we, lass?"

Feeling like the worst kind of traitor, Tess went to fluff the pillows at his head. "Mind you don't wear yourself out, Dad, with all this talking."

"You see how she looks after me?" Ben appealed to his friends. "How could anyone ask for a fonder daughter?"

Tess's hands were still shaking an hour after the visitors left.

When Rachel appeared to spell her that afternoon, she declined to leave. "I can't ride Linzy in this awful weather," she gave as her excuse, but the real reason was her terror that other, less discreet guests might come to see Ben. "Besides, I'm in the middle of reading to him. Aren't I, Dad?"

"We can both stay, then," said the widow. "I'm in no hurry to rush back out in that rain." She settled into one of the spare chairs. "And I like being read to, too."

That's where they all were still, with Tess reading the Song of Solomon, when the sitting-room door opened behind them. " 'Set me as a seal upon thine heart, as a seal upon thine arm,' " she read, " 'for love is strong as death.' " Then she smelled rain and spice at her back, and knew he'd returned.

"Tess."

She turned, meaning to caution him that her father had awakened, but found she could not speak when she saw him, so full was her heart. He was dripping wet, his black hair plastered to his head, his boots slippery with mud—he hadn't even stopped to take off his cloak, she realized, touched by this proof of his haste.

"Well, yer lordship," said Rachel. "Welcome home."

"Hello, Rachel," he said, his eyes never leaving Tess.

"Ben, his lordship's come back," Rachel noted.

After the way her father had carried on to Sam and Mungo about the new lord, Tess would have expected him to hail Gideon as a hero. But he was strangely silent as he considered the tall, sopping man who was staring at his daughter so fixedly.

"Dad's waked up, sir," Tess told her lover.

"So I gather." He tore his gaze from her to greet her father. "It's fine to have you back with us, Jericho."

Ben inclined his head. "I owe you thanks." Tess glanced at him. Why did his voice sound so stiff and cold? Then she looked at Gideon, and it didn't matter; nothing mattered, only that he had come back to her.

"Best get out of them wet things," Rachel chided her master, "afore I've got ye to nurse too. Teresa, why don't ye go see about yer father's supper?"

"I'm not hungry," Ben said shortly. "I'm tired. I want to sleep."

"All right, then, we'll leave ye. Come along, ye two, and give Ben some peace." Tess could have embraced them both—her dad for being weary, and the widow for suggesting they go. She was trembling with anticipation, aching to taste his mouth, feel his hands on her breasts . . .

"I'll be back later to say good night, Dad."

"Don't bother. I just want to be alone."

And Tess was so filled with excitement she didn't even think that queer.

Somehow they made it out of the room without touching each other. Rachel said she'd be in the kitchens; somehow they bade her good night and saw her off downstairs. And then somehow they were in Tess's room, and she was in his arms, and he kissed her, and she was crying, crying with joy and the awful force of her love for him.

"I've been thinking of naught but this moment for the past seven days," he told her, his mouth at her ear.

"Then you'll have lost at cards."

"I never lose." He backed her onto the bed, pulled out his purse, and let a hail of coins cascade onto her lap. Her eyes went wide.

"Good Lord, Gideon! How much is here?"

"Nearly a hundred pounds."

"It's a bloody fortune!"

He smiled at her awe. "Hardly. But it's enough to be sure no one in Windber goes hungry this winter, whatever the harvest brings." He traced her cheekbone with his fingertip. "I only wish there were more. Then I'd drape you with emeralds to match your green eyes and your new green gown."

She blushed, pleased that he'd noticed. "I've no need for such stuff."

"Not to make you more lovely, no. Nothing could do that. Just to show . . . I said some terrible things to you, Tess, in the past. I hope to God you know I didn't mean them. That you are more important than anyone else in all the world to me."

"Oh, Gideon." Her tears spilled over; she threw her arms around him, holding him tight. "I'm just so glad you're home!"

"It feels like home," he whispered, "now that I've got you here." He grinned and plucked at her bodice buttons. "Let's get you out of this."

"Don't you like it?"

"It's exceedingly becoming. I just like what's inside it even more."

"Wait." Tess pushed his hands away. "Swear to me you didn't see Suzette."

"Swear to you . . ." He made a horrible fierce scowl. "Tess Jericho, how dare you even think that I would."

"Then you didn't?"

"I'll vow up and down on a stack of Bibles that I never felt for Suzette what I feel for you."

"And what's that?" she teased still holding him off.

"The most desperate longing." He fell on her, sending crowns and shillings flying. "Oh, Tess . . ."

He made love to her like a man crazed with passion, furious and fast, driving inside her and exploding in a burst of flame. After that he took her again, but this time with such slow, maddening deliberation that she shuddered and clung to him and begged for release. When Oren knocked with their supper, they sent him away; they feasted on lovemaking, gorged on each other, rising again and again to the summit of ecstasy, until, toward dawn, they fell into numbed, satiate sleep.

It would not occur to Tess until a long time later that he never had sworn what she asked him to.

"So."

That was what Ben said the next morning as Tess, out of breath, belated, hurried into his room with the breakfast tray.

"So?" She laughed, still glowing, every muscle in her body aching delectably. "So what? What do you mean, so?"

"I recollect now why I was going to Stafford."

"Do you? Oh, Dad, that's fine! See, it is all coming back to you in bits and pieces, just as Rachel—"

"Sit down, Teresa."

"Just let me butter this toast—"

"I said sit down!"

Taken aback by his tone, she sat. "My, aren't we in a temper this morning!"

"And don't talk to me as though I'm some sort of idiot. I haven't gone blind."

"Well, of course you—"

"I suppose I was the last to know."

Tess paused. "Know what?" she asked finally, cautiously.

"Come, lass, I just said I'm not blind! Do you think I couldn't see the way you looked at each other last night? That you've become his concubine." He spat the word out as though it were poison.

"But I thought you liked him! Why, you were telling Sam and Mungo just yesterday—"

"You can respect a man for his way with crops without wanting him to tup your daughter!" His bandaged hands balled into fists. "Don't I feel the right ruddy fool. All laughing at me in the village, are they? 'Poor Ben,' is that what they're saying? 'Lying sick abed while his daughter whores about under his nose!' "

"Who cares what they say?" she cried, green eyes flashing. "They're nothing but a bunch of old busybodies, and I hate them all!"

The anger flowed from him so suddenly, like air from a pricked wine bladder. He closed his eyes, looking weary and old. "I recollect, too, why I turned back from Stafford. Because of all you mean to me, Teresa. I couldn't make you marry Tim's cousin knowing it would make you unhappy. And so long as there wasn't any chance of your taking up with Cade . . ." The hitch in his voice was so sharp, as though his heart were breaking. "But you lied to me, didn't you?"

"Dad, I—"

"That's what he's done for you, Tess—made you a whore and a liar. And I . . . I wish I'd died in that fire."

"Don't say that, Dad!"

"Jehovah help me, I mean it."

"I love him, Dad," she said helplessly. "I love you, but I love him as well."

"And what will that get you when he takes up with another?"

"He isn't like that, Dad! He loves me too!"

"Ah. He loves you too." The words were heavy, ironic; there was a world-weariness to him that Tess had never seen before, and it frightened her. "Asked you to marry him, has he?" Tess didn't answer, and he laughed shortly, coldly. "So I thought. Never yet known a man to pay for what he gets for free."

"What would you know about love?" Tess demanded, striking out blindly, cruelly. "A dried-up old sot who's had only one fling in his life—and that with another man's wife!"

"Shut your mouth, Teresa!"

"You're a fine one to judge who's faithful, aren't you? How faithful were you to that great lord you served? The one who treated you like his own son—"

"Shut up and get out!"

"The one whose wife you lay with time and again, day after day!"

"Teresa!"

"Oh, I forgot—she forced you into it, didn't she? How did she manage that, Dad? Hold you down, did she? Put a knife to your throat?"

He looked pitiful, shaken. "You know nothing about it!" he cried, spittle flying from his mouth.

"I know a Pharisee when I see one. Don't tell me how to live my life when you've only made a mess of yours."

"Now, you listen to me!"

But she steeled her heart against the pain in his voice and stood up. "No, Dad. I'm through listening. If loving Gideon makes me like my mother, so what? I'd sooner be like her than be a bloody old hypocrite like you."

18

There had never been such a summer in Shropshire. It was as though earth and sky teamed together to compensate in three short months for all the miseries they'd visited on the county's inhabitants since time began. The sun shone nearly every day, but never too hotly; the nights were balmy and breezy; the rains, when they came, were warm and gentle, with never a hint of storm. It seemed the soil itself had changed, that overnight some invisible giant had plowed the hard, rocky crust the local farmers had spent their lives fighting against, leaving a soft, rich loam as fine as any found in fabled Sussex and Essex, where (they'd heard) a man never needed a hoe. The laziest of lazy Shropshiremen could not complain of his life that year.

Nowhere was the miraculous weather more remarked upon than in Windber-on-Clun. Accustomed to the need to hack away at the tough, stony ground from sunup to sundown, Mort Brady and his son Jack and the others found themselves suddenly in possession of the strangest of luxuries: spare time. Without guilt they stood about in the evenings watching the sun set; their wives met them in the fields at midday, children in tow, for leisurely meals of roast chicken and pie. Mungo jested that the following spring would see such a bevy of new babies they should have to incorporate into a town, and he may have been right. For although business was brisk at the Swan, nearly everyone headed home by nightfall. The weather was simply too fine to miss a moment of it with bloodshot eyes and a muddled head.

Among those gathering at the tavern each evening was Ben. Once he'd come out of his fog, his recovery had been astonishingly quick. By the first of July he was sitting up unaided; by the middle of that month he'd taken a few steps; and early in August he'd moved back to the cottage by the well. If by leaving the big house he'd hoped to curtail Tess's liaison with his lordship, he was doomed to disappointment. Though she showed up to cook her father's meals and do his laundry, she spent her nights with Gideon Cade.

It was to Cade that the tenants credited the weather. Oh, they praised God too, on Sundays, with the pastor's prompting. But the rest of the week, all glory went to the hero who'd saved Ben, brought potatoes and maize to Windber, and got the pigs fat enough that they all had bacon with their morning porridge whenever they pleased.

As for Tess, if she'd hoped time would soften Ben's heart toward her, she was doomed to disappointment too. He was civil enough when they ate together in the cottage; he thanked her for the washing and mending she did. But he seemed so formal, so removed, that she felt more like hired help than his daughter, and when she bade him sleep well each night before she headed back to the big house, he never said a word in reply.

She tried to tell herself that so long as she had Gideon, what Ben thought of her didn't matter. But it wasn't so easy as that. A lifetime of seeking her father's approval couldn't be forgotten in weeks or even in months, and as she left the cottage every evening, she felt the weight of Ben's displeasure like a heavy hand. She longed desperately to confide in Gideon, but didn't dare for fear he would think she was angling for marriage; her pride demanded the first mention of that should come from him. And so her unhappiness grew and grew, tangling around itself like one of the lush twining vines in the glasshouse, until she met Gideon there one night in the long summer twilight and burst into tears.

"Here, what's this?" he asked, tilting her chin up toward him.

"N-n-nothing." And another torrent of tears burst forth.

"My Tess doesn't cry for nothing. Was someone from the village cruel to you? Was it Meg Mullen?"

Tess shook her head, surprised he was even aware of the cold shoulder the tenants gave her. "No . . ."

"What, then? Tell me, pet."

She might have regained her composure if he hadn't used the same endearment Ben so often did. "It's Dad," she confessed.

"My God. Has he had a relapse?"

"No, no. It's nothing like that. It's just . . ." Her fragile equanimity dissolved again. "Oh, Gideon, I don't think he loves me anymore!"

He nearly laughed, but caught himself in time. "That can't be so. What could you possibly do that would be so dreadful as to make him do that?"

"Fall in love with you, that's what."

The amusement vanished from his gaze. "Christ, Tess, the last thing I want in the world is to come between your father and you. But I thought he liked me!"

"Oh, he adores you." She couldn't quite keep the bitterness from her voice. "Everybody adores you, even Meg Mullen. It's me they despise."

"That's nonsense; you know it is. I'm surprised you'd let a few silly biddies like Meg drive you to tears."

"It's not just a few old biddies! It's all of them, the whole bloody damned village. They think I'm a whore and a slut, and Dad thinks so too. I see it in his eyes every time he looks at me. 'Just like your mother,' that's what he's—" She stopped abruptly.

"Did she leave him to run off with someone else?" he asked gently, and when she didn't answer, he stroked her hair. "That's all right. You don't have to tell me about it."

But Tess found she wanted to. "It was much worse than that. They weren't even married. Or rather, she was, but not to him." She recounted the story that Ben had told her. "So you see," she concluded, "it's hardly fair for him to act like a saint! What he did was more awful than anything I've done." She sniffed back her tears, green gaze slanting toward him as he said nothing. "I suppose you are shocked."

He shook his head. "Actually, I was thinking how sorry I am for him."

"What, for Dad? I don't see why you should be," she said spitefully. "He made his own bed, didn't he?"

"But that's when it's hardest to live with a mistake. When it's one's own fault." His blue eyes were distant; then he shrugged. "I'm glad you told me about it. It explains a lot about Ben."

"If there's anyone you should be feeling sorry for, it's me," Tess grumbled. "I'm the village pariah. I've half a mind to let everyone in Windber know the truth about poor wronged Ben Jericho."

He laughed. "But you won't, and you know it. Look here." He showed her the spindly bush he'd been tending. "Ugly, isn't it?" She nodded. "It's the night jasmine. See the buds?" Tess looked more closely and saw small pointed buds, furled tight as spindles, among the sparse leaves. "It will bloom any day now, and when it does, the fragrance is enough to make one forget completely how it looks the rest of the year. My . . . Someone I know says night jasmine is always a reminder that however awful life gets, something beautiful and unexpected always lies just ahead."

"Well, that's damned silly," Tess said, still out of sorts.

He chucked her chin, grinning. "My sweet sentimental Tess. Fetch me that bag of pig dung, would you please?"

She did, making a face. "You're sentimental enough for both of us, it seems to me. What sort of work is this for a man? You should be out slaying dragons or something."

"I'll have you know the happiest hours of my childhood were spent in a garden, with my mother teaching me about growing flowers." Tess looked at him in surprise. He'd never mentioned his mother to her before.

She heard a low buzzing sound; then Gideon's long arm stretched out close by her head and snatched something out of the air. He opened his hand, and she saw a flash of iridescent wings. "So I'm afraid," he told her, "you'll have to settle for dragonflies."

"Your jasmine-loving friend may have been right about surprises," Tess announced the next week over supper, her green eyes dancing.

"Why is it," Gideon wondered aloud, "women are so bad at keeping secrets? I knew you had something to tell me the moment I saw you. Let's have it."

"Just for that, I'm not saying."

"Suit yourself. Would you please pass the butter?"

"I'll tell you," she said, and kicked his shin when he laughed. "Linzy is carrying a foal!"

"No! Really?"

She nodded happily. "I suspected, so today I asked Dad. He says she's three months along."

"And eleven altogether, you said. That would make it . . ." He counted on his fingers. "Next April. Oh, Tess." He pulled her straight out of her chair and into his lap. "Nothing will go wrong this time, I know it! It will be the most beautiful, perfect colt in all the world."

"And it will belong to Lady Hardwick, for buying back Satan," she reminded him.

"That's all right. It's just the first of many." He kissed her nose. "We'll have to tell Emilia. I had a letter from her just the other day asking when we'd be by to visit."

"Me, go calling on the nobility?" Tess laughed. "Oh, I never could."

"Why not? She already adores you. And I want you to see Hardwick Hall. I think it's the most beautiful building I've ever seen."

"Grander than the big house?"

It was his turn to laugh. "Maybe not grander, no. But I like it better. It's the kind of house I've always dreamed of building someday."

"Then I would like to see it. I suppose if you're sure she wouldn't mind my coming with you—"

"On second thought, why don't you go by yourself?" he suggested. "I've a mountain of work to catch up on in the glasshouse; this would be the perfect chance."

"Go alone?" Tess's face fell. "I wouldn't feel right. After all, I scarcely know her. I wouldn't have the least idea what to talk to her about."

"Of course you would. You can talk horses, see her stables. And you can talk about me," he added teasingly, "which you couldn't very well if I was there."

Tess nibbled her lip; that notion was appealing. Wasn't it just what she'd been longing for, someone to talk with about Gideon? "Well . . ."

"It's all settled, then. I'll write back and say you'll come at the end of the month. The gillyflowers will be blooming by then."

"You needn't sound so eager to be rid of me," she said, pouting. "Won't you miss me at all?"

He nuzzled her throat, hands closing over her breasts. "I'll show you how much I'll miss you."

"After dinner," Tess whispered, even as she shivered with excitement.

He grinned, kicking back his chair with her still in his arms. "To hell with dinner. Let's celebrate."

Lady Hardwick responded to Gideon's letter suggesting the visit with such enthusiasm that any doubts Tess had regarding her welcome vanished completely. She insisted that Tess stay the night at Hardwick Hall, since otherwise, as she wrote, "You will spend a whole day coming and going, and there won't be time for a proper chat!" Gideon pampered the gillyflowers in the glasshouse until, the day before Tess's departure, they exploded into a riot of bright feathery petals. "The houseboy can carry them," he told her, showing them off.

"What houseboy?"

"Why, the one who rides with you."

"I'm not taking a houseboy. Why should I?"

"You're not going alone!"

"Why the devil not? I'm used to riding by myself, and I like it that way."

Gideon looked worried. "Around here, yes. But all the way to Hardwick Hall—there could be robbers and thieves."

Tess snorted. "What would they steal from me—gillyflowers?"

"That's another thing. You'll need money." He pulled out his purse. "Here, take five pounds."

"Why?" she asked, laughing. "So the robbers will have something to take?"

"In case something happens," he said stubbornly.

"Oh, honestly, you're like some old mother hen." But Tess was pleased by his concern. She fished in his purse. "Here, I'll take this sixpence and no more. And I *won't* take a houseboy."

"Then I won't let you go."

"Hah. Just try to stop me."

He frowned at her. "Has anyone ever told you you're impossibly stubborn?"

"Aye." She kissed him. "My father. Wish me luck; I'm on my way to tell him about this trip."

She chose the moment carefully: while he relaxed with his pipe after a meal she'd taken extra trouble with, of roast mutton and his favorite rosemary dumplings. He'd thawed so far during the meal as to compliment her cooking; heartened, Tess bided her time until he'd got the pipe going, and then told him he'd be fending for himself for supper the following night, as she'd be away.

He sucked at the pipe, then let out a dense cloud of smoke. "Away where?"

"Over to see Lady Hardwick. You know, the one that bought Satan back for Gideon. I'm going to tell her that Linzy's bearing. Gideon promised her the first colt from their breeding." She didn't miss the way Ben winced each time she used the lord's given name.

"Can't the man read and write?" he demanded.

"Of course he can, you know that."

"Then why don't he write her a letter?"

"Well, it's sort of a social visit too, seeing as she's a widow, and lonely."

"Ah. So she invites stablemasters' daughters over for pheasant and truffles and to discuss the latest court fashions."

Tess flushed, but stood her ground. "Lady Hardwick isn't like that, Dad. She's not frivolous. Gideon says she loves horses, even though she is crippled now and can't ride. And she's very kind."

Ben knocked the tobacco out of his pipe and filled it again. "My, my, all this rubbing elbows with the gentry. I swear, Teresa, you grow more and more like your mother every day."

"Damn you, Dad," she told him as calmly as she could, "I'm going to the big house now. Good night."

"Mind you tell Lady Hardwick all about your mum; I'm sure she'll find it charming!"

She slammed the cottage door and ran back home, ran back to Gideon.

Hardwick Hall was a revelation. It was no larger than the big house, and it was by no means as grand as some of the mansions Tess had passed on her way to London. But the moment she saw it, she knew why Gideon admired it so. Everything about it was so delicately balanced, so perfect, that it shone in its setting of green lawn and forest like an unflawed gem.

All along the road to the manor were miraculous shrubs shaped like all sorts of animals: cats and turtles, deer and dogs, peculiar creatures Tess couldn't name. "Oh, they don't *grow* that way," her hostess said in answer to her wide-eyed query. "You have to trim and train them. Topiaries, they're called. One of my dear Albert's hobbies. Chester keeps them up for me now. Quite out of style in London these days, I'm told, but I like them, so who cares?"

She made a grand fuss over the gillyflowers, blushing like a girl when Tess told her how Gideon had spent the past weeks pampering them. For one uncomfortable moment Tess was reminded of her father's accusation that the lord of Windber was buttering the widow up for marriage. But she soon forgot that as Lady Hardwick showed her through the lovely house, pushed by one of her maids in a chair set on wheels. It was obvious from the way she spoke of her late husband—almost as though he were still alive—that she had no interest in marrying again.

"But look at me running on, with you still in your riding clothes, and like as not faint with hunger!" she announced when they'd toured Albert's library. "What would you rather do first, wash up or eat?"

"Eat," Tess said shyly, "if you please, Lady Hardwick."

The old woman laughed. "A soul after my own heart, I

see! Very well, we'll eat—*if* you'll promise to call me Emilia from now on instead of Lady Hardwick."

"Oh, I couldn't."

"Nonsense. You must—if you want to eat! Take us to the dining hall, Nancy, if you please," she directed the maid, "and then run and tell Cook we'll have tea and cakes right away. Unless—" She looked at Tess. "Unless you'd prefer coffee?"

"I've never tried tea." Tess confessed. "I've tried coffee, though, and didn't much like it."

"Can't abide the stuff either! And I can't understand how an otherwise sensible fellow like Gideon's got addicted to it. I'd work to cure him of that if I were you."

"Me?" Tess echoed, and now she was blushing.

"Who better?" Emilia asked, so blithely that Tess was left with little doubt that the widow knew she was Gideon's paramour.

It was over fragile cups of tea—warm, golden-colored, sweetened with honey, and infinitely better, Tess decided, than coffee—and platters of biscuits and cold meats and cakes that she told Emilia about the colt. To see the way the old woman's face lit up made her more glad than ever that she'd made the trip. "I declare," her hostess said, dabbing her watery blue eyes with a napkin, "I feel, fool that I am, quite as though you'd told me I was having a grandchild. New blood in the stables! Well, God bless Linzy and Satan and Giddy and, my dear child, you." She leaned back in her chair, a mustache of powdered sugar crowning her lip. "Who would ever have believed from that disastrous first meeting that Gideon Cade and I should turn out to be friends?"

"Where did you and he meet?" Tess asked, hoping that she didn't sound too eager for information.

"Hasn't he ever told you?" Emilia laughed her loud, young laugh. "No, come to think of it, I don't suppose he would. Well, it was in Stafford. Chester had driven me in to see Dr. Burton—the same one who came out to treat your father. How is your father, by the by?"

"Ever so much better. He's up and about and more ornery than ever."

"Hmm." Those blue eyes had turned shrewd; she

seemed on the verge of pursuing that topic, but let it pass. "Dr. Burton couldn't do a thing for poor Albert either when he took ill. Where the devil was I?"

"Telling how you met Gideon."

"Don't call him Giddy, do you? I do. He hates it." The old woman grinned wickedly. "Strange name he's got. I don't think it's his real one."

"I beg your pardon?" Tess blinked.

"Well, do you know what it means? Not Gideon, but Cade." Tess shook her head. "Why, it's what my father used to call a colt or a calf that had lost its mother, that had to be raised by hand. That's what a cade is." How strange, thought Tess. That means I'm a cade too.

"And have you" ever heard of a family called Cade?" Emilia went on. I haven't, and I would have sworn I knew every family in England."

"Just because you don't know his people—"

"Oh, that's not the only reason. It's what Sebastian said too. My grandnephew Sebastian," she went on in response to Tess's puzzled look. "Because he went to Oxford—Gideon, I mean. He let that drop once, you see. As did Sebastian. And since Sebastian can't be more than one or two years younger than Gideon, I asked, but Sebastian didn't remember him. He seems the sort one would remember, don't you agree?"

"Why, yes, but—"

"Why would he change his name? I know, that's the question. It's not necessarily because of something nefarious, I suppose, but one does wonder. There's a strange element of danger about that man." She looked at Tess, faintly accusing. "You think I'm imagining things."

"Well . . ." said Tess, and couldn't help blushing.

"Well, quite so. Maybe I am. I'm an old woman with too much spare time on my hands, that's what Chester says. But I've made inquiries." She chose another cake and bit into it, sending out a small cloud of powdered sugar that lighted on her bosom and chin.

"What do you mean, inquiries?"

"I wrote to Sebastian again," Emilia said through her mouthful of cake. "Meddlesome, I know. But I never have been able to abide a mystery, and Gideon Cade's a great mystery to me."

Tess found the course of this conversation disturbing. She was sure Lady Hardwick wasn't malicious, but it seemed horribly rude to go poking around behind Gideon's back. Guessing her thoughts, Emilia turned defensive. "Well, has he ever talked about his past to you?"

"Of course he has. He's told me all about sailing to the New World and the Orient—"

"I don't mean that sort of stuff; he's told me that too. I mean about where he comes from, his family."

"Aye, he has," Tess said triumphantly. "He told me his father had a lot of wives—four, I think he said. And it was his mother that taught him to garden. That's why he loves plants."

Emilia snorted. "More than I've gotten out of him, I'll admit, but it's still not much. Aren't you curious?"

"Sometimes," Tess admitted. "But considering the circumstances, family background isn't one of my favorite topics of conversation."

"You mean because of the differences in your stations. Well, Gideon's no snob. But he is nobility; I've got no question of that. No, he's more than a clever rogue who won himself a lawsuit. Gideon Cade is somebody, mark my words. I knew that the first moment I saw him."

"You were telling me about that," Tess reminded her, glad to steer the talk back that way again.

"So I was, wasn't I? Well, I'd gone to Stafford in the carriage to see Dr. Burton; Chester took me. And we stopped afterward at a tavern I know that makes the most delectable pastries. Not *quite* up to the creamcakes in Stover's Mill, mind you, but awfully good. Anyway, we went in, and there was Giddy sitting at a table with a harlot."

Tess choked on her tea. "With a what?" she asked when she'd recovered.

"You heard me. A harlot. An expensive one, but there wasn't any mistaking what sort of woman she was. As soon as he saw her, Chester tried to make me leave. But having come all that way, it seemed a shame not to have a single sweet. So we sat down as far from them as we

could and gave our order. The next thing I know, the
serving woman brings over this whole huge apple pastry,
the most luscious thing you've ever seen, and bows and
lays it down on the table, and says, 'A tart, m'lady,
compliments of the tart over there!' Naturally I look
over, and the two of 'em are laughing and giggling at me.
Well, Chester wanted to call in the law, but the man
stood up and bowed ever so elegantly, and he was just so
handsome and dashing that I hadn't the heart. Besides, it
was a splendid-looking tart."

"What did you do?"

Emilia shrugged. "Ate it. They left before we were
finished. But a few weeks later I saw him again, out
riding on that monstrous stallion of his. I had Chester
stop the carriage, and I thanked him for the tart. He
turned out to be ever so nice. A nobleman, as I said—
even Chester could tell that. We just got to talking, and
he told me about the glasshouse he was building and how
he was going to breed racers, and I had him back here to
see my stables. You know, there aren't many men like
him who'd take an interest in an old crippled lady like
me. He's got a way of making one feel so special. But
then, I don't have to tell you that, do I?"

"No," Tess agreed, her brow slightly furrowed.

"Worried about that harlot, are you?"

"Of course not!" She reached for a cake to prove she
wasn't. "But how could you tell . . . what she was?"

"Oh, my dear, you should have seen her gown. Bright
red satin, and cut quite indecently low in the front. She
had reddish hair too, and a most remarkable complexion,
I will give her that, and a French accent! And dining out
in public with a much younger man—what else could she
be?"

"Suzette," Tess breathed.

"What's that?" Emilia asked sharply.

"Nothing. I just said . . . the cakes. Are they flavored
with anisette?"

"Oh, no. Lemon and mace; I can't abide anisette." A
clock behind her white head chimed the hour of five, and
she made a face. "Time for my nap, I'm afraid. Would

you care to rest too, or shall I have Chester show you the stables?"

"I'd love to see the stables."

"Ah, to be young again. Nancy!" The maid came running. "Fetch Chester, will you, and have him show Mistress Jericho the stables while I lie down."

Tess spent the next few hours admiring Lady Hardwick's infinitely admirable horses in the company of the droll coach driver. Later that evening, her hostess insisted on teaching her to play a card game called cribbage and then won five straight rounds. They had a delicious supper of broiled salmon from a nearby stream and venison stew made with leeks and carrots, followed, of course, by a sweet—butter cakes soaked in brandy sauce and topped with poached white peaches from the estate gardens. "Not bad," Emilia judged the confection, "but I do think it could use whipped cream."

After the heavy meal, Tess could scarcely keep her eyes open, but Emilia had one last surprise to show her. Chester carried his mistress, wheeled chair and all, up three flights of stairs to the topmost room in the house, while Tess trailed behind them. There she was shown Albert's fondest treasure: something called a telescope that, when one looked through it, made the stars and moon come near. Despite a lengthy explanation dealing with mirrors and curved glass and mathematics, Tess hadn't the slightest understanding of how it could work, but she found it enthralling all the same.

Emilia laughed when her third attempt to describe the process failed. "You're just like Giddy," she said fondly. " 'I don't care how it does it,' he says. 'I'd rather think it's magic anyway!' He sits up here for hours and hours when he comes to visit, just staring at the stars—sometimes the whole night long!"

As Tess peered through the cylinder at the pocked surface of the moon, she felt a strange peace come over her. Here she'd always imagined Gideon to be dancing with countesses and flirting with baron's daughters when he visited Hardwick Hall, and instead he'd been alone in this room contemplating the heavens. She quite forgot about Suzette as she pictured him perched in this chair, training the telescope's eye on the vast expanse of black velvet and cool white fire beyond the windows. Though this was the first night they'd spend apart from each other in months, she felt closer to him at that moment than ever before.

Emilia must have sensed her mood, for she beckoned to Chester to wheel her away. "You stay here if you like," she told Tess, who rose to leave too. "For as long as you like. It's past time that I was in bed. Just ring the bell when you're ready, and Nan will show you your rooms. Good night, my dear."

Left alone, Tess stared at the distant stars and made wishes on each one that sparkled, and every wish she wished was exactly the same.

19

The sense of peace Tess felt in the observatory stayed with her all through the remainder of her visit with Emilia and the long ride home to Windber the following day. It remained unshaken even by the peculiar encounter she had with Millie Brady as she crossed the bridge into the village. Jack's wife was sitting on the stone wall with her baby as Tess approached atop Linzy at dusk, just as shadows began to merge into darkness. Tess nodded, ready to pass without speaking, but Millie addressed her.

" 'Evenin', Tess. Been to see the toffs, I hear."

"Hello, Millie," she responded, surprised by the woman's overture. "The baby's looking splendid, isn't he? So big! I was visiting a friend of Gideon's."

Her former rival nodded thoughtfully, one bare heel tapping against the stone wall. "Some kind of countess or somethin', ain't she?"

"I don't know what her title might be, to tell you the truth," Tess said. "But she was very kind to me. I went to tell her that Linzy's going to have a colt. Gideon promised the first one Satan got to her."

That bare, dusty foot went on swinging, while Millie looked her over slowly from head to toe. "Who've ye promised yers to?" she asked then.

"My what?"

"Yer firstborn."

Tess stared at her, uncomprehending.

"Well, ye surely can't keep it, can ye? Wot would his lordship want with a bastard by the likes o' ye?" Millie let out a giggle and jumped down from the wall, running into her cottage with the baby clutched tight to her chest.

Tess paused, then nudged Linzy on. "Well, I guess living with Jack would drive me crazy too!"

Her father wasn't in the stables. Tess was glad not to have to face him; she groomed and fed Linzy as quickly as she could. Satan was in his stall; his black eyes kept close watch as Tess tended his mistress. "Don't fret," she told him over her shoulder as she rubbed Linzy down. "I didn't work her too hard. I wouldn't risk anything going wrong this time." For an instant she remembered the other pony's miscarriage, the grotesque colt's twin heads bathed in blood.

Blood. When was the last time she'd had her monthly? she wondered idly, pushing the colt's image from her mind. How glad she was it hadn't arrived to spoil her homecoming! She gave Linzy a final comb and pat and hurried off to the big house to find Gideon.

Prince Oren was in the front hall as she came in. "Hello, Oren!" she cried gaily. "Where is Gideon, do you know?"

"His lordship is in the glasshouse," the butler told her, so stiffly that she couldn't resist needling him.

"Do you know, Oren, I've just got back from visiting a very rich countess"—why not give Emilia that title, if gossip already had?—"and there wasn't one of her servants that was snooty and stuck-up like you."

The face he turned back to her reminded Tess of a snake, the eyes hooded and venomous. "I've told you where you'll find his lordship now," he said with icy coldness, "but you'll have to ask him yourself where he spent last night."

She laughed. "What's that supposed to mean?" He didn't deign to answer, just sniffed and walked away. "Jealous," Tess muttered under her breath. "You are all just jealous." And she ran back outside and down the hill to the glasshouse, determined to put what he'd said straight out of her mind.

Through the glass panes and tangled vines she could see a lantern inside the building, glowing an unearthly

green like the fires—fairy fires, Rachel called them—that
sprang up in the marshes on hot summer nights. She
stood for a moment by the door, watching Gideon's
gigantic shadow play over the mottled leaves as she ran
hurried hands through her hair and straightened her skirts.
He stood with his back to her, pulling twigs from a tall
woody shrub, twisting them between his long, strong
fingers and snapping them away. Impulsively Tess slipped
through the door and crept up behind him, planning a
surprise. When she was almost there, her foot caught
the handle of a wooden bucket and overturned it. Before
she knew what had happened, he'd whirled on her, whip-
ping a knife from his belt and holding it to her throat.

"Gideon! Jesus, it's only me!" In the fleeting instant
before he lowered the knife, the expression on his face
made her blood turn cold; his eyes were narrowed to
slits, and were harder than the chill steel of the blade.
Then they widened; he let out his breath in a rush.

"Don't ever, *ever* do that to me again, you damned
little fool! I might have cut your throat!"

"I only meant to surprise you," she said faintly.

"I don't like surprises. You should know that by now."
He tucked the blade back in his belt.

"You might at least act a little bit glad to see me
back!"

"I *am* glad to see you." His hand on the knife hilt was
shaking. "But I damned near killed you."

"Who in the world did you think it might be, you silly
man? You're in Windber-on-Clun! No one here merits
pulling your knife on."

"I don't know. I just acted from habit."

Tess swallowed her resentment at this spoiled homecoming. "Your past life must have been even more ad-
venturesome than you let on," she said lightly, putting
her hands on his shoulders, standing on tiptoe. "Give us
a kiss." That, at least, was all she could have wanted
and more, lingering and tender and loving, but with an
undercurrent of hot passion that made her heart beat
fast.

"I missed you," he murmured, his arm tightening around
her waist while his tongue traced her earlobe.

"Nonsense. I'll wager you were in here fussing with your plants for the whole two days." As he nuzzled her neck, she looked more closely at the shrub he'd been pruning. "Is that the night jasmine?" He nodded, kisses slipping toward her breastbone. "Why, what happened to the blossoms? Did I miss them? They couldn't have all come and gone so soon!"

"Bugs," he said briefly, reaching for her bodice strings. "Had to cut 'em away and burn them."

"Now I'll never find out what their scent is like," she said mournfully.

"It will bloom again. Besides, it doesn't smell any sweeter than you do here . . ." Her bodice untied, he kissed the hollow between her breasts, while his hand slid over her skirts to her mound of Venus. "Or here." His fingers reached lower, pushing between her thighs through road-dusty serge. "Or here. Oh, Tess. Oh, my heart . . ." He pulled her down onto his lap on a bench, mouth covering hers in a frenzied kiss, tongue thrusting inside her while he pushed her skirts aside and ran his hands up her calves, past her knees, to her thighs. Tess shivered and sighed even as she remembered the gigantic shadow she'd seen from outside the glasshouse.

"The lantern," she whispered.

He stretched out one leg and knocked it over, so the flame flickered out. "There."

He'd found the edge of her drawers and slipped his hand inside them, while he moved his mouth to her breast and pulled at the nipple till it swelled to hardness at his touch. Night had fallen beyond the panes of glass; lying across Gideon's legs, his manhood throbbing against her buttocks, Tess could see the stars spread across the sky.

"Emilia showed me that room where you like to go," she said softly.

"Mm." He relinquished her breast for a moment. "How is Emilia?"

"Fine."

"Good. Let's stop talking about her."

Tess giggled, then caught her breath, arching against him as he found the bud hidden between the velvet folds of her flesh with his fingers and stroked her there. "Oh," she whispered. "Oh, Gideon. Oh . . ."

He laid her on the bench, pillowing her head with his jacket, and knelt, stripping off her drawers, parting her knees with his hands. "But most of all, I love the smell of you here," he told her, and his tongue flicked against that stiffening bud, letting loose so strong a tide of pleasure in her blood that she longed to scream. She clutched the bench, the stars spinning above her, while he made a slow, thorough exploration of the secret places that were no longer secret to him. His touch drove her wild; she moaned and writhed beneath his tongue and hands until she begged him, frenzied, to finish, to bring her to ecstasy. In the darkness she heard his belt drop to the floor, and the pop of his breeches buttons, one by one, and then he entered her with one swift, deliberate thrust that made her gasp aloud.

"Is this what you wanted?"

"Yes. Yes."

"This?" Again he drove into her, so hard and deep that she did scream, hands gripping his shoulders. He groaned as his shaft sank into her flesh, which tightened around him with silken force. "Tess." With each pounding thrust he spoke her name again, faster and faster. They were moving together as one, one body, one spirit, rising up to heaven like the smoke from a sacrifice on the altar of love. When they came, in the same instant, it was in an explosion so violently strong that Tess expected the panes to shatter around them, glass bursting apart like a million bright shooting stars.

But instead Gideon collapsed atop her, panting for breath, seed drained from his loins. "I wish . . ." he said, and stopped.

"What?" Tess asked, mouth pressed to his throat.

"That we could stay . . . just like this, forever."

But we could! she ached to tell him. If only you would ask me to wed you . . .

If only she had the nerve to say so aloud!

Before she could, he pushed himself up from the bench, then pulled her up too so she leaned against him as he sat. "*Now* I am ready to hear all about Emilia."

Guilt at her thoughts made Tess shy; she nestled into his shoulder. "You tell me first what you did while I was away."

"Absolutely nothing," he said cheerfully. "Just fussed with my plants."

Alone with him in the sweet-scented darkness, Tess had a sudden vision of Oren's pinched reptilian face, heard the challenge he'd hissed: *You'll have to ask him yourself where he spent last night.*

"You didn't go away at all?" she asked, and instantly hated herself.

Did she imagine it, or could she feel him stiffen? His voice was perfectly calm, though, even amused, as he met her question with another: "Who's been telling you tales?"

"Oren," she confessed. "He mentioned you'd stayed out last night."

"Did he, now?" Gideon laughed. "Doesn't he know a man's butler is supposed to be the soul of discretion?"

"You were out, then. Where?"

"Chasing fancy women." Now he was teasing.

"I wouldn't be surprised." Tess echoed his carefree tone. "Emilia told me all about the first day she met you, and the harlot you were with. I imagine that was Suzette."

This time there was no mistaking the tensing of his muscles. "Suzette's no harlot."

"Oh, really? Pray forgive me. I just naturally assumed that a woman who runs a whorehouse must be a—"

"People assume too damn much in this life."

"If she's not," Tess cried, hurt that he defended her so staunchly, "why did you send Emilia that message about a tart from a tart?"

"Because she'd made the same assumption as you." His tight voice turned gentler. "Tess, don't let's quarrel, not when I missed you so terribly."

"You still haven't told me where you went last night."

"I am sorry to disappoint all the gossips, but the plain fact's quite dull. I had a letter from my solicitor saying he'd be in Shrewsbury, so I rode out to meet him. He had some papers for me to sign." Tess heard no hint of guile in his tone. "You believe me, don't you?"

"Of course I do," she told him, and found that she did. "Pity he couldn't have come to Stafford, isn't it? Then you might have met me at Emilia's."

"That's the sort of solicitor he is," he said ruefully. "Always in the wrong place at the wrong time. Still, at least this way you got to listen to Emilia's tall tales about me." He found her drawers on the glasshouse floor, slipped them on her, then sat back on his haunches. "I must be going mad. Why did I do that?" And he moved to take them off her again.

"Because you knew I had to go and see Dad," she told him, laughing as she pushed him away. "But do you know what I'd like after that?"

"More of the same?" he said hopefully.

"No. A long, cool bath." She kissed him. "*Then* more of the same."

"I'll draw the water. Don't be long. Wait, I'll light the lantern again before you trip over my poor jasmine plant."

In the lantern's warm golden glow, Tess looked into Gideon's eyes that were the color of October skies and felt heartily ashamed for having put him through such an interrogation. "I love you," she said.

He smiled at her and, for the first time ever, told her, "I love you too."

She left the glasshouse walking on air.

Ben's expression when she opened the cottage door brought her down to earth again. "So," he said, and knocked tobacco from his pipe into the fireplace. "Back from hobnobbing with your betters, are you?"

"Hello, Dad." She slipped onto the stool across from him, checking the scars on his face and hands with a practiced glance. No changes there, any more than in his attitude. "Did you have supper yet?"

"Rachel fed me."

"Did she? What did you have?"

He turned his face from her, looking into the empty hearth. "If it's the same with you, lass, I'd as soon not trade idle chitchat. Why don't you hie yourself back to the big house and get on with your sinful ways?"

"Oh, for Christ's sake. You're as bad as Millie and

Oren and the rest of them. I've told you before: I love Gideon. Tonight he told me he loves me. Why can't you be happy for me, Dad?" She reached for his hand.

He snatched it away. "Happy?" His voice cracked on the word. "You want me to be happy, lass? Then give up this carrying on and come home to me."

"Don't make me choose between Gideon and you, Dad."

"What choice is there between your own father, your own flesh and blood, and that man?"

"I thought you liked him!"

His chin had that impossibly stubborn set. "Aye, well, that was before."

"Before what?"

"Before he ruined you."

She sighed. "If anyone ruined me, it was Jack Brady."

"Jack would have wedded you."

"Gideon will marry me too, Dad, I know it! He just needs more time."

"More time for what?" he demanded, the pipe squeezed so tight in his hand that the shaft cracked with a sudden snap. "More time for sneaking out the moment your back's turned to dally with some other girl?"

Tess had to smile. "If you are talking about yesterday, Gideon's already told me all about it. He had a letter from his solicitor to meet him in Shrewsbury. Something about some papers he had to sign."

"His solicitor, was it? Tell me then, lass, does he always take a great bundle of posies with him when he goes to see his solicitor?"

"What are you talking about?" she asked after a pause.

"The flowers he took with him! Tried to hide 'em in his cloak when he skulked into the stables to have me saddle Satan. Still, he couldn't hide the scent of 'em, could he? The whole place was filled with it; it was stronger than dung."

The night jasmine that Gideon told her he'd cut and burned because it had bugs. Tess hoped her expression didn't show the sudden pang of doubt in her soul. "I'm surprised at you, Dad," she said lightly, "spying on your lord and master. Anyway, why shouldn't he take flowers to his solicitor? There are plenty of men who like flowers. God knows Gideon does." But that didn't explain why he'd lied.

" 'Have ye eyes and see not, and having ears, do ye hear not?' " her father quoted St. Mark mournfully. The broken pipe fell from his hand; he leaned forward on his chair. "Turn away from this wickedness, Tess, before it's too late. I beg you, come back here to your home." He dropped to his knees on the floor. "Come kneel beside me, and we'll pray together to Jehovah that he forgives your iniquity."

"Dad, please." Tess squirmed with embarrassment.

"I *beg* you, Teresa! Confess and repent your sins to almighty Jehovah and he will save you! He will forgive you!"

"Dad, I've got to go now. Good night." Avoiding his outstretched arms, she hurried to the door. As she touched the latch, he called her name:

"Teresa!"

She turned back to him, fearful, reluctant. In the light of the candles, his eyes burned like fiery coals beneath a wild thatch of white hair. "There will be no more chances," he warned her. "Pray with me now, or never cross that threshold again."

Tess hung her head, burdened with guilt but at the same time angry that he forced her to make this choice. "I'm sorry, Dad," she whispered. "I love you. I always will." And she slipped through the door.

On the night wind she heard a mad wordless cry, like that of an animal caught in a trap. Job, she thought at first, and then realized it was her father. She pictured him rending his garments, tearing his hair like Moses looking down from Mount Sinai on the children of Israel, and the temptation to run back inside, into his arms, was so overwhelming that she nearly collapsed where she stood.

But it was too late now. She'd made her decision— made the only choice she could. Her father, Oren, all the rest of them—they were wrong. They didn't know Gideon the way she did.

The big house loomed above her on the hilltop, windows ablaze with candles, the doorway dark and gaping. Like an open mouth, Tess thought, and shivered. About to swallow me whole . . .

"Tess!"

There was Gideon, leaning over an upstairs sill, beckoning to her. "Come on!" he called. "Your bath is getting cold!"

Damn you, Dad, she thought, now you have got me seeing things! Then she hurried up the hill and through the door that was only a door.

20

As the autumn harvest drew near, there was an air of excitement in Windber-on-Clun that infected everyone, even Tess in her isolation. The oat and wheat were bumper; the hops were thriving; the rye was flourishing. The new crops that Gideon Cade had introduced were remarkable, from potatoes to tobacco. Most astonishing of all was the maize. No one had ever seen anything like it: taller than Cade himself, brilliant dark green, with tassels that he called "silk" dangling from the fat ears. From the window of her bedchamber in the big house Tess watched the village children playing among the stalks, encouraged by their elders as a means of keeping mice and rooks away.

She spent too much time looking out from that window. Though she never would have admitted as much to Gideon, she was lonely. She missed the easy company of the villagers, the daily exchanges of greetings and gossip. Most of all, she missed her father. Each time she saw him, each time he walked past her without speaking, she felt a terrible ache in her heart. He never came to the new stables once they were finished. She looked after Satan and Linzy; he was helping Mort and the rest of the men in the fields.

At least ten times a day it was on the tip of her tongue to ask Gideon about the night jasmine. But she always held her tongue, knowing that no matter how she phrased the question, it would sound as though she didn't trust him. And without him, she would truly be lost.

Perhaps Ben would come around once Linzy's foal was

born, she thought one day as she walked to the stables. He never had been able to resist colts, long-legged and gangly. She could ask for his help with the birth when the time came next spring.

And on the subject of time, when exactly was the last time she'd had her monthly?

"Good mornin', Teresa."

The friendly greeting, a rarity these days, took her by surprise. Rachel Jonas stood on the path before her, herb basket slung over her arm. Tess smiled in return. "Good morning, Rachel! My, it seems like months since I saw you. You're looking well."

"And ye too." Those shrewd eyes perused her closely. "Put on a bit of weight, ain't ye?"

Tess laughed, embarrassed. "Everyone seems to have this summer, with so much good food to be had. Gideon was complaining only yesterday that his breeches buttons need moving." He had, too, in response to her own lament that her skirt didn't fit. "It will stand us all in good stead, though, come the winter." She nodded at the basket. "No one's ailing, I hope?"

"Millie Brady. Not ailin', exactly, but with child again. It's dried up her milk for young Thomas."

"With child again?" It didn't seem possible. "But Thomas can't be more than—"

"Four months come Tuesday," Rachel finished for her.

"You're sure it's not something else dried up her milk?"

The herb woman shook her head. "No. Millie knew it herself, right away. Once ye've borne one, bein' pregnant is hard to mistake."

But if you hadn't yet borne one . . . When *had* she last had her monthly? "What is it like, being pregnant?" she asked casually.

"I only knows wot they tells me, not havin' borne none myself. Tiredness in the blood, most says. The breasts turnin' tender. Some say they taste copper on their tongues."

"Copper!" Tess laughed even as she tested the taste at the back of her throat. Was there something metallic? Last night, in bed, Gideon had put his mouth to her breast, and though that had always pleased her, this time she'd winced, pushing him away.

"Of course," the widow went on, "so long as yer monthly comes good 'n' regular, why, there's nothin' to worry about."

"Of course," Tess agreed. "Well, I wish Millie luck." She edged toward the stables. "Good seeing you again!"

"The same to ye, Teresa." Basket swinging, the old woman trudged on down the path.

Tess darted into the stables and, in the cool, quiet darkness, sat down to think. This was September. The fire had been in April; she and Ben had moved into the big house then. She remembered having her bleeding that first month, because she'd been shy about making a mess on the linens of her borrowed bed. The month after that was June; what about June? Yes, because she'd first slept with Gideon in June; she clearly recalled her relief that her flow had ended just a few days before that fateful night when he'd asked her to dine.

What next? July. August. Christ, she couldn't remember. The golden days of that golden summer blurred together in her mind like a field of buttercups seen from a distance, into one lush carpet of light. Oh, *why* hadn't she paid more attention? What if she were pregnant, what would she do?

Sitting on the hard wooden floor of the stables, she felt sweat gather under her arms, behind her knees, across her forehead. Pregnant. With a baby. His baby. She could just imagine what Ben would say.

Gideon would marry her if she was pregnant.

That stopped her trembling. He would, of course. He'd have to.

But I don't want him to marry me because he has to—I want him to marry me because he *wants* to! she thought frantically. To trap him into marriage that way would be cheap and tawdry. Everyone in the village would say that was why she'd given herself to him in the first place; she'd be called a fortune-seeker and worse. And Gideon . . . She began to sweat again, imagining his warm blue eyes turned to coldness. She would sooner die than have him think she'd lain with him in hopes that she'd conceive and force their wedding day.

She didn't know that she was pregnant, though. She

clung to that thought like a drowning man to a barrel. She didn't *know*, and since she didn't know, if he asked her to marry him now, before she found out for certain, it would be the same as if she wasn't, even if she was. All she had to do was get him to ask her right away, she realized with mounting excitement. Then her spirits collapsed as suddenly as they'd inflated. It had taken Gideon this long just to reach the point of saying out loud that he loved her. If it took him another few months to decide to propose, she was sunk for sure.

What she needed was some foolproof method of making him love her forever and ever. Some kind of magic potion . . . She sat bolt upright on the floor. But she had such a thing already! The love potion Rachel Jonas gave her when she was supposed to marry Jack. Guaranteed to bind soul to soul, the herb woman had told her then, when you steeped it in wine.

What in blazes had she done with the stuff? She cast her mind back to that evening when she sat with the neighbor women sewing on her wedding gown, downing Rachel's dandelion wine. A little bundle wrapped in cloth. Dried leaves and twigs.

Dried leaves and twigs. It didn't seem much to set her future on, Tess thought wryly as she got up and went to search the cottage. But it was better than nothing. And right now, nothing was all she had.

"More wine, Gideon?"

Above the rim of the just-drained glass, his blue eyes glinted with amusement. "If I didn't know better, Teresa Jericho, I'd swear you were trying to get me drunk."

"Don't be daft," Tess scoffed, even as she warned herself to be cautious. She didn't want to arouse his suspicions. "I've never even seen you drunk."

"Drunkenness is for cowards and fools," he told her, and then flushed. "I'm sorry. I didn't mean to imply that your father—"

She brushed it away with a wave of her hand. "Dad may not be a coward, but he surely is being foolish these days."

"He'll come around, though, won't he?" he asked, and

frowned. "I'd hate to think I was the cause of a permanent rift between you."

"It wasn't your fault, Gideon. From the way he's behaving, it's quite clear we would have had a falling-out eventually." Tess sighed, leaning her chin on her hand. "It's a part of growing up, I suppose, separating yourself from your father. Was it hard for you too?"

In the midst of taking a bite of roast lamb, Gideon dropped his fork. "Damn. You see? I *am* drunk." He laughed, pushing his glass toward her. "But you may as well fill it up again anyway. By the by, what are we celebrating?"

"Celebrating? What do you mean?"

"Don't play innocent." He indicated the supper table. "All my favorite dishes at one meal—lamb, and leeks, and lettuce salad—and, if my nose didn't mistake me coming upstairs, a gooseberry pie yet to come. Not to mention this extraordinary spiced wine. Either we're celebrating or you want something from me." He leaned back in his chair. "And if it's the latter, I may as well tell you. It will cost you at least one kiss."

"How cynical you are! Can't a woman spoil her man sometimes without secret motives?"

"I think it unlikely."

Tess stuck out her tongue at him and poured still more wine. "You didn't answer my question."

"What question?"

"About your father. Did you have a hard time convincing him to let you go off on your own, sailing to the New World and all?"

"Not really. *Is* there gooseberry pie?"

Tess nodded, and he rang for Oren. "I only asked," she explained, fearing from his brusque answer that he was angry, "because I thought you might have some idea of how I can convince Dad that you mean well by me."

He was silent while Oren, grim-faced, bore in the pie and a bowl of whipped cream and cleared the plates away. "I'll serve," she told the surly butler, anxious that she and Gideon be alone again. The potion had to be working; Gideon had never been so open with her before.

"You know what the problem is with you and your

father, don't you?" he asked at last. "You are too much alike."

"Dad and I?" Tess laughed. "That's absurd."

"Look at the facts, Tess. You're both as stubborn as the devil. You hate as much as he does not to get your way. Not to mention that strange streak of Old Testament morality that runs through you both."

" 'Morality' is rather an odd word to use for me," Tess said, scrunching her nose.

"Why, because you're my mistress?" He'd finished his pie and leaned back in his chair once more, sipping from his wineglass. "There are plenty of mistresses in the Bible. Look at Ruth, who sneaked in to Boaz in the dead of night. Hell, look at Esther." The wine had made his face red. "No, you and Ben are cut from the same cloth, all right."

"How about you and your father? Were you alike?" Tess pressed, refilling his cup with the last of the wine from the pitcher.

He drained it, then stood up abruptly. "All that's in the past, Tess. I don't want to talk about the past. The future is all that counts. Our future together." He came and stood behind her chair, his hands on her shoulders. Oh, God, thought Tess, holding her breath. It worked. He is going to ask me to wed him. Could he feel her trembling, hear the pounding of her heart?

"I love you, Tess." His voice was low, nearly a whisper, with the faintest trace of a slur from the wine he'd had—nearly a gallon, she knew, for twice she'd gone to the kitchens to refill the pitcher. He laughed and pressed a kiss to the nape of her neck. "I've never said those words to any woman but you. They don't come easy to me."

"Oh, Gideon. I know," she began, twisting in her chair to face him. "And I—"

"Hush." He silenced her with the tip of his finger, swaying on his feet. "Hush, or I'll lose the nerve to say what I want to say." Tess clamped her mouth shut, staring up at him. He moved the finger to the side of her throat, tracing a red-gold curl that had worked loose from her braid there. "You're so beautiful, Tess. The most beautiful woman I've ever seen, do you know that? Beautiful, and brave, and good . . ." He swayed again and had to grip the chair. Damn, Tess thought, have I overdone it? But he didn't look sleepy or fuddled the way Ben so often had; the fire in his eyes burned steady and low, not drink-bright.

"I want to take care of you, Tess Jericho. I want to look after you, watch over you so you never need to be frightened or alone . . ." Though she tried to keep rein on her emotions, Tess couldn't; she had waited so long for this moment that she started to cry. He was even kneeling, kneeling on the floor at her side to make his proposal, just as though she were a baron's daughter, not a stablehand's. "Tess . . ."

"Yes, my heart?" she whispered through a haze of happy tears.

"I want to ask you something."

"Go on, my love!"

"Will you . . . ?" He paused; she nodded encouragement. "Will you remember that, Tess? That I love you, whatever may happen?"

"Of course I will," she said impatiently, waiting for that other, all-important question.

He lurched to his feet and caught hold of her hands. "Let's to bed."

He made love to her wildly, sweetly, as though there were no tomorrow. The wine seemed to free him from himself: he held nothing back, laughed and cried, called her name. He moved with her in a dance of impassioned transcendence . . .

And to Tess it was ashes, nothing but ashes, for all she could hear as he shuddered against her was the voice of her father, harsh and embittered:

Never yet known a man to pay for what he gets for free.

21

She couldn't sleep that night. Gideon lay curled beside her, snoring heavily, dead to the world, but she stared at the ceiling in the faint glow of moonlight for hours and hours, trying to make some sense out of her muddled life.

He loved her; she was sure of that. He'd told her so, not just in words, but in the way he held her, the pleasure he gave her, the fire that burned in his eyes. Why, then, did he never speak of marriage? Was he ashamed of her low birth? Did he despise the fact that she hadn't come to him a virgin? Or was it just, as Ben said, that she'd given herself to him too easily?

He snored and stretched beside her, flinging his arm across her breasts. She tried to push it away, but he only moved closer, adding the weight of his leg to the arm. "Lord, I won't get any sleep at this rate," Tess muttered, and crept out from beneath him, pulling on a robe and going to the window seat.

Through the open draperies she stared down at the sleeping village, the lush distant fields, the glistening glasshouse. That reminded her of the night jasmine. Why had he lied about those damned flowers; where had he taken them? Did he have another lover? Oh, honestly, she told herself, how could he? Except for that one night she'd gone to Emilia's, they'd been sleeping together for months!

Months. God, she didn't want to get started counting months again. The more she thought about it, the more certain she was that she hadn't had her bleeding in August. Now September was nearly gone too. She opened the robe and looked down at her breasts. How full and heavy they seemed . . . and tonight, when Gideon touched them, she'd felt less pleasure than pain.

If she were with child . . .

God, she'd grow haggard and fat, the way Millie had last winter. If Gideon hadn't got another lover already, he'd surely take one then. Unless they were married. I am running out of time, she realized, and I don't know what to do. If only I knew more about him!

That was when she remembered the papers in his desk.

"Gideon," she said. He didn't move. "Gideon, wake up!" All those years of putting up with Ben's drinking did have their uses, she thought wryly as she pinched his arm. Experience had taught her a man in such a state would sleep for hours.

She slipped out of the bedchamber and into his study down the hall.

There was no need for a lamp; she could see by the moonlight once she tied the curtains back. A new stack of notes he'd written to himself lay on the desktop. She paged through them methodically, not knowing what she was looking for but certain she'd recognize it.

The notes held no clues. She opened the top drawer and examined the writing paper, then sorted through the drafting tools in the drawer below it. In the third drawer was his correspondence. She read through the letters unashamedly. All were matters of business, except for some from Emilia, which were chattily gay.

All the way in the back of the drawer was a packet tied up in black ribbon; she hadn't noticed it on her last visit there. Now she untied the bow and unfolded the letter on top.

"M-o-n c-h-é-r-i," she read, and blinked, looking again. But she wasn't mistaken; that was how the letter began. The writing was small and delicate; she had to bring it close to the window to see. "J-e s-u-i-s," she read on, then stopped, realizing it was in some foreign language. She went back to the drawer for the next one. It began with the same salutation, then continued with more unintelligible words. So did the next letter, and the next;

there were dozens of them, all in the identical delicate
hand. A woman's hand.

She turned the first one over, looking for the closing,
and there it was, set apart from the body: "J-e t'-a-
i-m-e," and then a signature, fine and graceful: "Suzette."

Suzette. The name conjured up an instant image of
auburn hair swept into a cascade of glorious curls, of blue
eyes and porcelain skin. And her voice, foreign-tinged,
so lovely. *Oh, Gideon,* she'd sighed when Tess told her
whom she had come to see.

He'd said she wasn't his mistress, but clearly she had
been for years and years. There were so many letters!
The ones at the bottom of the packet were yellowed with
age. Were they lovers still? Tess searched the letter on
top for a date, but could find none. It might have been
sent years ago or only yesterday.

Somewhere in the Peacock Inn, amidst the gilt tables
and plush carpets, there would be another packet of
letters—those Gideon had sent to Suzette. The thought
chilled her blood. Were they, like these, in this language
the two of them knew and she didn't? The language of
love. Had he spent the winter making love to her there in
London? Was night jasmine her favorite flower?

Tess's father had told her a story once about a girl who
opened a box that she shouldn't have and let loose a
world of troubles. She had the feeling that by looking at
this packet of letters she had done the same thing. Quickly
she arranged the pages the way she'd found them and
retied the black ribbon, even as she wished she could
bind her thoughts up so tidily.

Then she closed the drawer and let the curtains fall,
shutting out the pale round moon. She'd lost her taste for
exploring Gideon's past; she was haunted by an awful
feeling that even darker secrets might lie hidden there,
pushed back behind his outward appearance of normalcy
like letters thrust to the back of a drawer. And if there
are such secrets, she thought, I don't want to know about
them. I just don't want to know.

She tiptoed back to their chamber and crawled into
bed beside him. He reached for her, rolling onto his side,
stretching out his hand until he stroked her face. She

could smell the wine still on his breath as he stirred and mumbled, "Suzette?"

It is only the drink, she told herself, hoping that might calm her sinking heart. But she couldn't resist whispering back to him as best she could the words with which her rival closed her letters: *"Je t'aime . . ."*

He smiled in the moonlight and curled against her, holding her tight.

She rose early the next day and was on her way to the stables before Gideon could awake to what would surely be a vicious headache. She felt the need to go riding, to be alone with Linzy high atop the White Moor, where everything always seemed to look simpler and clearer. But before she even got past the glasshouse she heard hoofbeats coming from the village, and looked down the hill to see Chauncey, Lady Hardwick's plum-coated footman, galloping toward her atop one of his mistress's steeds.

"Hallo!" he shouted, waving his crop. "Mistress Jericho! Just who I've been sent to see!"

Tess wasn't in the mood to see anyone, but politeness made her wait as he rode up. He was panting with exertion, so she waited still longer while he caught his breath. "Thanks," he gasped out at last. "Lady . . . Hardwick . . . insisted . . . set out . . . before dawn!"

"My Lord! She's not ill!"

"Oh, no! Nothing . . . like that." Beneath its plum-colored livery his chest was still heaving. "Wants to see ye. That's all. At Hardwick Hall. Can ye come right away?"

Tess glanced back at the big house. "I don't know. Gideon is still sleeping—"

Chauncey gulped in air. "Beggin' yer pardon, Mistress Jericho; I've not made myself clear. Not M'lord Cade. Just ye."

"Just me? But why?"

"Don't know, mum. She didn't say. Can ye come?"

"Why, I suppose so, if she needs me." She nodded toward the stables. "I was just about to go out riding anyway."

"Very good, mum!" Chauncey beamed. "I've just one stop to make on the way there, at Stover's Mill. Some very important business for her ladyship—"

"Cream cakes," said Tess, and relaxed a bit. Emilia's summons couldn't be too desperate. "But Stover's Mill is northwest of here, isn't it? That's the opposite direction from Hardwick Hall."

"Aye, mum," he told her. "I thought I'd ask if ye was comin', then ride on there 'n' fetch ye on the way back, once ye've packed 'n' all that."

Tess didn't want to go back to her room and see Gideon, not until she'd had time to think. "I'm already dressed for riding. Why don't you ride on to Stover's Mill, and I'll just get started?"

"I wouldn't want ye to ride alone, mum."

"Nonsense; I do it all the time. And I know the way. I'll just rub down that horse for you, and you can go and have some breakfast up at the big house."

"If 'tis just the same with ye, mum, I'll eat and rub the horse at Stover's Mill." He winked. "There's a serving girl there I've got my eye on."

Tess laughed and slapped the steed's flank. "Get on, then! I'll see you back at Hardwick Hall." He waved and galloped away. She went into the stables, nostrils curling at the thick scent of dung. Ordinarily she would have begun the mucking, but between feeling out of sorts and Emilia's summons she decided to leave it. She'd just got Linzy saddled when she heard the doors open again, and Gideon calling, "Tess!"

Instead of answering, she ducked down in the stall. *I just can't bear to face him now,* she told herself, keeping silent. *I need to sort matters out, to decide what to do.*

"Tess! Are you here?"

Satan whinnied at his master, and Linzy nickered, but there was no other sound. After a moment Tess heard the squeak of hinges and the bang of the door as he went out again.

She counted to a hundred, then led Linzy to the front of the stable and peered out. He was nowhere in sight, so she went out, closed the latch, and clambered into the saddle. The sun was rising directly ahead behind the

White Moor, blinding her as she rode down the hill toward the village. Its reflection off the water as she crossed the bridge above the Clun was so glaring that she turned her head, looking back.

Gideon was standing in the middle of the road a hundred yards behind her, staring after her.

He didn't speak. Tess had reined in without thinking as she saw him, realizing she must have ridden right past him, that he would have seen her leave the stables and known that she'd been hiding from him.

Go to him, a voice inside her whispered. *Tell him where you are going. Tell him that you love him.* But then she thought of how he'd whispered Suzette's name in his sleep, and pride rose and choked off the voice. *Let him wonder*, she decided instead, *and worry, as I do.*

She dug her heels into Linzy and galloped away. Once, as she started the climb up the White Moor, she stopped and looked back again. He was still standing there.

" 'Mornin', Teresa!"

The cheery voice made Tess jump; she glanced to her left and saw the Widow Jonas, herb basket over her arm, straightening up from a clump of moss she'd been examining. "Good morning," she said shortly, then asked from force of habit, "Is someone ill?"

"Millie Brady," the widow confirmed. "Poor thing, 'tis a devil of a time she's havin' with this pregnancy."

When was the last time I had my bleeding?

"Coming so close on her other baby," Tess said cautiously, "perhaps it would be best if she got rid of this one."

"Got rid of it?" Rachel echoed.

"Aye. Couldn't you make her miscarry? There must be something in that basket that would do the trick."

The herb woman's sharp dark gaze met Tess's. "There's some healers might do that, allowin' that the mother weren't too far along. But not me. It's not my way."

"Of course, Millie has got a husband," Tess went on after a pause. "I reckon that makes a difference."

"Not to the babe it don't," said Rachel. "How've *ye* been feelin'?"

"Me? I'm just fine! Never better!" Tess told her, and quickly rode away.

From the top of the White Moor she looked down on Windber-on-Clun, lying peaceful and hushed in this season of plenty. The glasshouse gleamed in the bright morning sun; the whitewashed walls of the cottages sparkled; the new stables stood ready to shelter Linzy's colt and dozens still to come. The fields were lush with unaccustomed abundance; even the rocks along the riverbank seemed freshly scrubbed clean.

She couldn't see Gideon any longer, but there was her father stumping out of the cottage with Job at his heels, on his way to the well. How beautiful this place is, she thought, and felt a lump rise in her throat. How awful if I never saw it again.

Goose, she told herself, swallowing hard. You are only going to Hardwick Hall, not the end of the world. You'll be back in time for breakfast tomorrow. And you can make up with Gideon then.

The sun passed behind a cloud, masking the valley in shadows. Tess shivered in the sudden chill. "Let's go, Linzy," she said.

The first person Tess saw as she neared Hardwick Hall was the droll coachman, Chester; he was on the lawn with a set of shears, trimming a boxwood into the shape of a camel. "Thank heaven you've come!" he called as she rode up to him.

"Her ladyship isn't ill, is she? Chauncey said—"

"No, no, not ill." He set the shears in the grass. "It's something much worse, I'm afraid. She's got a secret."

"A secret?"

He nodded sagely. "All of the symptoms are there. Restlessness, loss of appetite—"

"You're pulling my leg."

He flung an arm toward the house. "Go and see for yourself. Mark my words, she's got a secret, a great whopping one, and she's been dying for someone to tell it to. That's why she's asked you here."

Across the green lawns came Lady Hardwick's voice, so surprisingly young and robust. "Yoo-hoo, Tess!" She was leaning out from a window. "For God's sake, don't dawdle; I've something to tell you!" Chester grinned at Tess triumphantly, then frowned as his mistress went on:

"Chester, what *are* you doing to that bush? It looks like a hedgehog! Leave it be and take Linzy to the stables to rub her down. Don't you know she's carrying my colt?"

Tess squinted at the boxwood. "She's right, you know. It does look like a hedgehog."

Chester stuck out his tongue at her and took Linzy's reins.

After the long, hot ride, Hardwick Hall felt deliciously cool and smelled of rosewood and lemon polish. Tess had no sooner come through the door than Emilia rolled toward her, pushed along in her wheeled chair. "Hello, my dear!" she cried as Tess kissed her cheek. "How well you look! Put on a bit of weight, haven't you? My, it suits you." Then she whispered, "Just one moment, while I get rid of Nancy. . . . Nancy!"

"Aye, mum?" asked the maid pushing the chair.

"Take me out to the gardens, if you please, and then bring us something to drink—berry crush would be nice. And cakes, and fruit, and some jam and bread—and mind you have Cook slice the bread thin . . ."

She went on adding to the list all the way out to the garden, until Tess felt obliged to protest, "You mustn't go to such trouble!"

"Hush!" Emilia hissed. "I want to keep her and Cook busy, so I've a chance to talk to you alone."

Once Nancy got her mistress settled in the shade of the grape arbor and left them, Emilia beckoned Tess closer. "Guess what?" she demanded, blue eyes sparkling with excitement. "I've found out who Gideon is!"

"You've what?" Tess asked blankly.

Her hostess sighed with impatience. "Don't you recall I told you I didn't believe he was who he said he was? That he had to be *someone*?"

Up until then, Tess had forgotten that ridiculous conversation. "Oh, Emilia. Don't tell me you're going to start that all over again."

"Well, for your information, he *is* somebody!" Emilia declared. "Now, here's what I did. I had Chester draw a sort of picture of Gideon. It wasn't much of a likeness, but that didn't matter because I told him to make it look as though Gideon were much younger. Twelve or thir-

teen years younger, I said, which is what Gideon would
have been when my grandnephew was at Oxford. You
remember I told you about my grandnephew that went to
Oxford? Anyway, I sent the drawing to Sebastian—that's
my grandnephew, suggesting that he see if it seemed
familiar, or rather if there was anyone who'd been at
university with him that he thought it might be. I got a
letter from him two days past—he's a terrible correspon-
dent, Sebastian, but then, I suppose all the young are
when it comes to that."

Tess, weary from her long ride and devoutly wishing
she had a glass of water, never mind berry crush, tried
hard to follow the thread that led through all of this.
"And did he?"

"And did he? Well, my dear, he said there wasn't any
doubt in his mind the moment he saw it. That Chester—
who would have believed it! I shan't tell him, of course,
or I'll never get the shrubbery trimmed to my liking.
He'll get it into his head he's an artist, and that will be
that! Though perhaps you think that's selfish of me." She
paused, eyeing Tess as though daring her to admit it.

"I think Chester would walk across hot coals barefoot
for you," Tess told her, "and what's more, you know it.
Now, if you don't mind, what's all this about Gideon
being who he's not?"

Naturally Nancy chose that moment to appear with a
tray piled high with Emilia's requests. Laying them out
and doing the serving necessitated a good five minutes'
delay; then Chester showed up to inquire whether Linzy
should be left out to pasture or fed in the stables, prompting a debate that Emilia eventually won. Then the house-
keeper wanted to know whether to make up a room for
Tess, and the cook had some question about dinner. All
told, half an hour must have passed before Tess was
alone with her hostess once more.

"Honestly," Emilia sighed, "you'd think they hadn't
got a brain to split between 'em. Where was I?"

"You were about to tell me what your nephew wrote
to you."

"Ah, yes. He's the Duke of Clary."

"How nice," said Tess, thinking she meant her nephew.

"No, no, girl, not Sebastian, Gideon! He's the ninth Duke of Clary."

Tess set her crush cup down with a click. "A *duke*?"

Emilia nodded vigorously. "Sebastian took one look at the drawing and said to himself: Why, as I live and breathe! They weren't in the same college, mind you; Sebastian is a Balliol man, and he thinks Gideon was Christ Church—or did he say Corpus Christi? And Sebastian's a bit younger, but—"

"What would a duke be doing in Windber-on-Clun?" asked Tess, not even realizing she'd interrupted.

"Well, I suppose by law he never actually *became* the duke. Still, that's who he is. As I say, Sebastian no more than saw that drawing, but he said: Why, of course! It's James! And—"

"James?" Tess broke in again. "Who is James?"

"Why, Gideon, of course. That's his real name—James Anthony George Trelawny. And—"

James Anthony George Trelawny. Tess didn't notice any more of Emilia's excited chatter; she was searching her memory. Somewhere she'd seen that name before. Where? She let her mind roam and saw darkness, darkness lit by a candle, and the cluttered surface of Gideon's desk. In his study . . .

Not on her trip there last night. No, it was the time before, when he'd been in London. Not in the first drawer, with the writing paper, or the second, with his drafting tools. Not in the third, with the letters. No, it had been in the last drawer, the one with the pile of documents. It had been on a document. James Anthony George Trelawny. Coupled with another name. Suzette's. On a marriage certificate.

Emilia was still talking, but Tess didn't hear her. She couldn't hear anything except blood pounding in her head. Somehow she got to her feet and stood leaning on the pretty little garden table. Emilia stopped talking and stared up at her like a startled owl.

"Would you excuse me, please?" Tess heard herself say. "I've just remembered something, and I must go. Thank you very much."

"But—"

"Good-bye!" She gave a little curtsy and went into the house through the garden doors.

"Nancy!" her hostess called at her back. "Nancy, get out here!" Tess went on walking, through the long corridors of Hardwick Hall and out the front doors.

Away from the shaded gardens, the sunlight seemed blinding. As she crossed the green lawn toward the stables, Chester came toward her, grinning broadly. "Well? Was I right? Has she a secret?"

"There's been a change of plans," said Tess. "I'll need Linzy again, right away." She kept walking toward the stables.

He ran a few steps to catch up with her. "I hope there's no trouble."

"Nancy!" Tess heard again from the house.

"No," she said. "No trouble. Just a change of plans."

"Well, I've got her fed and groomed," he told her, "and I daresay she's ready for another thirty miles, your Linzy. She's a tough little lady."

"Aye, that she is. Here, girl!" Tess whistled her away from the feeding trough to saddle her again.

Chester gave her a hand up. "Look here, it will be dark before you get to Windber. Chauncey's back; I'll have him ride with you."

"I'm not going to Windber."

"Oh, then, if you're not going that far—"

"Thank you, Chester. Good-bye." She spurred Linzy across the lawn, past the outlandish figures carved into the shrubberies, and onto the road. Her world had just exploded, and yet she rode calmly, competently, sitting tall in the saddle, hands and head held just right, the way Ben had taught her years and years before.

Of all the possible reasons why he wouldn't marry her, it was the one she'd never even thought of—and yet the one she'd known instantly was true.

James Anthony George Trelawny. Suzette Marie-Louise de la Mare.

He couldn't marry her because he was already wed.

22

"State yar business, please."

State your business. "I've come to seek work," Tess said hesitantly, looking down at the handsome young guard at the gate. "That is . . . if it's allowed?"

"Oh, aye, right enough," he told her, rubbing a bit of dog dirt from the side of his boot with his pike. "What sort o' work?"

"I'm not sure exactly. Do I have to say?"

"Nah. I'll just mark another under 'Domestic'; that's wot most o' the young girls come for." He squinted up against the bright sun. "Brought the fine weather with ya, dint ya, lass? So, how long was ya plannin' to stay?"

"I'm afraid I don't know that either."

The young guard's mate came to join him, grinning at Tess. " 'Allo, luv. Wot they wants to know is, is ya on stayin' permanent, like, or is ya makin' money to take 'ome wi' ya."

"Neither. When I have enough, I'm going to the New World. To Delaware." She pronounced the strange word carefully. "I've family there." That was a bit of an exaggeration, perhaps, but hadn't Lord Halifax said that his tenants were like family?

"More's the pity," said the mate. "Dint I tell ya, Tommy, all the pretty ones is goin' to the colonies. Soon there'll be naught left 'ere but fishwives."

Tommy grunted agreement. " 'Ave ya got a place to stay, lass?"

"Why, Tommy! Are ya offerin'?" the mate asked, leering.

"I was planning to put up at an inn."

"Oh, well." The young guard's manner changed slightly, became more deferential. "If ya've got money—"

"Of course I've got money! You'd have to be daft to come to London without it." Tess pulled her cloak aside to show them the weighty purse hanging from her belt.

"Oh, ya'd be surprised, lass, wot some folk'll try," Tommy's mate said. "Come 'ere without a penny to their names, they do, 'n' wind up beggars on the streets. But ya oughtter do fine wi' wot ya got there."

"I saved up," she told them. "I've been planning this for a long time."

Those in line behind her at the city gate had begun to grow restless. "Either screw 'er or pass 'er, bub!" an impatient voice shouted.

Tommy brandished his pike. "Mind yar filthy tongue!" Then he turned back to Tess. "Good luck to ya, lass, on yar way to the New World."

"Thank you kindly," she said. "There's just one thing more. Could you tell me, please, where I might find an herb seller? My pony's got a burr-sore, and I want to make her a poultice."

"Smithfield Market," the two said in unison. Tommy glared at his friend, then went on: "Down this road 'ere to Farrington Street, then turn right 'n' it'll be on yar left. Ya can't miss it. Biggest herb market in the 'ole city." Tess reached toward her purse, but he waved her on. "Nah, luv, get on wi' ya! Glad we could 'elp. Good day!"

Tess rode on through the gate, then wiped away the sweat that had beaded on her upper lip. If the guard had accepted the penny she felt obligated to offer, she would have been down to a single pence piece beneath the pebbles she'd put in the purse to make it look weighty. There's one useful thing, she thought grimly, learned from Gideon Cade.

It was the last bit left from the sixpence Gideon had given her on her first trip to Hardwick Hall that summer. She'd had to spend the rest on food and lodging, more for Linzy than for herself. She didn't dare push her the way she had on their last wild ride to the city, for fear the pony would lose the foal she was carrying. That, she supposed, was what folks called irony. Now she had only to find a place to stay, and some work.

And there was one more thing to be attended to.

Smithfield Market was vast, acre upon acre of stalls selling everything from cattle to clothing to coffee. One entire section, with three rows of long stalls, was set aside for herb and flower vendors. Tess wandered through with Linzy on her lead, pausing now and again to finger a bunch of betony or lamb's-ear as she studied the faces of the men and women behind their tables of wares.

" 'Elp ya, pretty miss?"

Tess glanced up into the dark eyes of a small woman in a bright red kerchief. "I'm not sure . . ."

"Was it somethin' in particular ya was lookin' on buyin'?"

"Well, it's for a friend." The woman smiled encouragingly. "She's having . . . female troubles."

"Ah." The red kerchief bobbed. "Trouble with 'er monthlies?"

Tess nodded, relieved.

"Why, then, this'd be wot she's wantin'." The vendor tossed a bouquet of big silvery leaves toward her. "Lady's mantle. Nothin' better for easin' the pain 'n' cramps."

"Oh." Tess rubbed the soft silky leaves between her fingers. "But what if . . . what if she wasn't having her monthlies?"

The woman's smiling mouth pursed. "Wot d'ya mean?"

"I mean, what if she wants to, but isn't?" Tess swallowed. "And hasn't. For a long time."

The encouragement in those black eyes turned to wary fear. "Wot, are ya mad?" the woman shrilled, and snatched the leaves back. "I'm a God-fearin' woman, I is! I've got no truck wi' wot ya're askin'. Be gone wi' ya, then!"

"Hush!" Tess hissed. "You needn't shout at the top of your lungs! I'm going."

"Best get yarself to a priest 'n' ask 'is forgiveness!" the vendor cried. "Yar friend, indeed!"

Cheeks flaming, certain that everyone nearby had overheard and now knew her mission, Tess clutched Linzy's lead and stumbled away from the stall.

Beyond the rows of tables, close to a stand of willows bending over a stream, she saw some little sheds and headed for them, wanting only to be alone, to regain her composure. So you were unlucky on your first try, she told herself; the next time will be better. But her heart was beating so wildly she did not believe she should ever find the nerve to try again.

You must! she reminded herself. You came here to get to the New World, to make a new start. And you cannot do that if you are carrying Gideon's child!

Gideon. In her mind she saw him smiling at her, saw the love in his blue eyes, blue as these October skies above her, when he whispered, "I want you . . ." Liar, she thought, fist clenched around Linzy's lead as tears streamed down her cheeks. God, I hate you, you liar!

His child growing inside her. A boy, black-haired and laughing. Or a girl, tiny and lovely, with blue, blue eyes—

"Miss?"

The soft voice at her elbow made her jump. She turned and through her tears saw a spot of bright red kerchief, and the herb seller's sharp dark gaze. She took a hasty step away, fearful of another scene, but the woman caught her hand. "Didn't mean to scare ya back there," she whispered, "but wot ya're askin'—well, 'tain't the sort o' business oughtter be discussed in broad daylight. D'ya ken wot I say?"

A laughing boy. A blue-eyed girl.

Tess steeled her heart. "Can you help me?"

The woman put her finger to her lips and led Tess beneath the overhang of one of the sheds. "How far gone are ya, luv?"

"Three months, as near as I can figure." The herb seller shook her head. "That's not too late, is it?"

"Nay, not too late, though 'tis easier when ya're not so far along." She took a small stoppered bottle from her apron pocket. " 'Ere, this'll do ya. Drink it all down when there's naught else in yar belly."

Tess reached for the vial. "My stomach's empty now—"

The woman pulled it back. " 'Ang on, 'ang on! Don't ya know it'll cost ya?"

"Oh, of course! I didn't mean . . ." Tess's hand found the purse at her belt. "I have money. How much for the bottle?"

Those dark eyes flashed to the purse, then back to her face. "One penny'll do ya."

Tess scrambled eagerly to find a pence piece. "I can't tell you what this means to me."

"Faith, luv, everyone makes mistakes." The woman's crabbed fingers took the penny. "Mind ya don't flash that purse about now ya're in the big city."

"Oh!" Quickly Tess slipped it inside her cloak. "Thank you. I'll be careful."

" 'Ere ya go, then." The woman handed her the vial. "Mind yar stomach's empty. 'Twill take a few hours afore it works; ya'd best find someplace to lie down. By tomorrow ya'll be right as rain." Then she winked. "Forget where ya got it, though; I don't need no trouble, if ya know wot I mean." She patted Tess's shoulder. "God bless ya, luv." Then, red kerchief bobbing, she scurried back across the market to her stall.

Alone in the shadow of the shed, Tess uncorked the bottle and sniffed its contents. The liquid inside smelled reassuringly green and earthy, like the balms she and Rachel had rubbed on Ben's wounds. Linzy was watching her in the half-darkness, her black velvet eyes reproachful. "I haven't any choice," Tess said softly. "He lied to me. I've got to go away, make a clean start. It's the only thing to do." The pony looked back at her steadily. She gulped the stuff down.

The taste was horribly bitter. Hands clenched, she waited for something to happen, but nothing did.

"Well, she did say it would take a few hours." The sound of her own voice was oddly comforting. "I suppose the thing to do now is find an inn to put us up for the night." By the morning it would all be over. Come the morrow, she would have her own life back again.

His black hair. His blue eyes . . .

"God forgive me," she whispered, and led Linzy along the stream, away from the marketplace.

She turned onto a likely-looking cobbled street, found a mounting stone, and climbed atop the pony. Then they meandered through the city, with Tess looking for signs for inns. She saw several close by the waterfront, but they seemed awfully dingy, and a crowd of drunken men burst from one as she approached and began to call out to her, so she left that street and headed up another as fast as she could.

The buildings lining this road seemed somehow familiar. But then, so many of these crooked, narrow roads overhung by tall houses looked exactly the same . . . This one, Tess noticed, was rather deserted; when she heard hoofbeats behind her she turned in the saddle, feeling apprehensive. But it was only two shabby men tugging at an overburdened donkey, paying her no mind.

When she reached the top of street she glanced back again. The men were laughing together, sharing swigs from a bottle; they showed no sign of noticing her. Up ahead, on her right, was a sign that looked to be for an inn. A place to lie down, the woman had said. Perhaps this place would do.

The pain came on so quickly, with no warning. One moment she was riding along toward the sign, and in the next she'd doubled over, clutching her belly and gasping. It was as though someone had taken a dull, rusty knife and was twisting it deep in her bowels, or searing them with fire. Then, just as quickly, it passed, leaving her hanging halfway from the saddle, panting for air.

Linzy had stopped as her mistress pulled up on the reins; now she waited, whinnying softly, as though she sensed something was wrong. The healer hadn't said anything about pain! Tess thought, her muscles slowly uncoiling. A little bit of bleeding, that was all she'd expected—

She cried out as it seized her again.

The road ahead was black and spinning. Out of the darkness a boy's voice called to her: "Ey, lady, pretty lady, can ya spare a farthin'? There's a kindly look about ya. Just a farthin' fer a poor starvin' lad—"

"Help me," Tess whispered into the blackness. "Please. Help me—"

For an instant the pain receded, and she saw him: a small, ragged beggar boy standing by the road with his arm outstretched. "Alms, good lady, fer a poor starvin' lad! Won't ya take pity on me, good lady?" Linzy was moving again, moving past him, and he let out a curse: "Aw, to 'ell wi' ya then!" Then the pain came on once more, blinding her with its terrible force, sending her sprawling against Linzy's neck, facedown in her mane.

"Lady?"

The boy's voice, and then a chorus of others telling him to mind his own business, get away, get back. Hands tugging her from the saddle, grabbing at the reins. A woman speaking, low and harsh: "Inside 'er cloak there, mates, there's a great huge purse. Aye, there's the goods!" With a tremendous effort Tess looked up and saw a small face with bright black eyes beneath a red kerchief, and two men, and a donkey. She smelled herbs on the air.

" 'Ere, now, wot d'ya think ya're doin'?" That was the boy again; Tess could see his dirty freckled face hovering above her. Then the woman:

"Give the little shit a farthin', Roy, to be on 'is way."

"Are ye mad, Maire?"

"Wot, are ye? This purse must 'old fifty pounds!"

"I think she's comin' round," said one of the men, but the woman just cackled.

"Don't be a damned fool, Roy. Wot I gave 'er'll kill 'er."

And Tess knew the herb seller was right as the pain engulfed her one last time.

IV

23

Hell, it turned out, wasn't hot, but warm: a lovely toasty warm, neither damp nor dry, rather like sitting on a cold winter's night at just the right distance from a crackling fire. And it didn't smell of brimstone or sulfur, either, but of soap and clean linen and rosewater, of all things. Someone ought to tell that to Dad, Tess thought; he'd be ever so surprised.

The only truly unpleasant aspects of the place were the incessant whispers that surrounded her in the darkness— and, of course, the pain. But even that came and went. All in all, Tess decided as the whispers washed over her, as she braced herself for the next bout of agony in her belly, hell wasn't nearly so bad as everyone said. She'd expected far worse.

Gradually the intervals between the pains lengthened and the whispers grew clearer. Then one day the darkness lifted, just as though a veil had been pulled away from her eyes, and she became aware of shadows drifting across a wide field of light. They came toward her and then receded, and though they went on whispering, she wasn't sure anymore that they were demons, not angels, because it seemed when they were near her the pain grew less. One of them offered her water. She drank for aeons, and fell into a dreamless sleep.

When she woke it was dark again, and silent. She made some small movement and saw a light appear in the distance, like a candle flame. It moved closer, borne by a shadow that slowly resolved into the figure of a small, dark, smiling woman who was vaguely familiar. It took

Tess a long time to place her. Then she knew: the little foreign maid from the Peacock Inn. She reached out to Tess, who flinched in fright.

"What are you doing here?" she whispered.

"Mam'selle se reveille enfin, c'est très bien ça—"

"What are you doing here?" Tess demanded again, her voice high and hysterical. "Where am I? What is this place?"

The little maid took a step backward. *"Pardon, mam'selle,* but my English—I go and fetch Madame."

Madame? She couldn't mean Suzette, surely! "Wait!" Tess cried, but the maid only bobbed her head and retreated, leaving her alone. The last person in the world Tess wanted to see at that moment, next to Gideon of course, was his wife. Closing her eyes against a sudden wave of nauseous dizziness, she struggled to sit up, but soon lost the fight. All her limbs were weak as water, floppy as fish. Hearing whispering voices again, she lay quietly, waiting for them to go away. At last they did. She opened her eyes.

Suzette and the maid were standing over her, peering down worriedly.

She clamped her eyes shut again, but too late; Suzette had seen her. *"Chérie?"* she said softly. "Can you speak? Can you hear me?" Tess made no response. *"Eh bien,"* the woman's gentle voice went on, "I will send word to your home that you are alive now, at least."

That opened Tess's eyes. "No!" she said frantically, loud as she could. "No, you can't—"

"Chérie, I must," Suzette insisted. "They will worry and wonder—"

"No! No one must know where I am!" Even this brief speech exhausted her; she lay catching her breath. Suzette put a cool white hand to her forehead, gesturing for the maid to bring water. Tess sipped from the glass that was held to her mouth, waited, and realized she didn't know that herself. "Where am I, anyway?"

"At my house. The Peacock Inn."

The Peacock Inn. "How did I get here?"

"Do you not remember, *chérie?* Thieves set upon you. Gypsies." Tess thought of the small woman in the red

kerchief and shuddered. Again that soothing hand brushed
her brow. "But a boy, a beggar, he ran for my gatekeeper, and together they drove the Gypsies away." Suddenly she smiled. "I gave the boy five pounds for his
bravery. He said he remembers you from Christmastide—
your fire-colored hair."

Tess remembered him too, now. They'd traded jests
about blessings; he was the one who told her that in
London one got nothing for free. "He wasn't hurt?" she
asked anxiously.

"Oh, non, pas du tout. He said he would use the
money to buy a passage to the New World." Again she
smiled. "He will make his fortune there, he says, and
come back and marry you someday."

Tess didn't want to talk of marriage. "How is Linzy?"
she whispered. The foreign women stared at her blankly.
"My horse . . ."

"Ah, le cheval!" Suzette nodded. "She is safe, *ma
petite,* safe and sound in my stables. But you . . ." Her
worried expression returned. *"Le docteur, le médicin*—you
understand? I called him here, and he tell me that you
are *empoissonée*—poisoned! How could this happen?"

"Poisoned . . ." Tess hoped she was too sick for blushing. What a fool she'd been! The herb-seller never meant
for that potion to do anything but kill her, so she and her
friends could steal her purse. "I remember now," she
lied. "I was thirsty, and the woman gave me something
to drink. Then they must have followed me."

"Oh, Mon Dieu!" Suzette spoke in rapid French to the
maid, who wagged her head and clucked her tongue, and
then addressed Tess again. "Charmian, she agrees, this is
a terrible thing!"

Tess could feel herself growing weaker moment by
moment. She licked her lips, fighting for consciousness.
There was more she must know. "How long have I been
here?"

Suzette pursed her painted mouth, considering. "This
is Friday, and it was Wednesday that you came. So, two
days." She patted Tess's hand. "You must rest now, and
get strong. No more talking! Charmian will stay with
you. I have work I must do."

"Wait!" Tess seized her wrist, holding on with faint strength. "Please, you must promise me—don't tell anyone that I'm here! No one at all."

Suzette frowned. "But your family . . ."

How much did the foreign woman know about her? Tess wondered. Clearly not much. Certainly not that she was her own husband's lover, or she'd never have taken Tess in. "I've had a falling-out with my family," she lied again; it grew progressively easier. "With everyone at home. That's why I ran away. Please, tell no one. Promise me."

The Frenchwoman hesitated for a long moment, then nodded. "*Eh bien,* if you are sure that is what you want." There was a strange expression on her lovely face—as though, Tess thought, her worst fears had been realized. Then she wondered: Why should I think that?

"I'm grateful," Tess murmured. "I want to repay you—"

"*Chut!*" Suzette hushed her, smiling. "Later. Now you must work hard to get well, *n'est-ce pas?* You will do this for me?" Weak though she was, Tess started to laugh. The Frenchwoman's fine plucked eyebrows knit together; she and Charmian exchanged puzzled glances. "What? What did I say?"

Tess just closed her eyes, shook her head. How to explain, all barriers of language aside, the impossible irony of her lover's wife begging that she get better for her sake, when the root of the illness was her attempt to be rid of Gideon's child? As she slipped away into sleep again, she was consoled by the knowledge that that attempt had succeeded. Horrible though the cost was, she had her own life back again.

For the next fortnight Tess lay in her borrowed bed, sipping the broths that Charmian brought her, nurturing her strength. The room to which she'd been brought bore no resemblance to the pleasure bower in which she'd last stayed at the Peacock Inn; this one was simply furnished, meant for a servant, she guessed. She was comfortable enough, though from time to time the pain still gripped her belly and bowels. In a peculiar way, though, the agony reassured her that whatever the herb seller's intention, the end result had been a miscarriage. She even worked up the courage to ask Charmian if, when the gatekeeper first brought her there, she'd been bleeding. *"Ah, oui, mam'selle!"* the little maid assured her, nodding vigorously. *"Il y a beaucoup de la boue; nous devons laver tout ton corps!"* She made washing motions all up and down her body, then went back to her work, singing

> *Je t'aime, je t'aime*
> *Avec tout mon coeur;*
> *Je chant, je chant*
> *Les plaisirs d'amour.*

"What does that mean, that song?" Tess asked.

"Oh, *mam'selle*, my English—"

"Just the first part. The beginning."

"Ah!" Charmian's brow cleared. " *'Je t'aime, je t'aime'* —this is, 'I love you, I love you.' And—"

"Never mind the rest," said Tess. She'd suspected as much, but wanted it confirmed. She needed to make plans.

She found it hard to think clearly, though, with the multitude of questions that chased through her mind. If Gideon—if James . . . she must think of him as James now—was married to Suzette, why did they live apart? Perhaps it was because he took lovers. Or perhaps she did. And if he was a duke, why did his wife operate a brothel? Why had he changed his name? She might have understood if he'd done it so his wife couldn't find him. But he'd told Oren that Suzette always knew where he was, so it couldn't be that.

If he was a duke, what in God's name was he doing in Windber, of all places? And why hadn't he got any money—weren't nobility rich? Sometimes she made herself dizzy trying to sort through it all. Charmian would find her slumped in her bed and run to bring warm milk custard or broth; the Gallic temperament, Tess discovered, believed all woes could be assuaged with the help of food.

And yet the treatment worked. In time, beneath the barrage of bland meals, the pains subsided. She lost her drawn, wan look and the dark rings that circled her eyes. Finally she felt healthy enough that she asked Charmian to send for Suzette to come to her room so that they could discuss what Tess's future would hold.

She'd seen little of Suzette during the weeks of her convalescence, so little that she wondered if perhaps the woman regretted having taken her in. But when she appeared in the small bedchamber, she was gay and smiling, though evidently in the midst of making her toilette.

"Bonjour, chérie!" she cried, trailing lengths of feathers and unbuttoned blue satin. "How fine it is to see you out of your bed! Forgive me, *je suis toute déshabillée,* but Charmian will help me dress as we talk."

"Forgive *me,*" Tess said quickly, "I see you are busy; this can wait—"

"Non, non, chérie! The Duke of Buckingham comes tonight with a party of friends, this is all. But there is still much time." She gave directions in French to Charmian, who circled around her, buttoning and buckling and lacing the resplendent gown while her mistress eyed Tess expectantly. *"Eh bien, qu'est-ce que c'est?"*

Tess flushed, wishing that the maid weren't there to hear, but then it occurred to her that if she hadn't the nerve to speak of such things in front of another woman, she would scarcely be brave enough to *do* them with men. So she squared her shoulders. "First off, I want to thank you from the bottom of my heart for all your kindness to me. I don't know why you should have gone to such lengths for a virtual stranger—"

"Perhaps," Suzette said, smiling, "to make up for my mistake the first time you come here, when I tell Gideon you are with child."

Tess took a long, slow breath. It was the first time his name had been broached between them. "You don't need to call him 'Gideon' any longer to me," she said steadily. "I know who he really is. I know . . . everything."

Suzette's lovely sculptured face registered surprise; she glanced at Charmian, but the maid was busy with a stubborn hook and eye. "He told you this?" she asked softly.

"No. Someone else did." Tess shrugged. "I just wanted you to know. It's neither here nor there. You mentioned the last time that I was here. We spoke then of the importance of paying one's debts." Suzette nodded, as if to say she remembered too. "Well, I owe you the debt of my life. And I want to pay it back by working for you."

There was a pause. Then, "Charmian," the Frenchwoman said, and let out a long string of directions in her native language having to do, Tess gathered, with some jewelry she wanted to wear. The little maid darted out of the room; Suzette closed and then leaned against the door.

"Work for me," she repeated. "You mean, *peut-être*, in the kitchens? A cook, a maid?"

Tess shook her head. "I think you know what I mean."

Suzette let out a sigh that did not sound encouraging. *"Ma petite—"*

"I'm very good at it already," Tess told her, head held high, green eyes flashing, "and I'll work hard to get better. I could study your books—"

"I am sure you would, *chérie*." She smiled faintly, crossing to the bed and sinking down on it wearily. "But there is something I must explain. To give yourself to a man for money—it is not like having a lover, *tu comprends?* You must suit his caprice, *oui?* What you call his whims. It is not always pleasant."

Tess looked straight into her troubled blue eyes. "I've been beaten and raped by a man I thought I loved—a man I thought loved me. Nothing a stranger could do would be worse than that."

"Mon Dieu," Suzette whispered, and bowed her auburn head. *"Oh, ma pauvre chérie.* I am sorry."

Tess acknowledged the woman's pity with a negligent nod; that night in the barn with Jack seemed very long ago. Gideon—James—had hurt her far more cruelly, but that was because she'd let him into her heart. She did not intend to make that sort of mistake with a man again. No, she thought, the casual coupling of courtesan and client would suit her very well indeed. "Will you let me, then? Please?"

Still Suzette hesitated. "It is not so simple," she said

finally. "You have little experience, I think, with men such as come here."

"Gentlemen, you mean." Tess nodded matter-of-factly. "I know. But I'll learn. I can learn anything. I learn very quickly, my father always said." For an instant the pain returned, in her heart and not her belly. If Ben ever found out about this, it would kill him. She pushed his fire-scarred face from her memory, made her heart hard.

Suzette had seen the suffering cross her face and misinterpreted it. "You are still not whole, not well, *chérie*. You need more time—"

"If I don't soon get out of this room," Tess said frankly, "I'll go out of my mind. Let me at least start my lessons. And I must look after Linzy—though I'm sure your stableboy has given her good care."

The Frenchwoman laughed, relieved to have the subject changed. "Ah, *oui*, he adores her! He tells me that she is bearing; he clucks—that is right, clucks?—over her like the mother hen."

Charmian came back in then, with a small blue velvet case. *"Pardon, madame."* She curtsied. "I had trouble to find them, it has been so long."

"C'est bien, Charmian," Suzette told her, and gave Tess a clandestine smile as if to acknowledge that she'd set the maid a lengthy task on purpose, so that they might have time alone. "Finish now with my dress, *s'il vous plaît."* The maid handed her the case and did as Madame bade her, completing the intricate fastenings of the gown. *"Et puis—"* Suitably arrayed at last, Suzette smoothed down her skirts. "For Mademoiselle Teresa, Charmian, I would like you to find a pretty dress and to put up her hair." Seeing Tess's eyes widen, she wagged a finger. "Not to work tonight, *non*. But you can watch from the balcony. The Duke of Buckingham . . ." She made a moue of distaste. "If anyone can turn you from this notion you have, it will be he and his friends."

"And if he doesn't?" Tess asked eagerly.

"If he doesn't . . . well, then, we see." She smiled, opening the velvet case. Tess drew in her breath. Inside was a necklace crafted of deep blue stones. "Lapis lazuli," Suzette said fondly. "James brought them back for me years ago from the Holy Land. He said they matched my eyes."

In her mind Tess heard what he'd whispered to her once: *I'd drape you with emeralds to match your green eyes.* Her hands curled into fists. God, I hate you, she thought, you inhuman son of a bitch.

She looked at Suzette. "There is one thing more. If *he* comes here, I cannot see him. I don't want him to know where I am. I never, ever want to see him again."

The Frenchwoman nodded, her blue eyes clouded. *"Eh bien, chérie.* It will be as you ask. Of all people, I understand."

24

Later that evening, when Charmian had bathed Tess and dressed her in a red silk gown and put up her hair in a long fiery coil, she led her to a small gilt chair in the high balcony that encircled the gambling floor. *"Et voilà."* The maid showed her how to draw a few yards of the blue draperies so that she could watch what went on below and yet not be seen.

"Why bother with this?" Tess asked of the curtain.

Charmian shrugged. *"Monsieur le duc,* he likes his privacy. And sometimes he pays to come and watch."

"Watch what?"

"Who wins. Who loses. You stay here, *bien?"*

"Bien," Tess told her. Charmian smiled and hurried off downstairs.

Though Tess felt a bit foolish hidden there behind the curtain, she was tremendously pleased at the outcome of her discussion with Suzette. Some night soon, she would be among the poised, elegant women who glided over the floor below in their silks and jewels, readying the gaming tables, laying out dice and decks of cards for the expected guests. It was overcautious of Suzette not to let her do so this evening. Still, she supposed there were certain refinements of behavior one was expected to observe in dealing with dukes and such. She would watch and learn.

A troupe of musicians arrived and was led by Suzette into the balcony opposite Tess's curtained niche; soon the cacophony they made tuning their fiddles and practicing their pipes filled the air. Tess thought how strained

314

and tense her benefactress looked. Well, so would she be, she supposed, if the great Duke of Buckingham were coming to call! Windber-on-Clun hadn't much interest in politics, but a proper awe of George Villiers, the second Duke of Buckingham, had reached even there. He was chief minister to King Charles and his closest adviser; it was said he was the handsomest man in the kingdom, and the finest soldier, dancer, and swordsman England ever knew. Tess tapped her foot in anticipation, eager to view such a paragon of a man even from afar.

When all the tables had been readied, Suzette clapped her hands, and the score of women lined up before her. She went along the row like a general inspecting his troops, smoothing down a flounce here, straightening a wayward curl there, making small jests that earned sly, knowing laughs. When, satisfied, she dismissed them with another clap, they fluttered off through the room, looking for all the world like lovely butterflies in their bright finery. In the meantime, the kitchen help, with Charmian among them, had been laying out a vast table of cold meats and fish and fruit and sweets and bread along one side of the hall, as well as arranging another with ewers of ale and wine. Tess watched Suzette survey the hodge-podge of bounty, point out a few platters and dishes that she wanted moved, send for a bowl of roses, and thus create a gorgeous, unified display. The Frenchwoman would have made a fine lady of the manor, she decided admiringly.

At last all was in order. The kitchen help retired, leaving just the houseboys in their red liveries and, of course, the women. The candles in the vast candelabra were lit; the room glowed warm and golden and welcoming, while the beautiful women fanned themselves and waited. It is just as wonderful as I imagined it would be, Tess thought. I don't know why Suzette is making me wait. I wish I could be down there now.

Then the big front doors of the gambling hall were opened by two red-coated houseboys. Suzette signaled the musicians, and they blew a fanfare as a throng of men burst in. They were outfitted in costumes of colored silk and velvet, and they all wore masks. Their loud voices drowned out the music as they grabbed goblets of wine from the women and drank greedily. Their thirst slaked, they began to chase the courtesans around the room among the tables, laughing as they pinched and fondled them. They yanked up the women's skirts, goosed them, pulled their hair, tweaked their breasts—why, Tess thought in amazement, they are worse than the men in Windber on Midsummer's Eve! Who would ever have thought nobility could be so crude? Thank God Suzette hadn't let her begin work that night, before she knew what to expect! She watched in astonishment as two of them seized a squealing girl and held her down in a chair. Another unbuttoned his breeches and sat down atop her while his friends leered and laughed.

"*Mam'selle!*"

Charmian's excited hiss startled Tess as she rose from the chair. "I'm going back to my room now," she told the maid, "I don't care to stay another second. It's disgusting the way those men are behaving."

"You see him?" the maid demanded, seeming not to have heard or at least understood what Tess said. "You see him, *mam'selle?*"

"There's no one down there I care to see, I assure you." Tess tried to brush past her, but the maid seized her arm, pointing to one of the figures cavorting below.

"*C'est le roi, mam'selle!*"

She frowned, searching for the words in English. "*Votre souverain, oui? Le roi!*" And then it came to her: "King!"

"The *king?*" Tess repeated so loudly that Charmian clapped a hand over her mouth. Tess pulled it away. "Which one? Where?"

"*Là, il est là—*"

Tess peered more closely at the man to whom the maid pointed. He wore a doublet striped green and blue, a belled foolscap, and below that the head of a wolf, long-toothed and beady-eyed. "Charmian, you must be mistaken," she said dubiously.

"*Non, non, c'est le roi!* King Charles." She rolled the name from her tongue. "*Et là, c'est le Duc de Buckingham.*"

Only the way she said it was more like "Boogingam."
This, Tess could believe, for the reveler the maid indicated was tall and very slim and graceful in his ermine
cape and feathered bird's mask, and held himself a bit
apart from the general mayhem, sipping wine from a cup.
But the *king* . . .

"Charmian, are you sure?"

"Bien sûr," she said, with a touch of indignation. "He
has come here before, many times! *Et voici Madame.*" It
was true, Tess saw, that Suzette was paying special attention to the man in the wolf's head, making sure his cup
was filled, bringing him plates of dainties, presenting to
him one after another of the courtesans, whom he poked
and pinched and pulled onto his lap. For God's sake,
Tess thought, staring down at the giddy, gallivanting
sovereign, his own father had been dethroned and
beheaded for such willful foolishness; had the man got no
sense?

By now, their initial hungers satisfied, some of the men
were settling in to gambling, taking places at the gilt
tables while the women fetched them drinks or shuffled
cards. Not King Charles, though; he lolled in his chair, a
woman on either knee, and gobbled sweetmeats from
their hands. The wolf's head was interfering with his
eating. He swore an oath and pulled it off, flinging it at
an unheeding houseboy; it struck him in the kidneys,
making Charles laugh. Tess stared down at him. With his
long dark brown hair curling over his shoulders, he reminded her of Job.

With her guest of honor occupied, Suzette had snatched
a moment to check on the need to replenish the food and
wine and to send another of the boys around the room to
collect the masks which the courtiers, following the king's
lead, had now discarded. Charmian murmured something
and rushed off to the kitchens again. Tess had decided to
return to her room, king or no king, when she noticed a
man approaching Suzette as she surveyed the buffet. He
wasn't in costume, like the rest of the guests, unless he
was supposed to be a fellow down on his luck: he wore a
ragtag black velvet suit that was too small, torn stockings

and dusty shoes, and his bald head shone with sweat in the light from the great candelabra. There was something uncannily familiar about his portly figure and pigeon-toed walk.

From behind the curtain, Tess watched him tap Suzette's shoulder, saw her turn, frowning and distracted. The man, with his back to Tess, leaned close, as though he would share a private word with his hostess; she leaned away. He pulled her sleeve. She pried off his fingers. He seemed to be demanding something and Suzette refusing him, shaking her head. He repeated his plea, whatever it was; again Suzette denied him, looking anxiously to see if the king or Buckingham had noticed the intruder, and would have left him except that he caught her wrist. Was she imagining things, Tess wondered, or did he give it a brief cruel twist? Whatever the reason, Suzette faced him again and, blue eyes narrowed, slipped her hand into the purse at her belt, then gave him a fistful of coins.

That must have been what he'd asked for, because once he'd put them in his own purse, he turned and started from the room. As he passed directly below Tess, she caught her breath in surprise.

He was the spitting image of, a dead ringer for, Lord Andrew Halifax.

But Lord Halifax was in the New World, she thought in confusion. Still, the two were like enough to be brothers, with their pale eyes and florid faces. Though Tess had never seen Lord Halifax without his white wig, she supposed he might be bald. They did say everyone had a twin, she reminded herself. Of course, Lord Halifax would never be seen publicly in such clothes; he'd always been so dapper. But even the way they walked was identical!

If it were Lord Halifax . . .

It couldn't be, Tess assured herself. Nonetheless, she ran down the stairs to see if she could catch another glimpse of him.

In the hallway below, she found Suzette and Charmian arguing in French in low angry voices. They broke off guiltily as Tess came near, and Charmian hurried back toward the kitchens after suffering a final sharp rebuke.

"Did you want something, *chérie?*" Suzette demanded, looking cross and bothered.

"I'm sorry," Tess stammered. "I didn't mean to interrupt you. I can see you have enough on your mind."

The Frenchwoman sighed, straightening a single auburn curl that had slipped out of place. "It's that damned king of yours. Forgive me, *chérie*, but I am always put out of sorts when he visits."

"I thought perhaps it was your other visitor who upset you."

"Other visitor?" Those blue eyes were suddenly watchful.

"Aye, the man in the raggedy black suit."

"I'm not sure who—"

"The one you gave the money to."

"Ah!" The Frenchwoman's broad white brow cleared. "Monsieur Kelton!"

"Kelton—are you sure that's his name?"

"*Mais oui, chérie!* Monsieur Jasper Kelton. We are, how you say, old friends. Well . . ." She laughed and then grimaced. "At least, I have known him a long time. Whenever his luck is down, he comes to borrow money—always at the most inconvenient times! Why do you ask about him?"

"He reminded me of someone I know," Tess told her. "But I was mistaken. I am sorry I interrupted you and Charmian."

"I'm sure Charmian is grateful," Suzette said wryly. "I was angry with her for letting Monsieur Kelton in." Then she winked, blue eyes glinting with amusement. "Would you like me to present you to the king, *chérie?*"

Tess shuddered. "No, thank you! I couldn't believe Charmian when she told me he was here. Who would ever have thought a king would behave like that?"

"A king is no different from other men." Suzette laughed. "Except that it is not wise to say no to him! I must get back to my guests."

Tess went upstairs to her room, mulling over her first glimpse of the peerage of England. It just went to prove, she supposed, that a gentleman didn't have to be a gentleman. One thing was sure: she'd been mad to think Suzette's visitor could have been dear old Andrew Halifax. Why, he'd sooner die than be seen in this sort of place!

The king's visit to the Peacock Inn made Tess think long and hard about going to work for Suzette. But the fact remained that she could think of no better way of earning the money she needed to repay the Frenchwoman's kindness and get on with her life again. And as she got to know the rest of the women employed there, she felt better about the prospect. They weren't at all what she expected harlots to be like.

To begin with, they were working for the same reason she would be: because they had to. They had husbands who'd left them, or children got out of wedlock, or parents they supported, and there weren't that many honest ways for a woman to earn gold. They had dreams, too. One was saving toward a plot of land in the countryside, where she could take her two sons and raise chickens; another was trying to earn the money to get her father out of debtors' prison. Annie Perkins, a stunning brunette who'd come to London from Sussex, was raising her fare to the New World. When she found out Tess intended going there too, she began to make excited plans.

"Philadelphia, that's where I'm headed," she told Tess. "The biggest city in the colonies—twenty men for every woman! Any girl with looks and brains ought to be able to find a fellow rich as a lord. And I've got looks and brains."

"Is Philadephia near Delaware?" Tess asked.

"I reckon so. How big can the colonies be? Say, why don't we go over together? We could share a cabin on the ship."

"Wouldn't a cabin be expensive?"

"So what if it is?" Annie tossed her dark curls. "I've made my mind up, I'm going in style! Not as a bonded servant, or wedded by proxy to some man I never saw. No, I'll make my passage in a private cabin, thank you, dressed in silk. And when I get there, I intend to put up in the finest rooming house in the city and take the time to look about for the right man."

"You'd best leave without me, then," Tess said, laughing, "for it'll take me twenty years to save up that much gold!"

"All you need is thirty pounds or so." Annie studied her, black eyes appraising. "I'd say three months at most."

"Three months to make thirty pounds? Why, you're daft!"

"You'd have to work hard, but you could do it, so long as you know what you want. You've got the kind of looks most girls would kill for."

"Me?"

Annie giggled. "Aye, and you're sweet as well, or I'd hate your guts!"

Embarrassed, Tess turned the conversation around. "This fellow you'll find there—what will he be like?"

"Why, he'll be handsome, of course. Black hair and blue eyes, I think. I'm partial to blue eyes." Tess thought of Gideon. He'd certainly fit Annie's bill. "And gentle, and loving, and kind, and considerate." Well, maybe not. "Oh, and rich. Did I mention rich?"

"Will you tell him . . . what you used to do?"

"You mean about working here?" Annie cocked her head. "Sure I will, darling. Of course, I'll pick my moment." She pantomimed the act of lovemaking, leaning back in her chair with her legs spread, batting her eyes at an imaginary partner. "Oh, darling," she cried between quick short breaths, "there's something I must tell you now, before we go any further!"

Tess laughed. "But don't you sometimes feel . . . well, disgusted by the men who come here?"

"Disgusted? Nah, darling. I feel sorry for 'em. They only come to the Peacock because there's something in their lives that's missing. And whatever that something is, they won't find it here. I figure working here is only going to help me be a better wife! Now, what's waiting for you in Delaware? Is it a man?"

Tess nodded. "But he's none of those things you listed— tall and dark and handsome. He's not even rich anymore; someone cheated him of all his money."

"Well, I don't suppose that really matters," Annie said dubiously, "if you're in love with him."

The idea of being in love with Lord Halifax made Tess smile. "It's nothing like that. He's more like family. Though I think . . ." She remembered the chain he had given her. "I rather think he might have fancied me."

"He'd have to be blind not to. And what will this short ugly fellow do for you once you find him?"

"He'll help me. I know he will."

Annie pinched her cheek. "Then go to Suzette and ask if you can start working! The New World is just waiting for us, Tess Jericho!"

That very morning Tess went to Suzette's rooms and knocked on the door. *"Entrez!"* the Frenchwoman sang out.

"I hope I'm not interrupting," Tess said as she came in, seeing the desk in front of Suzette littered with books and papers.

"You are, but I'm glad. It is my day to settle the accounts. I hate numbers." She winced at the page of figures she'd been studying. "If the nuns who worked so hard to teach me two and two makes four could only see me now . . ." She laughed. *"Eh bien,* it is good they do not, *n'est-ce pas?* I do not think they would approve of this place. Come and sit down, *chérie."*

Tess slipped into a chair. "Are you a Catholic?" she asked in surprise. She'd never met a Catholic before, but she knew what her father said about them—that they were idolaters and traitors. Everyone said that in Windber-on-Clun.

"Once I was. Now I am not much of anything," Suzette said ruefully.

What a strange place this city is, Tess thought—where one was helped by beggar-boys and Catholics, and made friends with harlots, and saw the king behaving like an ass! "How did you ever wind up in this business, if you don't mind my asking?"

Suzette raised and then lowered her elegant shoulders. *"Qui sait?* It happened. I needed money, a long time ago."

"Well, I need money now," Tess told her, glad for the opening. "And I just came to tell you, I'm ready to begin working." She saw Suzette start to protest, and rushed on: "There's no sense trying to change my mind. I've talked to lots of the other girls, and thought it all over, and I know it's the right decision. After I pay you back the money I owe you, I'm going to start saving to go to the New World, like Annie Perkins. I've got it all figured out."

"The New World." Suzette sighed. "*Peut-être . . . oui.* It may be for the best. But I do not want you to pay me back, *chérie.*"

Tess straightened in her chair. "I insist that I do."

"But, *chérie.* Please. I feel that we are family."

That was rather a peculiar thing, Tess thought, for Gideon's wife to tell his lover. Then again, everyone knew foreigners were queer. And somehow she understood what Suzette meant, felt close to her too—not as if the woman were her sister, like Annie, but almost as though she were the mother Tess never knew.

Still, "I've told you before that I pay my debts," she said stubbornly. "If you don't let me repay you by working here, I'll just have to find work at another establishment like this to earn the money."

"*Chérie,*" Suzette said with pride, "there are no other establishments like this. My Peacock is one of a kind. But it is still too soon, *non*? You have not yet recovered from your sickness."

Tess snorted. "Oh, really. I've never felt better in all my life." It was true, too. She was no longer troubled by pains from the poisoning; she felt full of energy, and the bounty of the Peacock's kitchens was helping her more than recoup the weight she'd lost while she was ill. Despite the hearty meals she shared with the rest of the women, she even found herself sneaking downstairs at night for snacks of bread and pickles and cheese.

"*Et puis—*" Suzette raised a cautionary finger. "I must be careful. *Mon Dieu,* if one of my clients caught from you the sickness you had—"

"Poisoning's not contagious!"

"There was also the fever. *Non.*" she said decisively, "not yet. In one more month, perhaps."

"Another *month*?" Tess wailed. "But I'll never make it to the New World at that rate! I'll just keep owing you more and more!"

"I am sorry, *chérie*. But I cannot take a chance. I have the reputation of my house to uphold. Still . . ." She spread out her hands. "Until then, you can work in the kitchen. Not so much money, *peut-être,* but it is something."

Tess could see there wasn't any use in arguing further. *"Eh bien,"* she said in resignation. "The kitchen it is. But I start today."

By evening, after ten hours of paring and slicing and chopping and stirring, Tess had to admit that Suzette might have been right about the lingering effects of the fever. The work was far easier than horse-riding or stable-swabbing, yet she felt shaky and drained. She was so exhausted, in fact, that she couldn't sleep; she sat at the window of her tiny room overlooking the courtyard, trying to convince herself that a rich husband in the New World might make her as happy as Annie thought it would. As she sought to picture what such a husband might look like, another face kept intruding on her thoughts: Gideon, his black hair wild and windblown, his blue eyes dark with love.

"Well, that's surely not about to help me sleep," she said aloud, and turned from the window. As she did, a bit of movement in the yard below caught her gaze. Suzette, wrapped in a cloak against the November chill, but with the light of the full moon shining bright on her auburn hair, stood close by the eaves of the stables. Tess was certain from her stance that she was waiting for someone there.

I wonder, she thought, if she has got a lover? Though from what Tess could see, the Frenchwoman hardly seemed filled with anticipation; indeed, her expression indicated this meeting was one she would prefer to avoid.

Then a horseman rode into the court from the alley. Suzette raised her hand in greeting; the man reined in beside her and dismounted, and Tess saw he was stout

and short, shorter than Suzette by half a head. Even in
his cape and hat he somehow seemed familiar. Suzette
said something to him; he pulled the hat off to scratch his
head, and Tess, seeing it shine baldly in the moonlight,
knew why. It was Suzette's old friend Jasper Kelton,
who'd reminded her so strongly of Lord Halifax.

For old friends they were having one devil of a row,
she thought, watching as Kelton stomped his foot and
gestured wildly in response to whatever Suzette told him.
Even though she knew now it wasn't Andrew Halifax,
she couldn't help thinking it was; they were as like as two
florid-faced peas in a pod. Of course, sweet old Lord
Halifax hadn't had such a temper. As Tess watched in
horror, Kelton lifted his riding crop as though he would
slash Suzette's cheek. The Frenchwoman never flinched;
instead she reached into her cloak and drew something
out, holding it out to him. A purse, Tess was nearly
certain. Kelton paused, the crop in midair.

Calmly, almost regally, Suzette kept talking. Kelton
lowered the whip, then took the purse from her hand.
Turning on his heel, he put his foot to the stirrup, tried
to heave himself onto his horse, and failed, hampered by
his stoutness. Tess suddenly shivered. Lord Halifax had
slipped off his mount just that way on the day he left
Windber-on-Clun; she remembered thinking how stout
he had grown.

Longing for one more close look at the man, she
pressed her nose to the window. But on his second try,
with the poor horse cowed by his temper, he got into the
saddle, clapped on his hat, and rode out through the
alley once more. Suzette stood looking after him for a
long moment, then drew her cloak tight around her shoulders and walked back to the inn across the cobblestones.
Even allowing for the moonlight, she looked wan and
pale.

She's afraid of that man, Tess thought, though she tries
not to show it. I wonder why she pays him. I wonder why
she would meet him so secretly.

By now the courtyard was empty. The moon glittered
on the cobblestones, turning them to diamonds. Tess

heard Linzy nicker, or imagined she did, and suddenly she was looking from another window onto a valley flooded with moonlight, where two horses coupled together, and the man beside her whispered her name, passion darkening his voice, igniting his eyes.

"Leave me be, Gideon Cade!" she cried, hands clenched as she turned from the window, and on the wind heard his voice whisper "Tess" again.

25

The next four weeks seemed to Tess to pass impossibly slowly. Her work in the kitchens, while far better than doing nothing, was dreary and tedious, and the rides she took on Linzy were curtailed by December weather that was relentlessly sodden and cold. Not even the approach of Christmas could cheer her. The eager talk of Annie and her friends of plans for visiting home and kin over the holiday Suzette gave them, when the inn would be closed, made her homesick for Windber and Ben. She began to understand more clearly just how wrenching it would be to depart for the New World without ever seeing Shropshire again. How odd that she stood on the verge of fulfilling what had once been her sole dream in life—going on a grand adventure—and all she could think of was the rich butter yellow of sunlight pouring through the open door of the cottage, and Job, his dark eyes morose, his outlandish ears flopping, as he squeezed through the pasture fence to chase rabbits on a fine spring morn.

She didn't lack holiday invitations. Annie had asked her to Sussex to visit her sister and brother-in-law and their passel of youngsters, and three or four of the other women offered hospitality as well. Tess declined, though, fearing her low spirits might spoil their enjoyment of the festivities. She'd already asked Suzette if she could just stay on at the Peacock, and the Frenchwoman cheerfully gave assent. "We will have the house all to ourselves, you and I," she noted. "Even Charmian leaves at Christmas, to go back to France."

"Don't you want to go back there as well?" Tess asked her.

She shrugged. "*Pourquoi?* I have no one there. I have not been back since I left twenty years ago."

"Twenty years! Why, you must have been only a child!"

That made Suzette laugh. "You are very sweet, *chérie*." The deft turning of her compliment made Tess wonder anew just how old the woman was—*and* kept her from asking, as she suspected it was intended to.

On St. Thomas' Eve, the longest night of the year, Suzette traditionally held a party to thank her clients for their patronage. "It's just good business sense," Annie told Tess. "Madame spends a few hundred pounds, but it keeps the boys coming back and spending thousands all year. It's that idea of getting something for nothing, you know. Everyone loves that."

"Someone once told me you can't get something for nothing in London," Tess said rather wistfully, thinking of the beggar-boy who'd saved her life. Had he made it to the New World? Perhaps someday she would encounter him there.

"Well, where can you, these days?" asked Annie. Then she winked. "Except on St. Thomas' Eve at the Peacock Inn!"

That night Tess wasn't watching from the balcony as the hall was readied for the celebration; she was down on the marble floor, scurrying in and out of the kitchen with platters of roast quail and haunch of venison and ham, fetching serving forks and spoons she'd spent the last week polishing, laying fresh green linen cloths on the gaming tables and making sure the wine pitchers were filled. Suzette's poise as she prepared for an onslaught of what Annie had said was often five hundred guests was truly awe-inspiring; while the kitchen help and houseboys ran about like chickens with their heads cut off, she supervised with utter calm, tucking sprigs of mistletoe and holly in among the silver platters, checking that the proper barrels and tuns were brought up from the ale and wine cellars, counting cups and spoons and plates.

Tess saw her flustered only once: when a boy came in from the kitchens carrying a huge bundle tied in brown

paper. She tore away the wrappings, and a fragrance
sweeter than honeysuckle filled the air. "Night jasmine,"
Annie whispered to Tess, watching as Suzette buried her
nose in the enormous bouquet of waxy white flowers.
"Somebody sends them every year at Christmastide. She
told me once it used to grow wild on the walls where she
lived in France." Tess saw the woman's eyes fill with
tears as she lifted her head, and her own chest tightened
around her heart as she realized: *She still loves him too.*

She wished then that she'd accepted one of the invitations to spend Christmas away from the inn. How strange
it would be here with Gideon's wife and her own memories! But it was too late now to change her plans. And
she didn't want to offend Suzette after she'd been so
kind.

Once the tables were set, Tess retired with her cowork-
ers to the kitchens, where they'd stay through the night,
replenishing trays and washing cups and plates. "Still,
our lot's easier than them poor gals out there," one of
the cooks, a toothless woman named Molly, told Tess as
she stirred up a vat of raisin sauce for the venison. "Go
'n' fetch me more cloves for this 'ere from the spice
closet, luv." And she threw her the key to the little room
off the hall where such precious stuffs were stored.

Out in the corridor she could hear the sounds of music
and loud talk and laughter from the gambling room; the
evening seemed to be well under way. Behind her, the
door to the kitchen popped open, and Molly stuck out
her head. "Bring some nutmegs 'n' cinnamon too, luv;
that ass Carrie's gone 'n' burnt me stock!" she shouted.

"I did not burn the bleedin' stock!" another voice,
high and irate, called. "I'd like to know, I would, why
everythin's always my fault!" Tess acknowledged the ad-
ditional order with a wave and ducked into the closet,
biting her cheek.

She found the cinnamon and cloves readily enough,
but the nutmegs eluded her; in the day's confusion, someone must have misplaced them. As she hunted for the
proper box along the rows of shelves, Tess heard the
fight between Molly and Carrie come to a name-calling
head and then peter out. Just as she finally found the

nutmegs—on the bottom shelf, naturally, and turned backward so the label was hidden—she heard a new set of raised, angry voices through the half-open door: Suzette and some man who was all in a rage. Embarrassed to be eavesdropping, albeit inadvertently, she tried to decide whether or not to make her presence known, and at last chose to just stay put.

Of the two, Suzette seemed calmer, or at least had her ire under better control. The man had been drinking and was slurring his words, but beneath the burr of wine Tess thought she heard a hint of Shropshire that made her long for home. "You can't turn me out," he bellowed. "I've a right to be here!"

"The only people with a right to be here," Suzette told him, an edge of steel to her voice that Tess had never heard before, "are my invited guests!"

"I've been a faithful patron, haven't I?" the man demanded belligerently. "Hell, if you'd add up all the money I've lost here, I could buy the bloody place ten times over!"

"We had an agreement. You were to stay away. That is why I have paid you the gold."

"For Christ's sake, it's Christmastide! I've nowhere else to go!"

"And whose fault is that?" Suzette asked evenly.

"Yours, bitch, if you ask me! If it wasn't for you, I wouldn't be begging money in a stinking whorehouse!"

"You have only yourself to blame for what happened," Suzette told him, and then gasped. "How dare you raise your hand to me!" Fearful for Suzette's safety, Tess moved toward the door, then stopped as the Frenchwoman said more calmly, "If you do not leave now, I will have my servants throw you out on the street."

Tess held her breath, but the man backed down, his voice changing from anger to a mewling whine. "Please," he whimpered. "Please let me stay. I'm lonely, so lonely. You don't know what it's like, to have lost your home, to have lost everything . . ." Tess shivered as he began to cry in great slobbery drunken sobs. Suzette let out a sigh.

"*Eh bien,* here is more gold. But you must find another establishment in which to spend it."

"Let me have one of the girls," he wheedled. "Let me have Betsy or Annie, just for an hour."

"*Non!* I tell you, you must go!"

The man broke off crying, his sodden temper flaring once more. "I'll get you yet," he swore with a vicious oath. "You'll pay for having ruined me, filthy French bawd! See if I don't make you pay."

"*Monsieur.*" Now Suzette sounded weary. "I pay and pay already. Go, or my men will send for the law. I have friends in high places."

"So did I once—and I will again. Remember that, Madame de la Mare." Tess heard heavy bootsteps heading back to the gaming hall, and then a slamming door.

She waited until she was sure Suzette had gone too, not wanting the woman to know the unpleasant scene had been overheard. But when she came out into the hallway at last, she found Suzette was still there, slumped against the wall. Seeing Tess, she straightened with a start. "*Chérie!*"

"I'm sorry. I didn't mean . . . Molly sent me to get these." Tess held out the spices. "And I didn't know what to do when it started—when he started." She looked at the Frenchwoman more closely and realized that her face was streaked with tears. "Are you all right? Did he hurt you? I should have let him know I was there."

"*Non, non, chérie. Ce n'est rien.* It was nothing." She wiped beneath her eyes with a lacy kerchief.

"Who was he? What did he want?"

"You did not see him?" Tess shook her head and thought she looked a bit relieved. "No one. A drunken fool."

Tess touched her arm in a gesture of comfort. "You shouldn't let him upset you so."

"It is not that. It is . . ." Her voice turned surprisingly fierce. "I hate Christmastime. Everyone else with their families, so happy . . ."

Tess was suddenly glad she wasn't going away for the holiday after all. "We can have our own Christmas, just you and I," she told her. "We can start tomorrow after everyone else is gone. We'll make tarts and cakes, and roast a goose—"

Suzette laughed shakily. "*Chérie*, I am the worst cook in the world!"

"That's all right. I'm not very good either." They smiled at one another there in the corridor. Then Suzette squeezed the hand Tess had laid on her arm.

"*Eh bien,* that is what we do. Now I get back to my guests." As if on cue, the door to the gaming hall opened and Charmian rushed in with an empty tray.

"*Madame, les crevettes! Il n'y a pas assez des crevettes!*"

"We have no more shrimp?" Suzette's blue eyes were twinkling again as they met Tess's. "*Quel désastre!* Do you suppose all the guests will go home?"

At the opposite end of the hallway, the kitchen door opened as well. "Tess!" Molly bawled. "Where's me bloody damned nutmegs?"

With a rueful glance at Suzette, Tess hurried back to her duties, and at last there was a bit of Christmas warmth in her heart.

What was most remarkable about the Peacock Inn over the holiday, Tess told Suzette as they struggled to roll out a pie crust the following evening, was the silence. The women, the houseboys, the cooks, even Charmian, had departed. With only the two of them in the vast manse, no footsteps ran up and down the stairs or clattered across the floors overhead, and their voices, though they spoke softly, echoed through the big brick-walled kitchen as though it were an empty church.

There was a certain soothing quality to the quiet, though—"Like a winter afternoon up on the White Moor," she tried to explain to Suzette, "when you look down into the valley, and the sky is slate-blue so it makes the snow that color too, and it's so cold your teeth are chattering, but you can see smoke curling up from the cottage chimney, and you know Dad'll have hot milk ready when you get home . . ." She stopped, embarrassed at how she'd been running on, and then finished lamely: "Anyway, that's what that hush, that quiet, sounds like to me."

Suzette didn't laugh the way Tess feared she might. Instead, trying to pry too-sticky dough up from the marble pastry counter, she asked, "Is it very pretty where you come from in Shropshire?"

"I didn't used to think so. When I was younger I would have given anything never to see Windber-on-Clun again. But now . . . I don't know. Knowing I can't go back makes it seem more beautiful somehow."

Her companion nodded. "*Oui, je comprends*. When I think of France, I always think . . . the flowers. So many flowers! Jasmine and eglantine and roses, the sweet, sweet roses. And then when I came here to England, we had a garden at the house. That and James, they were all my joy."

Tess laughed, suddenly self-conscious. "It really is rather strange, don't you think, for us to be here together talking about him?"

"*Pas du tout*. We both love him, *non*?"

"*Loved* him," Tess corrected her tense. "I surely don't . . . What was that?" She'd heard a dull thud from the courtyard.

Suzette waved a hand. "*La neige*. The snow. Falling down from the roof. *Chérie*, this crust—what shall I do with it next?"

Tess looked at the mass of hole-studded dough and giggled. "Throw it out and begin again! Didn't those French nuns teach you anything?"

"They taught me very fine embroidery."

"Then maybe you can darn it and get it into the pan."

Suzette glanced slyly at the pitifully flat almond cakes Tess had just pulled from the oven. "*Eh bien*, after that I will sew enough of those together to make them look like they should!"

"Why, you . . ." Tess hurled a handful of flour across the room, and the white powder settled over Suzette's face and bodice, making her sneeze. In return the Frenchwoman tossed the pie dough; it landed with a splat on Tess's apron and slithered downward like some monstrous slimy creature. "Egh, get it off me!" she cried, beating it with her hands. Suzette burst out laughing.

"Here, let me help you." But as she tried to pull the dough away, it only clung to her too, stretching out in translucent loops as sticky as glue.

"Wait, I know!" Tess grabbed a long knife from the counter and began to hack at the stuff to free them. It stuck to the blade, and to her hair, and to the counter where she'd touched it, and . . .

"It eats us alive!" Between gusts of laughter, Suzette fought to untangle Tess from the clutches of the unruly dough, and only succeeeded in getting them both even more ensnared. At last they looked at one another in shared defeat. "Whose idea *was* this, you tell me!" Suzette wailed.

"Look at us!" Tess giggled, pulling dough from her hair with dough-covered fingers. "What a pair James picked for his wife and his mistress!"

Through a shroud of flour and water and lard, Suzette's head jerked upward. "James has a *wife*?" she said in disbelief.

The most peculiar feeling came over Tess, as though the earth had stopped spinning. "Well, of course he has. You're his wife," she managed to say.

Beneath its powdery mask, Suzette's face had gone flour-pale. "*Chérie*, I am not his wife! I am his mother."

Tess's legs disappeared from beneath her; she collapsed to the floor.

The next thing she knew, Suzette was kneeling beside her, pressing a cup of brandy to her mouth, urging her to drink it. "*Oh, ma pauvre petite*," she said over and over. "*Oh, mon Dieu*, his wife! Where in the world did you get that idea?"

Tess took a sip of the brandy, and it made her faint-headedness subside just a little. "The . . . the marriage certificate," she stammered. "He has it. I saw it. Your name and his—"

"Not his, *chérie*, his father's! They give the father's name to the son here, *n'est-ce pas? C'est le coutume*—the custom!" She sat back on her haunches, shaking her head. "How could you ever think James would be married to an old woman like me?"

"But you're not old! Surely not old enough to be his mother!"

The Frenchwoman preened, just a bit. "*Eh bien*, I am only his stepmother, true . . ." Abruptly she brought herself back to the subject at hand. "But when you came here, *chérie*, you said to me, I know everything—everything. What did you mean?"

"Why, that I'd learned Gideon's real name, that he was James Trelawny, the Duke of Clary, and married to you!" Outside in the courtyard, beyond the black windows, another chunk of snow must have fallen from the roof, but neither paid any mind to the sudden thud.

"That is all?" Suzette asked, a curious expression on her face. "The title, Duke of Clary, it means nothing to you?" Slowly Tess shook her head, and she sighed. "*Hélas, chérie*, now you make me feel old indeed. But it is true, you would have been an infant."

"What should it mean to me?" Tess demanded.

"*Ne rien.* It means nothing." She started to rise from the floor. Tess stopped her, holding to her wrist.

"For Jesus' sake, you've got to tell me! What should I know about the Duke of Clary?"

"*Chérie*, I cannot tell you. It is not my place."

Still Tess clung to her hand. "You must!" Her heart wrenched with pain as she thought of the child she'd destroyed in her womb. If James hadn't lied to her, if he wasn't married . . . God, had that been for nothing? "Please, I beg you!"

Her desperation moved the Frenchwoman to pity; she settled back down beside Tess, idly picking bits of dough from her elegant hands. "*Il y a longtemps,*" she murmured, "such a long time ago . . . every day I think, I hope, perhaps it is all forgotten. But here, in my heart, I know it never will be." She took a long deep breath. "James, my James—he killed his father, you see."

Killed his father! Tess could not hide the horror she knew had to show on her face. Suzette saw it and made an impatient, angry gesture. "*Oui, oui,* it is horrible. My stepson murdered my husband. I should hate him, *non?* I should fear him, despise him! But how can I?" Her voice rose in a mournful, passionate wail. "How can I, when he did this awful thing for me?"

She buried her face in her hands, shoulders slumped with despair inside her blue velvet gown. Tess hesitated only a moment, then put her arms around her, holding her tight, smoothing back her hair. Gradually the woman's anguished tears subsided. "Tell me," Tess whispered then. "Tell me about it, if you can."

Suzette straightened up slowly, leaning against the brick wall of the kitchens, rubbing her eyes with the backs of her hands. The sticky dough that covered them made her laugh faintly, shakily. "How many years have you, *chérie*? Nineteen?" Tess nodded. "I was two years younger, then, when I first saw the Duke of Clary. He had come to France to parley with King Louis. They went hunting together, and the stag gored one of their party. They brought him to the convent where I had lived since my parents died."

For a moment the depths of her eyes ignited with the warm glow of memory, and Tess caught her breath, seeing her as she must have looked at sixteen. "All the nuns, they have the eyes only for King Louis, *oui*?" she went on. "But I stared and stared at the Englishman. So tall, I thought, so handsome! He looked just like James does now—a little older, *peut-être*. And—*oh, mon Dieu,* I saw him stare back at me!"

She smiled in self-deprecation. "I was a schoolgirl, *tu comprends?* Young and silly. After the king's party left us, *la maîtresse*, the convent mother, she said: Suzette, this Englishman asked many questions about you. *Naturellement,* I think this is because I am so beautiful. I do not think it is perhaps because I am rich! My mother and father had left me a great fortune."

"I'm sure he must have admired more than just your money," Tess protested.

The Frenchwoman nodded. "*Ah, oui!* He also liked that I had no family to protect me, I think. *Eh bien,* the next thing I hear, we are to be married, the duke and I! The nuns are most excited. They make for me the beautiful trousseau, they put me on a ship, and I am in England before the drop of the hat!"

"Weren't you frightened?" Tess asked, trying to imagine such a drastic uprooting.

"*Pas du tout.* My head is filled by the nuns with stories of love." She waved her hand grandly. "*Tous les grands romans de l'amour!* I think I am living such a story. My handsome duke meets the ship, he puts me in a carriage, and we drive away to his house. It is . . ." Her blue eyes widened. "The biggest house I ever have seen! A castle! I take one look and I know we will be . . . how do you put it, what they have at the end of such stories?"

" 'They lived happily ever after,' " Tess said softly.

Suzette nodded. "*Oui, oui.* I know this is how we will be. And then . . ." Her lovely face darkened. "Then he introduced me to his son."

"You and James—you didn't get along?"

"*Non, chérie,* the trouble was not that. The trouble was I did not know his father had been married before. And not once, but three times!" She held up that many fingers. "The boy, his mother was the first. She died when he was very young. Since then, two more. And the poor child is not yet ten! I look at him and I see he is sad, so sad. He has the most sad face I have ever seen. I remember I wondered why. But I was happy still. That night, my duke and I, we were married. He promised to the nuns that he is Catholic; now I find he is not. That gave me a shock. But it is nothing to what came after." She clenched her eyes tight shut. "When he came to my bed."

In the long pause Tess heard her own quick breathing, and Suzette's, sharp and labored, and from the pantry a scuffling of mice. "If you don't want to go on . . ." she began.

But the Frenchwoman shrugged. "I think you can guess. He beat me until I screamed and screamed, and then he beat me until I stopped screaming, and then . . ." She broke off again.

"He raped you," Tess whispered.

Suzette shook her head. "But it is not rape because he is my husband, *n'est-ce pas?* That is what he told me the night after, when he came for me again and I said: *Non, non,* I will not let you into my room. He broke down the door, he was shouting that I am his wife, he will do what he will. And then I see the boy again, he is there in the hall, kneeling down as if he is praying, all white and shaking, and I think: *Oh, mon Dieu,* those sad eyes. He has seen this before."

Tess's heart ached for the woman who sat shivering beside her, and for someone else as well: Gideon-James, that little boy made old before his time, so frightened and alone. "What did you do?" she asked.

"What could I do? He was right, my duke. He was my husband; I belonged to him. All I could do was stop screaming, stop fighting, so that the boy would not be afraid. My duke." She laughed softly, bitterly. "Happy ever after. What a fool I had been."

"But there must have been someone you could tell— someone who could help you!"

"Who? We saw no one. He kept us as prisoners there in that castle. The servants were more frightened than we were. *Non, chérie.* There were only the boy and I. He became my one joy, my solace. We tended our garden together. He taught me English, I taught him French. We were secret friends. For two years we went on that way."

Tess thought of the brutal duke and balled her hands into fists. "It's a wonder the bastard didn't beat you to death."

"That is what happened to the others. *Oui,*" she insisted, seeing Tess's shock. "James told me. One after another, he killed them. That is why he picked me out in France, I think. I was an orphan, I had no family. In England there were whispers. No one would give a daughter to him."

"Why didn't someone *do* something?"

"*Chérie,* he was the great Duke of Clary. No one could touch him. No one dared accuse him openly. And to look at him—so elegant, so handsome—you would not believe he could be such a monster. Well, you know. My James, he is as like him as could be." Quietly, as though she didn't even notice it, Suzette had begun to cry. "We had a happiness of a kind, my James and I. But then the duke, he began to notice our happiness. And he could not stand it. He could not even leave us that. One day I heard voices, shouts, in the garden, and I ran to see. The duke, he was drunk, he was beating James, and he cut with his sword—from here to here." She pointed from her knee to her thigh on the back of her leg, and Tess shuddered, remembering the angry red scar her lover bore there.

Suzette's slim, proud shoulders straightened. "I knew then that to save James, I had to send him away from there. So I went to his father. I was very clever. I flattered him, *oui*? I said, the great Duke of Clary, his son must go to university, *n'est-ce pas*? He must wear the robes of a scholar; he has from you the brain—" She twisted her mouth. "Men. Just like a big baby he was. He agreed—only he pretended it was his idea."

"So James went to Oxford."

Suzette nodded. "He did not want to. He did not want to leave me, he was afraid for me. But I made him go. I swore to him his father had changed, that there were no more beatings. So he went, and I wrote, and I always told him all is well. And I was glad, because he wrote back and told me how happy he was, how he makes friends, how he learns many things."

"But the beatings hadn't stopped," Tess said gently.

"*Non*. They grew worse. Some days I could not write to James because my eyes . . ." She touched them, pressing the flesh as if she felt it even now swollen and pulpy beneath her fingertips. "Because I could not see."

"You were very brave."

"I did what I must," the Frenchwoman said simply. "To save him. Because I loved him as if he were my own." She was silent again for a few moments; then she roused herself with a sigh. "He wrote to me that he would come home for Christmastide. I wrote back— *non*, I say, you cannot, you must not. Stay with your friends, stay at your school. But I think he suspected. *Non*," she corrected herself, "*non*, I think he knew." Slowly she rose from the floor, putting her back to Tess, going to stoke the fire in the huge hearth before she went on:

"He came home in secret; I did not know he was coming. The duke was drunk as always, and he came to my bedchamber. He stripped off my clothes, and he began to beat me. I look out in the hall, and I see—there is James. The blows—I do not even feel them. What I think is: *Mon Dieu*, he is grown so tall!" She hugged herself tightly, still facing the fire. "Then I see in his hands the sword." Tess saw it too, in her mind: the boy, awkward and gangly, but with a terrible fire raging in his blue eyes.

"He calls out." Suzette's voice was breaking. "He says: Father, *non*! Father, stop! The duke, he turns around, he laughs. Whelp, he says. Why? Are you a man now, do you want your turn? Take her, then. He pulls me up from the bed and pushes me toward James, and I fall to the floor. And then James, he cries out: You bastard, you bastard, I hate you! I won't let you kill her! The duke, he laughs again, he says: How will you stop me? And James, he raises up the sword, and the duke, he draws *his* sword and comes toward him, laughing, and . . . and . . . oh, *Dieu en ciel*, he was only a boy! Only a child, my James, but he ran his own father straight through!"

Tess couldn't move, couldn't breathe for the ache in her heart that was huge and still growing, that filled all her chest, crowding out everything but the picture Suzette had painted in her halting English: the father, mocking and cruel, the woman, shamed and helpless, and the boy, made brave by his very terror, by his fear that the brute who had spawned him would murder the one human being he had ever dared love. Tears streamed down her cheeks as she imagined James's horror as he made his decision, and that moment when steel slid through flesh and sealed his fate inexorably. In her memory she heard the prating questions she'd once put to him: "What did your father think when you went off to the New World?" "Was it hard for you, too, separating yourself from your father?" And as she remembered, she saw the child in the eyes of the man and, too late, understood.

"I'm sorry," she whispered, half for Suzette, half for James. "God, I'm so sorry."

The Frenchwoman had composed herself, drying her eyes, turning round again. "We did not know what to do." Her voice betrayed only a hint of the anguish she and James must have faced as they stared at the fallen body. "And so we ran away. We took nothing. Only the clothes on our backs. We did not want anything that had been his."

"But surely you might have pleaded that James acted in self-defense!"

"How? James drew his sword first."

"On a man who was beating you!"

"Beating his wife. That was his right, that is what the law says."

"Where did you go?" Tess asked in dismay.

"We went to the coast, to Plymouth. I used my name I had before I was married. James chose a new one. Gideon. It is Hebrew, he told me, for a hewer, one who chops wood. Because, he said, he had cut off his family tree. And Cade—that is a calf or a colt that has lost its mother." Tess nodded, remembering what Emilia had told her. "Because he said he had to leave me. It would be too dangerous for us to remain together." She sighed. "That was the hardest of all, to be parted from him."

"Was that when he went to sea?"

"*Oui.* He signed on with a captain who gave him money, so he could give the money to me. The captain promised they would return in six months. But it turned out to be six years."

"My God!" Tess tried to imagine how lonely those years must have been. "What did you do? How did you live?"

"When the money ran out, I found work. In a tavern. I was afraid to leave Plymouth, afraid if I did, James would never find me. Afraid he was dead. But then one day he came in looking for news of me. All grown up, he was—a man!" She laughed, remembering. "And so angry to find me at work in that place! Suzette, he said, this will not do! You are too good for this—you are a lady! He gave me all the money he earned at sea. It was a lot of money. And I told him I wanted to use it for a gambling hall." Her blue eyes rolled. "Ooh, la-la! You should have heard what he said to that!"

"He didn't think it was a good idea?"

"He was horrified! He said: That sort of place is not for you! Don't you know what it will attract? Prostitutes!

he said." She smiled impishly. "And I said: *Oui*, I want to have them, too!"

"But why a gambling hall?" Tess wanted to know.

"So I could take money from rich men who have too much of it. Half of all my profits here—the half that should be Gideon's—I give to the poor. And prostitutes because it is a good way for women to earn money. It is important that women should have money of their own so that they can do what they please." She made a face. "Gideon does not agree with me, though. He will not take a penny of my money even now that I am wealthy. I will make my own way, he always says, and then off again to sea!"

"Except now he's in Windber-on-Clun."

"*Oui*," Suzette said sadly, "and you are here. When he first talked about you, I was so happy! I thought: Now he will marry, have children. But now, after you told me what he did to you . . ." Her voice trailed away.

"What he did to me?" Tess echoed, puzzled.

"*Oui, ma petite*. That like his father, he beat you and raped you."

"Do you mean you thought . . . ?" Tess drew in her breath. "Oh, Suzette, no! It wasn't James who did that to me!"

"Not James?" the woman repeated, dazed.

"No, no! That was another man—a boy, really, whom I was to marry." God, that seemed a long time ago. "James never laid a hand on me." Except, she thought, in love.

A mother's relief, clear and joyous, lit up Suzette's face. "*Chérie!* But then why did you leave him?"

"Because I'd seen that marriage certificate! Once I found out his real name, I thought he was married to you!"

Suzette's laughter rang out like bells. "*Ma chére* Teresa! Then it is all a mistake. You love my James, and he loves you! You must go back and marry him at once!" She pulled Tess up from the floor. "Come! We will go now, tonight!"

For the length of a heartbeat, Tess was caught up in this happy-ever-after ending. Then she remembered the child that would never be, and she shrank from the radiant woman holding her hand. "God help me," she whispered. "I can't."

"Can't? *Ma petite,* you must!"

"You don't understand." Tess backed away frantically, shaking her head. "I've done something awful. Unforgivable."

"Nothing is unforgivable, *chérie.*"

"This is," Tess insisted. "And I can never see James again. No. I've made up my mind. I'm going to the New World. I'll find Lord Halifax there and get work with him."

Suzette's expression changed, her mouth puckering as though she'd tasted green apples. "But you cannot do that."

"Why the devil can't I?"

"Because Lord Halifax never went to the New World."

Tess stared at her. "Then where is he?"

She and Suzette whirled around in tandem as a black shadow fell across the brick wall and a voice spoke from the entrance to the darkened pantry: "He's right here."

26

"Pray forgive the intrusion, ladies," said the stout bald man standing before them.

"Lord Halifax!" Tess turned to Suzette in confusion. "But you told me his name was Kelton!"

Suzette had gone ashen-pale; her eyes never left the man's face as she whispered, "How much did you hear?"

"Enough." He swaggered into the kitchen in his snow-damp cape. "And to think all I'd hoped for out of this evening was more of your charity." He turned his pale gaze on Tess. "Teresa, how very nice to see you again. Suzette, why didn't you tell me my old friend Teresa was here?"

Suzette pulled a handful of coins from her purse and held them out to him. "Here, take this. This is what you want. And then you must go."

He laughed, taking a step toward them. "You don't really think I'll settle for a few miserable crowns now, do you, when I've discovered your secret? The secret that will get back my house and lands—and see the son of a bitch who stole them from me hanged for murder."

"Don't be foolish." Suzette's voice was still steady. "No one would believe you—a drunkard, a madman."

With terrible nonchalance he pulled out a long, lethal-looking pistol and whipped the butt across Suzette's face. "Lord Halifax!" Tess cried in shock as Suzette stumbled backward.

"I'm not mad," Andrew Halifax said, his pale eyes gleaming. "Don't ever say I'm mad."

Suzette wiped blood from her mouth with a corner of

her apron. "It is all right, *chérie*," she told Tess in a low voice. "I will give him his gold and he will be on his way." She looked at Halifax. "How much do you need?"

He wagged his head from side to side. "None of it, you stinking whore. I'll be rich again, once I tell King Charles where to find the man who killed the Duke of Clary. Who knows?" He sounded absurdly cheerful. "His Majesty might even settle the dukedom on me!"

"He never would," Suzette told him, "not once he found out how cheaply you valued your birthright."

"Then I suppose I'll just have to make sure there's no one left alive to tell him, won't I?" Lord Halifax asked in that same sunny voice, and leveled the barrel of the gun at Suzette's heart.

She let her apron drop abruptly, revealing the knife she had hidden there, and sprang at him even as she cried, "Run, Teresa! Run!"

But before Tess could move, the pistol went off with a deafening roar that reverberated wildly from the brick walls and shook the crockery down off the shelves in a barrage of thunder. Suzette staggered, then fell face-downward on the floor, the knife still clenched in her hand.

"Dear God in heaven." Tess saw the dark stain of blood spreading at the back of the Frenchwoman's blue gown and knelt beside her. Dazed, acting on instinct, she helped her to a sitting position, cradling those slim straight shoulders in her arms. The jagged hole just below the woman's left breast was as big around as her fist. "Oh, God, Suzette. Hold on. I'll get a doctor—"

Suzette shook her head, ever so faintly. "There is . . . no need."

"Hush. You must save your strength." Tess tried ineffectually to stanch the rush of blood from the wound; it seemed a tide, an ocean.

"Save it for what? For dying?" Her mouth curved in a wry smile. "*Écoute, chérie.*" Blue eyes, wide and empty as the Shropshire sky, searched the room. Staring straight at Lord Halifax, she whispered, "He is gone, *non?*"

"Aye," Tess lied. "Aye, he's gone."

"*C'est bien.* Listen to me. You must not be afraid to go to James. Do you hear? There is nothing to be afraid of."

"Oh, Suzette—"

"You must go to him! Do you promise?" The French-woman's hand clung to hers with desperate strength. "Promise!"

"I promise."

"C'est bien." Suzette sighed; her eyelids closed. Then, quietly, like wind ruffling water, she died.

"How very touching."

Tess looked up to see Andrew Halifax reloading his pistol, pouring powder into the chamber from a pouch at his belt. "I don't understand," she whispered, blood covering her skirts, dripping from her hands. How had the man she'd grown up honoring, admiring, become this monster? "Why? Why did you kill her?"

He paused, about to aim the gun. "Get up." But Tess couldn't move. "I said get up!" The tip of the barrel came to rest against her cheek; he moved it downward, over her throat to her bodice, slipping it inside, rubbing it back and forth across her breast. "I'm going to enjoy this, lovely Tess. I'm going to enjoy taking something that's his."

"You *are* mad," she breathed, the chilly gun barrel teasing her nipple.

"Don't *say* that!" He jerked the pistol from her bodice, holding it instead against the side of her head. "Let's go. Up the stairs."

Tess didn't know where she found the strength to obey him, but somehow she did. She moved Suzette's lifeless body from her lap and stood. While Lord Halifax watched, she plunged her bloodied hands into a bucket and washed them, then splashed her face. The water was bracingly cold. Beneath the red half-moons of her nails there were still shreds of pie dough. The sight calcified her resolve. She would not let Suzette's death prove in vain. She would go to James and warn him that Lord Halifax planned to expose him. Perhaps in some small way that would atone for the terrible wrong she had done him when she rid herself of their child.

Drying her hands on a bit of toweling, she glanced over her shoulder at the madman with the pistol. Forcing her voice to husky seductiveness, in imitation of Annie, she moved toward the corridor and purred, "As you wish, milord. I know a room where we can be very comfortable . . ."

It was the measure of his lunacy that he accepted her abrupt volte-face, returning her smile—though he did not lower the cocked pistol. "Lead on, Mistress Jericho."

Upstairs in the gallery, the Peacock was pitch dark and deathly quiet. Tess took a few running steps along the curtain-draped hallway, hoping to slip away from the man following behind her, and instantly felt the gun pressed to her back. "Where to in such a rush, my pigeon?" came Lord Halifax's voice.

"I . . . I thought to fetch a candle."

"We've no need for light yet. You know your way."

Holding her skirts in one hand, feeling the wall with the other, Tess counted three doors down from the stairwell—the room with Suzette's books, where she and James once ate and slept and pleasured each other for hours on end. A room made for love. She remembered thinking that in that strange Christmastide one year ago. She opened the door.

Lord Halifax entered close behind her. Tess groped her way to the bedside, found candles and flint, and the room glowed with soft golden light. "Won't you sit down?" she invited, gesturing toward one of the chairs. He sank into it, still gripping the gun. "Some wine?" When he nodded, she found a bottle in one of the cupboards, uncorked it, and filled two crystal glasses up to their rims. "To this night," she said softly, carrying the glasses to the table beside him, touching hers to his. He made no move to drink, but she took a deep swallow of wine, needing its steadying strength.

"Now." She brought the three-stemmed candlestick to the table as well, putting it close to him, swallowing revulsion as he ran the gun barrel across her bodice again. Smiling, she stepped back, untying her apron, raising it over her head, and had to clench her eyes shut against the sticky bloodstains going past her face. She let it drop to the floor, reached for her bodice buttons, and undid them slowly from top to bottom. Lord Halifax's pale eyes narrowed; he settled back in the chair.

She removed the bodice, one sleeve and then the other,

and tossed it aside atop the apron. Next she unfastened the band of her skirts and let them fall too, stepping from the nest they made in her petticoat and chemise. Moving the gun to his left hand, Lord Halifax reached for his wineglass, his tongue moving over his lips. "My dear Teresa. You've filled out," he said appreciatively. "I had no idea."

"When you saw me last, I was only a child."

He downed the wine in a gulp, then wiped his mouth with the back of his hand. "Well, you're all woman now."

"And you . . ." She pulled the pins from her hair, letting it tumble loose over her bare shoulders and down her back. "Even when I was only a girl, I knew you were a special sort of man."

"Did you?"

Tess nodded, unlacing her chemise. The cloth shimmered in the candlelight, rippled with every movement she made. "Oh, yes. I remember—I thought you were the King of England, and the big house a palace."

"I'll live there again. Or someplace even grander, as the Duke of Clary."

Not if I live to help it, Tess thought as she bared a breast and said, "I know . . ."

His colorless gaze was riveted to her flesh. She pirouetted gracefully, pulling off the chemise; it fluttered to the floor like a wounded silk bird. "Perhaps you might live there with me, Teresa." He reached for his wineglass, found it empty, and frowned.

"Take mine," she suggested, loosening her pettiskirts, then stepping out of her drawers. "All that I have is yours." Utterly vulnerable, she stood before him and thought of the dream she'd dreamt on the night she was to marry Jack, the dream in which she'd danced naked in front of all the men in Windber. She'd been sick with shame in that dream; now she was far beyond shame, steady despite her fear.

But still he had his hand on the gun.

She knelt at the foot of his chair. He smiled and unfastened his cloak at the throat, then reached for his breeches buttons. "Let me," Tess purred, leaning over him. Slowly she undid them, letting her breasts rub against his thighs. He drew in his breath. His head fell back. His eyes closed. The hand in which he held the gun snaked out to pull her toward him.

She grabbed his balls and twisted as hard as she could.

He let out an unearthly howl and doubled over, lunging for her at the same time. Tess grabbed for the gun, but it was lost in the folds of his cloak. He sent the wineglasses spinning from the table as he lunged again. They fell to the floor just as Tess leapt back to avoid his grasp. The candlestick went flying. For an instant, as it sailed through the air, the flames lengthened and everything grew brighter. Then it landed. The flames flickered and went out, plunging the room into darkness just as Tess reached the door, slipped through, and slammed it shut again.

She headed for the stairway, one thought running through her head. If she could just reach the stables . . . There would be weapons there—pitchforks, knives, an ax. She knew her way around a stable. If she could just make it to the stable . . .

But somehow, groping her way in pitch blackness, she missed the door, or else she miscounted, for when she started down the stairs, there weren't any there. Hurriedly she retraced her steps, stumbling back out into the gallery—and screamed as Lord Halifax cursed and caught her round the waist.

Christ, how had he moved so fast? If she'd been wearing clothes she would have been doomed, but as it was, she managed to twist away, leaving him holding air. Her bare feet made no sound at all on the carpeted floor, but neither could she hear him coming. Either he wasn't moving or the soft wool muffled his steps as well.

She was headed away from the stairs, but it couldn't be helped; she wasn't about to try to slip past him in such narrow confines. Did he know there was no other way down from the gallery? She ran past the first turn, feeling her way by the banister, and thought she heard the opening of a door. If he did know there was but one escape route, she realized, he had only to bide his time for her there. The thought made her shiver. She waited, ears strained, heart thumping in the darkness, but could hear nothing more.

Where the devil had he got to? She didn't know whether to move forward or back; paralyzed by indecision, she stood shivering, clinging to the balcony rail. At last, minutes, hours later, there came a sound.

Such a peculiar sound it was. She'd heard it before. Tess was sure of that, though she couldn't think when or where. It reminded her vaguely of fast-running water, like the River Clun in spring, when snow from the White Moor swelled it to the head of its banks. Or of the crinkling pages of Ben's old Bible as one flipped through it quickly . . . or of cold winter nights at the Swan, when the whole village gathered, hoisting mugs of mead around a roaring fire—

God, that was it. It was the sound of fire.

Her head filled with horrible visions of the blaze that had come so close to killing her father. She stared down into the gambling hall below, but saw only darkness. She could smell fire, though—that harsh acrid stench that had seared her lungs as the stables collapsed around the screaming horses, that had clung to her hands and hair. She thought of Ben's burns, his awful pain, and she thought: God, I don't want to die that way!

She turned and raced back around the corner, raced for the stairs.

Though she threw open one door after another, she couldn't seem to find the way down. The smell was growing stronger; she imagined smoke wrapping around her in the darkness. As she grasped one more doorlatch, her mind registered that it felt warm. Then she yanked it up and screamed. She'd found the stairs—and the fire. The carpet, the walls, the floor of the corridor below, all were engulfed in flames.

Quickly she slammed the door shut. The fire was too furious, too hot to have spread so far in so short a time. Lord Halifax must have set it, perhaps with the gunpowder he wore on his belt. She took a few deep breaths, until she could think clearly again.

There was no way to climb down from the gallery without breaking her neck. Just the idea of dangling from that height on a rope, even if she could find one, made her head spin. She could wait until someone spotted the smoke and flames from outside—but what if that was too late? God, what should she do?

There in the darkness, an image rose up in her mind, of Gideon—James—coming out of the burning stables, carrying her father. He'd done it. He'd come unscathed through the flames. She could do so too.

She felt her way to the bedchamber where she'd undressed, found her boots in the darkness, jammed her feet inside them. Then she ripped the coverlet and blankets from the bed; she couldn't risk spending precious minutes putting on her clothes. Instead she wrapped the bedding tight around her, pulled it over her face, and rushed back out into the corridor.

As she opened the door to the stairs once more, as red-hot air and smoke roiled toward her, there was one dreadful instant when she lost her nerve, when she stared down into the inferno and very nearly backed away. But then she thought of Suzette's brave, desperate attempt to stop Lord Halifax—because of her love for James—and that gave her strength.

She filled her lungs with air, filled them full to bursting. She clutched the covers she wore, hiking them above her boot-tops to make sure she wouldn't trip. And then she ran downstairs.

It was the longest, strangest journey she had ever made, those few hundred feet of stairway and hallway. The roar of the fire was deafening; it made its own wind, high and howling, that soared toward the gallery, flattening the flames like meadow grass and blowing them up again. Despite the blanket that covered her face, her lungs ached; the smoke sucked the air straight out of them, leaving only heat.

Through a slit in the blanket she saw the open door to the kitchens, reached it, stumbled through. The brick-walled room had become one huge oven fed by the skeletons of cupboards, tables, chairs. In the center of a red-gold ring of fire, like some exotic flower from the glasshouse, she saw a heart of blue velvet, knew it was Suzette, and quickly looked away.

Then she was through to the pantry, across the tiled

floor, and—oh, blessed cold, holy snow and ice!—out the door to the yards. Slipping, sliding, she skidded over the cobbles to the stables. Dung had never in all her life smelled so fresh and sweet.

"Linzy!" she called, exultant, and heard the pony nicker in the darkness, found her by the sound. "Oh, Linzy." She buried her face against that beloved silver mane and clung to her sweet substantialness, wanting nothing more than to lie down in the hay with her and dissolve in tears.

But there wasn't time for that. Even now, Andrew Halifax would be on his way to see the king. Once Charles learned that Gideon Cade was really James Trelawny, there'd be soldiers riding to arrest him, bring him to London for trial.

"Linzy, love." She struggled into the filthy shirt and breeches the stableboy used for mucking. "I know it's cold out. And I know you're bearing." She grabbed a spare coat and hat as well, and then the pony's gear. "But you know I wouldn't ask this of you if it wasn't important. You've got to take me back home to Windber, Linzy, one more time." Home. She bit back tears, methodically tightening the girth, checking reins and bit. The home she'd never thought to see again. Home for the holidays . . .

"You see," she went on, the sound of her own voice holding desperation at bay, "we've got to warn James—I mean Gideon . . . we can only call him Gideon now—that they're coming for him." And tell him that Suzette is dead. Christ, what a terrible task.

And then . . .

"He'll be off again, I expect. Somewhere as a sailor, I reckon. We'll be off too, you and I, though God knows where."

But first . . .

She climbed into the saddle, drawing the blanket up around her shoulders. First she'd be telling Gideon Cade about another death, that of the child he had given her.

It was not a prospect to incline one to ride hard—and yet she did.

27

Christmas Day in the year of Our Lord 1671 dawned cold as winter ale and bright as silver—and with Tess still shy of Ludlow, more than twenty miles from her goal. But when the sun came up, it was from behind the White Moor far in the distance, just as it had every morning when she lived in Windber-on-Clun. And even as the roadbed grew more rocky and rough, the rocks and roughness rang unmistakably of Shropshire with each jolting clang of Linzy's iron-shod hooves.

The cottages she passed were teasingly familiar, with their thatched roofs and low walls and fat stone chimneys belching tufts of smoke. In Tenbury the villagers came tumbling out from doorways to hurry to church. "Come and join us!" they cried when they saw Tess riding through their midst. She turned them down even as she drank in their Shropshire drawls. There would be worse fates in life, she mused, than to stake one's place in some such village, still within the shadow of the White Moor. Her neighbors would come to accept her eventually, just as the tenants of Windber had accepted Ben. If it took years—why, she'd still have Linzy. And the colt—she could sell that and buy herself a long-eared hound to keep her company. The Widow Jericho, that was what she'd put herself about as. No. On second thought, it would be safer to pick another name.

The cold kept the road surface frozen, so Linzy didn't have to slog through slush and mud the way she had for most of the past few days. Despite her increased girth, the pony had been uncomplaining; it was as though she heard the same song of home that Tess did in her ringing shoes. One thing was sure, Tess thought: the pony was as glad as she to be out of London, away from the noise and smells, back where the air was clean.

The journey had been so hard that she allowed herself and Linzy the luxury of a mere trot now. After all, the soldiers who'd be coming for Gideon were still behind her. She knew, for she'd asked at each stop she made along the way; no one had seen any of the king's men pass. Perhaps Charles had decided to grant them the holiday with their families before they set out. Why not? So far as Lord Halifax knew, there wasn't any hurry. She and Suzette were dead. There was no one to warn Gideon Cade of the coming blow.

At noon, with the pale sun at its peak, she reached Stanton Lacy. A tantalizing aroma of roast goose hung thick in the air around the manor house; when she begged at the kitchens, she got white bread dipped in its grease. By the time she got as far as Clunton, where the river widened and ran like flat green window glass, the sky above had darkened. Living in London, with candles and lamps and drawn curtains, she'd forgotten the brevity of country winter days.

Linzy plugged on, but with her spirits lagging, looking longingly at every shelter they passed. Tess didn't blame her one bit. "Come on, girl," she coaxed, "it's just another five miles, and then there'll be hay and oats and your very own stall."

They rode for a long time in deep purple twilight. Stars came out, and a minuscule sliver of blanched moon. The road split away from the river, climbing into the heights of the Forest Clun; the White Moor rose and fell before them, and then, when the sky above had turned to smooth black velvet, they were home again.

The Swan was ablaze with candles. Tess gave it wide berth, sticking to the shadows, but still she could hear voices—Sam, Mungo, Tim, Meg Mullen—raised in cheery song. Her father would be there as well, no doubt drunk beyond singing in celebration. Ben always had loved Christmas. When she was a girl he used to craft calendars for her out of paper and wood, with little doors to open, one for each day until the Christ Child came. Lord, she hadn't thought of that in years; why did the memory come to her now?

"The holly bears a berry as sweet as lily flower," the voices from the tavern sang, "and Mary bore sweet Jesus Christ to be our own savior . . ."

A single window showed light at the big house: the librarium, draperies half-drawn against the winter chill. Tess felt the cold now, more than she had at any other point along the ride. She longed to deliver her sorry news and be gone, away from this place and her memories. But she'd promised Linzy a meal and a rub, and the pony had served her too faithfully to be denied.

A familiar snort sounded as she led Linzy into the stables. It was Satan, Tess saw as she lit a lamp at the doorway, with his ears back and nostrils flaring as he butted against his stall. "That glad to see us, then," she said with grim humor, then noticed the other horse—a powerful gray gelding, withers bathed in foam—in the stall beside him. "Someone's been riding you hard—and couldn't even be bothered to rub you down," she noted, disapproving. "I'll take care of that in a minute. Come along, Linzy, girl." Rubbing her sore back, she led the pony to the stall across from Satan's.

The building was still so new that it smelled more of oak and turpentine than manure and hay. Tess eyed the long rows of empty berths and thought of Gideon's dream of filling them with champion racers. That dream would end like all the others they'd shared together, once she made her confession to him.

"Go on, girl," she told Linzy, who balked at entering her stall. "Go on, pretty girl, and I'll fetch the oats and currycomb." The pony whinnied, high and wild, rearing back. From Satan's stall came an answering neigh, and the black stallion thudded into wood again. "What is wrong with you two?" Tess demanded, going round to Linzy's head to calm her. "You'd think you'd both seen a gho . . . " The word trailed away as she saw the man sprawled facedown on the floor of the stall.

"Dad?" That was her first thought: that it was Ben, victim of too much Christmas merrymaking. But the man was taller than her father, and stouter, and besides, Ben had never worn anything like that well-patched doublet. Only one man in the village did. "Oren?" She said his name again, more loudly, but he never moved. Behind her, Linzy whimpered, tugging at the bridle. With a sudden sense of doomed certainty, Tess poked the motionless man with her toe, then knelt and rolled him over. She could scarcely see the short-hilted knife sunk into his chest for all of the blood.

"What in God's name . . . ?" Who would murder Oren? True, he'd been the butt of jokes and jests so long as she could remember, but murder? On Christmas Eve, in Windber-on-Clun? It was incomprehensible. She whirled around, half-expecting to find some homicidal stranger looming over her. But there was only Linzy. "It's all right, girl," she said soothingly, letting the body fall forward again, leading the pony to another, empty stall. "But I'm afraid that rub and meal will have to wait." Another death to tell Gideon of, this one so recent the blood hadn't dried. Leaving the lantern behind to help calm the horses, she slipped up the hill past the darkened glasshouse to the big house. No sense knocking, not with Oren dead. She went in through the front doors.

Inside, all was shadows and silence. The housemaids and boys must have gone to the tavern, or home to their families. Unless . . . Tess shuddered at a sudden thought: what if she found their bodies too? Unable to bear the suspense, she called into the darkened hush: "Hello? Hello, is anybody here?"

There wasn't any answer. She waited, waited ten whole seconds in the cold black stillness. Then, "Hello!" she screamed, and heard sound from the floor above, and footsteps on the stairs.

"Tess?" that voice, so loved, so missed, made her start to tremble. "I was asleep. I thought I was dreaming." The footsteps stopped halfway down, at the landing. "Am I dreaming?"

"No," she said. "No. I'm here . . . James."

Such a long, long silence before he spoke again. "You know my name," he said slowly, wonderingly.

"I just found Oren." Her voice sounded dull in that

house, and eerily thin. "Out in the stable. Someone's stabbed him to death."

"Oren? Why in God's name . . ."

Tess forced herself to go on, pushing past his bewilderment. "There's more. Suzette is dead too. Andrew Halifax shot her at the Peacock Inn and set the place on fire."

"Jesus in heaven," he whispered, and then cried it out in anguish: "Jesus in heaven, *why*?"

From the darkness another voice spoke. "My felicitations on your resurrection, Mistress Jericho." And then came the sound of a pistol cocking. "What a pity it's to be so brief. Only three short days."

"Tess!" Everything happened at once: Gideon's shout, the sizzle of powder, sparks, thunder, and a blow that knocked her from her feet. Gideon's arms around her, holding her tightly as together they rolled to the floor . . .

"You're hurt," she said, blood welling up between her fingers as she touched his thigh.

"Hush, Tess, hush!" He scrambled to his knees, dragging her with him toward the front doors. Another shot rang out. Tess screamed, unable to stop herself. Gideon put his hand over her mouth and kept on crawling, grimly crawling.

"It's no use," Andrew Halifax called. "I know this house far better than you could. Or perhaps you've forgotten, milord Clary, that it used to be mine." Gideon stopped, stiffened as he heard that name. Halifax laughed. "That's right, Clary. Your little secret's out, thanks to your stepmother. Your *late* stepmother, I should say. It was really quite a touching scene. She died trying to protect you."

Gideon's groan was involuntary, an animal thing, wrenched from his heart. Andrew Halifax used the sound as a guide and fired again. The ball struck the floor so close to Tess's arm that she felt its heat, and splinters drove into her hand.

"Do what you want to me, Halifax, but let Tess go," Gideon bargained in the time he had before the man could reload.

Halifax clucked his tongue. "What a self-sacrificing lot

you Trelawnys are—except, of course, for your father. Alas, I can't spare her now. She knows too much, just as Oren did."

His footsteps were coming toward them; Tess could almost see him, a black shape coming out of the blackness. She smelled powder on the air and knew he'd never miss from that distance. Her lips moved, mumbling a prayer: "Our Father, which art in heaven . . ."

At her back the front doors swung open. Light poured into the hall. "I heard shots," Ben Jericho said, lifting up his lantern. "On my way home from the Swan." He blinked. "Great Jehovah, it's Lord Halifax!"

"Dad." Tess started to cry. "Oh, God, Dad, help us!"

He swung the lantern round to see her. Its glow obscured his face, but his voice was cold. "Well, Teresa. Come home to your lover for Christmastide, have you?"

"Dad, Lord Halifax is trying to kill us! He's already killed Oren out in the stables, and he's trying to kill us now!"

The lantern swung round again. Tess could just discern the craggy profile of her father's forehead and nose and chin as he contemplated Andrew Halifax. She'd never seen him look more unyielding. "What, his lordship try to kill you?" He let out a snort of disbelief. "There must be some mistake."

"There's been a mistake, all right." Halifax, damn his soul, sounded impeccably cool and calm; there was no vestige left of the lunatic Tess had seen in London. "I've just discovered, Jericho, this scoundrel's name isn't Gideon Cade at all. He's really James Trelawny."

"Trelawny, you say? Why does that name ring a bell?"

"I daresay you've heard of him," Halifax said smoothly. "He's the ugliest sort of criminal. A patricide. Murdered his own father, the Duke of Clary. Cut him down in cold blood."

Ben turned the lantern on the man crouched beside Tess. "Great Jehovah above. It comes back to me now—it must be twenty years past!"

"Believe me, Ben." Halifax grew ever more chummy. "If I'd any notion who he really was, I'd never have left Windber in his care."

Ben took a step toward the man he knew as Gideon Cade. "Well, what have you to say for yourself? *Are* you James Trelawny?"

"Aye," he said in so world-weary a voice that Tess ached to hear it. The shock of Suzette's death seemed to have pulled the life from him, like a sapling uprooted, like the blood that still seeped from his thigh.

"And you murdered your father?" Ben pressed incredulously.

"Aye."

"It wasn't like it sounds, Dad," Tess said desperately. "His father was a brute, an animal! James only killed him to save his stepmother's life. He—"

"I'll tell you the sort of woman his stepmother was," Halifax cut in. "A French slut who ran the biggest whorehouse in London. I regret to have to tell you, Ben, that's where I found Tess a few days past. Someone there had been teaching her well. She did her best to seduce me."

"No," Ben whispered. "Not in a whorehouse. Not my Teresa!"

"How can you listen to him, Dad?" she cried. "He killed James's stepmother, shot her down with that same gun! Dad, I saw him do it!"

"*Were* you in a brothel?"

"Yes, but—" He turned away from her, shaking his head. "Ask him about Suzette, why don't you?" Tess challenged him. "Ask him how James's stepmother died!"

Halifax patted Ben's shoulder. "The woman's house of iniquity burned to the ground earlier this week. Regrettably, Madame de la Mare was inside at the time. Loss of life can never be applauded, though I must say that in this case . . ." He let his voice trail away. "But you mustn't blame Tess, Ben. She was led astray by this evil man; she's not responsible for her actions."

Ben bowed his head. "No. The one to blame is her mother. Tess has got bad blood in her, the devil's blood. She's her mother's daughter; that's the cause of all this woe."

Tess saw with sudden blinding clarity how clever Halifax had been. The authorities in London would never be able to tell what had caused Suzette's death. Halifax could shoot Gideon right now and be hailed as a hero for bringing the murderous son of the Duke of Clary his due. Everyone in Windber would be convinced Gideon was guilty; look how easily Halifax had convinced her own father! The words Rachel Jonas had spoken to her on the night of the harvest tally rang in her ears: *How far d'ye reckon on letting things go before ye face up to wot ye've done?* Kneeling on the floor, still shielding Gideon, she reached for Ben's hand.

"Dad, listen to me. I'm not my mother's daughter. Her blood can't make me a harlot, any more than his father's blood"—she pointed to Halifax—"could make him a decent lord."

"She's talking nonsense, the poor creature," Halifax said, but with the faintest hint of a snarl in his voice. Ben tried to pull back his hand, but Tess wouldn't let go.

"And you can't blame Gideon either," she rushed on, "for what's happened to me. Up there in the cave that night—that wasn't his fault. It was mine, Dad. I seduced him, to get back at you for making me marry Jack."

"Oh, lass. You don't know what you're saying."

"That's right," Halifax assured Ben. "She—"

"I know *exactly* what I'm saying. I'm taking responsibility for what I've done the same way you took responsibility for me. I won't say I haven't made mistakes, because God knows I have. But it's what we do afterward, after our mistakes, that matters." She took a deep breath. "I'm *your* daughter, Dad. Everything I know in this world about faith and truth and love, all of it, you taught me. Now I'm asking you to go on loving me. To have faith in me."

"Oh, Tessie." The lantern-light glinted off tears in his eyes. "I do love you, lass."

"Then trust me, Dad."

Half-apologetically, Ben turned to Halifax. "I'll just go see, your lordship, sir, if I can find Oren."

The blast of the pistol took him by surprise. "I'm not about to be thwarted by the likes of you, Ben Jericho!" Halifax screeched. Tess, heart pounding, saw that the shot meant for her father had crashed into the front door instead. "I'll not be thwarted by anyone, damn you!" He was trying frantically to reload, spilling powder all over the floor. "I've come too far for that. I'll see you all dead!"

He got off another shot while Ben stared dumbfounded; Gideon was still struggling to get to his feet. Tess screamed as the lantern shattered in Ben's hand, sending a hail of broken glass and burning oil raining through the room. The spilled powder ignited with a hungry hiss, surrounding Halifax with a wreath of flame. He ignored it, pouring still more powder into the chamber of the pistol even as his breeches ignited. "Great Jehovah, man," Ben blurted out, "you're on fire! Are you mad?"

"Don't say that. Don't ever say that!" He raised the gun again just as Gideon flung himself forward into the fire, knocking him down.

Tess stared in horror as flames engulfed the two men. "Help me, lass!" Ben cried, ripping the draperies from a window. "Come on!" Together they hovered over the figures wrestling on the floor, trying to beat down the spreading blaze. The draperies caught on Halifax's spur; Ben tried to tug them free, but the fabric slipped through his hands. For a long moment the velvet thrust and heaved with the desperate struggle of the men beneath it. Then one last gunshot rang out, and all motion ceased.

"Oh, God," Tess cried, her hand at her mouth. "Oh, God in heaven . . ."

Ben bent down amidst the flames and pulled the drapery toward him. First he revealed Andrew Halifax, his wide-open eyes staring up at the ceiling, and then the man he knew as Gideon Cade, the pistol clenched tight in his hand.

"Come on," Ben shouted, fighting to help the survivor to his feet. "We've got to get out of here, ring the bell for the fire—"

"To hell with the fire," Gideon said. "Let the damned house burn."

They staggered out through the doors to the portico, and for an instant Tess thought the whole hillside was on fire. Then she saw it was the villagers, carrying torches: Mungo, Sam, Tim Whitaker, Mort and Ellie, Meg Mullen—everyone was there, bleary-eyed from celebrating and staring in disbelief at the growing conflagration crowning the hill. "Wot in bloody hell happened here?" Mungo asked in awe.

Ben had to shout to be heard above the roaring blaze. "Andrew Halifax is inside—or at least, his body. The poor man went mad and murdered Oren."

"He never," cried Meg, while the rest all gaped.

"That's not the half of it," Ben told them. Tess drew a deep breath, waiting for her father to reveal the awful secret of the man she loved. But Ben looked at her, and in the depths of his eyes there was no more hate, only hope and forgiveness. "Then," he said, "he tried to kill our Lord Gideon Cade."

28

They took his lordship to the cottage, at Ben's insistence. "Put me up in his house when I was sickly, didn't he?" Tess's father kept asking. "My hospitality's no match for his, but I'll do my best by Gideon Cade."

"I'll show Mungo and the others where they can find Oren," Tess said as Ben and Jack started down the hill with Gideon propped between them.

"Don't go," the wounded man whispered, reaching for her.

"But—"

"I reckon they'll manage to find him; he's not going anywhere, is he?" Ben asked, and gave Tess a sharp glance. "You come on to the cottage too, lass. You look all done in. Rachel, we'll need you to dress his lordship's wound."

"Ben, wot should we do about . . . ?" Tim nodded toward the doors to the big house, opened now onto a solid wall of flame.

Ben grunted. "Can't see the sense in live men risking themselves for a dead one—'specially not when the live ones are as drunk as you are. 'Tis a pity, but Lord Halifax is beyond feeling it, ain't he? Mind you don't let that fire spread." Between them, he and Jack humped his lordship down the hill to the cottage, with Tess and Rachel trailing behind.

"Anything more I can do here?" Jack asked, when they'd got their burden settled safely on Ben's bed.

Ben waved him toward the doorway. "Nah. You'd best

363

go make sure those fools out there don't ignite from all the ale on their breaths."

"All right, then." Jack started for the door, but turned back, twirling his cap in his hands. "I'm glad ye got out," he told the man on the bed. "I mean that. And ye, Tess." Then he hurried into the night.

"Well," said Rachel, slicing away the bloodied breeches leg, "how about that?" She probed the bullet hole with gentle fingers. "Ben, have ye got a clean bedsheet or somethin'?" He looked ruefully at the huge pile of laundry by the foot of the bed. "Nay, I didn't reckon ye would." She sighed and began to cut her pettiskirt into strips. "Shall I send to the Swan for some brandy, yer lordship?"

"Not unless Ben wants it."

Tess saw her father grin. "Faith, ye know I've given up the bottle—and for good this time."

Rachel wrapped linen around Gideon's thigh and pulled the ends tight. "There. Now, Teresa, come hold this while I fetch my herbs."

"I'll get them," she offered, wanting to postpone the moment when she must confess to Gideon about their child.

"Don't be daft, girl. Ye don't know wot I need." So Tess knelt by the bed and held the compress while the widow trudged outside.

Ben rebuilt the fire at the hearth, then stood and dusted his hands on his breeches. "Reckon I'd best go see to Oren. Do you know, it's the strangest thing. Standing there in that fire, with the flames all around me, I kept thinking I was seeing him."

"I don't think that's so strange," Gideon told him. "Remember, Tess, how when Ben was recovering from his burns he kept talking of Oren? I'll bet he's the one set that fire in the stables—and I'll bet, Ben, you saw him there."

"Oren may have been a prig, but he'd never have tried to kill Dad," Tess demurred.

"He didn't expect him to be there that day," he reminded her. "He'd heard Ben ask me for permission to ride to Stafford."

Ben looked bewildered. "Why would Oren do such a thing?"

"It's likely he and Halifax cooked it up together."

Tess nodded in sudden comprehension. "Remember, Dad, it was Oren who rode with Lord Halifax to London when he first left Windber. Halifax must have confided in him then, and asked him to cause trouble for Gideon. That would explain why Halifax came back here before going to tell King Charles who Gideon really was. He said in London he had to make sure no one who knew the truth about how he lost Windber was still alive."

Ben grunted. "And just what is the truth about how he lost Windber, I'd like to know."

"I won it from him in a card game," Gideon said.

"You what?" Tess and her father were staring.

"Halifax was an inveterate gambler," he confirmed. "He'd already lost nearly everything he owned; that's why the big house was stripped bare. All he had left was the land and the title, and one night at the Peacock he tried to put them up as stakes in a hand of vingt-et-un. The girl running the game came and fetched Suzette. She wasn't going to allow the bet, but I talked her into letting me play him."

"He gambled us away in a game of cards?" Ben couldn't believe it.

"I wouldn't put anything past that man," Tess said with a shudder. "What I don't understand is why Gideon took the bet."

"I knew he was gambling with his tenants' lives. If he didn't lose the stake there, he'd only lose it at some other hall." He shrugged. "I just didn't think it was right."

"Five hundred years there were Halifaxes in Windber," Ben muttered to himself. "Five hundred years!" He banged his fist against the cottage wall. "Great Jehovah, man," he cried, turning to Gideon, "why didn't you tell us? Why'd you let us believe his lies about the lawsuit and such?"

"I've never thought much of those who make themselves look bigger by tearing other men down. Andrew Halifax had trouble enough, so far as I was concerned."

His clear blue eyes darkened. "But then, I never expected he'd blame Suzette for his gambling debts."

"When I think of all the grief we caused you . . ." Ben swallowed. "The glasshouse that night—that was my fault, Jehovah forgive me. I spurred them on."

"He knows, Dad," Tess said quietly.

"But look here, what about that money Lord Halifax sent us last Christmas?" Ben demanded, not quite willing to relinquish all those years of allegiance to the dead man.

"I'll make a bet of my own," said Tess, "that it never came from him. You sent it, didn't you, Gideon? And said that Halifax had."

"I had to do something so you wouldn't all starve." He smiled faintly. "Considering how stubborn your father is, I thought he might convince all of you to turn the gold down if you knew it came from me."

"And just where did *you* get it?" Ben wanted to know.

"You sold Satan, didn't you?" Tess asked Gideon.

He nodded. "With the glasshouse gone, I hadn't anything else to fall back on. At least that gave me a gambling stake."

"I don't hold with gambling," Ben said, frowning.

"Oh, for God's sake, Dad." Tess bit off a smile. "It serves you right for getting us so worked up we tore the glasshouse down."

"Hmph," said Ben. "I reckon I'd best go see to Oren." On his way to the door he stopped by the bed and laid his hand over Gideon's with awkward tenderness. "I am sorry about your stepmother, son."

"I haven't thanked you yet," Gideon said, his voice husky, "for keeping my secret out there tonight. For not letting on who I am."

Ben looked at his daughter. "Well, the way I see it, Tess was right in what she said. We all make mistakes. It's what we do afterward to try to right 'em that matters." He paused. "Your letting the big house burn— does that mean you'll be leaving us?"

"I don't know."

"Well, I'm one would rather see you stay." Then he stumped out the door.

There was no sound in the cottage for a moment but the crackling fire. "I'm sorry, too, about Suzette," Tess said at last. "She was a good woman. A good friend."

"It is my fault she's dead," Gideon said, his voice breaking.

"You can't blame yourself!" Tess told him earnestly. "How could you have known Halifax was a madman? None of us guessed, and we knew him far better than you."

"She was so happy when I told her about you." He smiled, remembering. "It was the first time you visited Emilia. She came up to Shrewsbury. I met her there with a big bunch of night jasmine. She knew right away that I was in love." The smile faded. "She couldn't understand why I couldn't ask you to marry me. I tried to tell her—how could I ask you to share my life when it was spent in hiding? When everything about me, even my name, was a lie?"

"I think Cade's a fine name," Tess said softly. "It would have suited me well."

His laughter rippled, bitter and dark as cheap ale. "Aye, well, that's water over the dam. I would have had to confide the truth about my father sooner or later. Emilia told me how you ran off the moment you heard who I really was. That showed what you thought of having fallen in love with a patricide."

"Oh, Gideon, that's not why I ran off. It was because I'd seen your name on that damned marriage certificate with Suzette's. I thought you were already married! And there was a reason why . . . why, if you would not wed me, I had to leave," she said haltingly.

"What reason could there be?"

Tess didn't, couldn't, answer, could not admit the awful thing she'd done. She just looked at him, and saw knowledge dawn in the azure depths of his eyes. "A child," he whispered. She bowed her head. "My God. You're having a child." Pistol wound forgotten, he stumbled up from the bed and came toward her, holding out his arms.

"Don't!" she cried, reeling blindly away. "You don't know what I've done!" She put her back to him, hugging herself, eyes clenched shut. "I went to London because I knew Rachel wouldn't help me. I went there to be rid of the baby. I paid a woman in the market there and got rid of it!"

She heard the creak of the floorboards, and she prayed for him to strike her, hoping that might take away some of the wrenching pain in her heart. But when he touched her it was with exquisite gentleness, as though she were one of the glasshouse flowers that he tended with such care. "Oh, Tess. My poor Tess." He held her close, standing behind her, cheek against her hair. "I'm so sorry—"

"Why should you be sorry?" she cried. "You've naught to be sorry for; I'm the one did it!"

"You only did what you had to do. And now you must put it behind you, forgive yourself, and go on! Believe me, I know. Forgiving yourself is the hardest thing of all to do."

"I will never forgive myself," Tess whispered brokenly.

"But you must." He turned her to face him. "How else will we go on together, you and I?" She looked up at him, and in his eyes she saw love and hope and compassion and the strength she lacked. "Say you'll marry me, Tess."

"Aye," she told him, voice catching in a sob. "Aye, I'll marry you, Gideon Cade." Then his mouth covered hers.

That was how Rachel found them when she bustled in a moment later, herb basket over her arm. "Back on that bed, yer lordship," she ordered briskly. "As for ye, Teresa, kindly change yer clothes—ye stink of fire 'n' horses. Speakin' of which, yer father's seen to Linzy. Right pleased with her, he is, considerin' ye rode her all the way from London in her condition. Tell me again when she's due."

"April," Tess said rather distractedly.

The widow grunted, shoving Gideon down on the bed. "Ye know, another inch to the left and yer thigh bone'd be broken. This'll hurt." He winced as she poured a vile-looking potion over the wound. "So. Just a month afore ye, Teresa."

"What's that?" asked Tess, searching the disordered cottage for something to wear.

"Hold this," Rachel directed Gideon, putting a poultice to the gash in his leg. "Hold it tight! Wot's the matter, a great strong fellow like ye ain't got the strength to hold a bit of linen? I said, Teresa, Linzy'll be birthin' just a month afore ye."

Tess drew in her breath as her heart contracted. Gideon came to her rescue. "Tess isn't having a baby, Rachel," he said calmly.

"Wot's this? Not havin' a baby? Why, a soul's only got to look at her to see it. I'd guess she's four months along. Here, yer lordship, drink this."

By then Tess had found her tongue. "You're mistaken, Rachel. While I was in London—"

"Faith, girl, wot do I care wot ye did in London?" the widow interrupted. "Wot goes on there in the big city's naught to me. I'm tellin' ye, ye're havin' a baby."

"But—" said Gideon.

"There's no buts about it! Jesus blessed Christ, if I was ye two I'd stop arguin' with me 'n' start makin' weddin' plans; ye're late enough as 'tis."

"Rachel," Tess said after a moment, "I'm *not* having a baby."

The herb woman faced her, hands on ample hips. "Oh, ye're not, are ye? When's the last time ye had yer monthly?"

"Back in July, I think it was, or August. But—"

"Hmph. Feeling sickly of mornin's, was ye, up until a few weeks ago?"

"Aye, but not anymore."

"Well, of course not, girl; that part's past. Hungry all the time?"

Tess flushed; she'd just picked up a heel of stale bread and was gnawing it ravenously. "Maybe I am, but—"

"Tired?"

"Well, of course I'm tired, but so would you be if you'd ridden all the way from London!"

"So I would—'specially if I was carryin' a babe. Wot about yer breasts?"

"Why, what about them?" Tess stammered.

"Got bigger, have they?"

"Aye, they have," Gideon offered unexpectedly from the bed.

"Gideon!" Tess blushed.

"Well, I could hardly help noticing. Tess, maybe she's right."

"Of course I is!"

"But you can't be!" Tess insisted. "I'm telling you, when I was in London—"

"And I'm tellin' *ye*," Rachel said just as vehemently, "ye may have done this 'n' that 'n' the rest, but life don't always work out the way that we plan."

"Oh, Tess." Gideon looked at her with the first wild glimmer of belief in his eyes. "Do you think it could be true?"

Deep in her belly, Tess felt a sudden faint movement, like the fluttering of a fledgling's wings. She clapped her hands to her stomach. "Oh, dear God . . ."

"That'd be the quickenin'," Rachel said with satisfaction. "Didn't I tell ye so?"

"Gideon . . ." Tess ran to him. "Gideon, there's something inside me, and it's *moving*!"

"Not 'something,' " Rachel told her patiently. "A baby. Merry Christmas to the both of ye." And then, as Gideon pulled Tess into his arms, "Teresa! Mind the poor man's leg!" Neither paid her the least attention; they were holding one another, laughing and crying, kissing tenderly.

Ben came into the cottage, stomping his feet, with Job at his heels. "Snowing again," he said, and then saw the couple on the bed. "What's going on here?"

"Ye're goin' to be a grandfather," Rachel told him. "Now, come on and leave them alone, ye old fool."

"But I just got in!"

"Well, ye're goin' out again." She shooed him and Job into the night, then paused on the threshold. "Amazin', ain't it, wot a few open doors can lead to? But the Lord does work in strange ways."

That caught Gideon's attention; he raised his head. "Rachel, what do you mean?" But she was already gone.

"I wonder," Tess said slowly.

"What?" asked Gideon

"She said that same thing to me the night before I was to marry Jack. The night somebody left open the doors to the stables. And to Linzy's and Satan's stalls."

"You don't suppose . . ." He stared after the herb woman.

"I wouldn't be the least bit surprised."

"Of all the sneaky, low-down, underhanded, meddling . . ."

"If it's a girl, we'll have to name the baby after her," Tess said, and kissed him.

"Absolutely," he agreed.

Epilogue
Windber-on-Clun,
April 1672

Tess opened her eyes to butter-yellow sunlight and the sight of her husband standing naked at the bedchamber window, tall and slim and straight-backed as some proud medieval king. The unconscious nobility of his stance made her giggle as she pushed herself up from the pillows. "So, how does it feel being master of all you survey?"

"At the moment," he said without turning, "all I survey consists of Job, who is chasing a rabbit, and Mungo and Robbie and Sam, who are sitting on the front steps sharing a bottle of ale while they try to recoup the energy they expended coming all the way up the hill to work on the house."

"My poor darling." Tess bit her lip. "It's so hard, isn't it, to find good serfs these days?"

"God knows I don't begrudge them their nip and nap," he grumbled, "but don't you think they might at least get started before they take 'em? Makes you wonder how old King Edward ever got Westminster Abbey built."

"He had sense enough not to build it in Shropshire, that's how." She laughed again as he banged on the window, and shook his fist at the malingering workmen. "Well? Did that help?"

"Not a whit," he said as a cheery chorused "Good mornin', yer lordship!" floated up from the yard. "They're waving back at me."

"It will get done, you know," Tess tried to reassure him.

"Aye, but when? The kitchen's still a mess, they haven't started on the front hall—and what about the nursery? The baby's due any day now!"

"The baby's not due for more than a month, as you know perfectly well. And a month's an eternity to someone from Shropshire. Do you know what your trouble is? I think you miss life in the big city. All that hustling and bustling about."

He turned from the window, grinning, sunlight making a halo around his dark head. "And do you know what your trouble is? You're so filled with baby it's beginning to crowd out your brain. I *hate* the city. I've always hated cities. All I ever wanted in life was a bit of good land."

"Aye, and twenty or thirty lazy Shropshiremen to help you work it. Oh, I'm sure." She began to unbraid her hair to brush it. "That was most unkind, what you said about my brain and the baby."

"It was meant to be." He threw himself on the bed beside her, tugging down the lacy shoulder of her nightdress. "I wanted the chance to make it up to you. At length."

"What do you plan to do when the baby comes?" Tess demanded as his tongue teased her nipple.

"The baby will just have to learn to share. God, you're beautiful. How do you manage to grow more beautiful every day?"

"*You're* daft. How can you say I'm beautiful when my breasts are as big as those muskmelons in the glasshouse—"

"Nothing wrong with that."

"—and my belly's gotten fatter than Mungo's—"

"Aye, but his is all squishy. Yours is like a drum." He thumped it with two fingers, admiring the taut resonance.

"—and I've got so many of those horrid red lines on it that it looks like a map of England."

He leaned back, unbuttoning the front of the night-dress, perusing the marks she complained of. "Do you

know, you're right. Look, there's York way up here, and
Oxford, and London . . ." His hand slipped between her
thighs. "And down here is Land's End."

"Oh, no you don't." Resolutely she pushed him away,
clutching the nightdress shut. "Have you forgotten what
day this is?"

"Thursday. Grand day for an excursion to Land's End,"
he mumbled, tugging hopefully at her bodice.

"The only excursion I'm making right now is to the
stables. Don't you remember? Dad told you he thought
Linzy would foal today."

"We could make it a very brief trip."

"Hah. There's no such thing with you—though, mind,
I'm not complaining."

"You had better not be." He sighed as she swung her
legs over the edge of the bed.

Tess laughed. "For God's sake, don't look so bereft.
You know Rachel insists I have a nap every day. You can
take one with me."

"So I can," he said, brightening.

"You see? We'll make a proper loafing Shropshireman
of you yet. But for now, kindly ring for breakfast." She
pushed herself to her feet, grimacing at her belly. "Lord,
it's getting so I can't even dress myself."

"Let me help," he offered.

She snorted. "I think not. We'd never make it downstairs."

"Bonjour!" sang the small dark-haired woman who
bounced in a few moments later with a breakfast tray.
*"Voilà, le petit déjeuner. Madame, ton père est dans l'écurie.
Et—"*

"Whoa, Charmian!" Tess held up her hand. "In English, if you please!"

The French maid's mouth formed a pretty pout.
"Pardonne, madame, but my English, it is not very—"
She broke off as Gideon made a rude noise. *"Qu'est-ce
que c'est, Monsieur Gideon?"* she asked, looking offended.

"Your English is every damned bit as good as mine
and has been for years. Pull that trick with Tim and Sam
and the rest of your suitors; Tess and I have had enough
of it."

"I am sure I do not know what Monsieur Gideon means," Charmian said aloofly, though there was laughter in her dark eyes. Ever since Gideon had brought her back with him from London after Suzette's funeral, the exotic foreigner had been turning Windber-on-Clun on end. The bachelors of the village called her "Charmin' " and vied ceaselessly for her attentions. Just the other day, at the Swan, Robbie had been heard to declare that he understood now why the kings of England had always been so keen on conquering France. The sally had earned him a giggle from Charmian and dirty looks from Mungo and Tim and the rest, who all wished they'd come up with it. When Tess heard the story, she burst out laughing, remembering how suspicious her fellow tenants once were of foreigners. Windber had changed.

"But, *madame*," Charmian went on, "your father has gone to the stables. You wanted to be told."

"Already? Oh, Lord, Gideon, I'm going to miss it! Charmian, come and button me up, please, and hurry! Is there any sign yet of Lady Hardwick?"

"Non, madame."

"*Should* there be a sign of Emilia?" Gideon asked, helping himself to eggs and ham from the tray.

"I should hope so. I sent her word yesterday that if she wanted to see her colt born, she'd better hurry here."

"Poor Linzy!" he said feelingly.

"What do you mean, poor Linzy? Drat, Charmian, this skirt's not going to fit either, is it? Never mind, then, just bring me a pair of Gideon's breeches. You don't mind, do you, darling?"

"It wouldn't matter if I did. But, Tess, how would you like to have a whole stableful of people watching you when your time comes?"

She paused to consider it in the midst of buttoning the breeches. "I don't know. Would you want to be there?"

Charmian shuddered. "*Madame, Monsieur!* It is simply not done!"

"There, you see?" Gideon appealed to his wife. "She does understand English perfectly. I'll think about it, shall I?"

"But Madame Rachel, she would never permit you to be present at the birth!" Charmian protested.

"I don't know about that," Gideon said, just as Tess said, "She might." They smiled at one another. Then Tess bent down to kiss him, and waved, heading out the door. "I'll see you at the stables, then, shall I?"

"Hold on!" He lunged and hauled her back by a belt loop. "Eat your breakfast."

"But—"

"No buts. The baby needs food and so do you."

Tess smiled brightly. "I'll just go down to the stables ever so quickly and see how Linzy's coming along, shall I? And then I'll come straight back and eat like a pig. See you in just a minute or two!"

"I don't know, Charmian," he told the maid loudly as his wife made her exit. "She must be afraid she'll be sick to her stomach if she eats before watching the birth. I've seen it happen before at a foaling."

Tess spun around in the doorway. "Not to me you didn't."

"No, not to you," he acknowledged. "but in your condition, no one would blame you for being squeamish."

"I'm *not* squeamish." To prove it she took the seat across from him at the table and heaped a plate with food.

"Charming manners, your ladyship," he told her as she shoveled eggs into her mouth. Tess swallowed, stuck out her tongue, and uncovered another platter.

"Mush!" she said in delight. "We had this the very first time we had breakfast together, Gideon. Do you remember?" He shook his head. "Oh, but you must!"

"All I remember is sitting across from you and thinking: I am having breakfast with the most beautiful creature in all the world. I was petrified."

"You were cool as a cucumber," Tess countered. "It was I who was scared."

"You had me wrapped around your finger even then, as you know perfectly well."

"Hmph," said Tess. "Remind me not to let you teach our children the story of our courtship."

He grinned around a bite of mush. "Tell me, does Ben know you plan on being present today?"

"I can handle Dad. Are you coming?"

He pushed his empty plate away. "Naturally. I wouldn't miss this battle of the Jericho wills for anything in the world." ·

" 'Mornin', yer lordship, Tess," Mungo greeted them as they came out the front doors, and nonchalantly stashed the bottle of ale he'd been sipping from under his coat. He and Robbie and Sam were still sitting on the steps of the portico. "Comin' right along, ain't it?"

"Aye, that it is," Gideon said, patting Tess's belly. She stuck an elbow in his ribs. "Oh! Did you mean the house, Mungo?" He and Tess turned, gazing up at the handsome new manor that was rising—at a leisurely Shropshire pace—on the site of the big house. "Very nice. Very nice indeed."

"Ye'll notice, yer lordship, them there what-you-may-call-'em's around the windows. Robbie's carvin' every single one of 'em himself out of oak wood."·

"Westminster Abbey," Gideon murmured. "Do you think there's any chance, Mungo, you'll have finished the nursery by the time this baby gets here?"

"Why, no doubt about it, sir! Wot've ye got now, Tess, another three months till ye're due?"

"Closer to three weeks, Mungo."

"Nah! Three weeks? Ye don't say!" Mungo and Robbie and Sam all shook their heads in disbelief. "Where does the time go?"

"Where indeed?" Gideon echoed faintly. "Carry on, men. Mind you don't let the grass grow under your feet." He pulled Tess down the hill. "I don't suppose they've paid me any heed?" he asked when they were out of earshot.

She glanced over her shoulder. "Oh, yes, they have."

"They have?"

"Of course they have, darling. They moved up a step so their boots aren't touching the lawn."

In the cool quiet of the stables, Tess rather wistfully inhaled the smell of sweet hay mingled with manure. It was months since she'd been riding, and though the decision was her own, she couldn't help missing the exhilaration of galloping up the White Moor and down again.

"Jack?" Ben called from the birthing room. "Is that you?"

"It's me, Ben," his son-in-law told him, entering the stall.

"Hmph, even better. But how'd you know I was here?"

"Tess has had spies watching you like a hawk for the past two weeks."

Ben looked up from stroking Linzy's silver coat and saw his daughter. "Hello, pet. How're you feeling?"

"Splendid."

"Good. Now, get out of here."

"Dad—"

"Gideon, you're her husband. You make her go."

"Is that supposed to be a jest? You know perfectly well I can't make her do anything."

Ben grimaced. "Dangedest marriage I've ever seen, where the man's got no control over his wife."

"I know," said Gideon. "I put it all down to the way she was raised." Ben threw a currycomb at him. He smiled at Tess. "I'll go fetch you a chair."

He'd no sooner settled her on a stool close by Linzy's head than they heard Jack's voice from the front of the stables. "If ye'll just come this way, m'lord, m'lady . . ."

"Great Jehovah, what now?" Ben demanded.

"I knew you wouldn't mind, Dad," Tess said quickly, "if I sent for Lady Hardwick, seeing as she's been looking forward to this for so long."

"And who's she got with her, pray tell, the bloody House of Lords?"

"Ben Jericho, such language!" Emilia said sternly as she appeared in the entrance to the stall, borne aloft in her wheeled chair by Chester and a young man Tess didn't recognize. "You've none of you met my grand-nephew, have you? Sebastian, this is my dear friend Ben Jericho and his daughter, Tess. Oh, and her husband. Gideon Cade."

Tess's heart jumped into her throat as she watched the tall, slim young man who'd gone to Oxford with Gideon look him up and down. Emilia had long since committed herself to keeping Gideon's secret—indeed, she'd declared that causing Tess to run away had made her swear off gossip forever—but who knew what Sebastian might do when he saw his old schoolmate in the flesh?

What he did was to thrust out his hand to Gideon and grin. "How do you do? Aunt Emilia's said so much about you. She even sent me a sketch of you once. The wildest thing—I thought you looked just like someone I used to know at school."

"And do I?" Gideon asked, one eyebrow raised.

Sebastian tilted back his head, considering. "No. The boy you reminded me of never looked so happy."

"That would be Chester's fault," said his Aunt Emilia. "Got no more artistic talent than a mushroom, the poor man. You should see, Tess, what a mess he's made of my shrubberies this spring."

"Madam is too kind," Chester said, just as Linzy gave a sort of shuddering heave. "If I can be of no further assistance, perhaps Madam would excuse me before I make an ass of myself by fainting?"

"You can get yourself some breakfast in the kitchens, Chester," Tess told him.

"I think," said Chester, as Linzy snorted and moaned and shuddered again, "perhaps something stronger—"

"Come on, mate, I'll take ye to the Swan for a pint," Jack offered. "I've no stomach for this either."

"I would be forever grateful."

"Though, mind ye, it can't be much worse than my wife's last birthin'," Jack confided. "Not that I was there, mind ye, but ye couldn't miss her screamin' 'n' carryin' on. See, the Widow Jonas, that's the midwife, tells me the baby was in upside-down. Breech, that's wot they calls it. 'N' a big bugger he was, too! Anyways, he got stuck halfway in 'n' half out o' my Millie—"

"How perfectly fascinating," Chester said politely, rolling his eyes at his mistress as Jack led him away.

"Are you expecting anyone else, Tess," Ben asked, "or is it all right if we just go ahead?"

"Oh, no. Everyone's here," Tess said airily.

"It's a bit late to stop Linzy anyway," Gideon noted as the colt's head appeared. "Chester made it out just in time."

"Good girl, Linzy, good girl!" Tess cried as the pony heaved and strained. Emilia looked on, enrapt; Sebastian turned a bit green at the gills as, with Ben and Gideon hovering around her, Linzy proceeded to deliver a perfectly formed spindle-legged pitch-black colt.

"Is it male or female?" Emilia demanded, craning in her chair to see as the gangly thing fought its way upright beneath Linzy's mothering tongue.

"Male," Gideon confirmed. "And a more likely-looking racer I never did see, did you, Ben?"

"I don't hold with wagering on horses," Tess's father said. "Although, if I did, I'd lay a few bob on this fellow. What will you call him, Emilia?"

"Albert, of course."

"Albert?" Sebastian echoed. "What do you think Uncle Albert would have said to that?"

"I should hope he'd have been very honored. Tess, has the cook at the Swan got any hand for pastries?"

"Missus Backus is a very ornery woman—but she makes a mean raisin tart," Tess told her. "Dad, what's the matter with Linzy? Where's the afterbirth?"

"Hold on, lass, can't you see she's twinning?"

"She's *what*?" Tess and Gideon said in unison.

"Does this mean I get two colts?" Emilia asked hopefully.

"Don't be greedy," her nephew chided. "Only the first one's yours."

The second colt was pure silver, a female. "Would you mind if I called her Suzette?" Tess asked Gideon.

"I'd be as pleased as Albert," he said.

That night, after a celebratory supper at the Swan, he and Tess walked home hand in hand beneath the broad Shropshire sky. "Is there anyplace in the world that's prettier than this?" she asked, looking up at the bright spangles of the stars.

"Not that I ever found. Why do you think Ben and I both chose to settle down here?"

The moon rose over the White Moor. Tess turned to Gideon and saw its reflection, twinned, full and round, in his eyes. "Was it bad for you today, when you saw that Sebastian had come?"

"At first. A little."

"But he didn't recognize you."

"He did too, and you know it. But he'll hold his tongue."

"Aye. I think so too."

They walked up the hill past the glasshouse that shimmered in the moonlight like a palace of fire. "I'm so afraid," Gideon said suddenly, passionately. "Not for my sake, but for yours, and our children's. This village isn't all that isolated. Someone else could come along and recognize me someday."

"And what if someone does? We'll still have each other. I'd go to the ends of the earth with you, Gideon Cade." His arm wrapped around her in the darkness, and she laughed. "Hell, for you I'd even stay in Windber-on-Clun."

"Chin up," he said dryly. "If the harvest ever fails again, I'll take you with me to London to gamble."

"I wish you would. I'd love to find that woman in the red kerchief and see what she thought when she opened up my purse and found it full of stones."

He laughed with her, but when he spoke again his voice was husky and low. "If I could, Tess Jericho, I'd make every star in this sky a diamond, and give them all to you."

"Where would I wear that many diamonds in Windber?"

He grinned and kissed her. They walked on.

At the top of the hill stood a heap of brick and stone meant for the nursery. "Tell me the truth," Gideon said, contemplating the half-risen bulk of the new manor he'd planned. "Do you think this house will ever be finished?"

"I don't know. But I think it's got a grand beginning."

He put his hand to her belly, brimful with the future. "So it has, Tess. So it has."